What early readers say...

"Join teen psychic friends Jinx and Max on their adventure aiding in the Underground Railroad transport effort. This capable duo of white children venture from their homes in the present-day North to the Antebellum South and back to rescue a slave's missing two young boys. Along the way they are confronted with the nation's ugly past as well as their own roles in attempting to rewrite history. A smart and adventurous tale, in this History Mystery Detective Agency Series. Ages ten to thirteen."

Julie Eakin
Editor-in-Chief
ForeWord Reviews

"...truly an historical adventure. What a fun and exciting way to learn about the Underground Railroad! Even though a story of fiction there are so many true facts about the slavery issues before the Civil War...As a former elementary school librarian I would have loved to have this series as a way to keep kids reading and learning at the same time. It's like the Magic Tree House books were for the younger students."

Cindy Gehr
Elementary School Librarian
Solanco School District, Quarryville, PA

"Through research, entertaining stories, and the footsteps of those who have gone before, Martin invites readers to go with her on her creative historical journeys into the past. Using a sophisticated form of writing and vocabulary appropriate for the middle grades, readers are asked to join in the flow to see where these journeys lead. Along the way, the reader may be challenged to look at the reality of a situation, but also asked to wonder at the 'what if.'"

Sue E. Snyder
Fifth Grade Teacher
Lampeter-Strasburg School District, Lampeter, PA

For more words from our readers see page 398

JMP History Mystery Detective Agency Series

Ghost Train to Freedom

Jinx and Max travel the dark Time Tunnel to the past to attempt the most daring feat of their lives—a search and rescue using the most dangerous train in the world—the Underground Railroad.

COMING SOON

Lost and Found Colony

Teen Jinx MacKenzie didn't acquire her nickname easily, and she has the bumps, bangs, and bruises to prove it. Her 'gift' of communicating with visitors from the past has Jinx and her friend Max using clues to help a frightened little girl from 400 years ago.

Conestoga Courage

Two teen-age friends and their pets run a desperate race through the Time Tunnel of history. Their mission is to thwart a gang of ruffians who are intent upon murdering the last fourteen members of the Conestoga Indian tribe.

Pirate Problems

Modern day pirates, Blackbeard, and eleven sunken treasure ships! Psychic teen friends Max Myers and Jinx MacKenzie have their hands full of problems when they become stranded back in time during the hurricane of 1715 ... and Blackbeard is NOT happy!

Ghost Train to Freedom

An Adventure on the Underground Railroad

Faith Reese Martin

JMP History Mystery
Detective Agency Series

American
Literary
Publishing
TELL · YOUR · STORY

American Literary Publishing is an imprint of LifeReloaded Specialty Publishing LLC
Lancaster, PA

American Literary Publishing
an imprint of LifeReloaded Specialty Publishing LLC
Lancaster, PA
www.americanliterarypublishing.com

Design and layout—Mike Lovell
Artwork—Barry Sachs

ISBN: 978-1-60800-014-2

Publisher's Cataloging-In-Publication Data
(Prepared by The Donohue Group, Inc.)

Martin, Faith Reese.
   Ghost train to freedom : an adventure on the Underground Railroad / Faith Reese Martin ; [artwork by Barry Sachs].

   p. : ill., maps ; cm. -- (JMP history mystery detective agency series)

   Summary: Teen psychics Jinx MacKenzie and Max Myers swirl back through history in the Time Tunnel, landing in 1851 to become conductors on the Underground Railroad.
   Interest age level: 012-016.
   ISBN: 978-1-60800-014-2

   1. Underground Railroad--Juvenile fiction. 2. Teenagers--Psychic ability--Juvenile fiction. 3. Time travel--Juvenile fiction. 4. Adventure and adventurers--Juvenile fiction. 5. Underground Railroad--Fiction. 6. Teenagers--Psychic ability--Fiction. 7. Time travel--Fiction. 8. Adventure and adventurers--Fiction. 9. Historical fiction. 10. Adventure stories. 11. Fantasy fiction. I. Sachs, Barry. II. Title.

PZ7.M3785 Gho 2012
[Fic]   2011946291

If we don't
—Who will
?

Designed, published and printed in the
United States of America

Note from the PUBLISHER

The artwork that has been created for *Ghost Train to Freedom* brings to life the challenges and heart-pounding excitement experienced by runaways escaping through the Underground Railroad. It also illustrates the courage of those who risked their own lives and property to assist them in their pursuit of freedom.

The sketches also show readers today some of the horrors of the cruelties and deprivation endured by those who were enslaved.

The quilt art used at the end of each chapter depicts the quilt patterns of the era. They show some of the secret codes that were hidden by the black women in their quilts to guide the runaways. You will find the other secret codes that Mama put into her freedom quilt described in Appendix IV at the back of this book

The *Wagon Wheel* pattern was often used to alert slaves preparing to run to freedom that a conductor was in the area. When slaves saw a quilt with this pattern hung out, they knew it was time for them to gather supplies and any belongings and be ready to leave at a moment's notice.

Visit the *Ghost Train to Freedom* website to discover more about the Underground Railroad:

www.ghosttraintofreedom.com/historical

Inspiration for
Ghost Train to Freedom

A secret, underground passageway runs catty-corner between those two historic houses on the square in Lampeter, Pennsylvania! Runaway slaves used the passageway to escape the bounty hunters.

This rumor was passed amongst the students riding *Bus 17* to Lampeter-Strasburg High School as the bus traveled right through the square every weekday morning and afternoon. When I was an eighth grader studying the Civil War, I was captivated by the rumor. What would it have been like being on the run for freedom in the 1800s?

I'm hiding in the damp basement of the old brick house on the square, fearing for my life. I'm a black runaway who has fled from a terrible existence on a Southern plantation. Suddenly, I hear the family hound barking loudly at the pounding on the door upstairs.

A tousle-haired boy from the family who harbors me comes tripping down the steps with a message. "Slave hunters are here; follow me!"

The boy has an oil lamp. He pulls open a cupboard door and pushes on the back of the closet. Amazing to see, it swings open into a dark, dank tunnel that has steps leading to...where? We crawl in.

He pulls the cupboard door closed behind him and pushes the back wall until it clicks back into place. Down we go, into a packed dirt tunnel that seems to go on forever. We have to stoop low so we don't hit our heads on the wooden support beams.

Water drips here and there, and I hear the scuttling of little creatures. Rats? I shiver.

Finally, we reach another set of stone steps that lead upward and into another secret room. "You're in the basement of the gray-stone house across from us. You'll be safe here. If need be, we'll run back over to my house. We could fool those horrible slave hunters by goin' back and forth all night long!" the young boy says. He grins at me in the lamplight and pats my arm.

My pounding heart starts to slow down, and I can return a ghost of a smile. I'm on the Underground Railroad, at the mercy of the good people who risk their lives to help slaves like me reach freedom. God bless these families and this dirty-faced, brown-eyed little imp, I think.

Of course, this scenario is only my imagination trying to understand the magnitude of the Underground Railroad and the important role it played in the lives of so many enslaved black Americans. That school-bus rumor from years ago sparked the quest to explore the history of the Underground Railroad, especially since it ran through my home territory of historic Lancaster County, Pennsylvania.

My characters have an awesome, giant-of-a-tale to tell you, dear readers. I invite you to walk in their footsteps and to put yourself in their place. I hope I did each character justice in the saga of *Ghost Train to Freedom*.

Sincerely,

Faith Reese Martin

Dedication

In remembrance of those who have been enslaved,

and

For Sue—I'll miss you, Friend

ACKNOWLEDGEMENTS

How can I express my deep appreciation to so many friends who helped to strengthen my story and made it possible to bring *Ghost Train to Freedom* to press? By giving simple thanks from the bottom of my heart!

To my editor and publisher friend, Mike Lovell, of LifeReloaded: Your support and belief in me as a children's author is wonderful. Thank you for the endless hours of work you spent on the novel and your excellent insight into the story. Also, thanks to Pam Haines for your support.

Next come many thanks to my reader and editor friends: Susan Hendricks-Barry, Emily and Glen Vasey, Sherry Eshleman, Sue Snyder, Cindy Gehr, Cathy Kessler, and Philip Reese (my brother *extraordinaire*). You all gave many hours of your precious time to read my book and help me improve the story. That speaks volumes about you as special friends.

Also, warm thanks to Reverend Edward Bailey, Carolyn Godfrey, Doris Johns and Deborah Singleton from the community at Bethel African Methodist Episcopal Church in Churchtowne, Lancaster, Pennsylvania. The heart-to-heart, round-table conversations we had provided me with your very unique insights into the delicate subject of the American slavery era and the lives of African Americans today.

Special thanks and appreciation go to the extremely talented artist for *Ghost Train to Freedom*, Barry Sachs. Barry's artwork was drawn specifically to personalize each chapter in the story; it shows not only the wretched life the enslaved Africans had to endure, but also the triumph of their striving for a better life in freedom. Barry, I'm awed by your talent. Thank you for the hours spent to make my book so very special.

Contents

Appendix I

Appendix II

Historical Background

Appendix III

Appendix IV

Appendix V

PART ONE

A Special Load of Potatoes

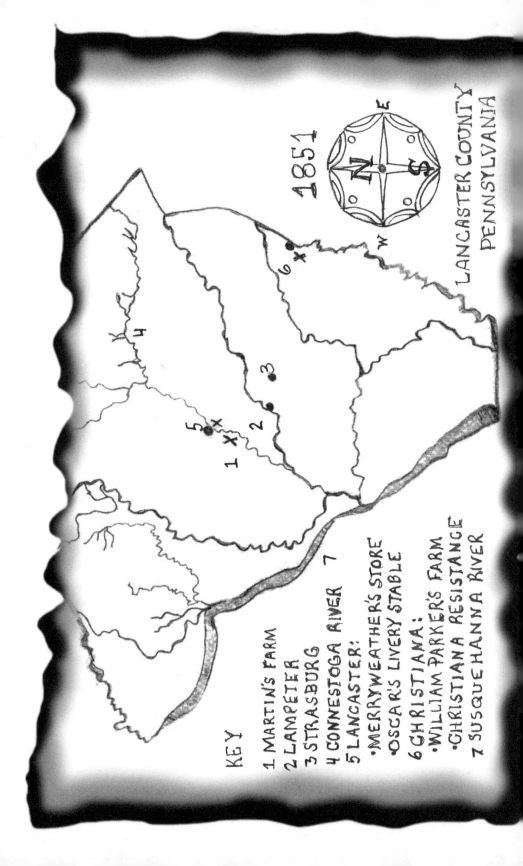

KEY

1 MARTIN'S FARM
2 LAMPETER
3 STRASBURG
4 CONNESTOGA RIVER   7
5 LANCASTER:
  •MERRYWEATHER'S STORE
  •OSCAR'S LIVERY STABLE
6 CHRISTIANA:
  •WILLIAM PARKER'S FARM
  •CHRISTIANA RESISTANCE
7 SUSQUEHANNA RIVER

1851

LANCASTER COUNTY
PENNSYLVANIA

Prologue

North Carolina Plantation of Arthur Young; September, 1850

A fierce pounding on the crude door, then it slams open, sounding like the crack of a rifle shot. The small group breakfasting around the old oak table freezes in fear. Who is the tall, white man wearing a scowl on his face following Master into the dim room? What could they possibly want this early on the Sabbath day? Papa knows this will be very bad news for his family, but his mind tries not to admit it.

It is barely sunup. Papa has just delivered plates of scrambled eggs to Uncle and the six-year-old twin boys. There was to have been some free time until church service in the evening.

Before they can react, Master slaps a small riding whip against the table and says, "Stand up when your superiors enter the room, you lazy, good-for-nothing rascals."

Chairs groan as they are shoved back across the rough floor-boards, some crashing to the floor. The two black men stand tall but lower their eyes as is expected of slaves on a plantation. The little boys run to Papa and hide behind his strong legs, each grabbing on to his cotton pants with frantic fingers. They sneak looks from behind.

Everything about Master and the stranger appears threatening. Master wears his fine breeches, a pure white, frilled blouse and a black waistcoat. His riding boots glisten and shine. His curly, black hair grows into a wiry beard that wraps around his face. Master's dark eyes are always as flint hard as his mouth.

The stranger is even taller than Master, but his clothes are much coarser. He wears a dusty hat, brown coat and brown riding breeches. His boots are scuffed and muddy. Dirty, long hair peeks from beneath a battered hat. His icy-cold blue eyes look the boys up and down, judging their worth.

"Is these the boys, Mister Young?" the stranger asks. "They look sturdy enough. Come here, boys. Let me look ya over."

"Yes," Master says, "you'll find them a handsome pair to be trained as house slaves. They are quite healthy and are fast learners. The mistress of your plantation will be well pleased. I hope this settles my gambling debt to Mister Smythe."

The twins wrap their little brown arms around their papa's legs even tighter. Fear shows in their dark brown eyes. The boys are identical copies of each other: smooth, round faces and black hair that curls around their ears. They understand what the men are saying. They have seen other children and adults ripped from the arms of their loving families to be sold Down South. Surely Papa won't let this happen.

Papa raises his eyes to Master's face and says, "Please Master, don't take my boys away from me. They's so young. If you must, send me instead, not my boys. They mean everything to me, I beg you."

"Or send me, sir," says Uncle. "I'll go. Please, not the boys. They's too precious to be sold down Deep South. Please, sir."

"Stop sniveling and send the boys over here now. They don't even understand what's to become of them. They don't have feelings like white children do. Their new mistress will take good care of them. They are certainly better off as house slaves rather than workers in the fields," says Master.

The boys now begin to cry out loud. "Papa, no, I don't want to go."

The white stranger grunts in disgust and strides over to the boys. He grabs one boy and jerks him away from his father. Holding him in an iron grip, he pries the youngster's mouth open to inspect his teeth. The boy clamps down on the man's forefinger and bites hard.

"Owwww, let go, you little..." He pulls his hand back and shakes his arm while glaring at the boy. "I figured I'd have trouble with two of 'em to deal with. Billy, git in here. Grab one of them boys, and I'll git the other. Bring the rope along, we'll have to hog tie 'em." A short white man walks in the door.

"I'll git 'im, Jackson," Billy says. He walks towards one of the boys.

Papa and Uncle both grab a boy and hug them to their chests. The boys hide their faces against the coarse shirts, their eyes pinched shut.

"Please, sir, no—there has to be another way," Papa begs.

Master strides to the door and calls in a couple of the slave men from the crowd that has gathered outside the cabin door. "You, Charlie...and you, Willie, hold them back."

He orders in a sharp voice that must be obeyed, because that is the way it must be, or there will be whippings. Papa and Uncle will surely be given ten lashes for disobeying and talking back to Master.

Several slaves hold Papa and Uncle back, while others help to tie large grain bags over the boys. They are tossed over Jackson's horse like thirty-pound sacks of potatoes.

All of their kicking and floundering around dies with their hope when the twins are trussed to the horse's broad back. Their sobs turn into hiccups as they feel Jackson mount his horse.

An older Negro woman with tears running down her face rushes over to the horse that carries the twins. She quickly tucks a quilt around the boys and whispers to them, "You keep the special quilt with you, no matter what. It's yours. Remember the secret of the quilt." She places her hand on the patch of the quilt that shows a dark-colored hand reaching for the stars.

"Old woman, get back from them boys before I kick you back," says Jackson. The old woman slips away out of sight.

"All this fussin' and fightin' is the least likable part of my job," he says. "We've a long ride ahead back down to Savannah, Georgia. I won't be delayed no longer. Good day to ya, sir." Jackson nods and taps the brim of his dirty hat with his riding crop. He

slaps the reins against his white stallion's neck and gallops out of the yard. His helper, Billy, gallops after him.

The crowd of black men and women murmurs; they shake their heads in sorrow. Mothers hug their children to their aprons, relieved that it is not their own child disappearing down the long, dusty lane.

"Go on, now, back to your own business. The show is over," Master says. He turns abruptly and marches across the broad lawn toward his white plantation mansion.

Papa and Uncle hang low, bent over in the men's arms, deep sobs racking their chests. The fight is all out of their bodies. The men let them fall gently to the dirt. Before Papa and Uncle stand, they exchange a long, teary look with each other. But instead of hopelessness, steely determination shows in their eyes. This fight is not over. They will find the boys someday, somehow, or die trying.

Jinx MacKenzie shudders awake, drenched in cold fear. The dream is so real that she finds her face awash with tears. Her black-and-white Jack Russell terrier, Petey, licks her cheek in comfort.

The boys were so small and helpless, and the situation seemed hopeless, Jinx thinks. She has studied about the Southern culture and slavery in school but never gave it further consideration after the test. Now the horror of it touches her personally and wraps its ghostly fingers around her. She feels a sense of power pulling her to the past once more. A mission awaits her action.

"I'll help, Jinx," Petey communicates silently.

Jinx hugs her small terrier to her chest and dries her tears in his fur. "I know you'll help, Petey. I love you. I'm sure the whole *JMP History*

Mystery Detective Agency will help. These things always play out in their own good time. We'll soon be with Max and Poppy when we go visit Aunt Merry at the farm. We'll talk it over with them when the time is right."

Jinx smiles to think of Poppy, the big orange-and-white cat, and her boy, Max. They are her best friends and fellow Time Travelers. She burrows back down in her covers, snuggling Petey to her side for comfort. Right as she drifts off to sleep she hears a soft train whistle in the distance. *"Whoooooooo, woo wooooooo..."*

Funny, Jinx thinks, *there's no train that runs nearby our house...*

Chapter One

The Delivery

I wonder what's inside the Big Dipper," Jinx MacKenzie says to her best friend, Max Myers. The two lie on their backs in the sweet meadow grass, their hands cushioning their heads. Their bellies are satisfied, full of fresh tomatoes, corn-on-the-cob, and hotdogs from suppertime with Aunt Merry. It's a late-summer eve, and they are at Conestoga Courage Farm visiting Jinx's Aunt Merry for a few weeks.

The crickets and grasshoppers are like fiddlers, sawing away with their back legs. The throaty *"ga-rumps"* of the pond frogs and the *"chit-chit-churry"* of the katydids add to the insects' chirping song.

Max smiles in the darkness at Jinx's imagination. "You'd think with our psychic abilities we could fly right up there and take a look. Let's see–I think it's full of ice-cold lemonade. I'm thirsty," he says.

Max is a tall, strong teenage boy. He shifts his lean body to get into a more comfortable position. Pushing the shock of blond hair away from his blue eyes, he crosses his arms above his head, accidentally bumping into Jinx's elbow.

"No, make it warm, melted chocolate for dipping strawberries and bananas," says Jinx. She elbows him back.

She is almost as tall as Max. Her tousled red hair and green eyes are a perfect match for her nickname. The only people who call her by her given name, Margaret, are her parents, usually when they are annoyed by her behavior. *That seems to be often,* she thinks, *since I've become a teenager.*

There is a rustling in the long grasses and a twenty-pound furry critter jumps onto Jinx's stomach. *"No, no, I think the Big Dipper's full of dog biscuits."*

"Oomph! Petey, take it easy," Jinx says. The wind is knocked out of her by her beloved Jack Russell terrier, returned from a game of tag with Poppy, Max's cat. Jinx hugs her terrier and rubs his furry ears. She feels his heart beating a comforting rhythm against her chest.

Poppy comes silently through the grass and rubs against Max. Her orange-and-white striped coat and her amber eyes glow in the moonlight. *"I'd like a bowlful of cream from the Dipper,"* she purrs.

The two teens sit up, watching the vast sky above them laid out like a velvety carpet of blinking fireflies. They're looking for a meteor shower named Perseids that is supposed to be at its height tonight. They sit in the comfortable silence that two good friends can share.

In the past year they have had many adventures together since meeting at the Outer Banks of North Carolina. They named themselves the *JMP History Mystery Detective Agency*. Fate brought them together back then and bonded them tightly; it is a force way beyond their understanding. It was no random act, but some higher force that was meant to be. Jinx's psychic ability of being able to communicate with people from the past and using time travel to help them is a gift that she sometimes wishes she did not possess. It is often a scary, dangerous ride.

With Jinx's help, Max's psychic ability improves day by day. Instead of wildly shooting off into the past and being stranded, as happened last spring in Florida, he is now able to control his time travel.

Both teens think the best part of their mental gift is the ability to communicate with the animals. They love being able to understand animals' thoughts and feelings, finding the wisdom offered by the animals very helpful.

Jinx looks much more like her Aunt Merry than her mother. They share the red hair and green eyes of the family. Jinx's mom is tall and dark-eyed, with beautiful black hair. She and her sister both have the psychic Gift that was passed on to Jinx. Their powers weakened when they reached adulthood, but they understand the call from the past. Aunt Merry's Gift was always much stronger than her sister's. She has gone through much of what Jinx is now experiencing, and she always tries to be there for her struggling niece. Jinx's father wishes they all would cease to have this Gift. He always worries for their safety.

Max brushes away a mosquito on his arm and scratches a bite on his ankle. Jinx and he are both barefoot, and their tee shirts and canvas shorts do little to protect them from the biting insects. He points upward. "See the Little Dipper close by?" he asks.

"No, where is it? The sky is so full of stars tonight," says Jinx.

"Look directly to the left of the Big Dipper. It's smaller and the same shape. The Big Dipper stands on its handle, but the little one is upright. See it?"

"I do, I do." Jinx is excited. She reaches her pointer finger into the air and traces the stars.

"Now follow the two stars at the rear of the little dipper, and then trace the three stars in the handle." Max says. "Look for the last star in the handle. That's Polaris, the North Star. It's the only star that stays in the same position all year. If you keep Polaris in front of you, you'll always know which direction is true north."

"Let's hope you're always around if we're lost in nature. I don't think Polaris would help me at all," says Jinx.

"True," Max says. "You tend to be perpetually lost, even in your own house."

"Thanks, Mr. Smarty. How do you know so much about the stars?"

"Astronomy in school this spring," Max says. "Good stuff. The dippers are actually called Ursa Major and Ursa Minor. Ursa means..."

"Don't tell me. I remember learning about that; Ursa means bear–Big Bear and Little Bear."

Petey jumps up and down, bouncing off his back legs like a leaping kangaroo. *Are there any dogs up there to chase the bears?* he woofs.

"Yes Pete-o, my buddy, there are," Max says. "Canis Major and Canis Minor—Big Dog and Little Dog. But you can't find them in the summer sky."

Big Dog, that's me, says Petey, continuing to bounce around the group.

Peter, really. Big Dog? Have you checked in the mirror lately? Now my constellation is what you would call big. Leo the Lion–check to the east of Big Bear, purrs Poppy.

Jinx and Max laugh at their furry friends. They aren't even amazed at Poppy's knowledge. Both animals have often saved the day in their past adventures. Though Petey often annoys Poppy, they all know she has a warm spot in her heart for her hyperactive canine friend.

In the midst of their camaraderie, two meteors shoot across the sky, their long tails flickering out within a split second. They are followed by three more in succession. They both catch the flickering tails.

"Ohhhhhhh, look at that...," Jinx whispers.

Without thinking, Jinx picks up a stick and traces her hand in the dirt beside her. She finishes the drawing by adding five stars surrounding the hand, and then looks at it, puzzled. "Max, did you ever see anything like this before?"

Max looks at her drawing and shakes his head.

Awed, Jinx begins to feel a familiar chill and tingling that starts in the tips of her fingers and toes and works its way up her arms and legs. She's about to have a calling from the past and can do nothing to stop it. She lies back down, keeping her eyes on the Little Dipper and Polaris, the North Star.

"Follow the Drinking Gourd," she says dreamily. "Follow the Drinking Gourd. Time to ride that train. Do you hear it? It sounds so lonely."

In the distance, a lone whistle sounds. *"Whooooooooooo... wooooooooooo, woooooooo."*

"Jinx, you're not making any sense," Max says. He looks over at his friend and sees her glazed-over look in the moonlight. "Hey, you're not going anywhere without me. Do you hear me?"

The ghostly whistle sounds again. *"Whooo, wooooo, woo."* Max tilts his head to the faint sound, puzzled. No train tracks run close to Aunt Merry's farm.

Jinx is vaguely aware that Max grabs her cold hand and holds on tight, but it feels like she is in a coma and can't communicate with him.

"Follow the Drinking Gourd, follow the Drinking Gourd..." she murmurs.

Everything around her goes totally silent. She is in a deep void of total darkness; no smells of the sweet summer meadow, no insects busily chirping, no stars...nothing. A great whooshing sound occurs as Max is spiraled into the cold Time Tunnel with her, off to the unknown. Something or someone is calling them back in time.

Both teens are dumped onto firm meadowland. Jinx and Max run to hide behind a big haystack to the rear of a nearby red barn. The summer-night noises are back, and with them is the faint baying of big dogs on the hunt. *"Ah-rooooooooorr, borr, borr, borr."* The sound is far away.

"Where do you think we are, or should I ask 'when' do you think we are?" Max whispers.

The full moon shines brightly on the scene. "I'm not sure. It looks like Aunt Merry's barn, but look at the dark paint on the sides. Aunt Merry's barn has peeling, white paint. It also feels later than August. *Brrrrrr*...it's much cooler." Jinx rubs her arms for warmth.

A low mooing comes from within the barn, along with a whinny and the shuffling of horses' feet. The two look at each other, thinking the same thought: Aunt Merry doesn't keep animals at her farm. She rents the land out to a neighboring farmer to plant crops. They may not have traveled away from the property, but they definitely are gone from their own era.

"Children, what do you think you are doing? Who are you? You're going to have to stay hidden for your own safety," orders a gruff voice. "This isn't the night for you to be out and about playing hide-and-seek. I've got a load of potatoes coming in right now."

Jinx and Max jump a foot high, hearts pounding against their ribs. *Load of potatoes? What could he mean?* They gape at the tall farmer, dressed in rough trousers with suspenders, dark boots, and a deep red cotton shirt. He is tall and has a bearded face. Bushy eyebrows grow almost together above dark eyes. He holds a glowing lantern in his hand and stands glaring at them.

"Now, no noise. After this is over, you'd better scamper home and forget what you see and hear." His voice softens, telling the children that he is more concerned for their safety rather than angry at them. The farmer turns and strides toward the woods, gently swinging the lantern in the pitch darkness.

"How is it that you always drag me to the wrong place at the wrong time?" Max grumbles.

Jinx fights back a nervous giggle. "Sshhhh, he'll hear us. I don't think he's dangerous, but he is annoyed enough to give us a good swat on the behind if we don't listen to him. Maybe he thinks we're neighbor kids. Something big is obviously about to happen." She grabs Max's hand again.

"Yeah, let's see why a load of potatoes is arriving in the dark of the night," Max says. "It's probably bigger than a load of potatoes." They stay behind a haystack near the barn.

The farmer continues to swing the lantern and peer back and forth along the woods' edge. Suddenly, three huddled figures dressed in dark clothes scurry from the woods and run to the man. After a short conversation with lots of arm pointing and gesturing, one form slips back into the woods, and the other two turn and follow the farmer.

"Ah-ruuuuuuuuuuuuu, boor, booooor boor...," the baying hounds call out, louder and closer.

The figures from the woods turn out to be two young men, both dressed in tattered pants and coats missing buttons and covered with patches. Their skin is as dark as the soft night. Neither wears shoes. The tallest man limps badly but is determined not to fall behind as the farmer urges them to hurry. Jinx and Max hear the low voices of the group as they walk by the haystack.

"Now don't you worry none; you're safe with us," says the farmer. "I'll hide you until the danger passes by. Then we'll take a look at that bad foot and get you some warm food to fill you up."

"Thank you, sir. We was afraid we wouldn't make it this far. The hounds picked up our scent a ways back, but our conductor told us to walk in the stream to throw them dogs off. My name's Henry, and this is my brother, Edward," says the thin, slightly shorter man. They speak with a soft southern drawl.

"Oh, sir, hurry. Where can we hide? I'm afraid the hounds got our scent again." Edward shifts his brown eyes back toward the woods. He grabs the farmer's hand.

"I won't go back to North Carolina," Edward continues. "Master say if we run one more time, he'll trade us to some planters in the Deep South. I'll never see my family again. That's as bad as bein' dead."

The farmer clears his throat with a gruff cough. "Come on; no need to worry. I've got a hiding place for you. Into the barn. Hurry." They go through a big back door.

Jinx and Max can't help but follow. The drama has them in its clutches, and they are as determined as the farmer to help the men.

The farmer hears them and stops in frustration. "Doggone it, children. I asked you to stay out of sight. This is deadly serious business. Where did you come from? Are you two runaways...or spies?" he says. He worries that the children were sent by the wrong people and will tell them about him helping the black men.

"No, sir, we're here to help," says Jinx. "What can we do?"

He looks into the eyes of the two young people and sees something he can trust. He nods his head.

"Hurry then and help shove these bales of hay aside. They cover a trapdoor to a secret room."

Everyone gets busy lifting and moving the stack of hay bales. The hounds continue to close in on their quarry, sounding louder and closer yet.

When the area is clear, the farmer grabs hold of an iron handle to a trapdoor and throws it back. The dim light of the lantern shows a dugout room big enough to hold four or five people for a short time.

"It will be stuffy and cramped, but the door has enough gaps in it to allow for air. The trick is to scatter enough loose hay and bales to cover its existence," says the farmer.

The farmer helps the two men jump down into the hidden room, where they crouch on feed sacks scattered on the floor. "Give me your coat," he says to Edward.

Edward slips out of his jacket and hands it to the farmer. Jinx gasps, as she notices raised scars that crisscross Edward's strong back in the dim lantern light. *This is really terrible,* she thinks. Cobwebs clear and ideas finally form in her mind. *These men are runaway slaves.* She glances at Max, whose lips are pressed in a tight line and his brow furrowed. He stares back at her and nods his head.

"Don't worry, we'll throw the dogs off track so fast they won't know what hit them." The farmer throws the trapdoor closed and begins to move some bales. "You, boy. Are you brave?"

"Yes sir, I'm braver than you'd ever think," says Max.

Jinx thinks of their past adventures, which included hostile gangs of men and Blackbeard the Pirate, and shakes her head in agreement.

"My friend Jinx is even braver than me," Max says. "Whatever you need us to do, let's hear it." Jinx grins her thanks.

The farmer hands Edward's jacket to Max. "You need to go back out into the woods. Follow the creek until you get to the first big bend. Then drop and drag the coat as best you can, heading away from here. Can you run two or three miles at a stretch?"

"I can do a five-minute mile if I have to. I'll take it way out." Max brags a bit and sounds so sure of himself. Jinx rolls her eyes at him.

"Good boy," says the farmer. He is beginning to be impressed with these children. "Take it as far as you can, then drape it up over a tree branch. Cross the stream before you head back. We'll throw off those big hounds' noses to give you some time. Go on, now." He throws the coat to Max, who tears out the door without a backward glimpse.

"Meet you back here later, Jinx," Max calls out.

The farmer then turns to Jinx. "Jinx, is it? Go get that can over in the corner, behind the plow. Now listen, hold it away from you and don't sniff it."

Jinx runs to the corner and wiggles between the plow and the rough barn boards. She sees a can the size of a paint bucket and grabs it. Her curiosity gets the better of her, and she peers over the rim.

Ahhhh-choo....ah-choo...ah-choo." It's pepper, and she can't stop sneezing.

"Jinx, I told you to hold it away from you. You children are the nosiest two children I ever did meet. Go outside the door and sprinkle pepper around, and then try to retrace the path we took from the woods and sprinkle some more. Doesn't have to be a lot–a little goes a long way. Won't hurt the dogs in the long run, but it'll mess up their noses for a bit and throw them off the track."

Jinx doesn't wait for further instructions. She heads out to do her part. *I sure feel sorry for the dogs,* she thinks. Petey comes to mind and she feels a bit guilty. *I hope it wears off all right.* Even though she feels guilty, the fate of the hidden men seems to be partly in her hands, so she begins to sprinkle liberally.

"Come in to the back porch when you're done. Hurry, girl," the farmer calls softly after Jinx.

Jinx soon meets the farmer back at the porch. They hide the can under the back steps. She sees a faint lamplight in the kitchen, and for a moment thinks it's her Aunt Merry waiting for her. Then she remembers that she has jumped back a couple of generations. *This must be one of the families who lived here first,* she thinks.

The farmer interrupts her daydreaming. "Come in quickly, Jinx. Meet my wife, Mary. She'll care for you until this blows over tonight. The good Lord willing, the men and their hounds will be turned away. It's in God's hands now."

Mary is a petite woman, with the strong hands of someone who is used to hard labor. Her light brown hair is pulled back into a neat bun. Her face is smooth except at the corners of her mouth and eyes, which wrinkle in a welcoming smile. A frilly, white apron covers Mary's dress.

Mary doesn't pause to ask any questions. She seems to understand exactly what to do, like they've done it many times before. "Hello, child. Hurry upstairs with me. We must all pretend we're asleep in bed. Those men mustn't see any light." She blows out the kitchen lamp and grabs Jinx's hand, leading her up the back kitchen stairs that are so familiar to Jinx.

The farmer follows them. He and his wife pause at the top of the steps and have a hushed conversation. Jinx can hear Max mentioned. Then Jinx is escorted to the bedroom she always uses when she visits Aunt Merry and is tucked into a feather bed under a lightweight summer quilt.

Will Max get back safely? What will happen to him if he's caught? What if the people chasing the runaways come to the farmhouse? Worries fly around her head like a whirlpool of bath water going down the bathtub drain.

"My friend, Max...he's in big danger. Maybe he shouldn't have gone out to the woods," Jinx says to the lady.

"I trust that your brave friend is going to do fine," Mary murmurs. "Stay here until he returns and the danger is over, and then we'll sort everything out. Including who you children really are. Have faith. My husband John told me you two tend to have minds of your own. Independent thinkers, I see."

She slips out of the door and gently closes it, leaving Jinx to her own swirling, troubling thoughts.

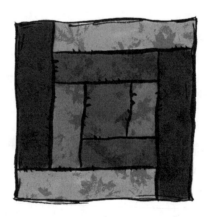

Chapter Two

Sneezes and A Five-Minute Mile

Less than ten minutes later, Jinx can hear the dogs barking and yelping as they reach the farmyard. She slips out of bed and peeks through the curtains. The moonlight shines on the strange scene. The bloodhounds roll around on their stomachs and backs and rub their eyes and noses, yelping and crying.

Two men ride up on horses. They are big men wearing slouch hats, dark clothes and riding boots. The tallest jumps down and calls, "Brute, come here."

The lead dog continues to yelp and roll around. The intruder looks down at the dogs and shakes his head at the other man. "I don't know what's got into them," he shouts.

He turns and strides over to the porch. Jinx can hear pounding and more yelling. "Open up. Open up the door, now." More pounding.

The door finally opens, and the farmer, dressed in a long nightshirt, goes out on the porch. Jinx strains to hear through the open window.

She sees the other man dismount, drag one of the dogs by the collar over to the watering trough, and dunk his head. The dog sputters and shakes his massive head with its huge floppy ears, then eagerly laps up water. Satisfied, the man goes for another hound.

"Yes, sir, who are you? Why are you disturbing the sleep of my family?" says the farmer.

"You hidin' runaway slaves here?" says the bearded stranger.

The farmer shrugs his shoulders and spreads his arms wide. "You can see for yourself that all is quiet around my property."

"Doesn't answer my question. I'm comin' in," says the man.

"No sir, I'll not have you enter my private property, continuing to disturb my family and me." He reaches behind the door for a shotgun. "I'd advise you to move along, now."

The man shakes his head angrily and raises a fist. "You folks all stick together up here," he says. "Thick as thieves, all of you. Hidin' other people's property. Same as stealin'." He hesitates, reaching for his pistol hidden under his coat, then thinks better of it.

He stomps off the porch and mounts his white stallion. He pulls the reins so his horse rears up and paws its hooves through the air. "Let's go," he shouts to the other man.

Jinx recognizes the two men. They were in her vision of the two little boys who were stolen from their papa.

The dogs are all rubbing their eyes, but when their master gallops out of the yard, they jump up, shake the dirt off their coats and run. The other man rides after them.

When he is sure they are gone, John pulls off the long nightshirt. Fully dressed, he heads for the barn. A short time later, he leads the two runaways, Edward and Henry, back to the farm kitchen and closes the door behind him.

Jinx can do nothing more but keep faithful watch for the return of her friend. She knows the hounds will be able to pick up the scent of Edward's coat again, and she worries about Max. *Please God,* she prays, *send an angel to be with my friend.*

Max races through the woods like a deer running for its life, giving little thought to the stones and rough terrain that bruise his bare feet. Other things are on his mind, like the two black men hiding in the dirt dugout under the barn floor. He saw the swollen ribbons of scar tissue across Edward's back and has no doubt about what era he has entered.

It is somewhere in the mid 1800s. These men are enslaved Africans, running for their lives from slave catchers, who are intent upon returning them to their masters for a huge reward. Frenzied bloodhounds are tracking the runaways. It's my job to bring the dogs back out to the woods and throw them off track. Max's thoughts race as fast as he runs.

Max judges that he is far enough away from the farm, somewhere near the stream. *Can I make it out far enough to hang the coat on a branch and then go back over to the stream before the dogs catch me?*

He drops and drags Edward's tattered coat, zigzagging back and forth. He suddenly becomes aware of the dogs' baying. They are coming towards him already, sooner than he thought they would. *I'm sure not doing a five-minute mile,* he thinks. Blood rushes to his head, along with a spurt of fear.

Max runs deeper into the brush; then he heads back for the stream. He looks for a tree branch to hang the coat. After that, he can jump in the stream's cooling water and forge back upstream to the farm.

Before he can act, the lead bloodhound, Brute, breaks through the brush and knocks Max over. His jaws snap shut over Max's leg. Luckily, Edward's coat protects him, and he pushes the huge dog off with a mighty thrust.

Max leaps for the branch and pulls himself up. The bloodhound jumps up and down, snapping his big jaws open and shut, all the while making an unearthly racket. More dogs burst into the scene, joining in the cacophony. They are trained to follow the scent of the prey and are so proud that they treed it.

He tries to quiet them so he can talk to the lead dog, but their frenzy is too heated. *"Booooooorrrr, boor, boor, booooorrrrrrr."* It's deafening. Max's heart beats a painful rhythm, and he puts his hands over his ears, trying to think. His breath comes in ragged gasps.

Two men on horseback catch up to the dogs. They plough through the underbrush and pull their horses to a stop. It takes all their might to control the agitated horses in the melee. "Brute, off. *Off!*" The older man with an unruly black beard and mean eyes yells at the dogs. The largest bloodhound gives one more leap, before running back to the men. The other three dogs follow his lead and stop jumping and snarling. "Down, all of you, down," he commands. The dogs flop down, panting heavily. Slobber drips from their jowls.

"Well, well, what kind of dirty little bear cub did we tree, now?" asks the other scrawnier guy. "Maybe we'll shoot him down outta there and have us some bear meat for breakfast tomorrow." He gives a mean snort.

"Git down here, boy. Where'd you git the coat? Doesn't look like it fits you. Looks like it mighta belonged to some escaped slaves we almost had tracked down," says the older man, obviously the leader.

Bunch of bossy losers, thinks Max. He jumps down and lands on his sore feet. *Better give them what they want.* Max looks up into the dark eyes of the leader. "Some farmer gave it to me, sir," Max says. He doesn't have to pretend to tremble.

"Is that so? Where you headin' anyway? Why you out so late? You ain't seen no runaways, have you?" says the leader.

Max hates to lie. *I try to be honest and do the right thing, but sometimes you have to do what's best in a bad situation,* he thinks. He decides to stick with the bare facts.

"I was out with my friend looking at the constellations. Now I'm heading home to my Aunt Merry's farm. Not sure about runaways–what do they look like?" he says.

The scrawny man snorts again. "Constell...what? What's this boy sayin'? Come on, Jackson. Them runaways is gittin' farther and farther away from us. This boy's talkin' nonsense. Let's git goin'."

"You're right, Billy," says Jackson. "Give me that coat, boy."

Max tosses it up to the black-bearded man, who grabs it as he gives Max a shove with his dirty boot. "Better not be helpin' people hide runaway slaves. Slaves're people's property. I'm warnin' you–pass the word."

Jackson gives a pull on his reins and says, "Yup, let's go, Brute," and the nasty men with their bloodhounds take off in a flurry of action. The dogs start their baying immediately. *"Boooor, boorrr booor..."*

A shaggy little form runs through the dark woods and jumps up in Max's arms, licking his face. *"Max, Max...you okay? You hurt?"*

It's Petey, who has tracked Max and Jinx through the Time Tunnel.

"Oh, Petey, boy is it good to see you," Max says, hugging the little terrier. "Can you talk to Brute; ask him to help us?"

Petey jumps to the ground and races after Brute and the pack.

"Brute, hey Brute, listen to me," Petey calls out to the biggest bloodhound.

The big dog circles around and comes back to Petey, a big question written all over his furry face. *"You callin' me?"* he asks.

"Please don't lead them back to the farm. Those men you're trailing— they're good men. We're trying to help them escape. Please?" says Petey.

The huge dog nods his head and grins at Petey. *"I know those men are back there, but I'm not headin' back to that farm again,"* he says. *"I think I'm allergic to that place. 'Bout burned mah nose offa mah face."*

"Brute, you lazy dawg, let's git goin'," Jackson yells from a distance.

Brute rolls his eyes at Petey and starts to run back toward his master.

"Thanks, Brute. I hope I can return the favor some day," Petey calls after him. He runs back to Max.

Max sits and listens until they become a faint sound in the distance. "Good job, Petey. Sounds like they're heading back out to my zigzag trail, and then away from the farm." He gets up, rubbing his sore back end. His tailbone had hit a rock when Jackson shoved him down.

What a job, he thinks. *I'm beat up, with scratches from head to toe. I wonder if I'll actually survive to be a grown-up.* Holding Petey, he wades in the cool stream water for a bit, to ease his bruised feet, and then he makes his way back to the farm.

"Where's Jinx? Is she hurt? Who are those men back at the farm?" Petey licks Max's arms in concern.

"I hope everyone is fine back at the farm. We helped to hide two men—runaway slaves. I'm sure Jinx is safe with the farmer," Max tries to assure Petey.

Max is anxious to get back to the farmhouse and make sure that everyone is okay. *I bet those slave catchers paid a visit to them before taking off,* he thinks. *They must not have found Edward and Henry, but I hope they didn't hurt anyone back there.* He tries hard not to let his imagination run wild.

When he rounds the last bend of the creek at the farm property, Max pauses to peer at the house. Petey jumps from his arms and waits by his side. The three-story stone farmhouse looks solemn but welcoming, with a soft glow in the kitchen. He cups his hands and gives a whistle. *"Whoot whooo, whoot whooo."*

The same is instantly returned, and he can see Jinx's form galloping across the yard. He leaves the woods behind and meets her halfway. Petey beats him, jumping all around Jinx and waving his front paws in the air.

For once, Jinx doesn't babble and hit him with a million questions. She hugs Petey and takes Max's hand to lead him back.

"You're scratched up," she states. "And what was that about running a five-minute mile? You're lucky if it's an eight-minute mile. More like ten."

"I've improved during spring track. I started to run cross-country. Okay, maybe an eight-minute mile," he admits with a grin.

"John and Mary are talking with the men," she says. "There's warm apple pie and plenty of hot tea. Are you okay?"

"Yes, although I about lost a leg to good old Brute when he treed me."

Jinx stops and looks at her friend. "They caught you?"

"Yeah, they caught me. I thought I was a goner. The men decided I was a stupid farm boy and took off again in pursuit. Petey convinced the lead dog, Brute, to take them far off the trail. What happened back here?"

"We sprinkled pepper and really messed up the dogs' noses. And John was so brave; he wouldn't let them into the house." She picks up Petey to carry him around the peppered path.

The teens enter the kitchen with Petey. The scent of cinnamon and sugar from the apple pies sitting on the table fills the air.

A teapot whistles cheerfully on the woodstove. Mary hustles over and removes it, using her apron for a potholder. She pours the boiling water with the loose mint and tea leaves through a strainer, then into the teacups in front of her guests. Mint fragrance mingles with the other good kitchen aromas.

Edward and Henry are seated with John at the table, talking quietly. Mary kneels and bathes the ugly gash on Edward's foot with some of the warm water and a soft bar of soap.

Edward nods his head at Mary and says, "Thank you for your kindness, Missus. Me and Henry, we can hardly believe the help we've received from the folks along the way. We almost got caught when a farmer smuggled us across the Susquehanna River from Wrightsville to Columbia, but he took the chance anyways. To know that some folks care about us...well, it's hard to tell you what that means, after bein' a slave for so many years." Tears start to trickle down his face.

Mary says, "We believe that all men and women are born with the same rights to freedom and peace. And I do believe for every misguided soul in the world, there are at least two good ones willing to help."

Suddenly everyone looks at the children, standing quietly beside the kitchen door with their little terrier friend by their side. Jinx knows the modern, summer attire that Max and she wear confuses the others. The question of who they are hangs so heavy in the air that Jinx imagines she can see a big black question mark hovering above their heads.

"I'm Jinx...Margaret MacKenzie, and this is my friend, Maxwell Myers," Jinx says. "And this is Petey," she adds, picking up the small dog.

John stands and shakes their hands and gives Petey's head a rub. "John and Mary Martin. I'm wondering where our two partners in crime come from, Mary," he says to his wife. Wrinkles around his eyes and mouth crease in a broad smile.

"Don't let John scare you off," she says. "We don't have children of our own, but John would make an excellent father. He's the kindest man around." She finishes wrapping Edward's foot in a clean bandage and gets up. "More pie, everyone?"

John chuckles. "Don't be giving away all of my secrets, Mary." Turning to the children, he says, "I haven't seen you two around. Have you moved in somewhere close by?"

Petey jumps out of Jinx's arms and goes over to the table to sniff the pies. Jinx and Max exchange a glance. "We're new in the area...it's kind of hard to explain, sir," says Max.

"No matter right now. Perhaps you'll tell us when you are ready. I'd like to thank you for your help. I don't think I could have pulled it off alone. Those hounds came in too fast."

John hugs each child. He seats them around the farm table. He cuts one of the apple pies and dishes a large piece, dripping in syrup, for each child. Mary pets Petey's soft head and gives him fresh water and a little piece of pie on a small saucer.

"It's almost sunup. I'd best start heating a kettle of water for Edward and Henry to bathe, then we'll get them into clean nightshirts for a good sleep," Mary says. "Would you children like to stay the night? We've plenty of room."

Jinx finishes off a large mouthful of apples in flakey pie dough. She gulps and dabs at her mouth with a linen napkin. "I think our aunt will be expecting us, thank you. What will happen next to Edward and Henry?"

Mary and John hesitate, again evaluating the character of the children. John nods at Mary. "When it is dark again, they will move on to another station along the way," says Mary. "We have plans laid for them to move on to Christiana."

"Station? I'm not sure I understand," says Jinx. She knows Christiana is miles east of the farm. "Will they take a bus or something?" She forgets where she is. Max elbows her.

"Bus," declares Mary. "Now *I* don't understand." She laughs, as she looks Max and Jinx over from head to toe. Henry gives the children a puzzled glance.

Jinx sees that everyone finally notices their shorts and tee shirts and begins to really wonder who are these two strange children.

"Um, I meant to say train, will they ride a train?"

Max comes to the rescue. "Jinx, I think we better head out."

Mary laughs again. "You might say they are riding a train. The biggest train in North America. Only noone sees this train...it's a ghost train."

Jinx and Max look at each other, thinking of the ghostly train whistles they heard earlier tonight. The children give their goodbyes. Going over to Edward and Henry, they shake their hands. The men return warm handshakes. "Thanks for your help, children," they both say.

"You helped save our lives," Henry says. He shakes his head and tears fill his eyes. "You're brave children."

Mary hugs them. "Whoever you children are, you should be safe if you hurry home. Come see us again. Maybe then you can tell us more about where you really come from and how you got to our farm."

After waving goodbye, Petey, Max and Jinx are heading for the rear of the barn when they hear a soft call.

"Children, wait."

Henry hurries after them in the dark. "I need to ask you somethin'. Can I trust you?" He looks into Jinx's eyes.

Jinx remembers the special drawing in the dirt that she made earlier. She drops to the ground and draws a box. She traces her hand in it, and then draws the five stars around it. Henry and Max stoop down to look at what she has drawn. Henry nods his head as his jaw drops.

"How do you know about that? Our mama made that square on a quilt to remind us to always reach for the stars, to follow the stars to freedom, if we decide to go." Henry looks at their clothes and thinks about the strange conversation back in the kitchen. "You aren't from around here, are you? I mean from...well, you look and talk so different," says Henry.

"You're right, we're Time Travelers," Max says. "From the future." He thinks Henry deserves the truth.

Again Henry's jaw drops open. "Time Travelers? You mean you can pop back and forth to any time you want...visit people in the past? That's somethin'!"

"About the picture of the hand reaching for the stars...I saw it in my mind and somehow knew it would be an important piece of this puzzle," Jinx says. "I'm excited to know it links to you." She grins at Max and Henry.

Henry gazes at them, amazement in his large brown eyes. He puts his hand to his brow and drops it again. "The wonderment of it all. I prayed for angels. I guess you're them. From the future?"

They all laugh softly. Henry hugs them.

Petey bounces up and down, pawing Henry's leg. He stoops and picks Petey up to pet his soft ears.

"I need your help. But it's so dangerous, I don't know if I have the right," Henry says. Big tears spill down his face again. Petey licks them away. "I have two sweet little boys, twins. They was taken from me and sold down to the Deep South. I'll never see them again unless... maybe you can help me? You's white and have some special gift...I think maybe you has the means of gettin' a trip together to go search for my boys." His brown eyes plead as he looks from Max to Jinx.

Soft, lonely sounding train whistles drift through the night air again. "*Woooo-woooooo, woo-wooooo...*" Everyone shivers.

Jinx can feel the fine hairs on her arms being caressed by an unseen hand. She hugs herself. Her mind flits to the vision she had weeks ago, before her vacation with Max began. *Twins...stolen from their papa and uncle...*

"It sounds so ghostly," she whispers. "It's the train Mary talked about, the biggest train in North America. I think we're all about to take a ride on the ghost train."

Chapter Three

Henry's Story

Max motions to a nearby log. "Let's sit. We have time to hear you out."

Jinx and Max sit on the log and Henry sits between them, with a hand on Petey's soft white back.

"Me and Edward are brothers," he says. "We been lucky to stay together. Worked on the same plantation down in North Carolina all our lives, 'til now. A master bought us together. We always worked in the fields. It was hard, back-breakin' work from can see to can't see, six days a week. Plantin' and weedin' big cotton fields. Then come harvest time we worked on into the dark sometimes, pickin' until our backs were aching and our fingers bled. On the Sabbath, though, we rested and had our church meetin's.

"When I was about fifteen, I fell in love with the prettiest little gal ever. May Ella was her name. Met her at Sabbath meetin'. She was visitin' from the neighborin' plantation. She had skin the color of coffee with cream mixed in, and the biggest brown eyes with long, long lashes." Henry grins.

"Master, he bought her to come work in the big house as Cook's helper. House servants, they have it a little better than field hands. But they still have to work early mornin' to after dark doin' hard jobs to keep a house runnin' smooth. I was so glad for her to have inside work.

"Well, we got married one Sunday. Had a great big feast and lots of singin' and dancin'. We jumped over the broom together to seal our marriage promises.

"One day we found out we was goin' to be a mama and a papa, and that was the happiest time of our life together. But when the time came for the baby to be born, a scary thing happened. They called in the midwife from the fields to help May Ella. But the baby was turned the wrong way to come out. Poor May Ella, she tried so hard to birth that baby..."

Henry pauses and looks down; tears slide down his dark face. He pulls Petey into his lap and strokes his soft ears. "May Ella died that night, bringin' our baby into the world. And on behind the first baby came a second one, twins. We didn't know ahead of time. I keep thinkin' I could've done somethin' more. But there wasn't a chance.

"But outta sadness come great joy—my twin boys. Henry Junior, he was the first born, and then Eddie. Two little half-pint babies they was, with their mother's button nose and big brown eyes and curly lashes. Too bad they got their daddy's big ears. Named them after Edward and me." Henry wiggles his big ears that stick way out from the sides of his head. "Now they's two young rascals, always makin' us laugh..."

Jinx and Max laugh with Henry, who wipes his eyes dry with his torn sleeve. Jinx lays her hand on Henry's arm. Petey scrambles out of Henry's lap and yips his support.

"Oh, Henry, I'm so sorry about May Ella." Jinx swipes her own eyes with the bottom of her tee shirt. Max hands her a bandanna from his pocket. "Today, I mean in our time, your babies would have had help in a hospital, and May Ella, too. She would have lived, maybe..." she says. Another thought hits her.

"Henry, you and Edward are twins, aren't you? Sitting side by side in the kitchen I could hardly tell you apart."

Henry gives a soft chuckle and nods his head. "Yep, must run in the family history. Edward may be a bit taller than me, but I popped out first. Don't ever let him forget that, either. I'm the real big brother."

Max puts his hand on Henry's strong back. He feels corded lumps through Henry's shirt. "Henry, we saw the welts on your brother's back, too. They are whiplashes, aren't they? I thought you said your master wasn't too bad."

"Oh, he was decent enough to us slaves. But he still took the whip to our backs for any problem reported by the Boss Man. Boss Man's in charge of the field hands, you see, and Boss Man's an evil man. He made up problems just to see us get the whip. He'd laugh out loud watchin' those beatin's. Half the time, he got to swing the whip.

"And Master's brother, Arthur, he's as evil as the Boss Man. Master caught consumption one winter when he was out checkin' the damp fields. He battled that cough for months until he finally died in the spring.

"Mistress, she no sooner buried her dead husband than his no-good brother moved into the plantation house and into her life. There she was with two half-grown young 'uns and a thousand-acre cotton plantation to run. She never dirtied her dainty hands. She didn't know what else to do. So they were married in the summer, and that devil took over the plantation. The new master cracked the whip, and his plantation caretaker, the same Boss Man, cracked the whip harder.

"We never could move fast enough. If you stopped to stretch your achin' back, you got the whip. If you asked for a drink, you got the whip. You darsn't look them in the eye or you got beat...the women, too. Our times of laughin' with our family in the evenin's ended. We always lived in fear of the whip.

"The Boss Man, he's a drinker, and when he drank too much he loved to call us all out any time of night to witness a whippin' of someone who made him mad. Maybe for being too sick to work, or spillin' a bag of cotton in the dirt. He'd make one of us tie the poor man to a tree and then watch while he gave twenty lashes, 'til the man couldn't stand no more.

"The first day my brother Edward heard he was to be sold down to the Deep South, he decided to run. I begged him to wait until we could plan more, but he said, 'Henry, if I wait one more day, I'm sure to die. And I'd rather die than be a slave anymore. I want my sweet freedom.' So he ran one night. But Boss Man, when he found him missin', he took off on horseback after him.

"We prayed he'd escape up to safety in the North, but two days later Boss Man come ridin' in pullin' Edward behind him in a neck chain, manacles around his hands and feet. I never saw Edward's eyes so dead and beat. He got his thirty-nine lashes that about killed him. Boss Man, he come by after and poured salt in his wounds. Y'all know what that feels like? Maybe you got salt in a little cut you had? It burns like hot brandin' irons all over your back. We nursed him back. Now both of us run here, months later. Sweet freedom or die tryin', that's our belief." Henry's eyes are now dry and defiant.

Jinx and Max exchange uneasy glances. What a horror story, worse than they have ever heard in their young lives. Petey has been listening intently to the story and looks around the circle at everyone's face.

"But Henry, what about your twins? What about Henry Junior and Eddie?" asks Max. "Where are they?" Max knows that Henry would never leave them to an uncertain, terrible fate on a plantation.

Jinx suddenly remembers her sad, sad dream of a few weeks ago, when she saw two dear little boys being dragged away from their father and uncle. "Your boys were taken from you and sold, weren't they?"

"Yes, my babies was taken from me and sold way Down South to Savannah, Georgia, for my punishment. Master says I knew about Edward's runnin' plans and didn't tell. And he owed a gamblin' debt. So I got twenty lashes, and he stole my boys out of my arms one Sunday mornin' and turned them over to a slave catcher for a plantation owner in Georgia. I can still hear them screamin' and cryin' for their Papa. And I couldn't do a thing about it." Henry thrusts his arms out, palms up, then he drops his arms in defeat.

Jinx and Max's eyes and mouths are wide open; they are outraged and stunned. Jinx knows this story–she has seen it in her vision. They both feel Henry's agony.

"I saw that in a vision, Henry. I saw your boys being kidnapped from you. It was awful. Now I know it's you I'm supposed to help."

Henry stares at her, again surprised at her strange talents. "You can see things...things that happen to people, like in a dream?"

Jinx nods her head.

"You're hoping maybe we can help you find the boys, aren't you, Henry?" says Max. "We want to, we really do, but I'm not sure how."

Max shakes his head and looks to Jinx for help. Jinx's head is tilted up, and she stares at the dippers. She reaches high with her left hand. "Follow the stars," she says, looking at her hand.

Max is startled. He thinks his friend is about to disappear again into the Time Tunnel. He takes her other hand. "Jinx, what are you talking about? You're not going to shoot off into the sky, are you?"

A former mystery hits Jinx. "Henry, do you know what 'follow the drinking gourd' means?"

"Yes, Miss Jinx, that's secret talk for runnin' away North. Find that ol' Big Dipper in the sky. It points to the North Star. Keep that shiny North Star in front of you at night, for headin' North to freedom.

"That's how we got us this far. There's a mighty train that's runnin' North, and many of us runaways try to hitch a ride. We got nothin' but the clothes on our backs and hope in our hearts. We had no idea how to go until word got passed on about a secret train runnin' North. Only this train's a ghost train, hidden from sight. You don't find it...it finds you."

"*Whooooo...woo woooooooo...*" That spooky train calls again. They all tilt their heads to listen. Petey lifts his head and softly howls. Chills run up and down Jinx's body.

"We'll think of a plan," she assures Henry. She takes Henry's warm hand, noticing his palm is a lighter shade than his brown arm. His hand is callused and worn. She turns his hand over and sees lighter brown, raised scars crisscrossing the skin. "Do you trust that if we leave you for a while, we'll come back to you to help?"

Henry gives Jinx's hand a warm squeeze. "I do trust you, Miss Jinx, I do. I know you and Master Max will help me get my boys back. I know the way. I can lead you. We just needs a good plan to get there."

Jinx turns to Max. "Max, we have to go home, talk to Aunt Merry and make some plans."

Max worries about how on earth they will be able to steal back two baby boys and find their way back North with Henry. "How old are your boys now, Henry?"

Henry tilts his head and looks at Max. "Master Max, they's not as big as you. They turned seven years old right after they was stolen away from me. They's little rascals, always doin' tricks and makin' people laugh."

Whew, Max thinks. He wasn't too keen on babies, but seven-year-olds are much more independent. "You go back in to John and Mary," he says. "We'll find you again."

Jinx drops Henry's hand. Henry gives them a hopeful smile, then turns and runs low, back towards the farmhouse.

Max gives a big sigh and looks at Jinx, who again studies the night sky as if the answer is written in the stars. Crickets chirp, and honeysuckle smells fragrant. Suddenly they notice the barn emitting a soft blue glow, as if beckoning them.

"Oh, Jinx, what have you gotten us into this time? This is dangerous business, very dangerous," Max says.

"We have to follow the drinking gourd, backwards," Jinx says with a big smile and a shrug of her shoulders. "No big deal, right, Petey?"

The excited terrier flips in the air, ready to head South.

Chapter Four

A Vision Lesson

Cold, dark and fast—the whooshing sound in the Time Tunnel is loud as it empties Jinx, Max and Petey out with a thump back into the sweet meadow of their own time. Poppy awaits them, pouncing on her young friends in worry.

"Where did you go so fast?" Poppy asks. She gives Max a lick and then licks her own orange shoulder. *"I did worry when you took off so fast. Then Peter decided to go after you. I see you all returned in one piece."*

Max laughs and strokes his orange-and-white friend. "Poppy, we're needed back in the 1800s to help rescue two little slave boys and bring them to freedom."

"Aha, another small task you've taken on," she purrs. *"I'm sure you'll be needing my help sooner or later."*

Max and Jinx pick themselves up and straighten their shirts and shorts. Jinx brushes the grass from her tee shirt and picks some sticks out of Max's blond hair.

"Whew, that always gives me such a heart-throbbing rush!" Max exclaims.

"What, the touch of my hand?" Jinx bats her eyes at him, teasing.

Max blushes to the tips of his ears. "Yes...no, I meant riding the Time Tunnel," he says. *I hate it when she does that to me,* he thinks. He always attempts to keep their friendship light, but finds himself more often thinking about Jinx in a deeper-friendship way. He wonders if she feels the same about him.

"Sorry, but I love to make you turn red. It's so cute," says Jinx. "Anyway, we've got business to discuss, important business. We need to talk to Aunt Merry about the farm, since the former owners of Conestoga Courage Farm helped the slaves to escape from the South."

The teens and Aunt Merry named the 1700s farm after the courageous tribe of Conestoga Indians last winter. They had been called back in time to try to help the small tribe escape from certain death at the hands of the Paxtang Boys Gang.

Jinx and Max talk as the animals lead the way through the meadow to the stone farmhouse. Fireflies light the path, blinking soothing messages in the air.

"Max, I had that dream awhile ago, and I didn't have time to discuss it with you. I was waiting for the right time. But the Time Tunnel grabbed us before I could share the vision." She glances sideways at her silent companion. But his eyes are focused ahead, as he thinks about all of the new developments.

"I saw Henry's boys taken away from him, like they were kittens to be used as cute little pets for a plantation mistress. There was nothing any of the slaves could do to help, or they would have been whipped. It was terrible..." Jinx's eyes begin to tear up again, as she thinks about the two little boys who were ripped away from their papa.

Max pats her shoulder. "I know these visions take a bite out of you. I'm sorry for that. I wish I could share the burden of having them for you."

Jinx glances at her friend. *When did he become so tall,* she wonders. *We're not little kids any more.* She gives a broken sigh.

"Thanks, Max. Talking with you helps more than you know."

They walk up the steps and onto the broad front porch that wraps halfway around the farmhouse. They settle on the big swing. Poppy and Petey flop onto the braided rug. The house is lit from within and gives off a comforting glow. The teens look around thoughtfully, noticing Aunt Merry's pretty flower gardens where once long ago there had been a farmyard for cows and horses.

Aunt Merry calls out a hello. "How about some lemonade?" she asks. "Be right out with some."

She soon appears with a tray of cookies and a pitcher of her freshly squeezed lemonade. Aunt Merry's red hair is longer than Jinx's and pulled into a ponytail. She looks calm and cool in her white tee shirt and pale-green cropped pants. She sits down in one of the comfortable rockers near the swing and pours everyone a big glassful of the sweet-tart treat. Sensing their mood, she rocks and waits for them to tell her about their problem.

"Aunt Merry, we took a Time Travel. We went back to the time of slavery. Our farm must have been a stopover for the fugitive slaves.

Mary and John Martin lived here, and they took in two men who were brothers. We helped John to keep them safe. Max got himself caught by the two slave runners and their hounds that were hunting the two black men. It was so tense."

Jinx lets the words tumble around in her chest and leave her, feeling the weight of them lifted to make her body lighter. She sighs. It always helps to talk with Aunt Merry. She once had the 'Gifts' that Jinx has: visions, Time Travel, and animal communication. Aunt Merry told her that as she got older, her powers lessened.

"Yeah, I felt like I was running for my life," Max says. "This job isn't going to be easy. I'd rather face Blackbeard all over again than these people who treat others so badly." He refers to their pirate adventure of last spring. "People treated their slaves like livestock, didn't they? Like they didn't have souls, or feel emotions like everyone else. I don't get it."

Aunt Merry lets the children unload for a while. She always worries for them, because of their special gifts, and never ceases to be amazed at their strength and willingness to face great odds to help others.

The warm wind caresses their heads and cools the sweat on their faces and necks. The teens sip the cold lemonade. Petey and Poppy jump up in their laps to listen better, causing the swing to gently sway back and forth. Crickets and grasshoppers still chirp. Off in the distance the sky flashes as a thunderstorm makes its way south of them across the county.

"You know," Aunt Merry says softly, "not to excuse this type of behavior or thinking, but it was the mindset of the era. Some plantations were hundreds of acres; they needed a couple hundred workers to plant and harvest the crops. Plantations also had dairies with cows and horse stables.

"So Africans were stolen from their homes and chained together in the bottoms of the ships; they were treated like the animals, given little more than shelter and food. Some early Americans thought that the black slaves were inferior to the whites.

"Maybe we should try a shared vision and go back to the beginning. The story is very tragic; it won't be pleasant. But I think it's necessary to help us understand. Max, Jinx, do you want to try? I've been feeling the same pull back into history as you two. But I can only share the vision if you take me there," says Aunt Merry. "I lost my strong powers long ago." Everyone nods.

The children join hands with Aunt Merry and she begins, "Feel the ship rolling and rocking in the deep ocean swells..."

Vision Story Part One:
1838—Atlantic Ocean, Aboard a Slave Ship

The boy can barely lift his head without bumping into the rack above him. He lies side by side with other sweating bodies, legs in manacles and wrists shackled by huge chains that run the length of the ship. When he does look, the sight is indeed an awful one to endure.

Everywhere he looks, he sees his village people and other strangers crying softly or moaning in pain. Last night two women and a poor little baby girl died a painful death from lack of food and water.

The ship rolls back and forth but does not soothe like a cradle. Instead it batters them and makes them roll side to side like logs. If the great ocean would only be calm and give them a little rest...

The boy still feels stunned and dazed. A few weeks ago the tribesmen from the closest village had turned against them and led the white men in a horrible raid on his village. He heard they did so for their own safety. His village had heard of these white men with weapons. The village elders warned them to run away into the jungle if they ever came upon them, but the white men had surprised them. They carried big sticks that cracked like thunder, causing men to tumble to the ground, bleeding from big holes in their sides. Many of the village people simply froze in fear, allowing themselves to be captured and bound in ropes.

If only his brother and the other children had followed the boy as he ordered, they would be safe in the cool, green jungle, not aboard this giant boat bound for a strange country called "A-mer-i-ca..." He rolls the word around his tongue, trying to say it.

He had been leading games and races with the village children when the white men burst upon them like tigers on the hunt. He shouted, "Run, run...follow me." But his twin brother and the other children had frozen stiff, as if they were encased in invisible cocoons. When he sneaked back to the village to get them, they were already tied to trees. The white men saw him and shouted at him. They chased him and threw him roughly on the ground to be tied up. Then came the weeks of torture on the large boat–lying on their backs, tied up like animals, only allowed above board for a brief time daily for exercise.

Now, some of the ship's crew hustles down the ladders from above. They shout strange words at the people. "Stinking animals...it smells to high heaven down here." What do these strange sounds mean? The white men do not like us; they hate us. Why?

The crew throws buckets of rotten vegetable and fruit scraps around the floor, along with some moldy hardtack—flat tasteless biscuits. Very little food is left for the crew this far into the journey, let alone for the captives. The sailors unlock the big locks that hold the chains tight and pull the chains from the manacles. They leave some buckets of brackish water behind. The Africans are able to roll over and get down from the racks, putting their feet on the wooden deck.

The women wait for the men to pass scraps, and then they feed the children before they eat. The boy gags on the smelly food. He hopes he will not throw up, like so many of the people are doing. But he knows he must keep his strength to stay alive. If he doesn't eat the food, the rats will.

Maybe soon they will come to take them above deck for their daily free exercise period. Then he will be able to breathe fresh air. Down in the dark belly of the ship, chained as they are, they cannot even move to the corners of the ship to relieve their bodies. They must relieve themselves right where they are, and then lie in the stinking waste. Like animals. Why do they treat us like this?

Suddenly, strange noises...the crew shouts in excitement. Ship movement slows. There is a great grinding as the anchor goes down. Sailors stomp and bang down the stairs once more. They shout, "Get up, move, move, move." They grab the boy, among some other men, and shove him towards the ladder. He gives his brother a frantic look. "Be strong," he shouts to him, before he is thrust into the bright sunlight.

The rough wooden planks scrape his feet. The sails are being dropped and lashed to the masts. Everywhere men scurry to do their jobs. He gulps in fresh salt air and tries to control the thump, thumping of his heart. It sounds like his drum at home. The boy bites his lower lip. He will shed no tears; let the seagulls screech and cry for him. The fresh air smells good and salty. The sun warms his skin.

They are chained to each other again, shoved into smaller boats and lowered to the waiting water. The land is very swampy, and swarms of mosquitoes attack the slaves. Since they are bound hand and foot, they can do little to save themselves from bites and stings.

The boy looks ahead apprehensively. Anything must be better than being shackled in the pit of a great boat. If only he knew what will happen to him.

The brawny sailors with tattooed arms row quickly to shore. The boy looks at the people watching as they bump into the wooden dock. More white men come and some white women and children, too. They are covered in strange material wrapped around their arms and legs from the neck down to the ground. Pants and shirts, boots and shoes, long dresses and shawls. Everything is so colorful and strange.

In his hot jungle home there is no need for covering your body with much clothing; it is the custom of his people to wear very little so they are cool. But these white people all point and laugh. He realizes that he is almost naked compared to the white people and feels overcome with shame for the first time in his life. I am so black and they are so white. We do look different, but don't they know that I have feelings, too?

On the dock the boy is shackled to the other men again. The sailors drag them towards a wagon hooked to a big snorting beast. The black men pull back a bit in fear. What kind of beast is this? It doesn't look like a leopard or monkey, but kind of like an antelope, without the twisted horns. He saw this beast, and smaller ones like it, being used as pack animals by his captors, back home in Africa.

The beast turns its head and looks at the boy; he feels better. The beast looks at him with tired, kind eyes. "They must work you hard," he says, and drags himself forward to stroke the beast's soft neck. The beast bobs his head.

"Hey, this one will make a good horse breaker," shouts a white man. The boy knows he is being talked about, but he does not care. He takes comfort in touching the warm neck of the beast.

"Come on, into the wagons, all of you," shouts another white man, shoving the captives towards the empty train of wagons. He is dressed in finery, with shining boots. His dark eyes snap with excitement as he thinks of the money to be made on this latest shipment of slaves.

Too bad he lost about one-third of his captives to illness and disease on the long sea voyage, he thinks. The sailors tossed the dead bodies overboard like they were dead rats. To make matters worse, his crew found a few other dead bodies while unloading his slaves here at the pier. Oh well, he thinks, still plenty of slaves made the voyage alive—it will be a good haul.

"Watch for the next slave sale posted, folks," Jackson Merryweather, Sr., the owner of the slave ship, shouts. "Looks like we got some good stock this time, good strong bucks for the fields, maybe even some brighter ones who will make excellent house servants. Lots of sturdy women good for breeding children, who will also be valuable as slaves. I expect they'll all fetch top dollar, so bring your moneybags."

Merryweather looks at the youth by his side. "Son, this is your legacy. When you grow up you'll have to decide whether or not you'll continue to run a slave ship. Since they made it illegal, it's more dangerous than ever to bring in fresh livestock direct from Africa. If government ships ever capture me, I could be slapped with immense fines, thrown into prison or worse."

Jackson Junior worships his father. He sees him as a brave hero, willing to defy the United States government. "Pa, I'll do you proud, don't you worry."

"That's my boy," Jackson Senior says. He claps his son on the shoulder and turns back to the loading of the slaves onto the wagons. His son helps him prod them to move faster by poking them with a riding whip and shouting orders. The boy gets a thrill out of frightening the captives and making them jump in pain.

The black men climb aboard the wagon. Another old black man is driving the beast, the boy notices. He is clothed like the white men, only his clothes don't look as fancy. He wears a tan shirt tucked into coarse brown trousers. His brown boots are scuffed. A broad-brimmed hat perches on his head, and a red bandanna is tied around his neck. He has white hair and a white beard.

"Hello, do you understand me?" the boy asks in his language. The driver gives a start and glances back over his shoulder.

"Quiet, boy. They hear you talking, they'll take the whip to your bare back," says the driver. "I'll talk with you on the road." He coughs and says, "Ha-yup." The beast responds to the gentle smack of the reins on his back and jerks the wagon into movement.

They rumble over the dock and off onto a road that winds through city streets. There are tall houses made of stone and brick, so different from their simple grass huts. The boy sees the fancy-dressed white man gallop ahead on another fine beast of a different color. The beasts must come in all colors, he thinks. I'd like to be friends with one of those. He smiles for the first time since he was taken from his village. He sits in the cart, thinking and wondering. Soon the crowded streets full of buildings turn into country roads, bumpy and rough, that lead over meadows and into wooded land. The air smells sweet, and the sun feels warm on his bare back.

"Now, Grandfather?" he whispers to the driver. He uses the name out of respect for his elder. "Is it safe to talk?" The boy is amazed and excited to find another who speaks the language of his people. "What is this pretty beast? I like him very much. What will happen to me? Where are we going? Will they hurt me? I'm afraid..."

The old man speaks in the language of the boy's village. "Wait, Little Man. You ask so many questions, all at one time. I remember when I first come here from my village. We must have lived close by, since I recognize your language after all these years. I'll try to remember it. I know how scared you are. First off, the beast is a horse." He chuckles at the young boy.

"Hor...sss," the boy tries out this word. "Horse." He smiles again. "I like this friendly beast, the horse."

"You will get to see more horses after a few weeks. First you're going to a slave pen. It's not a nice place; they'll keep you chained up. But the food is not too bad, and you'll have lots of water. They want to scrub you down and clean you up. The food will fatten you up so you look good at the slave market," says the old man.

"Chained up again? Will I live the rest of my life in chains?" The boy's eyes glaze over as he considers this horrible fate.

"No, the chains come off after a time," says the old man. "But only if you listen and do everything your master says. At the slave market, you hope a plantation owner who isn't too cruel buys you to work in his cotton fields, picking cotton all day long. If you work hard, you might get a special job living in the mansion house, or helping Boss Man in charge of the field hands. Maybe driving the wagons and carriages for the master, like I do. But you must always, always listen to Master, or you will be whipped or given worse punishment."

The boy cannot imagine punishment much worse than what he has been through so far. He cannot understand many of the words that the old man used, either. *Mansion? Carriage?* But he listens closely so he can learn.

"How long do I have to stay there? You mean to say I must always stay on this...plan-taa-shun? I can never go where I want to go?" asks the boy.

"That's right, boy. That's what the word 'slave' means. You're not free anymore. From here on out, you belong to the master who buys you. You work hard for the man for barely anything...a rickety cabin and a tiny garden to grow your own food. Your freedom is gone."

Not to be free? He has never thought even once about his freedom until he has had it taken away. This is the worst punishment of all. He ducks his head and puts his brown arms over his tight curls. The tears finally come, great racking sobs that cause him to rock back and forth.

The other black men who have been listening pat the boy on the back in sorrow. Slaves, not ever free again? They talk softly among themselves, feeling the same sorrow. Some of the men and women cry along with the boy. What a horrible fate, they think.

"Now, now, Little Man. Life is what you make of it. You can make it better, or you can make it worse for yourself. I'm telling how you can make it better. Now, you listen to me; we're almost at the slave pen. You do everything the white men tell you to do. Never look them in the eyes, always lower your head, and say 'yes sir.' Practice it, 'Yes, sir.' Even if you're angry, don't let it show. If you do, you'll be beaten. Do you understand? You're a slave now, and there's nothing you can do about it." *The old man looks at the boy in sorrow.*

"Yessss, ssirr," says the boy. *He wipes his tears on his arms and looks at the old man, feeling sorry for him. The old man has a broken spirit and has given up.*

The boy looks up at the broad blue sky peeking through at the lush woodland of this new land called America. He places his hands on his broken heart to begin healing it, and he makes a pact with himself. I'll never let my spirit be broken. I'll never give up. Someday I'll have sweet freedom once more.

The sky flashes and lights the farmyard for a moment before releasing a grumbling rumble. A stiff breeze picks up and turns the leaves of the old oak tree upside down. The tire swing begins to sway back and forth as if a phantom swinger is visiting. The barn throbs with a light blue glow, and then darkens. No one catches the odd glow.

Jinx breaks the handclasp first, shaking her head and pushing up off the porch swing. Petey barely jumps to safety in time. "I...I'm sorry, Petey." She places her empty glass on the tray and picks it up. "I have to go be alone," she mutters. Petey and Poppy follow her, along with the worried glances of Aunt Merry and Max.

Max stands up to follow her, but Aunt Merry holds him back. "Let her go. She'll be okay. How are you?"

Max sits back down on the swing and collapses backwards onto the flowered cushions. He places his arm over his eyes. "Wow, what a headache. I told Jinx I wished I could help share some of the burden and pain of her visions. I had no idea how tough it really is to have these visions."

"May I get you anything to help the headache?" Aunt Merry says.

"No, thanks Aunt Merry." Max stretches his full length out on the cushions. The swing is so long that there is room to spare. "It feels good to lie here. I'll stay put and think about everything. We need to figure out how to help our new friend from the past get his twins back."

The sky continues to flash, but the grumbling thunder is further away. The summer storm is taking another route tonight.

"Okay, Max, I'll say good night then. I'll come check on you in a bit."

Miss Poppy comes through the front pet door and leaps back up on the swing. *"Jinx is fine,"* she purrs. *"She's exhausted and fell fast asleep with Petey. Quite a day for your first full day of vacation, right, Max?"*

Max answers with a soft snore. He's fast asleep, too. Aunt Merry edges the screen door open and disappears. She returns with a cotton blanket and places it over Max. She smiles at Jinx's friend before she places a light kiss on his head.

"Yes, quite a day for my mystery detectives. Keep watch over your boy, Poppy. You and the angels will have your hands full with this trip."

Then she heads upstairs to check in on Jinx. Jinx is sprawled on her stomach on top of her oak bed, lightly sleeping. Petey is curled up beside her. She awakens when Aunt Merry enters. Jinx sits up, rubbing her forehead.

"Wow, Aunt Merry, that shared vision was more intense than any I've ever had before. I have the beginnings of a real headache, for sure."

Aunt Merry perches on the edge of the bed. "I know how it is; I've gone through the same thing when I was in my teen years. You'll be able to handle everything better with experience. You learn how to protect yourself from the bad stuff, as if putting yourself in a plastic bubble. You can see it all, but the vision doesn't affect you as physically. Emotionally...that's bad enough."

Jinx hugs Aunt Merry. "I'm glad I have you, Aunt Merry. I love Mom so much, but she doesn't get it. Her special powers were different than mine. She has no idea what this is like with the visions and Time Travel. You do, because you've done it all."

"I'm here for you, kiddo. Now try to rest. I guess you and Max have a huge task ahead of you." Aunt Merry pulls an old, brightly patterned quilt over Jinx. As they both touch the quilt, they feel an odd buzz tingle through their fingers and up their arms. It stops as quickly as it started. Petey jumps down to the floor.

Petey springs up and down on his back legs and then bounces up onto the bed. *"It's about a mystery, a mystery quilt that helps you find the way,"* says Petey.

Jinx hugs the quilt around her and studies the patterns. "Did you feel that buzz? Petey's right, I think this old quilt is trying to tell us something."

Aunt Merry looks at the quilt and smiles. "Quilting played an important role in history. Women got together for quilting bees as entertainment. They'd make blocks in special patterns and sew them together. Almost every household had quilts for comfort on those chilly nights. And it is thought that the slaves used the quilts to send codes about how to run away safely."

Jinx yawns and pulls the quilt up to her chin as she lies down. Petey curls up against Jinx's side. The quilt surrounds her with peace. "I know what you mean about quilts being a comfort. I remember something about a quilt in my very first vision of the twins being taken from Henry...I wonder..." Jinx slips into sleep.

Aunt Merry sighs, turns out the light and tiptoes out.

Chapter Five

The Glowing Barn

Jinx sits at a table in Aunt Merry's library the next morning, sipping hot chocolate and nibbling peanut-buttered toast. She is so deep into old reference books that tell about Lancaster County's history that she doesn't hear Max enter the room. Only when he places his plate of toast on the table does she raise her head.

"Well, well, the sleeping dead awaken. Good morning, Detective Buddy, about time you get awake," says Jinx. She gives a big grin to Max, who returns it with an even bigger one.

Max's blond hair is wet from his morning shower. He wears his navy-blue Mets shirt and baggy cargo shorts, with flip-flops on his feet.

"I see we have our rival shirts on again," he says, sitting down with a plop.

Jinx stretches her arms, then shoves the red sleeves back on them and lovingly brushes her hands across her Phillies sweatshirt.

"Yes, your poor Mets aren't looking too good again this year. Too bad your ace pitcher was sidelined with a hamstring pull," she says.

"Yeah, you look real sorry," says Max. He takes a big bite out of his toast and licks the peanut butter off of his fingers. "Yum, love Aunt Merry's homemade bread. What have you found?"

"Before we start, thank you for going into the vision last night. I didn't have quite as serious a headache afterwards," says Jinx. She looks into his bright blue eyes with a question. "I hope you were okay. I worried about you."

Max holds back the truth. *She doesn't have to know,* he thinks, *because then she'll want to protect me. I need to be able to share the load.*

"I was fine, very tired," he says, breaking off eye contact. He really doesn't like to tell little white lies to his friend. "So, spill it. Anything good to help answer some of these questions we have?"

Jinx becomes all business again. She loves researching, especially when it helps them in a new case. She tells Max about the strange experience with the quilt, and then she moves on to the research.

"Guess what? John and Mary Martin did own this farm, back in the mid-1800s. In fact, the Martin family continued to own the farm all these years until selling it to Aunt Merry. They were abolitionists, against slavery. This house was a safe house on the Underground Railroad route that ran through Lancaster County."

"A safe house? Is that a term they used for a place that would help the runaway enslaved Africans?" asks Max. He's as excited as Jinx.

"They knew what they were doing, too. You could tell it wasn't the first time they received runaways. John and Mary were really prepared with that hiding place in the barn floor."

"You're right. This is great news. No *wonder* I was attracted to the property," Aunt Merry says.

She comes into the library with plates full of bacon, sausages and eggs. The good aromas trailing from the kitchen attract Petey and Poppy, who follow her on the run. "You two need more than toast if you are planning on heading back in time," Aunt Merry adds.

The two friends attack the plates like starving puppies, smiling their thanks at Aunt Merry. Petey places his front paws on Jinx and wiggles his whole body.

"Oh boy, bacon, bacon, bacon. I love bacon."

"Petey, you're so goofy. You sound like that dog on the TV commercial. I'll save a piece for you, don't worry," says Jinx. She tickles him under his chin.

Poppy takes a much more sedate approach to begging. She winds back and forth around Max's ankles and purrs, then jumps into his lap and pretends to have no interest in the food. Licking her front paws, she says, *"If I may have one tiny morsel of sausage, I would appreciate it."* Everyone laughs.

Aunt Merry continues. "There were so many routes to take on the Underground Railroad. Many of them ran right through Lancaster County. The runaways would come across the border from Maryland into York County, then cross the river from Wrightsville into Columbia to head further north. Our farm is so close to the river, it would have made a perfect safe house.

"Did you know that many former slaves risked settling in Pennsylvania, instead of heading to Canada with others? Canada declared slavery to be against the law and refused to return runaways to the United States, so it truly was a safe haven for them," she says.

Through the open windows comes the whistle of a train way off in the distance, "*whooooooo, woo woo...*" Jinx cocks her head and looks at Max. He nods his head; he hears it, too.

"Aunt Merry, I keep hearing a soft train whistle in the distance, like it's calling to me. Can you hear it?" asks Jinx.

"No, I haven't heard it. I guess I've lost that part of the gift, too," Aunt Merry says.

"Why was it called the Underground Railroad, anyway?" Max asks.

"Well, railroading became a big means of transportation in the 1800s. Someone once was talking about how the African Americans kept disappearing from sight when they ran away, like they rode an underground railroad. They decided it would be a good code word to describe the secret routes and helpful people and homes for the slaves to use. It became so organized that even the words used to describe things were given railway names. The *conductor* was a person who would lead the slaves along the route to the next safe house, or *station;* the *station master* was the keeper of the safe house; and a *passenger* was code for a fugitive slave."

An idea pops into Max's head. "I'll bet *load of potatoes* is code, too. Yesterday when we were with John, he said he was about to get a load of potatoes, and it was Edward and Henry. Jinx, we saw a third person with them that left in the dark. That must have been the conductor, the guy who led them to John's house."

Jinx nods her head in agreement. "This is all making sense now. I guess you and I are about to find out what it was like to travel on the great Underground Railroad."

She and Max dive back into their plates of scrambled eggs, making sure they keep one piece of bacon and one-half sausage for the furries.

Jinx and Max splash each other with whirling windmill arms in the deep, cool pond, until they both beg for mercy at the same time. They have decided to take a swim to talk over some plans.

"Stop, you're drowning me," says Jinx, holding her hands over her face.

"Only if you stop, too." Max coughs and sputters.

"Okay, on three we stop," says Jinx, as she keeps slapping the water. "One...two...three...stop."

They both keep up a whirlwind of splashing and laughing, finally calling a truce. Petey doggie paddles around them; his eyes sparkle with fun.

"You are so devious, I knew you wouldn't stop," says Max, toweling off on the shore. He tries not to stare at Jinx in her red-striped bathing suit. He feels his ears turning red and hopes Jinx doesn't notice.

"Yeah, you know me too well. It's my red hair. Makes me devilish." Jinx lies down in the sun on her blue beach towel. Petey comes out of the water, shaking his furry body, starting with his head right down to his tail. Water sprays everywhere.

Poppy jumps up from Max's towel where she had been basking in the sun. *"Peter, please. You know how I detest water."* She runs away to groom the water off of her shiny coat.

Max flops down beside Jinx on his stomach.

"So, I've been thinking of a plan. What if we were to go back in time as Northern cousins of some family, traveling down to the plantation that bought Henry's twin boys? Maybe Henry could go along with us as our servant. Two kids would never travel alone; they'd have a servant with them," says Max.

"How would we travel? I guess we could ride a coach, or take the train. But we need money from that time period. It would have to be a lot of money to tempt them to sell back two useful little house

Ghost Train to Freedom

servants. We sure couldn't use modern money. It would be a dead giveaway that something was off," says Jinx.

"We'll say we live near the plantation that sold the boys, and we heard about what good workers they are and would like to purchase them. Henry will know the path back Down South through North Carolina, where his plantation is located. Then we'll make our way further south to Georgia. I wonder where exactly the twins were sent? It'll be really dangerous, though. Professional slave catchers will be everywhere, hunting down escaped African Americans for a reward," says Max.

Jinx's eyes sparkle and she gets a faraway look in her eyes. "Well, we know the name of the twins' new owner from the vision is Smythe. And his plantation is near Savannah, Georgia. Henry told us that, remember?"

Max knows that look. Jinx thrives on danger and proving herself worthy of the challenge. But it's a righteous attitude. She will defend what is good and right even if it leads to danger first. He worries about Jinx throwing herself into so much danger. *Jinx would also be really mad at me for worrying about her,* Max thinks.

"I can see us now. We'll be dressed as two wealthy children of the 1800s." Jinx pauses, and her forehead creases a bit. "Oooo, I guess I have to dress like a girl, in a long dress and lace-up boots. Blech."

Max laughs. "Yes, you will have to be a perfect little 1800s girl. All about embroidering and baking and leaving the real work to the men."

"Yeah, right. That'll happen," snorts Jinx. "We should go tonight. It's easier to catch the Time Tunnel at night. So the goal is to meet up with Henry and head Down South after the twins. Simple."

"Oh yeah, simple," says Max. They bump fists and grin. It's never simple, and they both know it. "Let's head back so we can pack our bags," he says. He worries about the authentic money that will be needed.

Max always goes traveling prepared for everything: rope, tape, his all-purpose scout knife, a compass, a flashlight, anything that might be useful. Jinx loves him for his preparedness, knowing that she never thinks things through in advance.

"We'll work out the details when we get there. I know John and Mary will help us," says Max.

The two friends pack up their towels and head back to the farmhouse, both wondering how they will find the money. That's the key element to purchasing the twins' freedom. They both put their thoughts about needing 1800s money on hold, hoping the money problem will be solved.

As they head towards the barn, Jinx has a sudden thought: "I wonder if the hidden room is still in the barn. We didn't think to look for it," she says.

Rounding the corner, they both pull up short. Petey begins to wag his tail, and Poppy says, *"Well, well, look at the glow. I think perhaps the barn is calling us to come in and discover something special."*

Indeed, the barn is radiant, surrounded in a blue glow that pulses like a beating heart. It even emits cool air, drawing them closer in the warm afternoon.

"I don't know if we should go in right now," says Max. "The last time the barn glowed, we were threatened by that mean old Jed character from the Paxtang Gang. Remember? He told us to keep our noses out of the past. I don't need to visit with him again."

"Chicken. The barn was sickly green that time. Now it's a cool blue. I have a good feeling about it," says Jinx. "Look at Petey. He's wagging his tail."

"What do you think, Poppy?" asks Max.

"For once I agree with Jinx," says Poppy. *"There's something good for you in there. Let's go exploring."* She purposefully leads the way, her long tail straight in the air twitching away.

As the gang opens the barn door, a cool, mint aroma fills the air. They stand still and scan the area, checking to make sure there is no danger.

"Over here, over here." Petey tears off to the middle of the barn floor and begins digging through the scattered straw and a light layer of dirt. *"Help me dig,"* he says. Hay flies in all directions as he digs.

They finally find the wooden floorboards and the trapdoor. Jinx stops and looks at Max. "Bet it's the door to the hiding hole. This is about where it was during our trip back in time."

"Yes, it probably was forgotten over time when it wasn't needed anymore," says Max. "Here's the iron handle."

The animals stand back as Max and Jinx grab the cold handle and begin to tug. *Crash!* The handle pulls away from the rotten board, and the two children fall back on their behinds with a great thump in the dust.

"Ouch! Now what do we do?" says Jinx, rubbing her backside.

"Find a spade or something to pry it open," says Max.

They scan the walls to locate the tools Aunt Merry uses in her garden. Jinx runs for a shovel and hands it over to Max. He slides the edge of it under the slit in the floor. With an extra "oomph" the door opens enough to grab it and throw it back. Late-afternoon light filters into the dark hole. They all get on their stomachs and peer into the hole. Another surprise glows in the dark. In the far corner of the hiding place, a raised bump of ground gives off the same cool blue light.

"Who's going down first?" says Max.

"Not me. You're the one with the shovel. You go first and scare away the spiders and mice." Jinx shudders.

"Oh, my goodness. You faced pirates but are afraid of little arachnids and furry creatures? I'll go first," says Miss Poppy. She leaps in.

"Follow us, follow us, something good in here," says Petey. He dives in next, headfirst.

Jinx holds her arm out and flicks her hand. "After you, detective," she says.

Max grins and lowers himself down into the hole. Jinx continues to lie on her stomach, peering into the dark space.

Max joins the digging animals in the corner. He has to go about a foot down before he hits metal with a loud *clang*. Max continues to dig, and a buried metal chest appears.

"Come on, Miss Chicken. I need your muscles to help me pull up this chest," says Max.

Jinx finally jumps into the hole and grabs a metal handle on the side of the chest. A round of grunting and pulling finally unearths the whole chest. It's about two feet by three feet and as heavy as a box of rocks. They can barely hoist it up to the barn floor.

Up on top again, the two teens grin at each other.

"Who would have guessed? Buried treasure under the floor of Aunt Merry's barn," says Jinx. "What could it *possibly* be?"

Chapter Six

The Treasure Chest

The animals gather around Max and Jinx to look at the rusty metal chest. A big iron lock holds it closed. No key is in sight. How to break it open?

"It's so heavy—I hope it's not filled with bricks," says Jinx.

"If it's bricks, let it be gold bricks," Max says with a grin.

"Or dog biscuits," says Petey, leaping around the circle.

Poppy stares at Petey and shakes her furry head.

Max grabs the shovel and says, "Stand back, everyone. I'll try to break the lock." He stands and positions the shovel like a pole-vaulter getting ready to jump, then he jabs at the lock with mighty thrusts. *Bang...bang...* On the fifth or sixth jab the old lock opens, and Jinx takes the lock off of the chest.

Max falls back down on his knees. Everyone stares at the chest.

"Ready?" says Jinx. "You go ahead and open it, Max. It's only fair, since I made you do all of the dirty work."

"Thanks, Partner." Max lifts the creaking lid.

The box is filled with...old coins, lots and lots of old coins. It also has bundled paper bills. The teens lift some coins out to inspect them.

"Would you look at this? They are dated in the mid-1800s. This is exactly what we need to buy our way South and rescue the twins. The money is an answer to prayer. We'll need clothes, transportation, lodging and food, and lots of money to pay for the twins' freedom. This is plenty to pay for it all, with money left over," says Max.

"How do you suppose it got here? This is a miracle," says Jinx. "Do you think the Martins buried it?"

"Could be. Our farm is close to Gettysburg. Maybe they were afraid the soldiers would come raid the farm. I read that people buried their valuables to hide them from the raiding armies," says Max.

"Then we'll have to tell John and Mary about the money and return it to them," says honest Jinx. She notices Max's worried look. "What's the matter?"

"I don't know how that would work. Time Travel is a strange thing. There are certain rules to follow or bad things can happen."

"What do you mean?" says Jinx.

"Well, you can't show people things that they didn't do yet. When we go back to John and Mary, it will be before the Civil War is going on. They wouldn't have buried the money yet. They can't get the money back before they even buried it—we might get stuck in some kind of freaky loop and not be able to break out."

Jinx tries to wrap her mind around what Max is trying to say. "Interesting. But we're not sure who buried the money. We'll have to see how it plays out. We can at least tell them about the money."

Max agrees. "Let's show Aunt Merry and see what she says. Then we'll get ready to head out."

They lug the heavy chest in to the porch and call Jinx's aunt.

"What's up, you two? Did you enjoy your swim? Uh oh, now what?" says Aunt Merry, coming to the porch door. She puts her hands on her hips and examines their findings in disbelief. "Wow. You two struck it rich this time."

After filling her in, Jinx says, "So, whose money do you think it is now?"

"Well, the statute of limitations on any stolen money would be long gone. We can report it, but I feel sure it belongs to the finder by now. This is a real treasure for you," says Aunt Merry. "Half of this will be more than enough to help you in your journey. This is a wonderful find."

And I know what to do with the other half, thinks Jinx. The leftover money would sure help Henry and Edward get a new start in life.

They talk plans over with Aunt Merry and tell her they are leaving soon. She shakes her head in worry.

"I don't suppose I could convince you to let this one go?" Aunt Merry asks the teens. They both shake their heads no.

"Then I'll pray for your safe trip. But you need to know what you're getting yourselves into. There were wicked people back then who broke the laws and stole enslaved African Americans to resell and make money, no matter how dangerous that might have been.

"I remember reading about this one outlaw woman, Patty Cannon, who was the leader of a renegade gang of thieves."

"You're kidding, a woman bandit?" Max asks. He arches his eyebrows in surprise.

"You'd better believe it. At one time she lived in an old inn in Maryland. She and her gang not only stole freedmen and women, but they also would go to plantations in Maryland, Delaware and Virginia, steal slaves right out of their cabins at night, and smuggle them back to Patty's inn.

"They would chain them together for months at a time, in the attic and hidden basement rooms, with little food and water, until they had a bunch to sell Down South. If any slaves gave the gang trouble, she'd murder them and bury them in shallow graves on her property," says Aunt Merry.

Jinx and Max swallow hard and look at each other. The trip suddenly becomes less glamorous and scarier.

"Patty used an African American named Big George as bait to get runaways to trust him. Then Big George would lead them right into Patty's trap. The Negroes knew they really couldn't trust anyone, totally," Aunt Merry adds. "I just thought of something...remember, if you and Max are ever caught and put in prison, you won't be able to catch the Time Tunnel to come back home." She furrows her brow in worry.

"Aunt Merry," Max says, "it's the risk we have to take. We really must go."

Aunt Merry slowly nods her head. *Max is right,* she thinks. But she still worries.

"So Patty Cannon was a kidnapper, a smuggler and a murderer? Whatever happened to her?" Jinx asks.

"Her crimes finally caught up with her. She rented her land to farmers, and one plowing season her tenant got stuck in a sinkhole. Imagine his surprise when he looked down and saw a skull with arm bones and leg bones staring back at him. He called the sheriff, who found three more graves with bodies on the property. They think one body was a missing slave catcher she murdered for his money. The other bodies were two children and an infant.

"Her friends and gang members turned against her when she was arrested and put in jail. But before she went to trial, she died in prison. Some people say she swallowed poison that she smuggled along into the prison. They say it was the same poison she used to get rid of one of her husbands. No one is really sure what caused her death."

Jinx pulls back and gives a "phew" with her mouth. "What a horror story, Aunt Merry. Are you trying to scare us on purpose?" she says.

"You bet I am," says Aunt Merry. "These are the types of people you'll run into. Are you prepared to meet up with them?"

Max slowly nods his head. "I see what you mean, Aunt Merry. You're trying to prepare us for the worst. But we still have to go; we promised Henry that we would find his boys."

"Oh yes, one more weird thing about the story. Years later they had to move her bones out of the burial ground to a new location. Someone stole her skull, and it was passed around from one private home to another. Kind of a ghoulish ending for her, don't you think? It's supposed to be in some back room of the Dover Museum in Delaware, now." Aunt Merry watches the teens to see their reaction.

By this time they both have their hands around their necks, thinking about what it would be like to have their skulls passed around.

"Ew, Aunt Merry; that does it. Lesson learned. We'll watch for all kinds of awful people on the trip," says Jinx.

Aunt Merry winces and looks out of the window at the sun beginning to set. "I know; you must go. Please be safe, and do the right thing." She hugs both of them.

The teens head to their rooms to pack a few things, while Aunt Merry goes to the big farm kitchen to feed the animals. On the way to her bedroom, Jinx stops in the library to put away the books that she has been studying that morning.

The early-evening light shines through the windows, some of the sun's rays falling on the open pages of one book. As Jinx is about to close it, her eyes fall upon one word highlighted by the rays: Christiana. *Christiana? Where have I heard that mentioned recently.*

As she scans the page her heart thumps against her rib cage, and her breathing becomes shallow. Something feels wrong, dangerous. The air vibrates with the buzz that tells her she is about to have a vision. No, not right now when she's trying to prepare to go on a journey. Light fades to a tiny pinprick in the darkness...

A black man stands tall, shoulders back, on the porch of his farmhouse, waiting. Two dark faces peek out of the second-floor bedroom window. A crowd of black people starts to gather from the fields. They mill around and mutter in low voices. Their eyes watch the dusty road that leads in to the farmhouse.

"They're free now—no one can take them back."

"They better not try or there'll be trouble."

"Now, William says no violence, no guns."

"Don't matter what William wants. If those whites try to capture 'em, they won't go. We won't let it happen."

There is more rustling around. Someone shows a knife in a pocket, another shows a hidden gun. Horses on the road kick up a sudden dust storm as they head up the farm lane. Some white neighbors join the black people. Nerves stretch tight across faces, ready to break loose and urge fighting.

White horsemen gallop right out of the mist and into the yard, draw up reins and dismount. The oldest man with a beard and moustache shouts, "I hear my property is being hidden here. Better send those slaves of mine out here right now, or the sheriff will arrest you all."

The crowd is angry, and starts to advance. They push and shove and shout now.

"No man should own another man. We want freedom. Get out, go home. You are not wanted here."

The white men step backwards, and their hands go to their gun-belts...

✹ ☙ ✵

"AAhhhhh..." Jinx shivers and shakes out of her vision. Her hands go to her forehead, and she rocks back and forth while sitting on the floor. Petey licks her face.

"What's the matter? What did you see?" he asks. He places his paws on her arm. Jinx grabs him and buries her face in his warm fur.

"We've got to warn Henry and Edward. I think I saw the beginning of ugly trouble at a safe house in Christiana. The next place they are going to stay. Oh no..."

She jumps to her feet and flies up the steps, taking them two at a time.

She bursts into Max's room where he is loading his backpack and grabs him by the shoulders.

"Whoa...Jinx, you scared the dickens outta me. What's the matter with you?" says Max. "Sit down here, and calm down. Talk to me." He pats the quilt at the bottom of his big brass bed.

Jinx plops down and grabs hold of Max's shirt, shaking him again. "Hurry and finish packing. I saw some trouble brewing at the safe house in Christiana, where Henry and Edward are supposed to go next. We've got to stop them before they get involved. I think some plantation owner from the South is coming to grab them back. Maybe he's their owner. People started shoving and drawing guns and knives."

Max nods his head in agreement. Poppy has been listening, too. She jumps up in Jinx's lap and licks her arm with her sandpaper tongue. *"Ah, yes, the Christiana Resistance,"* she murmurs. *"Bad, very bad. It is written in history."*

Max jumps up and crams the rest of his stuff into the pack. Poppy knows her history. This sounds serious. "Okay, Jinx. Go pack. You need your backpack, too. We'll have to take along the money. We'll split up the bills and coins. Grab your canteen and any other useful things you can see. Don't worry about clothes; we'll be borrowing and buying some. Meet me in twenty minutes behind the barn, where we met John the last time."

"What about me, what about me?" says Petey. *"I need to come, I can help, I can help."*

Jinx and Max look at each other and make a split-second decision. "You'll come, Petey. Poppy, stay back here and monitor the situation. Come if we need you," says Jinx.

"Of course," says Miss Poppy. She knows she will have to come to the rescue, eventually. *Such a silly boy and girl to think they can handle everything. But they try so hard,* she thinks fondly. Poppy rubs against Max, who pauses his frantic packing to run his hand down her back.

Jinx and Petey run for her room.

Twenty minutes later the little group of Time Travelers draws close together in a circle, behind the barn. Jinx and Max are dressed in simple black tee shirts and jeans, with sturdy socks and leather hiking boots. They both wear their backpacks on their shoulders.

Aunt Merry puts her arms around Jinx and Max, with Petey and Poppy joining them in the middle. They stand in silence for a few minutes, whispering prayers for safety, until Aunt Merry kisses them both on their foreheads.

"Be safe and do what's right," she says. "Your travel angels will go with you."

She and Poppy stand back and watch Jinx pick up Petey. Then Jinx and Max join hands. It is important for them to block out every thought except that of going to John and Mary, back at the farmhouse, in the correct time era. Eyes closed, they stand tall. It is a still evening, darkness settles down over the farm in its valley. Then a great whooshing sound seems to surround them, sucking them into a black hole, and they blip out of Aunt Merry's sight, gone.

Jinx becomes aware of traveling in the frigid darkness of the deep, black Time Tunnel right before it dumps Max, Petey and her out in the farmyard.

"Ugh, you carry Petey next time," she says as she lets Petey down. "Between him and the money, it's a lot of extra weight to lug around."

Petey licks her leg and jumps up and down a few times. Max laughs softly. "No grumping around, it's too early in the trip to be complaining," he says. Jinx sticks her tongue out.

It's late evening, like the last time. Birds are silent, gone to roost. Crickets and tree frogs chirp and chatter. The clouds scud by, partially covering the moon. The air is humid, typical of late summer-night weather in Lancaster County. They look around for any sign of danger and then sprint low for the porch.

Max raps a soft little patter on the wooden part of the screen door. He sees Mary and John at the big oak table reading by lamplight. They both jump and look up when they hear the knock. John pushes back his heavy chair and strides to the door in two giant steps. He opens the door, his eyes widen and his mouth drops when he sees the children again.

"Well, our strange little helpers return," he says. "Come in, come in. I see you bring your furry friend with you, again." He reaches down to pet Petey, who licks his hand.

They all pull up chairs around the table, and Petey settles on the multicolored rag rug. Max and Jinx peer around the room. The big, black cook-stove, a woodpile, a comfortable rocker by the window, a big old iron sink—everything a large farm kitchen needs in the 1800s. On the wall a cross-stitch sampler shows the alphabet and a Bible verse: "Do unto others as you would have them do unto you."

"It's our way," gentle Mary says, watching their eyes. "You are looking for Henry and Edward?"

The two teens nod their heads. "Are they still here? We're very worried about the next stop." Jinx can't exactly tell John and Mary how she knows. "I'm afraid that it's a very dangerous place right now."

John says, "Yes, not every safe house is always safe, especially William Parker's house. But they did move on, to Christiana. Henry said he trusted that you were coming back to help him. He wanted to go on with Edward until you found him again. But he also wanted to meet Brother William Parker. He's a fugitive slave who settled over there in Christiana. Brother Parker has helped so many other enslaved Africans by sheltering them at his farm along the route to freedom, a brave man indeed. He himself could be taken any day by slave hunters."

Max's chest tightens; his heart feels like a huge balloon about to burst. He clenches his fists under the table. "When did they leave, John? Maybe we can catch them if we hurry."

John and Mary frown and glance at each other, picking up on the teens' worries. "They left last night. They were to stay over a few nights to rest before Edward left for Canada. Henry thought that he would wait for you there..." says Mary. She looks back and forth at Jinx and Max.

"I can take you over in the buckboard at first light," says John. "We need to clothe you the right way and pack some food for you. You should also rest a few hours."

Jinx is ready to disagree about the time to leave, but Max squeezes her hand below the table. "We need some time to prepare, Jinx. Listen to Mr. Martin," he says.

Mary hustles to the icebox to get some ham and cheese to wrap up. John goes into a back room and drags a green wooden chest out into the kitchen.

"Here, look through the clothes to find something your size. Our church gathers donations of clothing for us to keep handy for our runaways. They always need fresh, clean clothes and are so thankful. Find something to wear and pick out an extra outfit," says John.

Max grabs some cotton pants and shirts. He watches as Jinx holds first one dress, then another up to herself, frowning. Max bites both lips to keep from laughing.

"Can't I pretend to be a boy, Max?" she begs.

"You'll be more convincing as a girl, trust me," says Max. His ears turn red.

Mary laughs. "You can try on the clothes in the back room," she says.

Jinx takes the dresses and turns with a flounce. "Fine. I'll be the best girly-girl of all times," she says between clenched teeth. She stomps to the back room to try on the long dresses.

While Jinx tries on clothes, Max tries to explain Time Traveling, and how they found the buried money.

"*Ummm*, Mr. and Mrs. Martin, I think we owe you an explanation about who we are. I know you noticed our strange clothes. Jinx and I come from the future. We're Time Travelers. We know how to travel in the Time Tunnel to go into the past." Max pauses to see how the Martins react so far.

John sits at the table with his chin cupped in one hand. He watches Max with piercing dark eyes, weighing every word the boy says. Mary's pale blue eyes take on a faraway look. She glances between Max and John, head tilted and a small smile on her lips.

"Jinx has visions from the past, when someone in need tries to contact her for help. Or sometimes she sees things happen, and we have to decide if we're being contacted to go back and help. It can get really complicated..." Max finishes.

John and Mary both break into wide smiles.

"Well, the wonderment of it all," Mary exclaims. "But it's not for us to question. This world is full of strange and marvelous things."

John nods in agreement. "Don't look so distressed, son. You're right, it does sound complicated. But given the circumstances of how you two seem to appear out of nowhere, it all does make some kind of sense."

Max grimaces and continues on about the money. "Another thing...when we checked back into our time zone, we found a chest of money buried in the dugout room in the barn. It's money from the 1800s. Could it be yours?"

John and Mary look perplexed, eyes crinkled and brows furrowed.

"We've only got a small amount saved in the bank in Lancaster. Can't imagine where that money would have come from," John says.

About that time Jinx appears, dressed in a blue-checkered dress that buttons all the way up to her neck and reaches down to her boots. She does a circle, holding the wide skirt out to the side. She also wears a straw hat with a blue ribbon tied under her chin.

"Do I look like a lady?" She smiles, in a better mood. Petey scampers around her feet, barking.

Everyone breaks into applause and compliments until Jinx blushes.

"Max told us about your Time Traveling and the money," says Mary. "I believe the money is meant to be yours. Right, John? It certainly doesn't belong to us. We live a simple life."

"Yes, I believe it's yours to use in this great adventure. It will definitely help you along the way. You'll need hundreds of dollars to purchase the boys' release," John says. "It's quite a bold plan to go back Down South to find Henry's twins. I don't think you realize how far and how dangerous this will be. I recommend you buy a carriage and horse in Lancaster before you leave. When you have the boys, you'll have to travel by night, for sure."

"John, if anyone can do it, these two gifted children can. Let's get some rest for the weary until first light. You've quite a trip ahead of you," says Mary.

The lamps are soon extinguished, and the household rests. But Max and Jinx huddle together, sitting in the hallway outside of Jinx's room. Petey curls up between them. No one speaks. The house, so familiar to them, feels alien now back in the past. They wait and worry, wondering if they are too late to warn Henry and Edward about the Christiana Resistance. *I could kick myself for not remembering to check the exact date,* Jinx thinks.

Jinx reaches for Max's hand as she begins to sway and hears the loud buzzing sound starting in her ears.

"Max, stay with me. I think…I'm going back into a vision…"

Max grabs both of her hands. *Wherever she's going, I'm going too,* he thinks.

Vision Story Part Two:
1838—Slave Camp, Savannah, Georgia

Wagons full of slaves in shackles bump and rattle through a wooded area, finally reaching a large clearing. A few wooden huts stand around the edges of the clearing. White men dressed in big-brimmed hats and cotton pants and light-colored jackets stand around in groups, talking and bartering for slaves in chains. They poke and prod the black slaves, turn them around, and look them up and down.

Elsewhere are thatched-roof, open-sided shelters acting as pens for slaves. The enslaved Africans wear iron necklaces chained to rough support beams. Some even have their feet cuffed in iron, or have wooden stockade beams pegged shut around their ankles.

"Over here, Cyrus," shouts Jackson Merryweather, Sr., in charge of his shipload of new arrivals. The old black driver wheels the horse and wagon to a stop at an empty corral.

"Um hmm, boy, jus' remember what I told you. Eyes down and say 'Yes, sir' and you'll do fine," he whispers to the boy. He helps unload the shackled slaves and stand them in a row. Then he jumps back in the wagon and wheels it away without a backward glance.

The boy takes in the sights, too startled to cry. He watches some black men in plain shirts and cropped pants bring buckets from the nearby trough. In the blink of an eye he is doused in cold water. More and more buckets, then men with wet rags on poles scrubbing the dirt off of the new slaves. He coughs and spits, blinking the freezing water out of his eyes.

Next, they are given pants and loose-fitting shirts or dresses to put on; then they are taken to the empty corral and shackled to beams. Most of the new slaves hang their heads and close their weary eyes, hoping for some sleep to take them away from this new horror.

A doctor comes through with one of the white men in charge. He is elderly, and has short white hair and green eyes. His rough hands check for bad teeth and cuts or sores. The doctor pats medicine on those sores, and he gives strange medicines to some of the slaves who hold their stomachs or heads in pain.

"Hey," he calls to the overseer. "I believe I saw his double in the other pen. Have him brought over here. The pair of them together should fetch a bigger price."

The boy doesn't trust the old doctor. "Yes sir," he says, because that is what he was told to say. The doctor laughs.

Within a few minutes, the boy cries out in happiness as his twin is brought to him and chained with him. "Anwar," he shouts. They hug each other as if never to let go.

The old doctor shakes his head and grins. "I thought so; they look like two peas in a pod—brown peas that is." He chuckles at his joke and shuffles on down the row with his black bag.

Food buckets and water buckets are brought to the penned slaves. The food isn't too bad: fresh vegetables and fruits, cooked potatoes and peaches and apples, thrown in with the other slops. The two boys eat until their bellies are stuffed full.

"Alem, what will happen to us?" the boy's twin asks. "Are we to live like chained animals in this new world?"

"No, don't talk that way," says the boy, Alem. "An old man told me we are to go to a...plaan-ta-shun. I think it is a place where they grow things. A master will make us work. But it will be better than this, I hope."

"I hope that we will go together," says Anwar. "We need to cling to each other as if we are one."

They fall asleep that night, each holding the other close.

Chapter Seven

The Christiana Resistance

It's a beautiful, foggy September morning in 1851. Leaves on some trees are beginning to show hints of red, orange and yellow. The air smells fresh and earthy. John's horse snorts as he trots in the long lane of William Parker's farm, his breath like puffs of smoke messages.

Jinx adjusts her bonnet and draws her cotton shawl closer around the shoulders of her checkered dress. Petey rests in her lap. She glances at Max. He looks great in his dark-brimmed hat, black coat over a white shirt, and brown pants. Max feels her look and grins at her. His eyes say, "We can do this." Jinx nods at him, feeling his excitement of the beginning of a new adventure.

"This is William Parker's farmhouse. He rents from the Pownall family, close by," says John. "William is a fugitive. Even though it is risky, he chooses to stay here in Pennsylvania to help other runaways seeking freedom." Through the swirling fog, the two-story stone farmhouse appears. Two windows on the second story are placed directly above two below. Smoke puffs out of the chimney on the right side of the house and mixes into the soupy fog. There is no sign of people, nor have they encountered anyone along the road at this early hour. John reins in the horse near the front stoop.

The door opens and a tall, thin man steps out onto the stoop. He has mulatto skin like the color of coffee and cream mixed to a shade of light brown. His brown eyes are friendly as he greets them.

"Good mornin' to you and your friends, John Martin. What brings Brother Martin to my home this fine day?" says the man.

"Children, this is William Parker," says John. "The children, Miss Jinx and Master Max, are friends of Henry and Edward. They have promised Henry they will help him go back Down South to rescue Henry's twin boys."

William looks at the children with respect and amazement. "Come in, all of you, to our warm kitchen. My wife, Eliza, is mixin' up fresh biscuits as we speak. Come have breakfast with us. It's fresh eggs and ham. You're welcome to come in," says William.

John laughs and strokes his beard. "I'm tempted," he says, "but I've still got a crop of late corn to harvest before the frost takes it all." He turns to the children on the seat beside him and hugs them close. They jump down in the dust with their heavy bags. Petey goes over to lick William's hand. A couple of beagle hounds come over to sniff Petey. *Come play,* they say. The dogs rush off, yipping and yapping, to play tag.

"Godspeed to you both. Mary and I send you on with our love and blessings," says John. "Goodbye, William. I'll continue to pray for you and your work." John touches his brim, nods and slaps the reins to turn the wagon back towards home. Everyone watches until the wagon is out of sight, and then they follow William into the kitchen.

Inside the kitchen, the good aromas of frying ham and bacon and eggs fill the air. Henry and Edward jump up from the big table and run to the children.

"I knew you'd come find me," says Henry, with his dark eyes full of optimism. He and Edward hug them. "Hang your coat and shawl over here on the pegs and come meet the best cook around."

Eliza wipes her flour-covered hands on her apron as she greets the children.

"Men, you all shove down and make room. Looks like you both need some fattenin' up, um hmmm." Eliza rushes to the wood-burning oven and whips out a tray of brown biscuits. She dumps them into a basket and delivers them, along with plates of eggs and ham, to the hungry men and children.

Soon everyone is eating and talking in high spirits. Back from their races and fun, Petey and his friends, the beagles, chow down in little bowls over by the stove.

Henry explains who his young friends are, "This is Master Max and Miss Jinx. They's goin' to help me go back down South and get my boys back. It's a big danger, but I know we can do it." The others are excited to shake hands with these two white children who are brave enough to help Henry.

Then the conversation turns somber. William calls the table to order. "I expect trouble from the Gap Gang bounty hunters to come anytime, now. I received word days ago that Edward Gorsuch, from Maryland, is comin' with the Federal Marshal for his two runaways," William tells the group.

Everyone looks down the table to the end, where two black men are shaking their heads back and forth. Joshua Kite and his friend had stolen some crops and run away from Gorsuch's plantation. William Parker is helping them to find jobs and a new home.

"Brother Parker, we're not goin' back," says the one dark man with curly, short hair. His partner, with longer black curls, agrees.

"We've tasted freedom–it's not right to take us back like we was some horses that escaped the corral," he says. "We're human bein's and shouldn't be treated like we's someone's property."

"Don't worry, Joshua. No one, includin' you, is goin' back into slavery as long as I'm still standin'," says William. "My *Black Self-Protection Society* will make sure to come if they're called. Ring the big bell; blow a horn. Everyone comes runnin' to help when there's trouble. We're ready to defend the right of freedom for every black man and woman to death, if we have to."

Jinx sits next to Henry and pokes him in the side. "Henry," she whispers. He looks at her, startled. "I'm afraid there's going to be big trouble; please, let's leave before it starts."

"Hush now, Miss Jinx, let the man speak," whispers Henry, but he looks more worried. "Me and Edward are here with you–we'll help if needed," he says out loud.

William nods his appreciation. "Now let's go on about our daily business. We can't be paralyzed by fear," he says.

Jinx and Max watch Joshua head out the door to his farm job on down the road. Jinx decides to help Eliza clean up the breakfast dishes, and Max heads out to the porch to make plans with Henry and Edward.

Barely five minutes later, everyone hears a man yelling with all his might. They rush out to the lawn to see what is wrong. Joshua

Kite tears in the lane, holding his hat and screaming, "Kidnappers, William, kidnappers!"

A cloud of dust shows a group of men on horses galloping in the lane right on his tail. Joshua stumbles into the kitchen, where William shouts, "Upstairs, all of you."

The men grab Jinx's and Max's hands and pull them along up the steps to the second story. Petey yips up the stairs after them, growling, *"Let me get them...grrrr."* The beagles are outside, baying the alarm. *"Baarrrk, bark barrkk..."*

A bunch of white men on horseback gallop right up to the house. Two of them dismount and throw their reins to the rest of the posse. They fly through the door right into the house, shouting.

One is a middle-aged white man with a round face and brown hair that grows right down around his chin. He is dressed in riding clothes, a long coat and dark trousers with tall riding boots. He wears a broad-brimmed hat and carries a gun.

"My name is Edward Gorsuch, from Maryland. I believe you are harboring my runaways," he says. "You turn them over to me right now, or there'll be big trouble. I've got the deputy marshal on my side, with a warrant."

The hulking body that follows Gorsuch in the door shouts orders, too. "I am Deputy Marshal Henry Kline. I do have warrants for the arrest of the fugitive slaves that belong to Mr. Gorsuch." He throws them on the kitchen table. "Now, you know that Fugitive Slave Law says it's against the law to help runaways, Parker. It's your duty to turn them over to me, or I'll arrest you, too," says Deputy Kline. "You've gotten away with too much these past months."

Edward Gorsuch yells up the steps again. "If my slaves come with me peacefully, there won't be any trouble or punishment for them. I'll forgive their stealing wheat from me, and running away. I would like them to come back peacefully with me."

Deputy Marshal Kline starts up the steps to get the men. An angry William towers above him, holding something long behind his back.

"Don't take another step, Marshal, or I'll break your neck," says William. He is a giant protecting his own race against the evils of slavery.

"I'm a United States Marshal...you can't talk to me like that," says Deputy Kline.

"I don't care for you or your United States. There's no freedom for my people in the United States, so I won't obey your laws," says William Parker.

Deputy Marshal Kline sees William whip an ax out from behind his back and swing it through the air. He backs down the steps. *They must have weapons stockpiled up there,* he thinks. *We could get ourselves killed.*

Edward Gorsuch is disgusted with the deputy's cowardice. He urges him on. "It's your sworn duty to arrest my runaway slaves, Deputy. Go get them." When the deputy doesn't go back up, Gorsuch starts up the stairs himself. "I want my property, and I'll have it now!" he yells.

"You might come up the stairs, old man," says William, "but if you do, you won't be goin' back down, because you'll be mine." William heaves the ax at Gorsuch, and it comes so close it could have shaved the whiskers off his chin.

Jinx stares with wide eyes and open mouth. She grabs hold of Max's arm and squeezes. "Max, we have to do something," she whimpers.

"Ouch, Jinx, let go. We're not magicians. We have to stay low and let the adults deal with this, " Max says.

Jinx and Max watch Eliza grab a horn and go to a window, where she begins to give a mighty blast over and over. They peek out the window and see people begin to appear over the fields.

"Stop blowing that horn, woman. Men, *shoot* her, don't let them call for help, *shoot* her," says the deputy.

Outside, two men from the posse climb up some peach trees to get a better shot, lift their guns and shoot at the window where brave Eliza continues to blow her horn. Ten shots, twelve shots...still Eliza blows her horn. Someone from the house returns fire.

More black and white neighbors, some of them Quaker farmers, now gather in the yard, making the rest of the posse nervous. The neighbors have heard Eliza's horn and know that means trouble. Good neighbors run to help when they hear the horn. It's the common law of neighborly behavior. They stand like a solid brick wall in front of the house. Gunfire ceases.

The deputy marshal is furious. "All right, the warrant says to take you dead or alive. Go get some hay; we'll burn the place down," he says.

"Burn us if you want. You'll still not take us. You'll see my ashes scattered all over the ground before you'll take us," says Brother William Parker.

A young man from the posse comes forward. He looks much like Edward Gorsuch, with his bearded face and brown hair. "Father, *please,* I can see into the upstairs windows. They have guns and swords and mean to harm you. Come back, away from danger," says Dickinson, Gorsuch's son.

Meanwhile, the group of black men and women in William Parker's upstairs bedroom begin to fret and worry. "Maybe we should give up and go with them," says Eliza's sister, Hannah.

Eliza brandishes a corn cutter and says, "I'll cut off the head of the first one of you who tries to surrender." Hannah backs off in a big hurry.

The standoff rapidly gets more heated. Shots ring out from both sides again, until a yell cuts through the air. Edward Gorsuch is hit and falls to the ground.

"Father, no..." Dickinson runs to his father's side and takes a hit in the shoulder before he falls on his knees beside him. He gently cradles his father's head in his lap, tears streaming down his red face. Edward Gorsuch is dead.

The posse stops firing guns and retreats as William calls for a ceasefire among his supporters. The runaways will not be returning south with Edward Gorsuch.

The Deputy Marshal gathers his men, and they mount horses for a quick retreat. He doesn't wish to lose another life in today's battle. The message is clear—these people will fight to the death rather than go back into slavery.

Some of the neighbors who witnessed the shootings help Dickinson with his dead father. It is decided that they will take the body to the Pownall family farm further down the lane, where Dickinson can be treated for his gunshot wound and make arrangements for his father's body to be returned home for burial.

Before he is led away, Dickinson faces William Parker, the brave leader of the revolt. "You may have won today's battle, but this is not over," he says. "I *will* have justice for my father's death."

It has been a day of terror. Now in the evening dusk, the people in William Parker's house gather around the farm table once more for soup and bread. The injured have been attended to and the house and yard cleaned of any evidence that violence and bloodshed have occurred. No one speaks. The only sound is the clanking of spoons against bowls.

Max and Jinx sit huddled in rockers close to the warm, pot-bellied stove with a savory bowl of beef vegetable soup and hunks of brown bread clutched in their hands. Petey laps warm soup from a bowl; then he slurps a bit of cool water from another. He places his paws on Jinx's lap and whines a bit in worry.

Max reaches over and pats Petey on the head. He worries about Jinx. She stares into her bowl of soup without eating or moving. Her hands tremble slightly. Max places his soup bowl on the tiny table between them and gets up to place a knitted coverlet from the back of his rocker over Jinx's shoulders. She barely notices.

"Jinx, talk to me. What are you thinking?" No answer. "We can go home, Jinx. Maybe this is more danger than we can handle."

Jinx finally stirs and looks into Max's eyes. Her green eyes glisten with tears.

"I've never seen a person killed before, Max. I don't know if I'm strong enough to go on. This is big and ugly. Such hateful talk. We've really been sheltered in our lives, haven't we?"

Max agrees. "Why don't we rest here tonight and decide in the morning. Henry will understand. After all, we're just kids. He would respect our decision."

Henry has been watching the two children. He walks over and pulls up a chair in front of them. "Miss Jinx, you all right? That was mighty bad business that went down today. But now you see how strong that urge for freedom is for my people. We'll do anythin' to be free, even break their laws and fight for it. Can't you see, Miss Jinx?"

Jinx nods her head and covers her face with her hands. She rubs her eyes and sighs. "I see, Henry. I understand."

Eliza joins the little group and takes Jinx's hand. "Come, young lady. Time to rest a bit. Ya'll let her be." She leads Jinx to a small bedroom off the kitchen and helps her to settle under a downy quilt on the big brass bed.

"I'm so sorry you had to witness that ugliness, Miss Jinx. You was brave, for sure."

"Oh no, Miss Eliza, you were the brave one. How could you keep blowing the horn for help even when those men were shooting at you? But, would you really have hurt Hannah with the corn cutter when she wanted to give up?" Jinx cannot imagine the gentle little woman being violent, herself.

Eliza smiles and shakes her head. "I truly don't know, Miss Jinx. People say things in the heat of battle that they'd never think of or say under normal times. Sometimes it takes a threat like that to slap some sense into a person, you know? Now don't you fret none, you're safe here tonight." She leaves a lamp lit on the table.

Petey jumps up and snuggles with Jinx. *"I'll keep watch, Jinx. You rest."*

Jinx wraps her arms around her terrier friend and slips into sleep. She doesn't see her other best friend slip into the room and wrap up in a quilt on the rocker beside her bed. In Max's arms is a shotgun, borrowed from William Parker. He plans to keep watch all night.

Shortly after midnight, Jinx begins to tremble and shake. She calls out in her sleep, "Max? Max, come with me...it's the vision story. I'm slipping away..." Max nods awake and quickly grabs her hand to go along.

Vision Story Part Three:
1838—Savannah, Georgia, at the Slave Pen Camp

The two brothers have been in the camp for a few weeks now. Twice a day, food is brought to the pens and dumped into troughs. The boys quickly learn they must push their way in to get some food. There is never enough, but the food is better than what they had onboard the ship. They are unchained for a short period each day and exercised in a big pen with lots of other black men carrying rifles watching over them.

They sleep on piles of straw, chained to the fence. Like onboard the ship, there is no privacy for anyone. There are only two buckets in the corner for all the men to relieve themselves. The women are kept in a separate cage.

The constant rolling of the ship and seasickness have been replaced by the relentless itching from the bites of mosquitoes and other insects.

Once, they saw a big man break away from the group and climb the fence to escape, only to be shot and carried away. Another time, two men tried to run at night. They actually broke their leg chains, crawled under the stockade fence, and made off into the deep woods.

Everyone rejoiced for them, until a day later when the men were dragged back into the camp behind horses, all beaten and bleeding. The boys watched in shocked silence as the escapees each had a finger cut off. Then their heads and feet were put in wooden stocks, where they were forced to stand in the hot sun all day and night. The boys did not dare to even think about an escape after they witnessed these acts of terror. Maybe someday, but not now. Besides, where would they go? How would they get food? At least they were fed daily and exercised.

Today, after the morning meal, there is a murmur of excitement in the air as ten wagons arrive in the camp.

"Alem, what does it mean?" asks the boy's taller twin. "Will we travel on to a different pen? Are we always to be tied up as animals?" He grabs his brother's hand and squeezes tight.

"The old man in the wagon who brought us here said we'll be fattened, then sold to a master to work for him. I think we're fattened enough." The boy pats his stomach and points at his brother. "You look even taller, Anwar, and much fatter than me." He can't help but tease. They cannot take away his sense of humor.

"How can you laugh, Alem? Some days I think I'd rather be dead than to be here in this strange land and feel so frightened," says Anwar. He begins to cry.

Alem grabs his brother by the shoulders and gives him a good shake. "Never say that again. You must have hope that our lives will have some great meaning. Remember our parents and aunts and uncles. Honor them by fighting for survival. Promise me you will always fight for survival and freedom...promise me."

Anwar sniffs and wipes his face with his dirty shirt. He admires his brother's bravery. "I will fight with you. I promise." He seals the promise with a hug.

"Everyone, up on your feet. Let's go. Time to clean up and look pretty for the slave market. Your master wants top dollar for you...stand up." A white man with a cracking whip hustles all to their feet for a scrub-down with buckets of cold water.

The enslaved Africans are given new shirts or dresses to wear. Groups are shuffled over to the waiting wagons and loaded, still in ankle chains. By luck, the boy and his twin are put into the wagon driven by the old man who had brought them to the slave pens. Alem can't believe it. He has many new questions.

"Grandfather, tell us what will happen," Alem says.

The old black man, Cyrus, grins through his white beard and scratches his curly hair. "Do I see double, boy?" He remembers the scared boy from weeks back. "I see you survived so far. You look good."

Alem grins back. "Yes, Grandfather. You see double; this is my brother and twin, Anwar. I am Alem. A white medicine man found him and brought him to be with me. We hope to stay together."

"Well boys, you hang tight onto each other. Chances are, you might be sold together. How old are you?"

Alem answers, "We have been on the earth ten years."

"Then you's about ready to work in the fields. Your new white master will probably put you with a new mama and papa. They'll take care of you in a little cabin. It won't be too bad," says the old man. "It will be like a new family. But they won't let you be called by your African names; they'll give you new ones, for sure."

Anwar has a question. "Please tell us, how do we get picked by a new master?"

"That's the bad part. When we get to the slave market in Savannah, you have to go up on the stand. You'll be stripped of all your clothes. They'll sell you to the man who pays the most money for you. Sometimes the buyers look you over good. The crowd can be mean and laugh at you. But you keep your head down and take it. There's nothing you can do about it."

The boys look at each other. They can't imagine being sold like animals in front of the white people.

The white man with the whip rides by and flicks it against the shoulder of the old black driver. "Hey there, no talkin'. I can't understand you, and talkin's against the rules, anyway."

"Yes, sir, yes, sir, I'm sorry," says the old man. He turns away from the boys, but not before he gives them a tiny nod of hope. He pats his chest. "Keep your heart strong."

The white owner of the slaves rides atop a white stallion to the beginning of the lined-up wagons. Slave-trader Jackson Merryweather, Sr. looks splendid today in his black riding pants and high black boots. His ruffled, white shirt peeks out from beneath a black vest and red riding coat. A black, broad-brimmed hat tops the outfit.

"Wagons, ho," he shouts. He looks forward to the thousands of dollars he will earn today at the slave market. The drivers all smack the reins against the backs of the horses and the wagon train begins to roll.

Alem and Anwar look backwards at the slave-pen camp and stare at the few enslaved Africans left in chains. They both think it is better to be in the wagons leaving the hated pens. Alem pokes his brother in the side and takes his hand. "Let's look forward, brother. Let's hope for the best in this new life."

Anwar wishes he felt as confident as his brother. He wishes the dark cloud hovering over his soul would go away.

Chapter Eight

Stop or Go Decision

Jinx wakes up in her downy bed with a throbbing headache and a stiff neck. Petey immediately stirs and places a paw on Jinx's arm.

"*Bad headache?*" he asks. "*Let me help.*"

Petey places his head and paws gently on Jinx's forehead and rubs his soft chin against her skin. Jinx's headache lessens and then leaves.

"Petey, you are amazing. Thanks, little buddy. Wait 'til I tell Max what a good massage therapist you are. Your talents always surprise me," Jinx says.

The events from the prior day flood back into her mind, and she sits up with a bolt.

A gentle tap at the door, then Max enters with a big grin. He is dressed in his 1800s clothes: brown pants, black boots, a neat white shirt and black coat. "Eliza says come to breakfast, sleepyhead." His grin falters when he sees Jinx's serious expression and furrowed brow.

"I know, yesterday was bad. There's some serious talk at the table this morning. And we need to decide what to do next, if we should go home or leave for the South with Henry. They say the local sheriff will probably come soon, maybe try to arrest people who were involved," Max says. He rubs his forehead and frowns.

Jinx asks, "Max, do you have a headache, too? I had a vision last night about the two slave boys, Alem and Anwar. I really like their names—it makes them even more real in my mind. They were picked up from the slave-pen camp and are on their way to a slave auction. Did I call your name to go along?"

Max nods. "Yes, and I do have a bit of a headache, but it will lessen. I stayed in your room last night, right there in the rocker, to watch over you. I was really worried about you. In the middle of the night you got very restless. I knew you were about to enter a vision, so I grabbed your hand to go along. I saw everything..." He pauses.

"I wonder, who are those boys? Don't you feel like you know them, somehow? We seem to be following their lives as they were captured in Africa and brought over to America. Max, what's happening to them is horrible. I never knew how bad the conditions were for the enslaved Africans. I can't imagine being captured from my home and taken to a new country. That was so wrong."

Max drops his head, thinking. "I know we're supposed to learn from these experiences, maybe to understand the history of the black Americans better and try to help where we can. I feel so bad I can hardly stand it—so helpless right now. Maybe helping Henry get his boys back is positive action we can take to make a difference."

The air is heavy with their guilt and sorrow. Jinx jumps up from bed and stands on the cold wooden floor in her nightgown and sleeping cap. "Yikes, I need to get dressed. It's cold in here," she says. "You're right; it's time to take action. We keep going, heading south. I'm sending Petey to your room with you. Lie down on your bed, and let Petey help with your headache. He's like a little massage therapist. He lays his paws and chin on you to take away your aches and pains, right, Petey?"

"Let's go, let's go." Petey jumps off the bed and races out the door. *"I'm a good massager. I learned it in the Time Tunnel."*

Max says, "I'll try anything to get rid of this headache, believe me." Max's grin returns as he turns to go. "I'll meet you in the kitchen. By the way, you're so cute in your long nightgown and frilly nightcap. A real 1800s girl."

"Max, be an 1800s gentleman and get out of here," says Jinx. She throws a pillow at him, just missing his back as he closes the door. "So I did wake up last night and see you sitting over in that rocker with a shotgun," she adds. But Max is already gone.

A washstand with a pitcher and bowl sits beside the window. Eliza must have brought hot water when Jinx was still asleep. *How kind of her,* Jinx thinks. She pours the warm water from the pitcher, grabs a coarse bar of homemade soap and gets busy scrubbing her face and arms.

Jinx joins the men and Eliza in the kitchen right in time for a fresh batch of pancakes and sausage. They all welcome her, but the atmosphere is tense with fear.

"I expect the sheriff anytime now," says William. "We'll try to have no more violence today. I got a message from our secret militia that the sheriff and his posse have already taken some of the Quaker men who were here yesterday to the prison in Lancaster. I reckon he'll be after some of us, too."

The men stir and talk amongst themselves. "We won't go. No, we'll run before he gets here..."

"Yes, it's best for me to head for Canada, now. I'm goin' on ahead and hope to send for Eliza later. Have faith that we'll win out over this demon slavery one day," William says, trying to calm the men. "The Philadelphia papers are already calling it the 'Christiana riot.' I also heard that word was sent to a very good lawyer in Lancaster, an abolitionist, named Thaddeus Stevens. He's a United States congressman, real outspoken for our rights. I'm hopin' he'll defend our friends who were arrested at trial."

Horses are heard galloping up the lane to William's house. Before they can stir, stomping and banging begins on the porch. The local sheriff and Deputy Marshal Kline have returned to the scene of the tragedy.

"Open up, Parker. We have a warrant for the arrest of you and your men for the murder of Edward Gorsuch," says the deputy.

William signals the men to follow him through a trapdoor under a colorful rag rug. The cellar leads to the back of the house and outside. William and a few of the fugitives escape, but Edward, Henry, and one of Gorsuch's slaves are trapped in the kitchen with Eliza, Jinx and Max.

Eliza kicks the rug back in place, barely in time. Petey growls and bares his teeth at the sheriff as the men storm through the door and enter the room.

"Shhhh...Petey, quiet," says Jinx. Max thrusts her behind himself and picks up Petey.

Eliza whispers to the children, "It's the Gap Gang again, with the sheriff. They're very hateful slave catchers from a nearby town. Don't talk; if you're lucky, they'll leave you be. It's William and the other men they want."

Eliza walks toward the men. "You've no right to burst into my home like this," she threatens.

"Out of the way, woman. You're harboring murderers now," says the local sheriff. He pushes his way by her, sweeping her aside with his arm. The Gap posse who accompanies the sheriff is a mean-looking bunch. Their clothes are dusty and their boots are scuffed and dirty. They also wear holsters heavy with guns.

One of them walks over to Edward and grabs him by the shirt, ripping his collar as he drags him to the door. "He's one of them that fired, I seen him yesterday," he yells. They tie Edward's hands and take him outside. Edward's face is pinched and terrified. He looks frantically back at the children and Henry.

Two other men grab one of Gorsuch's slaves by the throat and slap handcuffs on him. He is shoved out the door, after Edward.

"Where's Parker?" Marshal Kline says. "If he's hiding, we'll find him."

He looks around the room, searching. His eyes fall on the rumpled rag rug. Kline walks over and kicks the rug away. The posse pulls up the trapdoor, and a few of them scramble down the steps. But William is gone, escaped out of another hidden door to the outside. They troop back up the stairs with scowls on their faces. The room is filled with tension. The air smells of the sweat and anger.

"All right, men, let's ride on. Parker can't have gotten far. These escaped slaves are in far more trouble than only being runaways. Now they'll be brought up on trial for murder," Deputy Marshal Kline says over his shoulder.

They place the two men under arrest into a wagon with an armed guard watching over them. The whole group of dusty riders moves out, determined to hunt the other men involved in the tragedy.

Henry pulls a stunned Jinx and Max over to a corner. "Sit here," he commands. Jinx and Max sit without a word, like trained dogs. Petey jumps out of Max's arms and runs out the door, growling and snapping at air. He is so angry that his hair bushes out like a giant puffball.

"We have to move out this afternoon, before the sheriff comes looking again. He won't be satisfied with one visit," Max says.

"But Master Max, I can't leave my brother behind, in jail. He'll die there, for sure. They'll probably hang those men. Edward didn't fire no gun; we don't even have guns. I have to go tell the sheriff the truth," says Henry.

Max places his hands on Henry's trembling shoulders. "Henry," he says gently, "Edward and those others will soon be in good hands. You have to trust me. You know that congressman William talked about this morning? He is a hot abolitionist and a great lawyer. We can't be sure of the outcome, but if anyone can defend them, Thaddeus Stevens can do it."

Jinx jumps to her feet, as determined as Max is to take action. "Max is right, Henry. I feel it in my bones. Our main goal has to be to find your boys and bring them back up to safety, so you can go on to Canada and freedom. We'll hope and pray for Edward and the others."

"Oh, Miss Jinx, I don't think you and Master Max should go through with the plans. You've seen now how bad it gets. I couldn't bare it if somethin' bad happens to you children. I never should have asked you," Henry says.

Jinx hugs Henry. "It's already settled," she says. She turns and runs to Eliza, who has been comforting the others. "Miss Eliza," she calls out, "do you know where we can buy a carriage for our trip South... and a good, dependable horse? We need to leave this afternoon."

Petey storms back into the kitchen, out of breath and barking. *"I chased them out, I chased them and nipped at their boots. Bad men... bad,"* he pants.

Jinx picks him up and smoothes his fur. "Good for you, Petey," she tells him. "I'm proud of you. I don't much like them either, but they're only doing their job. What a mess."

Eliza and Henry give tight smiles and reach out to pat Petey's furry head.

"It does seem like this little dog understands everythin' that happened, don't it? He's a bright little dog," says Henry.

Eliza thinks a bit; then a real smile lights up her brown face. "I did hear that Oscar's Livery Stable in Lancaster has a used carriage for sale. We'll go see what it looks like. May be exactly right for your trip. He'll have good horses for sale, too. Next door to the livery stable is a dry goods store—you'll find all sorts of items for that long trip Down South. You children are truly brave ones, sent from above, *umm hm-mmm,*" Eliza says.

"I'll go hitch Eliza's wagon," Henry says. "You children gather your belongings."

As soon as Henry pulls the wagon up to the kitchen door, Eliza and the gang hop aboard. The ride in to town is filled with questions and discussion of plans to head South.

Eliza says, "Maybe you should take the train; it would be faster."

Max says, "Henry can get us back down to North Carolina, then we'll have to ask for help along the way to get further south to the plantation in Georgia where the little boys were taken. We're worried that the train is too public; our chances of getting the whole way down are better if we travel by carriage."

"It will be so dangerous every step of the way," says Henry. "The slave catchers, they don't care if a man has documents sayin' he's free, or belongs to someone. Some of the catchers, they steal you away and sell you way down Deep South to make money."

Max claps Henry on the back. "Trust, Henry, have trust." But he takes a big breath and looks up into the sky, saying a little prayer. *Lord, help us...*

Chapter Nine

Supplies and Spies

As the small group of travelers enters Lancaster and makes its way to the town square, Max and Jinx look around in amazement. They have been in Lancaster before, in their own time. Nineteenth-century Lancaster is very different. Wagons full of produce rumble around them, heading for market. Some wagons carry cages of clucking chickens or squealing pigs heading for the stockyards. People bustle in and out of stores carrying parcels wrapped in brown paper. A street vendor cooks his chestnuts in hot oil and sells small bags full of them for pennies; the scent of roasting chestnuts fills the air and makes them hungry.

"Turn here, Henry. Down this next alley is Oscar's stable," says Eliza. A big, red sign is nailed to the brown barn, and it says exactly that: "Oscar's Livery Stable."

Henry pulls back on the reins and jumps down to tie the horse to a hitching post out front. He helps Eliza and Jinx from the wagon while Max leaps down from the back. Petey scrambles off the wagon and heads out to explore. A small, very dark man comes out of a large building. He is stooped over a slight bit and has bright-white curly hair circling a bald spot and sparkling brown eyes. He wears a leather apron over his loose white shirt and brown pants.

"Howdy, folks. What can I help you with this fine day?" He stops short when he spots Eliza. "Miss Eliza," he gasps, "I hear you had bad trouble out your way yesterday. Is it true?"

Eliza walks closer and says, "Yes, Oscar, it's true." She looks over her shoulder and all around, and then says, "William is tryin' to make it to Canada. He'll send for me one fine day, I know it. Our days livin' here are done."

Oscar shakes his head and looks downward at his boots. "Troubled times, that's for sure, Miss Eliza, when a freedman has to fear for his life." He is quiet for a few moments. Then is brown eyes snap back up, and he smiles at the children. "How can I help?"

"I'm Max, sir. We hear that you have a carriage for sale. And we'll need a good horse to pull it. We have business Down South. Our servant, Henry, will help us look them over." Max shakes Oscar's hand, as he looks him in the eyes, wondering if they can totally trust this man.

"Ah, yes, Master Max. You heard right 'bout the carriage. I'm sure I can find a fine carriage for gentlefolk such as yer-selves. I've also got some good-lookin' quarter horses for sale." Oscar smiles at Jinx.

Jinx also offers her hand. "Hello, Oscar. Nice to meet you." She curtsies and bobs her head, then looks at Max. Max grins at her.

Oscar walks them into the big barn. On one side is an office with a big battered desk and chair, littered with paperwork. The other side is filled with stalls full of horses of all colors and sizes. They can hear gentle snorts and shuffling sounds, as the horses eat oats from the feed troughs. Many of them stop eating and look up, very interested in the children. Max and Jinx can hear them talking amongst themselves.

"*Hmmm, strangers.*"

"*They look friendly. I wonder if the dog is with them.*"

"*I heard them say they need a fine horse. I'd fill that order.*"

"*No, no–I'm taller and stronger than you.*"

On go the comments as Max and Jinx hide laughs behind their hands. No one else can hear the horses; it wouldn't do to laugh out loud.

The barn has a mostly pleasant smell of leather, hay and horses. There's only a slight odor of manure, as each stall they pass is clean and orderly. In the rear sits a large, closed carriage. It is black, has two doors with windows, two bench seats facing each other inside, and a high bench seat outside for the driver. Even though the carriage is a bit battered around the edges, it looks fancy to the children.

This is where Henry takes over. He looks it over from front to back. He checks the spokes of the four huge wheels, the hitches, the glass windows and the doors, the roof, and then he steps back. "Yes, sir, it looks mighty fine. It'll do us a good ride. Don't leak now, does it? Wouldn't want the children to get wet."

No, it sure don't leak," says Oscar. "It's a few years old but in good shape. A fine family traded it in for a newer model. Sure do wish I had 'nough money to do that every year." He eyes the children with a question on his face.

"Oh, yes, Oscar. We have enough money. Let's look over the horses and choose one," Max says. "Then we'll check with Henry and talk over a price for both."

Oscar leads them all to a different section of the stable. They see Petey visiting in their stables, chatting with the horses. "Some of them horses is bein' put up while their owners is in town. But here's a few up for sale. I only deal in good, solid horses. I stands by my livestock and wares," says Oscar.

The horses all seem sturdy and majestic. Max looks at Henry and nods at him. "What do you think, Henry? I bow to your superior knowledge."

Henry takes his time looking over the half-dozen horses. He pats them all down from forehead to tail end. He glides his palms over their well-muscled shoulders. He checks their legs and hooves and shoes. He looks into their warm eyes and whispers something into their alert ears. The horses all react to Henry with gentle nods, as if they are answering his questions.

Then Henry looks at the children. "Miss Jinx, come pick your horse. It's between these two." He points to a large black stallion with a white blaze on his nose and a pretty sorrel mare that stands a bit shorter. She has a round white circle on her forehead. They are sleek and strong, and their coats are glossy.

Jinx walks over, one foot in front of the other, and stops short of the horses. She looks at Henry. "I...I never had the experience to meet horses nose to nose," she admits.

Henry laughs and leads her closer. "It's all right, Miss Jinx. They's friendly just like your dog, only bigger."

Jinx hears the big stallion give a neigh. *"We won't hurt you, Miss,"* he says. *"If you choose me, I'll get you there fast. I can beat any horse in the stable."*

"*Now, no bragging, big guy,*" says the mare. She shakes her head at Jinx. "*All the boys in here brag like that. Don't pay him any mind. It's not how fast you can run when you pull a carriage. You need a steady trot to do it.*"

"*I know that,*" says the stallion. "*But maybe they'll need a speedy fellow like me in an emergency.*"

Jinx is enchanted with both horses. She reaches out and pets their noses, and is treated to soft rubs on her shoulders from the horses. "Max, I like them both."

"Master Max," Henry says, "that might not be a bad idea. One can trot along behind, and they can take turns pullin'. It's goin' to be a long journey."

Petey leaps on a stool and barks his approval. "*They're both nice. We talked about where they've been. Both have been South before. I like them...I like them.*"

Max, Henry and Oscar head to the office to settle up, while Eliza leads Jinx down the street to Merryweather's Dry Goods. The store is filled to the brim with everything needed to stock a home or plan for a trip.

"This will be good for me, Miss Eliza," says Jinx. "Max says I never plan ahead, so I'm going to prove to him I can. With your help, I hope."

"Some nights we'll be camping out, so we need bedrolls and a cook pot, canteen sets and three pewter mugs for water, sets of tin plates and forks, some matches, a lantern, some candles, oh...some rain slickers for us, and Henry, too..." Back and forth she went, from aisles to counter, as she piled up supplies that would come in handy.

"Don't forget some bandages and ointments," Miss Eliza says. "Heaven forbid, but you may get some scratches and bruises on the road."

Jinx nods her head in thanks and adds some first-aid supplies to the pile.

By the time Max and Henry join them, she has the lady storeowner totaling and packing the items in a trunk. Max is duly impressed with the supplies when he looks through the trunk.

"Max, here are presents for you and Henry," says Jinx. She hands each a brand-new pocketknife. The knives are polished metal with shiny blades.

Henry opens and closes each blade and grins from ear to ear. "Thank you, Miss Jinx. What a fine tool. It will come in mighty handy on our trip," he says.

"I got one for me, too," Jinx says. "You boys can't have all the fun. And check out Petey."

Petey jumps into Max's arms about knocking him over. *"Look, look, Max...new leather collar, new scarf...handsome me,"* he says. He wears a new, tooled leather collar dyed red and a fancy red bandanna. Petey turns his head from side to side so they can admire him.

"Henry, you get some new clothes, too. Since you're going to drive our fancy carriage, you have to look the part of a fine footman and driver. I have some shirts and pants put back in the dressing room for you to try on, and then you must pick a new pair of boots," says Jinx. She loves the role of taking responsibility for her friends.

Henry is speechless. He hugs Jinx and pumps Max's hand up and down. Then he turns and heads back to the dressing room.

The middle-aged storekeeper watches this odd group of people with great interest. She has her gray-black hair pulled back into a tight bun and wears her glasses perched on the tip of her nose. She wears a flowered dress covered with a matching apron.

Who are these children, and what relationship is this black man to them? And isn't this Eliza Parker, from over Christiana way? She has heard of the standoff between the slaves and the sheriff and that someone was killed.

The storekeeper watches Max take Jinx aside and count out money from a big wad of bills. More money than she has seen for a while. All her cash is tied up in inventory for the store. She feels like she has to tread water to stay afloat and keep the store open, since her husband, Jackson Merryweather, Sr., was shot and killed in his slave ship during a shootout with government agents. *Hmmmmm–wait until my son returns from his latest trip Down South. I'll have some interesting news for him.*

Henry returns, dressed in black shiny boots, black pants, a soft white shirt and a black jacket. He carries a small pile of another set of new clothes folded neatly, with a new broad-brimmed hat on top. Jinx hands him a satchel to pack his belongings.

"Thank you very much, Miss Jinx, Master Max...I don't know what to say," says Henry. He has a few tears on his eyelashes.

Miss Eliza takes charge again. "Mrs. Merryweather, if you will kindly settle the bill, the young man will pay, and we'll be on our way." Eliza lowers her eyes and head, but she has observed Mrs. Merryweather's interest in the children and Henry and feels uneasy. Time to get them off on their great journey.

Mrs. Merryweather stares at Eliza for a few moments. *What an uppity black woman,* she thinks. *She better watch herself, her and that troublemaker husband of hers...*

Henry and Eliza carry the chest and bags out the back door to the awaiting carriage. Mrs. Merryweather tries to get some information from the children. She pastes a fake smile on her face as she totals the bill. She adds an extra fee on the bottom, hoping they won't notice.

"Well now, Master Max and Miss Jinx, I wish you the best for your trip. Did I hear you are to head Down South? Do you know people there to visit, or is it a business trip? I don't remember seeing you around before," says Widow Merryweather.

Max and Jinx exchange a look. Petey lays his ears back and his hair begins to rise along his backbone. A tiny *grrr* comes from Petey. Jinx knows that sign. Petey does not like or trust Mrs. Merryweather.

"We were visiting our aunt nearby," Jinx says. "We are now heading out with our friend...er, I mean servant, Henry, for another visit." She figures the least amount of information they give out, the better.

"Oh? What's your aunt's name? Perhaps I know her," says Store-keeper Merryweather.

Max slams the money on the counter, making Jinx and Mrs. Merryweather jump. "Oh, excuse me, Mrs. Merryweather," he says, acting innocent. "Here is the money. I believe you made a slight miscalculation at the end of the bill. I adjusted the amount for you. Come on Jinx, Petey...look at the time. It's getting late, and we must be off." He claps his hat on his head, tips his brim to the storekeeper and grabs Jinx by the arm. They march out the back door, with Petey growling all the way.

"Does she remind you of anyone familiar?" says Jinx

"You mean like the Wicked Witch of the West? I expected her flying monkeys any minute," Max whispers. They both love *The Wizard of Oz* movie.

Jinx giggles. "Exactly. She seems way too interested in our business."

When they round the corner they come upon their carriage, with the black stallion hitched up and ready to go. The pretty reddish brown mare is tied to the rear. The trunk is tied to the carriage, along with some saddles and harnesses. Both horses give soft snorts and paw the ground when they see the children. Henry stands at the hitching post, back straight, shoulders back, a proud look in his eyes.

The black stallion with the blaze on his forehead snorts, *"Could we pu-leeese be off? I'm ready for some high adventure. I've spent way too much time in Oscar's stable lately."*

The red mare shakes her polka-dotted head. *"I decided to let Mister Impatient lead the way. I'd never hear the last of it had I insisted to go first. Whatever happened to 'ladies first,' Miss Jinx?"*

Petey scrambles up to the driver's seat. *"I'm with Mister Impatient. Let's go...let's go..."*

Of course Henry and Eliza can't hear any of the animal communication going on between the furries. Henry turns to Eliza with concern.

"Are you sure you don't want us to take you home first?" he asks.

"I'll be fine. I've been drivin' a horse and wagon since I was a child. Y'all must go now. I don't like how that Widow Merryweather watched y'all. Her mind was calculatin' how to make some money off of you, sure as I'm standin' here. I don't trust her, never did," says Eliza.

"Yes, she tried to cheat us by adding an extra ten dollars on to the tab. Good thing I checked over the bill," says Max.

"Rumor has it that she and her son are not friends to the colored folks around here. Her husband ran a slave ship from Africa for years, even after it was declared illegal. They say he got himself shot and killed in a tussle with a gov'ment ship that was chasin' him. I heard her son is involved with slave huntin'...well, never mind now. No use worryin' up somethin' bad. Please, be very careful headin' Down South. Did you work on papers for Henry, Master Max?" Eliza says.

Max goes to his bag in the carriage and comes back with a document. "Henry, I guess you'd best keep this on your person at all times. It states that your name is Hiram, you're a freedman and servant to our family, and you have permission from my family to accompany us on a trip south, signed and dated for September, 1851.

Henry nods his head. "Thank you, Master Max. If we're stopped, I'll be asked to show my papers. But, in the end, if we run into the wrong men, no paper in the world can save me from bein' captured and taken away to be resold to another plantation owner, or sent back to my old plantation."

Jinx is horrified. "Miss Eliza is right; we won't think about the bad things that might happen along the way. Everyone should think about good things. I can't wait to meet Henry's twins."

"That's right, Miss Jinx," says Eliza. "Let's have hope and trust in the Lord. Now off you go." She takes Jinx in her arms and hugs her against her soft body. Giving Jinx a kiss on her cheek, she then reaches for Max. "Master Max, you take care of Miss Jinx and Petey and help Henry get those precious babes back. Umm hmmm...I have great faith in you all." With tears in her eyes, she hugs him and Henry both and then strides back down the alley, heading back to Oscar's Livery Stable and her wagon.

Max takes a big breath. "One more item of business," he says. "Our new horse friends need names, or maybe they have one..."

Both horses shake their heads no.

"Well, would you look at them," Henry says. "They act like they sure do understand you, Master Max."

"Of course they do, Henry. If you listen hard enough, you can understand what they say."

Henry wrinkles his face and watches the horses for a few moments. "Nope, I can't hear them."

"*They're not talking, silly,*" says Petey.

The children grin. Max goes over to the black stallion. "You first, big fellow. You look like a storm on a dark day with your white blaze of lightning. I think you should be called 'Thunder.' Do you like that name? It feels strong, like you."

The black stallion lifts his head and neighs. His eyes light up as he rubs his face against Max's chest.

"Great! Thunder it is. Jinx, you pick a name for our lady horse friend."

Jinx walks back to the red mare and rubs her forehead again. "How about 'Dot'? You have a beautiful round circle right here, girl." She traces the white dot on her forehead, feeling its cottony softness. The mare paws the ground and neighs, as Thunder did.

"All right, I believe Thunder and Dot are ready to head out, Miss Jinx. I'll help you into the carriage," says Henry.

Jinx takes Henry's hand, gathers her skirts, and steps up into the carriage. "Thank you, Henry."

Max jumps in and slams the carriage door. Both children settle on the cushioned seats facing each other. Henry hauls himself up onto the driver's seat with Petey. Max opens the small window behind his back and calls up to Henry, "We're set. Let's start this big adventure. We can do this, everyone. We're off to rescue Henry's twins." He smiles at Jinx as they both take a big breath of air. Jinx reaches across for his hand and squeezes it.

Henry says, "Ha-yup," and gives a smart slap of the reins to Thunder's sides. He guides Thunder down the alley to the main road leading south out of Lancaster. The road smoothes out, and Thunder picks up speed, head held high and legs trotting into a rhythm. Dot keeps up the pace from the rear. They look beautiful in the late-day sunlight.

No one notices Widow Merryweather standing in the shadows of the late afternoon on the front porch of her store. Her lips are pressed together in a thin slash across her face, and her steel-gray eyes are calculating a profit to be made. She watches the carriage until it is out of sight, and then she rubs her hands together with a malevolent smile, turns her back and disappears into her store.

PART TWO

Deep South

NY

VT

NH

MA

CT

RI

PA

NJ

OH

DE

WY

VA

KY

NC

$\stackrel{N}{\wedge}$

ATLANTIC
OCEAN

2

3

SC 4

WILMINGTON

GA

CHARLESTON

5

SAVANNAH

KEY

X MARTIN SAFE HOUSE
1 JEFFERSON & JANIE
2 TORNADO
3 DOC ALEX ROSS
4 AMBUSH
5 SMYTHE PLANTATION

PART 2
DEEP SOUTH

Chapter Ten

Maryland–Visitors

Max and Jinx sleep soundly as the swaying carriage makes its way through the wooded landscape. They are both so exhausted that even the rocky path and branches brushing and scraping against the windows do not awaken them.

Jinx's forehead furrows in her sleep as buzzing sounds, like a whole nest of wasps flying around in her head, make her break out in a sweat. She jumps awake, eyes wide open but non-seeing. It's the beginnings of the vision that has been following her and intruding in her thoughts. There is nothing to do but ride into the vision.

"Jinx, are you okay? Jinx?" Max cannot get her attention. She's going into the vision again, he thinks. Grabbing her hand is like completing an electrical circuit; Max immediately feels the buzz. It fills both teens' heads in living color, as if they are watching another part of a lengthy movie together...

Vision Story Part Four: 1837 Savannah, Georgia Slave Market

*L*arge posters are tacked up all around town, on hitching posts, storefronts and the post office. They have crude pictures of two black African men dressed in loincloths, with headbands, arm bracelets and necklaces. The men have their arms out, fists clenching ten-foot spears beside them. The posters announce:

TO BE SOLD AT AUCTION

ON MONDAY THE SEVENTH DAY OF JULY

A NEW CARGO

OF SIXTY-FIVE

HEALTHY NEGROES

30 MEN, 21 WOMEN, 10 BOYS, 4 GIRLS

NEWLY AQUIRED AND

OWNED BY

MASTER JACKSON MERRYWEATHER, SR, ESQ

Alem and Anwar perch on their wagon loaded with men, looking around with owl eyes. The wagons are parked in an alley close to the town square in Savannah. White people throng the town square and alleyways, inspecting the captive Africans and chattering away in this new language that is so foreign to the twins.

The air is heavy with the warm sweat of animals, and of garbage in the gutters.

These smells mingle with scents of food vendors' wares: browned chicken on a stick, buns and breads, roasted nuts, and candies. In contrast to the fear of the Africans about to be sold into slavery, there is a feel in the air of a bazaar or market for the white people. Stand holders hawk their wares—live chickens, fish, oysters, and fresh garden vegetables. Flower vendors are everywhere, offering an array of fall flowers.

They hear a man yelling from atop a platform, but the Africans have no idea what he is saying. "Step up to the center stage, folks. The auction is about to begin. We have good, affordable slaves to add to your plantation stock–all ready to do hard work to help turn your crops into cash for you this fall. Step right up."

The two boys cling to each other in fear. They watch as groups of Africans shackled together in their chains are marched onto the stage; some include women with their children held tightly to their sides. No one holds Alem and Anwar. They are parentless. They know they are about to be stripped of their clothing and paraded up on the stage for their turn to be sold. The captives are terrified and ashamed to be stripped naked and sold off like cattle.

Bidding begins; slaves go to the highest bidder. The strong men sell for an average of $1,000, the women and children slightly less. White men walk right up on the stand to inspect the Africans. They check their muscles and teeth, look in their ears and eyes, and generally pat them down much like they are horses.

Finally, Anwar is grabbed by the wrist and wrenched away from Alem. He gives a mighty cry of alarm. "NO, my brother and I must stay together..."

The crowd laughs to hear his strange language. But a white man says, "Put the two boys together; see how much they look alike? They're probably brothers. They'll grow up into fine, strong field workers. Look how well muscled they are already."

"That's right, folks–this fine pair of twins is up for sale now. Come check them out," shouts the auctioneer.

Another group of men jumps up the stairs to the platform and begins to poke and prod the boys. The other white gentleman shakes his head sadly. He feels for the boys. They look so young and frightened. He decides he will bid the highest, no matter what, so he can take them home to his plantation.

One man starts the bid. "I'll give five hundred dollars for the pair."

"Come now, gentlemen. You can do better than that. Do I hear six hundred?"

"Here–six hundred dollars," says another.

"Seven hundred fifty for the pair," says the first man. He is tall and everything about him is square; he has square shoulders, a square head, square hands, square feet in big boots. His chin is square and his eyes are mean. The boys are afraid of him. The man looks like a big block that would squash them flat if they angered him.

"Eight hundred fifty dollars," says the second man. He does not look much better. He has greasy blond hair that comes to his shoulders, and black slits for eyes that keep looking the boys up and down.

"Nine hundred," says the first man, with a sneer on his face. He wants the boys for hard labor and plans to put them in the sugarcane fields right away.

The older gentleman has remained silent, but now he puts a stop to the bidding. "I'll pay one thousand a piece for them. That's two thousand dollars total, for those of you who can't do hard math." He smiles at the boys and sees them begin to look relieved when they hear his softer voice. The crowd laughs.

"Ain't no way I'm payin' that much for a set of boys," says the square man. He walks away in disgust.

The other bidder shakes his head in disbelief, also, and turns away.

"Sold to the highest bidder. Two thousand dollars for two strong slave boys. Bet you won't be sorry, sir," the auctioneer says.

The man smiles and strides up to pay his fee to the auctioneer. "Come on, boys," he orders. "Move quickly...I have a nice family for you to stay with. Don't look so afraid."

Alem doesn't know what the man said. "Ye...yess, sir," he stutters. He pokes his brother in the ribs.

"Yes, sir," Anwar says. He eyes his brother. "I wonder what will happen to us in this new life," he says.

They shuffle after him in their leg chains. The man takes them to his wagon along the street. There are already two strong men and a young woman in the wagon being guarded by a white man with a gun. The woman holds the hand of one of the young men.

"You boys sit here with this couple," says the white man. He looks at all of his new slaves and pats his chest. "Master Willard Young," he says. Again, "Master Young."

They nod and call after him, "Master Young." Strange sounds for their new master's name, but they get the idea.

The other man who has been guarding the new slaves with a gun grunts his name, "Alfred Dunn. Foreman Alfred Dunn." He has harsher eyes and a frowning mouth, much different than the master. Alfred doesn't believe the slaves should be coddled. They exist for one thing only–to work hard and make money for their master. Alfred's job depends on turning over a profit in crops every fall, and making sure each slave works hard.

Alem and Anwar do not trust Foreman Alfred Dunn.

Master Young takes the reins of his brown stallion, goes to the mounting block to swing his leg over his mount, and says to his foreman and the black wagon driver, "Time to head home to River Bend Plantation in North Carolina."

The young woman is trembling and has the mark of tears showing on her dusty face, but she puts an arm around each of the boys and hugs them tight. She looks in each boy's face and says, "You're mine now. I'll watch over you and love you like you're my own." She kisses each boy on the cheek.

The boys don't recognize her dialect, but they know comfort when they feel and see it. They rub the tears out of their eyes and lean into her warm embrace as the wagon heads out of town towards their new life in America. They have been so brave. Now they can lean on someone else for a while.

A few of the black men try to speak with one another, but the Boss Man, Alfred Dunn, rides back and slaps them with his whip. "Quiet!" he yells. The troubled men lower their heads and try to shrug their bodies away from the whip. Everyone is subdued and frightened. Their future seems full of horror!

Jinx and Max violently shake the remnants of the vision from their minds and come back to reality with a jerk. Petey jumps into Jinx's lap and nuzzles her face. She buries her face in the soft fur on his back.

Max rubs both eyes with his fists. "The boys, Anwar and Alem, are heading to a plantation in North Carolina. At least their master seems to be nice. I hope he treats his slaves better than some we've heard about," he says.

"Max, it's Henry and Edward in the vision. No wonder their faces looked so familiar."

"Yeah, it's got to be them. What a horrible way to come to America. Do you think we should say anything to Henry?"

"No, we'd better let it be for now. Maybe later. I have a feeling there's more of their story we're meant to see. Thanks for going into the visions with me."

"You have to admit, it's a unique way to learn our history lessons," Max says.

Jinx raises the shades and looks out the windows. The carriage rocks back and forth as Thunder trots down a rutted woodland road.

Henry guides the horses down a less-traveled path, deeper into the woods, to stay away from people. They come to a small clearing where he finally stops. A brook bubbles across smooth stones, and the air is pine fresh. It is starting to get dark. Henry helps Jinx jump down from the coach while Max and Petey jump out the other side door.

"I think this is a safe place to stop over for tonight," Henry says. "We's down into Maryland and no town in sight. No inns tonight, huh?" He looks up through the heavy leaves in the treetops. "Don't look like rain. Guess we'll camp out for our first night on the road."

"Henry, this place is so pretty. We can build a campfire and make some supper. Max and I can look for some twigs and wood while you take care of the horses." She goes to the rear of the carriage and strokes Dot's silky nose. Unleashing her from the carriage, she walks Dot over to the brook for a long drink.

"Thank you, Miss Jinx. This cool water tastes so refreshing," says Dot.

Henry leads Thunder over for his drink. *"Ahhhhh...so good,"* Thunder agrees. *"Didn't I do a marvelous job of pulling the carriage?"*

Petey looks up from slurping the water. *"I wish I was a horse like Thunder. He's big and strong."*

Thunder noses Petey. He likes the little dog. *"You can ride on my back,"* he offers. Dot shakes her head and gives a soft neigh.

"That boy sure likes to brag," she says. *"But I do have a soft place in my heart for him. Tomorrow is my turn,"* she reminds him.

Henry wonders what all of the barking and neighing is about. He laughs with Max and Jinx, anyway. He walks over to the rear of the carriage and gets a large brush and two blankets from a trunk. "Master Max, come watch–I'll show you how to brush down the horses." He begins to groom the horses.

Max helps Henry groom both horses while Jinx scurries about finding wood. They soon have a blazing campfire started. They set up metal legs with a rod over the fire to hold a cook pot. Jinx gets out her new knife and tries to puncture the top on two large cans of pork and beans. "Sure could use an electric can opener," she mutters to Max.

Max reads the directions printed on the label. *"Cut 'round the top near the outer edge with a chisel and hammer."* He laughs and looks at Henry. Henry grins and goes to the toolbox on the side of the carriage. He volunteers to pound away at the top of the can.

Meanwhile, Jinx finds the matches she bought at Merryweather's Dry Goods store. They are large sticks about the size of her pointer finger with some rough chemicals on the tips. "Uh, Max, are you supposed to rub these against something to light them?" she asks, while striking one against a rock.

The matchstick explodes and Jinx drops it with a yelp.

"*Yikes*. Careful, Jinx. I read about early matchsticks. They have pure phosphorous on the tips. Very unreliable," he says.

Henry has the baked-beans cans open and watches the teens with interest. He saves the day again. "Get a bunch of dry leaves to put under your sticks," he says. "That's right...now watch." He reaches into his pocket and pulls out two pieces of flint. He strikes them together until a spark lights a few leaves. Down on his hands and knees, Henry softly blows until the rest of the leaves catch fire, lighting off the kindling.

"You're good, Henry. I guess we need a few lessons on how to survive in the wilderness, for sure," says Jinx. The beans soon bubble merrily in the pot.

"Look Henry, I even got you a coffeepot and some coffee to boil," Jinx says. She runs to the brook to fill the pot. "Do you like your coffee strong?" she asks. "Dad says I make the best coffee." She proceeds to put spoonfuls of coffee into the top part. She places it on a flat rock close to the flames. When the water starts to boil, it bubbles up over the coffee and back down into the pot, making a potful of black coffee.

"Miss Jinx, you sure do take care of ol' Henry," he says. "Coffee, black and strong, is a real treat. We never had no money for coffee."

The horses munch grass near the stream, and Petey munches some beans in a little dish. As the humans sit around the fire to enjoy some late supper, they talk over plans.

"How long do you think it will take us to get to Georgia, Henry?" says Max. He pulls some printed sheets of paper from his pocket. "It's about 700 miles from Christiana. I printed this off the Internet before we left, Jinx." He shows the map to Henry.

"Good thinking, Max," says Jinx. "At least I packed a compass." She pulls her compass from her pocket. "I figure we keep heading South and ask for help along the way."

Henry takes the map from Max and looks at it in amazement. He traces a line from top to bottom with his finger. "We won't do much better than fifty miles a day, prob'ly less. We'll have to stick mostly to the back roads to be safe from slave catchers. 'Specially when we get to North Carolina, where I run away. I'm afraid the master has a reward out on me and Edward's heads. I never seen a map like this; show me the states, Master Max."

"Look here, Henry. This shape is Pennsylvania, and here's Christiana where William Parker's house is located. This here is Maryland.

Then we'll head into Virginia and stay near the coast. On to North Carolina, then South Carolina, then finally to Georgia." Max watches Henry trace each state and repeat the names.

"It's a far distance, ain't it? Gonna take weeks to get Down South," Henry says.

"Would you like me to teach you the letters and how to read, Henry?" asks Jinx.

"Yes, Miss Jinx, I'd sure like to learn. I'd like to teach my boys. There's power in words and reading," says Henry.

"Then we'll do it. Every day we can practice. I know you'll learn fast, Henry," says Jinx.

The night begins to turn a bit chilly. A fog rises from the brook. Jinx shivers and goes to the carriage to get the bedrolls and blankets. Henry throws more wood on the fire.

"You'd best bed down in the carriage, Miss Jinx. Master Max and I can take turns watching," says Henry.

"Oh, no; no one goes to bed until you have your first lesson, Henry," says Jinx.

Max and Henry laugh. "She's a stern teacher, Henry. She'll have you reading the newspapers by the time we get to Georgia," Max says. "I'll take first watch. That way you can begin to read with Jinx."

Max goes to the carriage, jumps up to the outside driver's seat and gets something. He comes back with a shotgun. Jinx is stunned.

"Max, a shotgun...do you really think we need that? Where did you get it?" says Jinx.

Max looks serious. "Yes, I really think we need a gun. We're not in Kansas anymore, Toto." He quotes again from their favorite movie, *The Wizard of Oz*. "We're in 1851 Maryland and heading for the Deep South. You know it's dangerous. William Parker gave it to me before he ran for Canada. Henry and I will take turns with the watch and the shotgun. During the time that Henry is driving, he'll have it with him."

"Fine, but I take a turn with the watch, too. You should have discussed something as important as a gun with me," Jinx says. She glares at Max.

Max knows the look. He sees it every time he alludes to the fact that she's a girl and shouldn't be doing men's work. Big mistake. "All right, you take a turn at watch."

"And the shotgun will be by my side, too," she says.

"The shotgun will be by your side. But, it's not a toy, you know," says Max.

"I know that," she snaps. Jinx turns away and storms to the carriage. She gets in and slams the door.

Henry stifles a smile and says, "I'd best check the horses." He leaves Max alone at the campfire.

Ten minutes later Jinx returns with her tablet, in a better mood. "Okay, Henry, time to practice the alphabet." She smiles at Max and sits down on the log beside Henry. "This is letter 'A.' You can see it in front of the word apple. But it can also make the sound like at the beginning of angel." She prints the two words and Henry repeats them with a grin.

"Good job, Henry. You read your first two words," she says.

Max grins, too, while watching the dark woods around them. They must be very vigilant, and he knows he won't be able to sleep when Jinx is on duty. But she doesn't have to know that. The seriousness of the journey threatens to overwhelm him. The night continues to be very calm as Henry and Jinx practice letters and words.

A snap crackles in the chilly air. Max startles awake. He sees Jinx burrowed into her bedroll, asleep beside him, as Henry's back jerks upright. The campfire pit is low and filled with red coals. The wood smoke smells good; it hovers close to the fire and then snakes upward into the tree branches. Max sits up and touches Henry's sleeve.

"Is someone out there?" he whispers.

Henry nods and eases himself to his feet while Max scoots out of his bedroll. Max pulls a pistol from under his bedding. Henry grabs the shotgun and motions for Max to stay put while he checks around the other side of the carriage.

The horses snort and paw the ground. *"Someone coming in the path, I see two people,"* says Thunder.

Petey crawls out from Jinx's bedding, awakening Jinx. He barks out a warning. *"People alert, people alert...it's okay, they're not enemies,"* he tells them and takes off down the path.

Jinx scrambles out of her covers and to her feet. "Henry, it looks like two people coming. Don't shoot them," she says. She looks at Max who holds the steel-gray gun with both hands, pointed to the ground at his left side. "Max, what are you doing? Do you even know how to handle that thing?"

"It's okay, Jinx. I had weapons training at the academy last spring." He attends a military prep school. Jinx never thought before about the training he goes through starting at a young age, and he sometimes doesn't tell her everything.

A young man and woman edge closer, hesitating as they get near. Petey escorts them. They have very dark skin and are dressed in dark clothing.

The woman wears a brown woolen skirt and a dark blue top. She huddles in a gray knit shawl, shivering from fear and coldness. Her hair is tied up in a knotted red kerchief. Her oval face is worried, her lips slightly parted.

The man is dressed in brown pants, beat-up boots and a checked, loose shirt. His jacket is threadbare and doesn't offer much protection against the chilly night air.

"Please, Sir, Miss...we've lost our way. Can you help us?" says the man.

Henry lowers the shotgun and says, "Miss Jinx, they's runaways, I know it. Should we hear them out?"

Jinx looks at Max who nods his head, then she says, "Come over by the fire to warm up. We have some leftover beans to offer you. I know you must be hungry. Henry, could you please throw a couple logs on the fire. Max, do you know how to make coffee?"

"Yes, Jinx," he says. He knows she is very upset about the extra gun.

Soon they all sit around the warming campfire, sipping hot coffee, and watching each other. Petey sits next to the woman, who pets his soft back and feels his velvet ears. They can see the woman is expecting a baby.

"This is our friend, Henry, and I'm Jinx. This is Max and Petey. You can trust us to help you," says Jinx. Henry nods his head at the young couple to encourage them to speak.

Something seems to speak to Jinx. She tilts her head up, with a distant look. Then she smiles, picks up a stick and traces her hand in the dust, placing the five stars around the hand. Jinx looks at the young couple. They nod their heads in excitement when they see the secret symbol.

"Follow the stars," the young black man says, and he smiles in relief.

"My name is Jefferson, and this is my wife, Janie," says the man. "We're goin' to have our baby in a few months, and by golly, we *will* have our baby in freedom.

"We run away from our plantation in southern Virginia. Partway up we found a safe house. Them folks took good care of us. They hid us beneath hay in their wagon and got us to the border," says Jefferson. He is slim, with a strong chin, wide mouth and tight black hair. His brown eyes glisten in the firelight.

"A Negro man conductor took us from the border about ten miles to the next station at a farmhouse. We hid there during the day and slept in the barn loft. Them good folks fed us well and told us where the next stop was," Janie says. She is a pretty young woman with delicate cheekbones and a nice smile. Her hands are worn, though, used to hard work.

"Did you run into trouble anywhere?" Max asks.

"Well, we had a lucky run of it 'til we got into Maryland," Jefferson says. "It was late, and there was no moon. We thought it was dark 'nough to hide us, so we tried an open road. But all of a sudden we heard dogs in the distance. We had to run back into the woods and wade in a waist-high stream for miles to throw them dogs off our trail. Lucky for us it worked, but we got mixed 'round and went miles backwards. That added another day onto our route 'til we found the right trail again. My poor Janie, she gettin' mighty tired of all this runnin'." He takes her hands in his and rubs warmth into them.

Janie smiles at her husband. "Now, Jefferson, we talked it over. I'm a strong woman, and we'll have this baby in freedom. I be fine. We's only a bit off our track. After we rest with these nice people, we be on our way."

"Did you see a small, white house with two chimneys and a red barn in your travels today? The house has a white picket fence all 'round it," says Jefferson. "That's our next safe house. They supposed to be ready for us."

The other travelers look at each other and smile. "We did see that place. I remember, because I said to Max how nice it looked when we went by. They have beautiful roses growing all around the fence. It's not more than half an hour up the road, right, Max?" says Jinx.

Max agrees. "Yes, we noticed a woman putting a quilt over the fence to air it out."

Janie gives Max and Jinx a big grin. "That's it, the quilt's sign that means a safe house for us folks runnin' for freedom. It have a wagon wheel on it, to mean it's time to run. I'm so glad we found you tonight. You's our angels. We can rest there for a day or two so I can get my strength back." Janie hugs Petey, then Jinx.

The runaways eat some cold beans and finish the leftover coffee. They all get to their feet; best wishes and handshakes go all around the little circle. Jefferson and his wife, Janie, head off North, following the Drinking Gourd to their next destination.

Jinx demands to take a watch, so Henry and Max settle down into their blankets around the fire. Petey climbs into Jinx's lap. The night settles back into stillness.

"*I feel bad, like something's going to happen,*" Petey whimpers.

"Petey, don't scare me. Let's feel good that we helped Jefferson and Janie. We're conductors on the Underground Railroad now," she says. "Try to rest."

Jinx notices the horses are restless, too. They move back and forth, shifting their weight and blowing small puffs of air. The breeze rustles the leaves on the trees and makes the hairs on Jinx's neck stand up stiff. She looks all around as she picks up the dreadful shotgun. *I don't want to be a baby and waken Max, but something is going to happen,* she thinks. Henry gives a loud snore and makes Jinx jump.

Max says in a low voice, "I feel it, too." They often read each other's minds, so Jinx is not surprised that he is awake. He sits up and watches with Jinx.

The air goes from silent one moment to an explosion of noise the next. Two huge horses push through the underbrush, with slave catchers Jackson and Billy astride. Henry jumps to his feet along with Max and Jinx. She holds the shotgun and Max holds the handgun.

"I think we found the source of the wood smoke, Jackson...what do ya think?" says the other skinny man.

"Yeah," laughs Jackson, "and I'm sure these folks will want to answer some questions about two runaways, won't you?" He dismounts and takes two steps over to the campfire.

Henry lowers his head and pulls his hat over his brow. Max and Jinx remember these men. They are the slave hunters who rode into John and Mary's farm looking for Edward and Henry. They are in big danger if either man takes a close look at Henry.

Even though the men have other runaways on their minds tonight, they can't help checking out the children's situation. They always look for an opportunity to make money on any runaway.

"So, who are ya? What are ya doin' out here in the middle of the night?" Jackson asks. His dark beard is even more unkempt than when they last saw him. His clothes are wrinkled and his riding boots muddied. He glares at them with his dark eyes and harsh mouth.

Max steps forward, holding the pistol pointed down. "We're traveling South with our servant, if it's any of your business. You're not invited to our campsite. You both need to leave now."

"You better have papers on that servant," Jackson says.

Max walks over to Henry, who looks even lower. "Documents please, Hiram."

Jinx smiles to herself at the use of a false name. *Max is always able to think fast in stressful situations,* she thinks.

Henry passes the papers to Max, who hands them over to Jackson. Jackson steps closer to the fire to look them over.

He gives Henry a hard look and then shoves the papers back into Max's chest. "Fine." He glares at Henry one last time from under hooded eyes, then he turns back to Max. "We're after two runaways, a man and a woman who's going to have a baby. They pass through this way tonight?"

Max doesn't even blink an eye. "Yes, we saw them. They lit out through the woods headed that way. I can't tolerate runaways." He points in the opposite direction from the route that Jefferson and Janie took, hoping to give them some valuable time to reach the safe house.

Petey has been growling all this time. *"Grrrrrr, better get outta here before I bite you, grrrrrrr..."*

"Well now, that's mighty neighborly of you to help out," Jackson says. He turns toward his mount, shoving Petey out of the way with his booted foot.

Petey yelps before he leaps up and grabs the man's calf through his trousers. He digs in and shakes his head back and forth. *"Ggrrrrrrrrrr..."*

Jackson is the one who yelps now. "Owwww, git off me, dawg..."

Jinx runs over and grabs Petey with her free arm. "Petey, that's enough. Calm down; the men are leaving." Petey finally releases Jackson's leg.

As Jackson backs away, he comes a bit too close to Dot, who reaches down and nips his backside.

"Owwww, Holy Hannah, let's get away from these devil animals," Jackson says.

Billy laughs behind his hand. "Yeah Boss, hope ya can sit on yer saddle."

"Ain't funny. You shut yer face," says Jackson. "*Ow*, my calf's throbbin' and my butt hurts. You all better not be lyin' to me about them runaway slaves," he snarls at Max and Jinx. They can hear him grumbling the whole way out through the woods, headed in the wrong direction.

Chapter Eleven

Virginia–Stormy Weather

The next several days are trouble-free for the travelers, but Max worries about Jefferson and Janie. He hopes they escape the slave hunters and soon reach safety in the North. He told them about Eliza Parker in Christiana, so they were hoping to travel in that direction to stay with her.

Jinx sits on the seat against the window facing the driver. The window is open, and she and Henry sing the alphabet song, *"A, b, c, d, e, f, geeeee, h, i, j, k, l-m-n-o peeeee..."*

Dot trots down the road, neighing along, while Thunder neighs his own song from the rear of the carriage. Petey sits up high with Henry, his favorite place to ride, and he wags his tail to the beat.

"Good job, Henry," says Jinx. "You know all the letters now, plus a lot of words, so we'll work more on the sounds they make when you put them together."

"Thank you, Miss Jinx," Henry says. He is proud of his progress.

The day is overcast, and thunder rumbles in the distance. They travel through some beautiful, rolling farmland in Virginia, with hundreds of enslaved people toiling in the fields, weeding crops of tobacco and cotton. Log fences surround some of the fields, and horses and colts frolic in those green pastures. It is an unusually warm September day after the chilly nights they have spent camping out. Broadleaf trees show signs of turning into fall reds and yellows, but the temperature hovers around ninety degrees.

"Did you notice the overseer on horseback?" Max asks. "I saw him whip a man who stood up to stretch his back. No wonder so many of the enslaved workers want to run."

"Max, little children are dragging bags as tall as they are, following their parents. They should be free to play. It's a terrible life for them. I don't get it; how do the plantation owners think this is right?" says Jinx.

"It's like your dad told you one time, Jinx, about trying to walk in someone's shoes to see their point of view. But that's hard to do when you have such strong feelings that something's wrong," says Max.

"I know; it's not for us to judge others. That's hard, too," Jinx adds. The two friends are very troubled about slavery. They have been talking about this often.

Fast-approaching clouds cover the sun. Deep thunder rumbles closer. Thunder the horse whinnies his concern. The children lean out of their open windows and check the sky. It is black as night off to the west with strange tinges of yellowish orange at the edge of the horizon.

"Ooooh, I don't like the looks of that," Max says. "It's going to be a wicked storm." He reaches through the open window to Henry and tugs on his jacket. "Henry, do you see anywhere to take cover?"

"Master Max, I seen tornadoes come out of skies looking like that. You're right, we'd best get under cover," says Henry.

About that time, the wind begins to blow hard, turning leaves over backwards and snapping branches. Hanging out of the window, Jinx shouts, "Henry–over there...quick, I see a big stone bridge crossing over the stream. See if you can get the carriage under there, down by the streambed," she says.

Now Dot lifts her head and neighs her concern. She picks up the pace, heading for the bridge. *"I can do it. I can get us under there in time, don't you worry."*

Thunder puts in his two cents. *"Faster, old girl, you can pick up your pace."*

Petey barks and yips in alarm, *"We have to get under cover, now... storm, bad storm..."*

The rain comes in torrents, and the downpour drenches the ground and everyone out in the storm. The wind gusts are ferocious. Henry swipes at his eyes, trying to see through the waterfall rolling off the brim of his hat.

They hear the field slaves screaming as some drop to the dirt, while others run for the outer buildings. The rolling black clouds put terror into their hearts.

The carriage flies along the last bit of muddy road and careens around the corner, down the bank and under the stone bridge. Henry jumps down to calm the horses, and Petey leaps onto the slick bank.

"Jinx, Max, hurry, get out of the carriage and lie down here with me," says Petey. He springs from his back legs, *boing...boing.*

Jinx and Max stumble from the carriage and huddle flat down on the bank, watching Henry hold Dot's reins on the other side of the stream. He begins to unhitch her with quick, practiced hands. The carriage is in the streambed, and Thunder is with the children up on the slippery bank. Max thinks it's a good idea to unhitch Thunder from the rear of the carriage, too.

At least we're all under some cover, Jinx thinks. It does little good as the rain blows in sideways and hail the size of quarters begins to batter the stone bridge. Max slips off his coat and makes a small tent over their heads with Petey underneath.

All of a sudden the rain stops. The sound of a roaring train hits the air, and a tornado is upon them. It hits the ground, bounces up and down like a ball a couple of times, then stays down as it cuts a wide swath of damage. It roars on by, missing the bridge by a narrow edge.

Then they hear a different kindof roaring, as the stream becomes a monster of raging water from upstream. Max sees the wall of water coming towards them. Wide-eyed, he jumps up, dragging Jinx and Petey with him.

"Come on! We've got to get away from the streambed. It's flooding fast," he yells, above the storm. Grabbing Thunder's reins in one hand, he hauls Jinx up the slimy bank and onward, away from the stream as fast as they can go.

Jinx prays Henry and Dot have gotten away from the raging stream. The rain and hail end; the storm moves on with lessening winds.

They stand with Thunder and Petey, wet and cold, and survey the damage around them. They can see the exact path the tornado took: trees are uprooted, crops are squashed flat, and some of the outer buildings on the nearest plantation look like a pile of splintered boards. Slaves cry out in anguish as they try to help those who were hurt in the storm. The overseer is nowhere to be seen. He has fled for cover, like the Cowardly Lion.

"Max, the carriage! Oh no, it's ruined," Jinx says. The carriage lies further downstream on its side, water rushing around and up over it.

The old, arched bridge stands strong against the rushing water, but the water floods up over it, also. They see Henry and Dot across the way. Henry waves his arms to show them that Dot and he are unhurt. Relief fills both children. Max thinks it's a good idea that he and Henry unhitched the horses, or they would have been dragged downstream with the carriage.

So much disaster has happened already, Jinx thinks, *and we're only in Virginia. What could possibly happen next? A blizzard?*

"Max, we should go see what we can do to help the field hands who are hurt. Henry will see where we go and come over to the plantation."

"I guess we should check the plantation and help out where we can. Then we'll see about pulling the carriage out of the stream," says Max.

This time Jinx takes Thunder's reins. The big horse is agitated and prances around, rearing a bit.

"Steady now, Thunder. Everything worked out fine," says Jinx.

"But Dot...where is she? Is she all right? I can't find Henry and Dot," he says.

"They're fine, Thunder. They're on the other side of the bridge. Soaked like us," says Petey.

Jinx notices Thunder is limping on the way to the plantation house. She stops to check.

"What's wrong, Jinx?"

"I think Thunder is hurt."

They both pat him down. When Jinx gets to the muscle on his right foreleg, Thunder jerks and neighs, *"It hurts, it hurts."* She sees he has also thrown a shoe.

"Ahh, you'll be fine, Thunder. A day's rest and a new horseshoe will make you feel better," says Jinx, trying to calm the horse. She hopes it's true.

"Yes, thank goodness he didn't break a leg," Max says, without thinking.

Thunder whinnies in fear, *"Noooooo, no broken leg."* He has seen other horses put down because they broke a leg.

Jinx pats him and strokes his head to calm him. She whispers in his ear as she saw Henry do, until Thunder is finally ready to finish the short trek to the plantation. The storm is over, and the sun breaks out. The air is much cooler and smells of rain and wet vegetation.

As they near the plantation house, they can see it is a beautiful building. It is white, longer than two large barns side-by-side, with two stories full of large windows. Four thick, white columns stand from ground to roof, edging a wide veranda. The whole length of the veranda is filled with scattered, upset wicker chairs and small tables that were tossed about by the winds. Old oak trees line the pathway into the house. The tornado did not damage the oak trees or house, but it did flatten a barn and many of the slave quarters.

The plantation owner and his wife stand outside on the front lawn, surveying the scene and deciding where to start. The house servants who were huddled in frightened groups nearby are already organizing to help where needed.

"Hello friends, welcome to Acorn Acres. I'm sorry it's under such terrible conditions, but how can we help you? I'm Chester Matthews, and this is my wife, Melody," says the master.

He is dressed in elegant clothing: riding pants tucked into tall black boots, a pure white shirt and a golden-brown jacket with long tails. His wife is elegant in a navy blue dress, with wide hoops holding the frilly skirts out. She has a tiny waist and a pleasant face framed by long red curls.

The children tell them their adventure with the storm. A slave is called to lead Thunder away to be groomed. He is the head groom, named Buster. Chester orders him to take Thunder to the blacksmith after his grooming for a new horseshoe.

"And don't forget some liniment for that right leg, Buster. Send someone out to watch for their servant and the other horse. You can rub her down, too, and check for injuries," says Chester.

"Yes, sir. We take good care of ol' Thunder and Dot. We got some medicine that'll feel real good. Heal that muscle in no time flat," says the kind old groom.

"Now children, you must come into the house to get some dry clothes," says Melody. "Surely we can find something near your size to wear."

"Mrs. Matthews, we want to help with the injured field hands," says Max. He can't bring himself to call them slaves. "We don't need dry clothes yet, please."

"Well then, I will send the staff out to set up a first-aid station. I'm glad you and your animals were not injured in the storm." She smiles at the children before calling into the house, "Betsy is already getting the house staff organized. They will need all the towels, basins and bandages that they can find. Also, soap and medicine for their injuries, and scissors and knives, too."

They hear a *Yes, Missus,* from a thin black woman dressed in an apron over her long black dress. She has a bandanna knotted around her head as do most of the other female house slaves. She turns to the other house slaves and claps her hands, ready to give orders.

"You, Rodger, get your workers busy gatherin' towels, basins and soap. Fannie, git your girls lookin' for bandages and balms good for cuts and scrapes. Kitchen peoples, you gather up knives and scissors. Let's get hoppin'–our friends are hurtin'."

Chester bellows for his white overseer, "*Frank,* where are you? We need to go out and check the grounds and fields."

Frank slinks from the shadows of the barn left standing, where he had taken shelter from the storm. "Yes, sir, I stayed with the field hands the whole time to keep order. I just got back from the fields," he lies to his boss. "Lots of slaves got hurt."

"Well, go get Manny to saddle our horses while we have daylight to survey the property to see what needs to be repaired. I must make a list for tomorrow. We'll order materials to begin rebuilding the damaged outbuildings and the slave quarters. Oh, and the fields–we'll have to clear the damaged plants and replant fall crops. I have so much to think about and to do. All this new trouble on top of those two runaways we have to look for...

"Children, I leave you in Mrs. Matthews' capable hands. Thank you for your kind offer of help. Our plantation is open to you, afterwards, to rest and freshen up," he says. He turns and goes into the house for his hat and riding crop.

When Melody returns to the house, the children go to the devastated slave quarters to find chaos. There are so many injured field hands they don't know where to start. But Betsy soon takes charge as the house servants arrive with supplies.

One of the larger storage buildings beside the apothecary building becomes a field house for the injured. The apothecary is loaded with everything they need for first aid. Bedding is brought out for the injured field workers who must stay overnight in the makeshift hospital.

Jinx and Max join Betsy in checking them over, one by one, for hours, until the line finally ends. The worst of the injuries are broken bones. The children are surprised to see how efficient Betsy is, even at setting broken bones.

The slaves who lost their homes double up with those who didn't. Betsy and the kitchen staff soon have hot soups and bread ready for everyone. Max decides to slip away to see if Henry made it to the plantation.

"Jinx, I'm going to the blacksmith stable to check on Henry and the horses," Max murmurs to her.

Jinx nods. "We'd best use Henry's fake name, Hiram, and stick with our story of going South to visit relatives. It's so dangerous for him," she says.

"Right. We'll probably check on the carriage to see if we can pull it out of the stream. It might not be as bad as it looks. Hope for a good report," says Max. He gives Jinx a quick hug, crosses his fingers and is gone.

Betsy walks over to Jinx. "I think we can leave the first-aid station to Fannie, now. She's the head of the cleanin' staff in the house. She a good girl–learned from me how to treat everythin' from a cut to a broken bone." Fannie hears the praise and grins.

"I best be gettin' back to the big house. I'm the cook, and they's gonna want a big meal even though that tornado ripped through. Follow me, Miss, I'll walk you up to the house," says Betsy. "No rest for the weary, child. Even us house workers are busy 'til the wee hours of the night."

Jinx finds Melody sitting in a comfortable chair in a large room off the main hallway. Melody pats the chair beside her. "Come rest,

Miss Jinx. I see Betsy is back; I'll have her brew a big pot of tea." She rings a bell, and a servant steps up from behind her chair. Jinx hadn't even noticed him there.

"Jasper, tell Cook we need tea and some muffins, right away," Melody orders.

"Yes, Missus, I'll bring it fast as I can," Jasper says. He bows and leaves the room.

"They are good people," Melody says to Jinx. "Sometimes...well, it bothers me how hard they are worked. I don't like how Frank, the overseer, treats them. I don't believe in...slavery." Melody gasps and covers her mouth with her hands.

"Well there, I've finally said it out loud. But we Southern women don't have a say in such matters. I love my husband; he's basically a kindhearted man. But his mindset is the workers are slaves and are stock, like the cattle and other farm animals. They are listed as assets, along with our other livestock. They are bought and sold so he will have the strongest workers for his fields. Mr. Matthews always worries about money and his crops; the storm damage will set him back, I'm sure."

Jinx gives her a smile. "It must be hard for you," she says.

"It is, so I do what I can to ease their way. I insist that Sunday is the field hands' day off for rest. Now, I do need my house staff every day, but we allow a few to come to church with us. After all, we need assistance getting in and out of the carriage.

"They always get a set of new clothes for Christmas, and Christmas Day is a holiday for the field hands. Their cabins must be kept weatherproof and must have stoves for cooking and heating in the winter. They also get to build their own sturdy, basic furniture. And Mr. Matthews may not have a say in how I run my house slaves–that's my domain." Melody looks defiant, and tosses her red curls.

Jinx laughs. "You are small but mighty, I can tell."

Melody gives a vigorous nod. "Now, let's go get you a warm bath and clean clothes. Mr. Matthews will expect a big supper later tonight when he comes in from the fields. We'll get you all dressed up," says Melody. "I'm so glad you happened by to help us. Besides, I love to have company. My, what an exciting day it has been. Thank God we had no deaths."

Jinx thinks about the many enslaved African Americans who are forced to live a basic, hard existence, working their fingers to the bone. Then she follows Melody up the grand staircase in the majestic plantation house, so different from the slave quarters, thinking about the long road ahead in history until equality and freedom are reached.

Chapter Twelve

Southern Hospitality

A pretty, young house slave named Beauty draws Jinx's bathwater. She then helps Jinx dress in a soft, clean nightgown, and fixes her wild red hair into a pretty style. Beauty is exactly that; she is a beautiful girl, not much older than Jinx. She is small and pert, with smooth skin the color of cocoa. Her curly lashes frame her big brown eyes. She chats with Jinx the whole time and puts her at ease.

The bedroom has lavender-flowered paper covering the walls. Two, ceiling-to-floor windows look out on the front lawn with its gardens and paths. The bed is made of cherry wood and has a canopy. It is so deep and wide that Jinx feels sure she'll get lost in it.

"Now, Miss Jinx, you rest under the quilt in this pretty nightgown. When it's time for dinner, I come back and help you dress in the prettiest evening gown of all. You'll be the rose of the night," says Beauty.

"But you don't need to help me anymore. I can dress myself. You've already made me feel so much better," says Jinx.

"Miss Jinx, the Missus say I'm to be your handmaid the rest of the time you here. I'm glad to do it. It's been real excitin' with the tornado and meetin' new people. Takes the drudgery away for a bit. So, I'll be back soon."

Petey arrives after a while, all fluffy and dry from his bath given to him by Beauty. He jumps way up high and lands on the bed, where he sinks into the soft covers.

"*Ummmm...feels good to sleep in a soft bed...zzzzzzz...*" Petey snores off to dreamland. He whimpers in his sleep, and his little legs twitch as if he is running.

Jinx pets him until he is calm and is almost asleep herself, watching a beautiful sunset out of her windows, when she hears a rap at her door. "Come in," she says.

"Will you look at the lady of the house, all primped up," Max teases. He closes the door and sits in a chair beside her bed. He is bathed and dressed in shiny black pants, a creamy shirt and a fancy, stitched vest. His blond hair is smoothed back on the sides, but his long bangs keep falling down past his eyebrows.

Jinx pulls her quilt into her lap and sits up against the downy pillows. "Hello, Sir Max. If you had black hair and a moustache, I'd say you're the spittin' image of Rhett Butler in *Gone with the Wind*. Quite handsome, you are. So how bad is the damage to the carriage?"

Max turns red. *Drat it all,* he thinks, embarrassed. *I hate blushing all the time.* He pushes his bangs out of his eyes. "Um, not as bad as we thought. Henry and Dot and Thunder are safe and warm in the livery stable quarters. The rear axle and wheel are broken, and one of the doors got ripped off," says Max. "But Buster, the head groom, says they can have the carriage all fixed up and ready to go for tomorrow.

"Jinx, this place is like a small village. They have a little store, a blacksmith shop, a smokehouse—all kinds of shops to fix equipment and a big cookhouse that has lots of brick ovens. There's a covered pathway from the cookhouse to the rear of the plantation house. The overseer has his own cabin, nicer and bigger than the slave quarters."

"Wait until you tour the house," says Jinx. "It's beautiful. Such an obvious difference from the slave huts. So, what about our belongings?"

"The servants are washing and cleaning our other belongings and laying them out by the fireplace in the kitchen to dry. They're very nice and helpful," Max says.

"The workers are really skilled, too. Some of them are great artisans, good at their craft. Ironsmiths, tinsmiths and furniture makers... They should be getting paid, not have to work as slaves."

Max looks off to the side. He knows Jinx is uneasy about the guns. "I also recovered the shotgun and the pistol. Mr. Matthews wants to replace our ammunition for the guns for free, but I'm going to try to pay him. Their hospitality is already more than enough."

There is a little knocking at the door. Before Jinx can answer, Beauty bursts in the room to help her get dressed for the big evening dinner. She holds a soft pink dress with white embroidery on the sleeves and skirts, and frilly petticoats with hoops.

"Oh, 'scuse me, Miss Jinx, Master Max. I'm sorry to bust in like that. Please don't tell the master..." says Beauty, her voice training off. She looks terrified. "I was so excited fer Miss Jinx to see her pretty gown."

Max blushes again and scrambles to his feet, knocking the chair back. "No, no, of course we wouldn't tell on you for something so trivial, or for anything else. I'll head downstairs to the study to talk with Mister Matthews. Bye, Jinx..." He almost runs out the door.

Jinx laughs aloud at Max's apparent embarrassment, awakening Petey. *I'm hungry, I'm hungry...oh, Miss Beauty, I love you..."* he says. Petey jumps over the bed to give Beauty kisses.

Beauty's hands are full, so all she can do is laugh as Petey covers her face with licks. "Here, Miss Jinx, let's get these petticoats on you. Your waist is so tiny we don't need no corset to pull it in. The women don't like them corsets anyways—they pinch them so tight they can't even enjoy their supper. What we women do for the menfolk...*um hummm.*"

Jinx laughs at her image in the mirror when she sees the swaying hoops under her dress puffing out her figure. "I've never worn petticoats with hoops before, Beauty," she says. "I feel quite grand."

Ten minutes later, Petey leads Jinx down the thirty steps of the curving staircase that lead to a grand hallway. The hall is wallpapered at the top, with dark wainscoting on the bottom. There are solemn portraits of family members hung along its length. A large grandfather clock rings out eight deep bongs.

Max awaits her with his eyes bugged out. He takes in the beautiful rose-colored dress, dainty slippers and string of pearls that Melody gave Jinx as a present and gives a low whistle. "Wow, who are you and what have you done with my friend Jinx?" he jokes. He is now wearing a dinner jacket with long coattails. Max offers his arm and they enter the dining room, off to the left side.

Now both teens take in the scene with bulging eyes. The dining room is decorated with huge pictures in massive frames; most are landscapes of serene countrysides or English hunting scenes with horses and hounds. Candle sconces are lit all along the walls.

Beautiful dark mahogany sideboards hold an array of steaming silver serving dishes that give off delicious aromas of roasted chicken, ham, roast beef, and roast pork. Salvers hold breads, cakes, and pies. Other silver bowls are filled with mashed sweet potatoes, round red potatoes, creamed corn, peas and onions, and soups.

The serving staff, all house slaves, is positioned around the room, standing straight, eyes down and hands folded. They wear black uniforms and white gloves. There is even a boy about Max's age waiting to pour beverages for the children and the adults.

Max and Jinx feel almost faint from hunger. There is enough food to feed an army. They look around, expecting a large group of people, but they only see Melody and Chester, chatting over coffee. They are seated near one end of an oblong mahogany table with sixteen chairs around it. The table is decorated with blue willow dishes, silver forks, spoons and knives, soft cloth napkins, and bowls of yellow and pink roses from their own greenhouse.

Mr. Matthews rises from his chair and pulls a chair out for Jinx, across the table from Melody. "Miss Jinx, you are looking especially beautiful tonight." He seats her, and then he pulls a chair out for Max. Jinx can't help but bat her eyelashes at Max to make him blush.

Melody asks a short blessing over the food as they bow their heads. Chester then rings a tiny silver bell. The servers get busy, offering the guests each tasty dish: first soup, then vegetables, meats, breads, and sweet rolls.

Max is uneasy–he and Jinx aren't used to this lavish a meal. *"More forks and spoons and knives than I know what to do with,"* he thinks at Jinx. He nudges her under the table.

Jinx tries hard not to giggle. *"I know...I wish I were with Petey out in the cookhouse with the cooks and other house staff. They're probably laughing and having a great time while they're eating. Watch Chester and Melody, and pick up the utensil they use. We're learning real Southern social manners, aren't we?"*

"Yeah, well, don't dribble gravy on your beautiful dress, Miss Jinx," Max thinks.

Jinx nudges him back under the table.

Chester and Melody Matthews are perfect hosts, telling the children about their plantation life instead of grilling them about personal details. Before they retire to the music room for dessert, the Matthews give Jinx and Max a grand tour of the other downstairs rooms: Melody's sitting room, Chester's den and office, and a large parlor for entertaining guests. Each room is more lavish than the last, with ornate furniture, tapestry wall hangings, and plush rugs; everywhere are signs of how rich the owners are compared to how very poorly their slaves live.

By the time they reach the music room, both children feel stiff, sore, and very tired from their tornado adventure. Melody sees their signs of fatigue. "You all sit down and let me serve you tea and dessert. Then I'll play some soothing music on the harpsichord that will ease you right on up to your big, fluffy beds for a good night's rest."

Melody rings for the servants to bring trays of tea, pies, cookies and cakes, and then she dismisses them for the evening. She leaves the room again and comes back carrying Petey, who looks at her with adoring eyes. "I thought your little Petey might enjoy the music, so here he is. You're a good little boy, aren't you, Petey? I'd love to have a little dog." She looks at her husband.

Chester smiles. "We'll see, dear one. Maybe a puppy for Christmas, *hmmm?"*

Petey leaps into Jinx's lap. *"A cookie, a piece of pie...please? Please?"* he begs. Max breaks a tiny piece of peach pie off and feeds it to Petey, who licks his chops and begs for more.

They are finishing up their dessert when banging and scuffling sounds occur outside at the front door. The overseer, Frank, is escorted to the music room doors by the black butler. He stands, hat in hand. His head is lowered, greasy hair falling over his shifty eyes, but his dark eyes are on Chester.

"Excuse me, Mr. Matthews, sir, but we have serious trouble out front. Bounty hunters have caught the two that run away a few days ago. You'd best come outside to control the situation." He nods, turns away and leaves.

Chester sighs and shakes his head. "What more can happen today?" he says, to no one in particular. He gets to his feet, goes into the hallway and out the front door.

Melody clutches her hands and follows, sadness written all over her face. Max and Jinx and Petey can do nothing but go along. They dread the punishment that will be meted out to the unfortunate runaways.

Jinx has to hold up the hoops of her skirts to run. She and Max are horrified when they pass through the great wooden doors to the verandah. A large crowd of slaves has gathered. They see Henry at the back of the crowd, taking care not to get in the slave hunters' view. Petey is agitated and barks at everyone.

The slave hunters, Jackson and Billy, have steel grips on the two runaways' arms. Jefferson and Janie stand in muddy, tattered clothes with manacles around their necks and chained to their wrists, hanging their heads in defeat. Janie protects her unborn baby by holding her arms across her belly.

"Max, we have to do something, they'll get whipped for sure."

"What can we do, Jinx?"

"I don't know...grab them and go into the Time Tunnel?"

"You know we can't do that, Jinx. Even I know that is forbidden territory for anyone who isn't a Time Traveler. It might kill them."

Jackson spies the teens and his face turns furious. "You two lied to us, didn't you? You helped these two runaways by feeding them and giving them directions, right? *The Fugitive Slave Law* says it's against the law to help runaway slaves. You should be arrested," he spits out at them.

Melody looks at the children, and then says to Jackson, "Did you see them aid these two?"

"No, but I caught the runaways soon after we left their campfire." Jackson nods at the children. "They sent us in the wrong direction, but we found them anyways."

"Leave this to me please, Mrs. Matthews," says Chester. "Let's move this nasty business along. You men caught my slaves, so I'll give you the bounty money I put out on their heads, $1,500 in cash." He pulls a leather pouch out of his jacket pocket and peels off the money. Jackson grabs it and stuffs it into his pants pocket.

"Now my slaves will take them from you. Be off with you," he says to Jackson and Billy.

"You could say thanks, ya know. It's hard work catchin' these runaways for you rich plantation owners. We're doin' you a service," Jackson mutters. He and Billy stalk back to their horses tied up at a hitching post, mount and rear their horses away without a backwards glance.

"Take them to the whipping tree, and I want all field hands and house slaves out there to see the whipping," says Chester. He strides toward the side of the big barn, where there is an old ash tree with a low bough.

The crowd murmurs in sadness and follows Chester to the whipping tree. Jinx and Max turn to follow, but Melody takes Jinx's hand.

"Stay with me, Miss Jinx. This is no sight for a young lady to see. They'll need help afterwards with their cuts." Melody pulls Jinx back to the plantation house.

"Max, please stay with them," Jinx says. He nods. Petey sticks by Max's side.

A few of the head field hands walk Jefferson and Janie to the whipping tree. Someone removes the manacles. Chester speaks to them.

"The punishment for running away the first time is thirty lashes with the whip. I abhor the thought of hitting a woman who is expecting a baby, so Janie will only get fifteen. Jefferson, you will get your thirty and the fifteen remaining lashes from Janie's punishment."

He turns to his other slaves gathered about. "Let this be a warning to you all, once again. I will not tolerate running away from my plantation. You are well treated here, and you belong to me. Frank, Janie will get her fifteen lashes first. Tie her to the tree."

Janie's hands are tied up to the branch above her head. Frank enjoys ripping her dress open in the back, stepping back and cracking his whip once to make the crowd jump. Some of the women hide their eyes and moan. Then Frank winds up and cracks the cruel leather against her soft back as hard as he can swing. The first leaves a long, red welt. The second lash lays her back open; the red welt appears and quickly begins to bleed. The third adds another bleeding slash. Janie stands silently, her head down, as she endures her punishment. When they cut her arms down, the women wrap her in a soft quilt and lead her away to the slave quarters.

Frank smiles, and his eyes glint in the darkness like a wild animal. He looks evil.

Jefferson is tied the same way to the whipping tree. The beating begins. Max thinks he is going to be sick. He closes his eyes and flinches every time he hears the crack of the whip, knowing that forty-five lashes from Frank's whip will feel like fire on Jefferson's brown back.

After it is over, Max leaves when the group takes Jefferson away and goes to a quiet place behind the barn. There, he throws up until he empties his stomach. Then he cries, alone in the dark.

Chapter Thirteen

North Carolina–Stuck in the Mud

Jinx sleeps in the rocking carriage with Petey in her arms. Max sits up top with Henry, taking a turn at handling the reins.

After a restless night's sleep, they have left behind Acorn Acres in southern Virginia and are well into North Carolina. Breakfast wasn't the jovial feast that yesterday's dinner had been. The Matthews were polite, but Mr. Matthews treated them a bit cooler after the slave hunters' accusations of the teens helping the missing slaves.

Jinx has not yet asked Max about the whippings, and Max does not offer any information. He can't make himself talk about it. Henry found him that night, behind the barn, and held him in his arms for a bit until Max calmed down.

"Henry?" Max says.

"Um hum, Master Max, what is it?"

"Aw Henry, why can't you call me Max? I'm not your master. No one is your master."

"I know that, but it's a habit I can't break yet. You and Miss Jinx, you's the best thing that ever happened to me. Next to May Ella and my boys, that is," says Henry. He gives Max a big grin. Henry and Max feel a closer bond after the night of the whippings.

"Anyway, what makes you and the others want to run when you know your chances are so slim for reaching freedom, and you know that you will receive whippings or worse? I think you are awfully brave," says Max.

"Well now, that's a good question. Some folks is satisfied with their place in life, and they make the best of it. But others, like me and Edward, we know what freedom is like. We wasn't born into slavery; we had our freedom taken away from us. There's nothin' better than takin' a big breath of air and knowin' you're free to do what you like, to make somethin' out of yourself, to find out your purpose in life."

Max shakes his head in understanding. "I'm starting to think about what I want to do when I grow up. I go to a military academy, Henry. I think I want to serve my country. Maybe I'll be a Navy flier."

Henry looks at Max. "A Navy flier? I heard about the Army and Navy, but do you mean to say you want to fly like a bird? Did you get a knock upside your head in that tornado, son?"

Max laughs. "I keep forgetting that I'm in the past. Maybe we figure out how to fly." He stops short of telling Henry about the Wright Brothers and the first airplane flight.

Now Henry laughs. "Boy, I sure do want to see that. Talk about sweet freedom...to think of flyin' through the air like a bird..." Henry gazes into the sky for a long time.

Then Henry frowns. "I'm thinkin' 'bout my brother, Edward, day and night. I sure do hope he's safe and not bein' punished too bad. I don't know how we'll ever get him back."

"Now Henry, you've got to have faith. We *will* get him back. I know Thaddeus Stevens and his lawyer team are really sharp. They have no time for slavery. Maybe we can get some news about it when we get to Wilmington."

"I don't know, Master Max. Some days I feels like this whole plan is doomed. It's awful dangerous to ask you to go Down South to fetch my boys. Slave catchers jumpin' out of every corner ready to snatch me and have you and Miss Jinx arrested for helpin' a runaway..." Henry shakes his head. "I shouldn't of asked you to do it."

Max looks deep into Henry's dark eyes, seeing the misery swimming in them. He lays a hand on Henry's arm. "We want to help you, Henry. You've got to understand; this is our mission, and we won't be satisfied until we complete it successfully."

Henry finally gives Max a ghost of a smile and nods his head.

The day is cloudy and cool. September is coming to an end. Everyone wears a heavier coat now. Max does worry about getting Henry and the boys back to Pennsylvania and straight up through New York to Canada in the late-fall weather. *I'll need to have faith, like I told Henry,* he thinks. Cold raindrops begin to fall, and Henry reaches under the bench to get the rain slickers.

"You're doing a fine job of driving the carriage, Master Max. Couldn't do better myself," says Henry. Thunder trots along at a steady gait.

Henry begins to sing in a low, sorrowful voice:

Follow the drinkin' gourd.
Follow the drinkin' gourd.
For the old man is a-waitin' for to carry you to freedom,
If you follow the drinkin' gourd.
When the sun comes back and the first quail calls,
Follow the drinkin' gourd.
For the old man is a-waitin' for to carry you to freedom,
If you follow the drinkin' gourd.

"Henry, that's a beautiful, sad song," says Jinx, through the window behind the driver's seat. "Remember I told you that that phrase, 'follow the drinking gourd,' kept running through my mind? You explained it's code for finding the North Star to help you go northward. Now here it is in a beautiful song."

"That's right, Miss Jinx. And this song is a secret code that tells us runaways how to keep goin' in the right direction, findin' that ol' North Star. If it weren't for the secret songs passed on, us slaves might not have no idea how to run or where to go. We'd just run blind, and likely get picked up by slave catchers right away. That's what happened to Edward the first time he ran. He wasn't ready to go, 'cause he didn't plan," Henry finishes.

"That line, 'follow the drinkin' gourd,' was trying to give me a clue about helping you on the Underground Railroad," says Jinx. "That's how it works for me; I see things or hear things, and then I have to connect them to figure out what is to be my mission in the past."

"Is that right, Miss Jinx? Ain't it strange how it all works out? It just takes time," says Henry. "Out in the fields we use hollowed-out gourds like cups to hold water. That's why those stars is called the drinkin' gourd.

"The song tells a story about an old sailor man with a wooden leg, named Peg Leg Joe. He comes South and teaches the slaves the song. It tells how to find him at the big O-hi-o River, where he's waitin' with a boat to take you safe across. He tells slaves 'bout the first safe house on the other side, and how people will help 'em get all the way to Canada.

"That's the way to go if you live off, farther to the west. There's a path across the Ohio River runnin' up through that state to them big cities, then on to freedom. There's so many good people along the way to help us runaway folks, no matter what state we runnin' from."

"Teach us the whole song, Henry, please. Singing will help pass the time," says Jinx.

"I will, but they's secret songs, not for you to sing out there in public. Too many slave hunters would figure 'em out, and then them songs wouldn't help the runaways," says Henry.

"I understand. We'll only sing them when we're together. Do you know more songs?" asks Jinx.

"Sure do. Here's the rest of the song." Henry's deep, mellow voice takes up the song again.

> *The riverbank makes a very good road,*
> *The dead trees will show you the way.*
> *Left foot, peg foot, travelin' on,*
> *Follow the drinkin' gourd.*
> *The river ends between two hills,*
> *Follow the drinkin' gourd.*
> *There's another river on the other side,*
> *Follow the drinkin' gourd.*
> *When the great big river meets the little river,*
> *Follow the drinkin' gourd.*
> *For the old man is a-waitin' for to carry you to freedom*
> *If you follow the drinkin' gourd.*

The road has become sticky with mud, and the cold rain keeps falling, but the group sings the soulful song to pass the time. Petey woofs along, and the horses neigh their version, too.

❈ ◍ ✹

Far up in Pennsylvania, Mrs. Merryweather, the storekeeper, lights a candle in the window for her son, as she does every night. She expects that he will be home any day now to give her a report about how much money they made turning in runaways. Her husband, Jackson Sr., owned a slave ship when he was alive. When he died in a shoot-out with government agents, they lost that huge income, so his son turned to catching runaways to make money. Sometimes he is gone for weeks at a time. It is hard work, but her son enjoys it, as his father enjoyed the profits of running captured Africans from Africa to America.

She turns to make herself a cup of tea, but suddenly she hears stomping on the backdoor porch. Her son and his sidekick burst into the kitchen.

"Hello, Ma. Me and Billy just got back. Did ya miss me?" Jackson gives his mother a big hug.

"Welcome home, Junior. Hello, Billy. Come sit down at the table. I can warm some dinner in the oven," says Mrs. Merryweather.

The men sit and eat the warm roast beef and potato dinner placed before them with great relish.

"Ma, we made $6,000 this trip. Of course, Billy gets a quarter of the profits. The last couple runaways we caught was closer to home. Got 'em in Maryland. A man and his wife expectin' a baby. Why on earth do they run? They don't get it. A free roof over their heads and food in their bellies. That's all they need, and they run."

"Well, that's all the more money in our pockets," says Ma. "Good job, boys. I know the family bounty-hunting business is dangerous, but it's

very profitable. It puts us right up there with Patty Cannon and her slave-stealing gang down in Maryland." Ma is proud that her family is becoming as notorious as that gang of thugs.

"Now, I have some news for you—did you hear about the trouble over at William Parker's house in Christiana?"

"Yeah, news traveled fast," says Jackson.

"Well, that next day his wife Eliza brought a couple of children over to buy the carriage from the livery stable, and they had a servant with them. They were all whispering about secrets—very suspicious. The children were heading South, but they were very close-mouthed about where they were going. And they have a huge amount of money. The boy pulled out a big wad of bills. Paid cash for everything," says Ma.

When she mentions the big wad of money, Jackson's eyes light up. "Ma, I think we had a couple a run-ins with them kids. They helped that last runaway slave couple—sent us off in the wrong direction. Then we had trouble with them at the plantation when we finally turned the runaways in. Couple of real brats."

"I know that 'servant' of theirs don't really belong to them. I think he was one of them runaway slaves that shot at the marshal over there in Christiana. I think there's some more money to be had; what do you boys think?" says Ma.

Billy and Jackson look at each other with gleams in their eyes. "Think maybe we should head out on another hunt come sunup, Jackson?" says Billy.

Jackson nods his head with a huge grin on his face.

"Good, boys," says Ma. "More roast beef and mashed potatoes?"

By the time the carriage gets within a few miles of Wilmington, Thunder must pull with all his might, because the road has become filled with deep, muddy ruts that suck at the carriage wheels. Henry takes the reins and sends Max into the carriage to dry off and warm up. Dusk is now fast approaching.

"Max, I think we should try to pick up Jefferson and Janie on our way back to Pennsylvania. I feel awful about them getting recaptured," says Jinx.

"*You* feel bad...I feel like it's my fault they were captured. I should have played it another way—said we never saw them."

"No, it's not anyone's fault. Don't be so hard on yourself, Max. Those kidnappers would only have headed North right away if you hadn't sent them the wrong way. What brave people. It seems almost impossible for so many enslaved African Americans to have actually made it to Canada. Some people estimate up to 50,000 slaves escaped along the Underground Railroad routes."

"I agree with you, Jinx. I want more than anything to rescue Jefferson and Janie," says Max. "We'll try hard, but our main goal now is to focus on Henry and his boys."

Petey says, *"I want to rescue the nice man and lady, too."*

Jinx lifts him and kisses his nose. *"What's the plan, Big Guy?"*

"I'm working it out, don't you worry," says Petey.

The carriage comes to a halt. Max opens the window to talk to Henry.

"What's up? Why are we stopping—trouble ahead?"

"There's a carriage off the road in a big gully, Master Max. Their horse can't pull it out. They need help," says Henry.

"You all wait here. I'll check it out. It may be a trap for you, Henry," says Max. He slips the pistol into his belt, pulls his rain slicker back over his head and opens the door.

"Enough of this pretending I'm some helpless 1800s girl. I'm coming with you, and don't you say one word about it," Jinx says. She pulls on her rain slicker and jumps down in the mud, following Max up to the carriage. The gooey mud almost pulls their boots off their feet.

The heavy rain runs off the brims of their hats like Niagara Falls. They see a black man in the driver's seat gently slapping the reins on the sides of a pretty brown mare, and a bearded white man pulling on the mare's reins from the ground. They try to guide her out of the gully, but the deep mud sucks at the carriage like quicksand.

"Come on, Dolly–you can do it. Easy, now one more big pull, girl," says the driver.

Max runs up to the white man, who has a graying beard and ice-blue eyes, and says, "Hello, sir. My name is Max Myers, and this is my friend, Jinx. How can we help you?"

"Ah, thank goodness you've arrived. My name is Alex Ross. This is my servant, Daniel." Daniel touches the brim of his hat and nods his head, water streaming off his face. "If we could use one of your horses to help Dolly, I think we could pull my carriage out of this dastardly mud."

Jinx volunteers to get Dot. On her way back, Thunder begs her to allow him to help. *Pleeeease, I can pull it out. I could do it on my own,* Thunder says.

"Don't be silly, Thunder. You're in harness. It would take too long to unharness you. Besides, you've been pulling through the mud all afternoon. We don't want to strain your weak leg any more."

"I'm ready," Dot whinnies. She trots smartly along, head in air, on by Thunder, who is pouting. *"Stand back, Thunder. Let a lady show you how to do it,"* says Dot. She allows herself to be harnessed alongside Dolly, and the two mares give a mighty pull to free the carriage from the mud.

Alex shakes hands all around in the rainy deluge, including his servant's hand. "Please, join me at the Cape Fear Inn for the night so I can properly thank you for your help. We're not far from town."

Within the hour they all pull up in front of the Cape Fear Inn in downtown Wilmington, North Carolina. Two livery stable slaves take the reins of the horses and lead them and the carriages around the rear to the stables. Henry and Daniel retire to the stables where they will stay. The children can hear the horses talking as they go.

"That was so easy with your help, Dot," says Dolly.

"Oh, we girls are good together, aren't we?" says Dot.

Thunder is very annoyed. *"It took two of you to do the work I could have done myself,"* says Thunder. *"Must I put up with this all evening?"*

The mares laugh, neighing together. They are good friends already and plan to chat all night.

Two other slaves take the baggage upstairs, while Alex and the children go to the front desk for their keys.

"Your rooms are already paid for, with my thanks for your help on the road. You were truly Good Samaritans to stop. These days, with such distrust going around, it's not everyone who would stop to offer help," says Alex.

"Oh no, sir," both children say at the same time.

"That's not necessary. We only did what's right," Max says.

"And you are good people for it," Alex says.

"What about Henry and Daniel?" Jinx asks. "Will they be taken care of?"

"They will be warm in the stables with the stable hands. You can have hot food sent out to them," the desk clerk snaps, as he turns away with a sneer on his thin lips.

Jinx feels reprimanded and embarrassed. Alex takes her hand and says, "Don't feel bad, Miss. They'll be fine. Let's all go to our rooms for hot baths and fresh clothes. We'll meet in an hour in the dining room for a good, warm meal. And I'll take care of our friends, Henry and Daniel, don't you worry."

Once more Jinx shakes her head at the unfairness of it all.

"When all those adults told us life isn't fair, they really meant it, didn't they?" Max says.

Jinx nods. "And I'm learning the hard way exactly what they meant," she says. "Come on, Petey, let's go get a nice, hot bath."

"Another bath? Too many baths on this trip," says a very muddy, wet Petey, who struggles in Jinx's arms the whole way upstairs to their room.

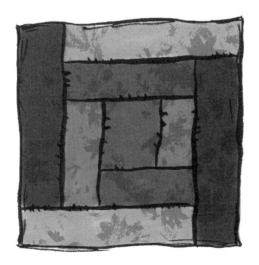

Chapter Fourteen

A Canadian Friend

An hour later Max taps at Jinx's door. He has dropped Petey off in the kitchen, where the delighted cook volunteered to feed the little terrier.

"Come on in," Jinx says.

"Wrong answer...you're supposed to say, 'Who is it?' Now what if I were a bandit?" says Max, entering the room.

"Good evening, Sir Galahad, my knight in shining armor. Don't start with the protectiveness stuff," Jinx says. She always turns to teasing to hide her muddled thoughts about how much she adores Max. It feels safer that way.

"*Ooooh*, a bit cranky?" says Max, grinning. He smells of perfumed soap and is dressed in the fancy black pants and vest that Chester and Melody Matthews insisted he take along. His boots have been polished and shine in the oil lamplight. He notices that Jinx has put on her pretty pink dress for dining with Alex Ross.

They walk down the stairs and enter the inn's dining hall. It is very busy tonight with many travelers who came in out of the weather. Alex waves at them from a table way back in a more private corner of the room. They join him there.

Alex arises when they come to the table. He is a tall man, rather heavy, with a full beard and moustache. His black hair is combed straight back. Alex is dressed in a gray suit with a vest, and polished black shoes. He walks around and pulls a chair out for Jinx. "Why, Miss Jinx, you look lovely tonight. I couldn't even see you today under all the rain and mud. Please, both of you, sit with me," Alex says.

They notice his accent is different, not southern, and not northeastern.

"Thank you, sir," says Jinx. She thinks she could get used to the males paying her compliments.

A waiter comes over and takes their orders. The specialty for tonight is a hearty chicken stew with potatoes and carrots. That sounds good to all of them.

"So, Mr. Ross, tell us about yourself," says Max. It's safer if they get their host talking about himself first.

"Actually, my full title is Dr. Alexander Ross, and I'm from Canada," he says. "I am a physician, but I am also a naturalist and an ornithologist. I love visiting the United States when I can, to document trees and plants, especially the birds. I'm working on a nature book. What about yourselves?"

The children look at each other. This has become the part they dread when meeting people on the trip.

Jinx takes a deep breath. "Well, Dr. Ross, we are very close friends, going South for a visit with relatives. We're traveling with our servant, Henry."

"I see," says Alex. His eyes twinkle, reminding the children of Santa Claus.

He pulls his chair closer to the table and leans in. He speaks in a low voice. "It's all right, children. You can trust me." He places his hand on the table and traces it with his other pointer finger. Then he traces the five stars around the hand. He looks at Jinx.

"Follow the stars," Jinx and Max both murmur.

Alex smiles and nods his head. "You see..." he stops and looks around, making sure no one is near, "I have spoken with my friend, Daniel. He is no more my servant than Henry is your servant. They have exchanged news with each other. I know that you are helping your friend Henry find his little twin boys. Daniel helps me on my secret missions to the South, pretending to be my servant."

Max and Jinx lean in closer. This mysterious, jolly man intrigues them. "What are your secret missions?" Jinx asks.

At this time the server arrives with hot bowls of chicken stew that give off savory aromas. He places the bowls around the table. Another server comes with a big loaf of brown bread, still warm from the oven, and fresh milk for the children. When they leave, Alex continues.

"The rain has stopped, but the night remains overcast. Perfect for my secret trip. Would you like to help me tonight? It is dangerous but important work. We will have to be very alert," says Alex.

Both teens nod yes without another thought.

"Good for you. You won't be sorry," says Alex. "Bring Petey. He'll be a good watchdog. Meet me at midnight in the livery stable. If you go down the back stairs to the servant quarters, the cook in the kitchen will let you out the back door. I've worked with the servants here many times; you can trust them."

The rest of the meal passes pleasantly, with chatting about the differences between the United States and Canada. Alex Ross tells them all about the different birds and flowers that he has catalogued in the South. He especially loves to visit the islands where the huge, three hundred and fifty to one thousand-pound loggerhead turtles come to make their nests. Alex lists the birds he has sketched: pelicans, herons, egrets and terns. Max and Jinx listen, excited to learn about some of the wildlife in the South. Finally, exhausted, they all retire to their rooms to rest until midnight.

At midnight, Max stops by Jinx's room again to pick up Petey and her for the mysterious secret mission with Alex. They tiptoe down the hallway to the servants' back-stairs door. There is only one dim lamp at the end of the hall. Jinx takes the glass chimney off and tips her candle to light it. Replacing the globe, they sneak through the door and go down the dark, narrow servant steps into the big kitchen. Petey follows them.

They see a smiling, brown lady wearing a cook's apron and headscarf. She motions for the children and takes them to the door. "Doc Alex, he says to hurry over to the barn. He's a-waitin' for you all. Thank you for helpin' him, children." She gives Jinx a basket of wrapped muffins and cold fried chicken. "You pass these goodies out tonight, child. You gonna meet some fine people." She hugs them both.

They dimly see Alex across the way at the barn. He holds the reins of the three impatient horses. When they get closer, Alex pulls one smaller pouch out of his big saddlebags. He motions them closer and then opens the pouch to show them what's inside: a folded map, a compass, a pistol and ammunition, and some loose coins.

Now the children understand who Dr. Alexander Ross really is—a conductor on the great Underground Railroad. He risks his life, probably many times a year, to help enslaved African Americans escape to Canada.

Alex grins at them and asks, "Will you help me with some special passengers tonight? I'm stopping at a plantation to pass out escape kits. One group is leaving tonight with me. I have a false bottom in my carriage that can hide four people. If you hadn't pulled me out today, I might not have been able to meet them tonight, as planned."

"But how will they know to watch for you tonight?" Jinx asks.

"Good question," Alex says. "I had Daniel lay my quilt over a fence at the back of the stable to air it out. My quilt has a very special pattern on it–the wagon wheel pattern. Only agents on the Underground Railroad know that it's code for 'the wagon is coming,' be ready to go. So the agent sent the message out to the plantation through other agents.

"You'd be surprised how easy it is to be organized. The Underground Railroad is a whole secret world that most people have no idea is happening right under their noses," Alex finishes.

Jinx and Max grin back at Alex and say together, "Let's go."

Alex mounts his horse, Dolly. Jinx takes one look at Dot, takes a big breath, and steps on a mounting block to put her foot in the stirrup. Tonight she wears her jeans and boots under her dress. Up she goes and takes the reins. Max hands Petey up to her, and Petey settles himself in front of Jinx, across the saddle. Max mounts Thunder and looks like a natural horse rider.

"Take care of me, Dot," Jinx whispers in her ear. Dot turns her head and nods.

"Hold tight, Jinx. We're going to gallop sooner or later," Max says.

"I suppose you had riding at the academy, also, right?" Jinx says.

"Of course," says Max, as he grins at her.

"Uh...this is my first ride, so pick me up if I fall off," says Jinx.

Alex leads them out into the shadows of the night in a slow walk. When they clear the town, he heads off into the woods. "Ready to gallop, Miss Jinx?" he asks.

Jinx gives a thumbs-up sign, tightens her grip on the reins, and nudges Dot with her heels. Dot takes off after the other horses in the dark. Jinx leans low to Dot's broad back. The air rushes by Jinx's ears, and her heart pounds like a hammer against her ribs. But she is exhilarated, loving the thundering sound of Dot's hooves. It reminds her of when Max first taught her to snowboard at Aunt Merry's house last winter.

Petey loves the ride. *"Go faster, Dot, faster."*

When Alex finally slows, the other horses also ease back to a walk. Alex leads them along the side of a large field of corn, by some wheat fields, and behind a grouping of shacks. All is quiet and dark. The sky is moonless, and no stars shine tonight.

Alex cups his hands around his mouth and gives an owl sound, *"Who whoot...who whoot."*

Another owl answers, *"Who whoot...who whoo."*

At least fifteen people slide through the shadows and form a silent group of dark faces in front of Alex. He dismounts and shakes their hands; some hug him.

"Welcome back, Doc Alex, we was waitin' for you, every night for the past week. Knew you'd be back soon," one man says. "We heard that wagon wheel quilt was airin' out today."

Petey jumps down and receives lots of petting. Both teens dismount, awaiting orders.

"Miss Jinx and Max are my helpers tonight. They'll pass out kits. Those of you not moving out tonight, hide your kit someplace really well," says Alex.

"Don't you worry about that, Doc Alex. I already pulled up the floorboard under my bed. Got a good hidin' place there. Boss Man, he'll never find it," says another man.

The group chuckles softly. Jinx gives everyone a muffin and shares the fried chicken to munch on from the good cook back at the inn. They all murmur their thanks. A man and woman with two small children and a bundle of belongings move closer to Alex. Alex hands the father the first kit.

"Good to see you're ready to go, Harry. This is in case we get separated–a map and a knife and a gun. The map shows the way North. The rest of you, good luck when you decide to go. God be with us all," says Alex. He hands kits to Jinx and Max, who pass them out to the remaining men. Offering thanks, the men melt back into the shadows.

Max feels his excitement mix with a new level of terror. *I can't believe we're here passing out guns and knives to the men,* Max thinks. *We're already breaking the law by helping them run, but arming them puts us in terrible danger if we're caught. Doc Alex seems so calm...*

Jinx hears Max's troubling thoughts. She turns to Max and grabs his arm. Using her mental telepathy, she talks to him. *It will be all right, Max; don't think about it. We're almost ready to go. Stay strong.*

"Harry can ride with me. Ruthie, you carry Sammy and ride with Miss Jinx, and JoJo can ride with Max," says Alex. He and Harry help everyone mount up again, and then Alex mounts and gives a hand up to Harry. "It will be a slower ride back to the inn with our extra passengers. If we run into trouble, scatter in the woods and try to hide in a creek bed. Ready?"

This time the horses can't do much better than a trot. JoJo is a wiry little boy about ten years old. He grips Max around the waist and lays his head across Max's back. Max feels him trembling. "It's going to be fine, JoJo. You're going to make it all the way to Canada, you'll see. Doc Alex has done this many times and never gotten caught," says Max. His heart goes out to the little guy.

Ruthie sits behind Jinx, one arm around Jinx's waist and the other wrapped around young Sammy's waist. Sammy is a cute little boy, about five years old, all bundled up in a warm coat and hat. "Miss... thank you for helping us," says Ruthie. "We been talkin' this over for more than a year. Now it's time to go, Lord be with us."

"I think you're the bravest mother ever," says Jinx. "Now try to rest against me. Dot's a gentle horse. She'll take us back to Doc Alex's carriage."

They ride in silence for almost an hour. Then Petey's ears prick up.

"What is it, Petey?" says Jinx.

"Dogs...getting closer. Two hound dogs." Petey growls and his hackles rise.

Jinx cannot hear the dogs, but she warns the others. "I think Petey is picking up some sounds..."

About that time they all hear a faint baying of hounds. "I'm afraid someone sold us out," says Alex. The family is terrified.

"What should we do, Doc Alex? I don't want us to go back, please," Harry worries.

"Now Harry, let us handle this. Children, follow me into the stream. We'll have to hurry."

In a flash Petey jumps to the ground and races off. "Petey, no...stay here," Jinx calls after him.

"*Tell everyone not to worry, I'll take care of the hounds...*" And Petey is gone in a streak, faster than a leaping deer.

They urge the horses into a trot, the riders holding on for dear life. Water splashes up and over them as the horses wade quickly into the knee-deep water of the stream. They go on for fifteen or twenty minutes, through the water.

After a bit Alex slows them to a fast walk, then slows and stops. "Listen..." he says.

There is nothing but the rustling of the tree leaves and the flowing of the stream. No hounds baying, no men on horseback chasing them, only the quiet of the woodland night.

They look at each other in relief. Next comes the sound of a small creature rustling through the underbrush. Petey comes tearing out of the woods and onto the stream bank. He is so excited that he jumps up and down off his back legs, yipping in delight.

"*I did it...I did it. Ran with the big dogs—they were great! Yip, yip, yip. Told them to follow me after a fox. We chased the fox forever... the wrong way. Bark, bark. It worked. Then I cut away back here. They'll never trail you now—yip, yip, yip...*" says Petey. Of course ,only Jinx and Max can understand him, or so they think.

The horses are excited, offering their cheers for Petey by neighing. "*Good job, Petey.*"

Jinx leads Dot over to the bank, and Petey springs high into her arms. He is muddy and has twigs and burrs tangled in his long fur, but Jinx doesn't mind. She hugs him to her chest and whispers into his ear, "Petey, thank you for saving the night. I love you so much."

Alex watches in amusement, then says, "I don't know where your little Petey got to, but I think he distracted the hunting hounds and the slave catcher. What about it, Petey, old boy? Let's get moving. We'll stay in the stream as long as we can; then we'll cut over to town and the livery stable. We must get these people hidden."

JoJo pulls on Max's sleeve and whispers in his ear. "Petey says he ran with the big dogs. He asked them to follow him, and they chased a fox a long way in the wrong direction. Petey really did save us. He's a great dog."

Max turns so he can look in JoJo's eyes. "*You* are an animal communicator?" he whispers in amazement. JoJo nods his head. "Jinx and me, too. Someday I think you'll be able to do great things, JoJo."

JoJo screws up his face and looks over his shoulder at his mother to make sure they are far enough behind, then says, "I can see things... things that happen in the future. They's like stories, but then they come true, like the one about Master gettin' married. I had one last night when I was asleep. My parents and my little brother, Sammy, they was free in Canada. They had their own pretty little house and some chickens and pigs and a big barn. Mama had a garden full of daisies, all different colors, like she always wanted.

"But Mama and Papa, they was real sad. At the supper table there was only three place settings; I wasn't there. And Mama had tears runnin' down her pretty face when she said the blessin' to the Lord. I'm afraid, Master Max. Where was I? Why wasn't I there? Do them stories always come true?"

Wow, Max thinks, *how do I handle this? This boy sees into the future, not the past as Jinx and I do. And is he a Time Traveler like we are?* Only time itself would answer that question.

He pats JoJo's shoulder. "Don't you worry, JoJo. Doc Alex, Jinx and I will make sure you are there with your family, safe in Canada," he blurts out. "We'll check up on you." He can feel JoJo relax and lean into him. *Why did he promise the boy? Oh well, for now it comforts the little boy. But this adds one more important thing to worry about.*

Alex soon leads them out of the stream and back into town, to the rear of the livery stable. It is late at night, and the town is asleep. Henry and Daniel pace the alleyway, watching for them. Big grins break out on their faces when they see the horses walk into the alley. They help the family and rescuers dismount and lead the family into the stable to change into dry clothes. The cook sends out more food and warm coffee and cider.

Max, Jinx and Petey share the warmth of the barn with the others. They look around in amazement at these new friends. It feels like they have known them forever. The boys are excited for the trip and explore the false bottom in Alex's carriage. They climb in to practice hiding. They know they must always watch for slave catchers and hide for safety. Petey climbs in with them, making them giggle.

Their thankful parents, Ruthie and Harry, hug Jinx and Max one last time. Harry looks each child in the eye. "Thank you, young friends. You're very special to have the goodness in your hearts to help other folks like us. God bless you."

Ruthie cries when she speaks. "Y'all come to Canada to visit us in our new home."

Alex herds his flock to the rear of the stable, where there is a trapdoor to a secret room. They will be safe there for the night. He touches the brim of his hat and winks at Max and Jinx. "Welcome to the Underground Railroad, young conductors. Fine job you've done so far. Best wishes for safe travels. We'll be leaving at first light tomorrow morning, so I bid you a fond farewell."

Henry leads Thunder and Dot into the stable to rub them down. Max takes Jinx's hand, and with Petey cradled in his arm they slip in through the back servants' entrance and up to their rooms.

At his door, Max tells Jinx to wait a moment. He gathers his quilt and sheets and follows Jinx and Petey into her room.

"I don't like to be separated at night," Max tells her. "I'll sleep on the floor. Besides, I think we should try to go into the story vision together. There may be clues or important information for us. Can we try?"

After they splash water onto their faces and arms to clean up, Jinx flops into a cushioned chair, exhausted from their latest adventure. "You're right–we should try it." She reaches for Max's hand. He settles against the chair on top of his quilt.

Jinx sets up a scene as it flashes behind her closed eyes: "Here we go...close your eyes and picture a plantation with its slave quarters...try to see Alem and Anwar with the woman who is their mama. They're in the little slave cabin at the end of a hard day of picking cotton...

Both Jinx and Max feel the warm buzzing going through their clasped hands and they slip into the vision...

Vision Story Part Five: *1842 The Plantation of Willard Young, North Carolina*

Mama, what you always workin' on that old quilt for?" asks Alem. He and Anwar have come in from the fields late in the day, and now they wash up for dinner. The quilt lies across the rocker with Mama's sewing box, ready for her nightly attention.

"That's an important quilt, boys. You'll find out someday, when the time is right to learn its secret," Mama says.

Anwar towels off and hugs their mama, the woman who adopted them as her own when they were bought by Willard Young five years ago at the slave auction in Savannah, Georgia.

"Now don't be givin' Mama a hard time, or you might not get her good ham and beans for supper. And you need your supper, 'cause you got to grow big and strong to catch the eye of that cute little gal over there on Owl Hollow Plantation. Hey Mama, did you know Alem is sweet on that little gal over there? He's not payin' attention at all to Sunday prayers—he's busy makin' eyes at May Ella."

Alem grabs his brother and wrestles him to the floor, where they roll around laughing. Alem rolls on top and pins his twin to the dirt floor. "How you know I'm not payin' attention during prayers? Your eyes must be open, too."

Mama laughs and says, "You two bear cubs stop that wrestlin' before you knock the chairs over."

The boys have grown taller and have filled out with strong chest, arm, and leg muscles from hard work on the plantation. At fifteen, they are both field hands and work from sunup to sundown year round, planting, weeding, picking, and hauling cotton, wheat, and corn.

They look exactly alike, strong faces, squared-off chins, and sparkling brown eyes. Both have ears that stick out, but the other boys in the fields don't dare tease them, because they know the twins can beat them hands down in arm wrestling and racing. Side by side, Anwar is taller than his brother; other than that, no one can ever tell them apart.

Pap joins his family in the little cabin. He and Mama wanted to have other babies, but poor Mama always lost the baby before birth because of being expected to work in the fields right up to birthing time. She looks up at her adopted boys with love in her eyes, thankful the good Lord blessed her with them.

Mama dishes up the ham and beans and potatoes. The boys smell fresh biscuits in the wood stove's oven. An elderberry pie cools off in the open windowsill. Sitting at the rough table, they all join hands while Pap asks the blessing over the good food. He also thanks the Lord for a kind master and asks for help so the Boss Man in the fields will be nicer to the field hands.

Alem grumbles under his breath. Pap looks at him with firm eyes. "What was that you say, Alem?"

"Pap, I don't know why you thank the good Lord for a kind master. We shouldn't be slaves—no man should be a slave under any other man. We's people. It ain't fair. And Boss Man, he's just plain mean. Ain't no prayer ever gonna change that. I'd rather ask the Lord for him to fall off his horse."

Anwar stifles a laugh, choking over a piece of potato. Pap glares at both his boys. "We raised you boys better than that—never wish ill on no one, not even an enemy. And from what I hear about some plantations further down Deep South, we got it mighty good compared to them. Daily beatin's and whippin's, not 'nough food, barely a roof over their heads; you don't know how good you got it with our master."

Alem lowers his head. "Sorry, Pap. But none of us gots the most important thing of all—sweet freedom."

Pap nods, more gentle now. "I know, boy. Maybe someday... but I don't want to hear any more talk of runnin' from you boys. That's plain foolishness. You don't know where to go or how to git to freedom. You'll git yourselves caught and whupped within a inch of your lives." Mama listens to her men talk. She glances at her quilting project.

They finish their meal by candlelight. The boys help their mama clean up and wash the dishes in a pan of warm water. Pap goes to the little front porch to smoke his corncob pipe and talk with the other men. Mama goes over to her rocker to work on her quilt by candlelight. The big boys stretch out on Mama's clean rag rug by her feet.

Alem admires Mama's quilt work. "I was teasing you, Mama. Your quilt is beautiful. It's got a pretty pattern, all crazy like." He tilts his head and studies the quilt close up. "It reminds me of how pretty nature is...look here, Anwar. Looks like a flowin' blue stream in this patch and a big boulder scooped out on the top on the next." He pokes his brother out of his sleep.

"Hhhmmmmm? What you say?" Anwar pushes up off the rug onto his elbows. He rubs his sleepy eyes and looks closer at the quilt with his brother. "I see what you mean. This here block has four tall trees. Are these little brown dots on the ground acorns, Mama?" He feels the small knots of thread with the tip of his pointer finger.

"That's right. You can call this my Nature Quilt," says Mama.

"Look at this patch—it has a hand with stars around it. What does it mean, Mama?" says Alem.

"It means to reach for the stars, boys. If you have a dream, you follow it."

"When will it be finished, Mama?" Alem asks.

"Oh, not for a while, yet. But when it is, my Nature Quilt will have a new name, and it will be for you two boys to share. Umm humm." Mama squints her eyes in the shadowy darkness. "Now you boys better get yourselves to bed. That ol' rooster will be callin' your names before you know it." She stops to kiss her two boys on the top of their heads.

Late at night, after even Pap is asleep on their straw bed, Mama works on her quilt. She hears a scratching at the window beside her rocker. Instead of being frightened, she smiles and stands up. Mama leans her head out the window, whispers with

someone, and then goes back to her rocker, smiling. She picks up
some green scraps and some white pieces and begins a new patch.
"Yes, they'll do fine for a green meadow with a white picket fence.
Umm hummm..."

"It's Henry and Edward. Exactly like we thought," whispers Max. "I feel...I don't know...humbled to be allowed to see their lives. They've been through so much."

Jinx nods her sleepy head. "Maybe someday soon they'll allow us to call them by their true names," she says. "It's a privilege to be able to watch their story. It helps me to understand Henry so much better. He's such a brave man, Max."

Jinx crawls into her downy quilts with Petey, while Max makes a bed on the floor. They drift off to sleep, thinking of their friend, Henry, and his awesome story.

Chapter Fifteen

South Carolina–Ambush!

Thunder trots smartly down the road on the way to Charleston, South Carolina. The weather is warmer now, the farther south they travel. It is October; this trip has taken weeks, so far. The sunset will be spectacular on this warm evening, with rose and purple backlit clouds along the horizon.

Thunder looks back over his shoulder at Dot and neighs to her, *"Keeping up, old girl? It's been a loooooong daaaayyy."*

"You keep your eyes on the road, Thunder. I'm keeping up fine," she neighs back.

Petey rides up top with Henry, who has no idea the animals are talking with each other. *"Wonder what's up ahead? I have a bad feeling,"* Petey barks to both horses.

"I feel it too," Thunder says. *"Maybe you should talk to the children."*

"Thunder, help Petey keep watch up there, and trust your instincts," Dot says.

Meanwhile, Max and Jinx talk together in the carriage, trying to figure things out and put them in some kind of order.

"Max, there's so much to think about, my head is spinning. This is the biggest job we've had yet. And woven in all around everything is the vision story of the two African boys that Aunt Merry started with us back on the porch. That seems so long ago... And to think that it's Henry and Edward's story that we're following. It's like seeing a movie of their lives."

"I know, my head's spinning, too. So, we heard Edward tease Henry about May Ella. They're about fifteen years old in the vision story now, right?" says Max.

"Yes, and what's going on with the quilt? That's a new mystery. It must have to do with the pattern, because the boys started to notice each block and talk about it being a Nature Quilt. I wonder who their mama talked with when everyone else was asleep?" says Jinx.

"Probably someone giving her a secret message. I bet it has to do with the quilt, because she went right back to it and started a new block. Something about a white picket fence."

They look at each other, thinking about the safe house with the white picket fence they sent Jefferson and Janie towards. They both have an *'aha'* moment at the same time, when they figure out what Mama was doing with the quilt.

"She's stitching a safe path to freedom right into the quilt's pattern," Jinx says. "What a *great* idea. No one but the boys will know the secret."

"*Wow*, this is the ultimate road trip, isn't it? I never dreamed we'd be touring the southern states by carriage in 1851, learning so much about the Underground Railroad," says Max. "Oh yeah, I want to tell you about JoJo. He talked with me that night about seeing visions like you get, only they're about things that are *going* to happen."

"You mean he sees into the future?"

"Right," Max says. "He told me he saw his family in a little house in Canada, but he wasn't with them. He asked me if those visions always come true."

"Oh Max, what did you tell him?"

"That we will all check up on him and make sure he's safe. What could I say? I wanted to comfort him."

"And we will check on him and help if we need to. Visions of the future don't always have to come true. Sometimes you can change the course of action. All of this sure feels like a big responsibility, doesn't it?" asks Jinx.

They can hear Henry singing a pretty song. It soothes their troubled minds. Max opens the window so they can better hear him.

"That's nice, Henry. Is it another slave ballad?" asks Max.

Henry nods. "Yes, sir, Master Max. I can teach it to you. It's called 'Swing Low, Sweet Chariot.' It talks about the sweet chariot of the Lord takin' us home to heaven. But it also has code words in it–a message for us slave folks. Here goes..." Henry's deep voice begins again:

Swing low, sweet chariot,
Comin' for to carry me home,
Swing low, sweet chariot,
Comin' for to carry me home.

I looked over Jordan,
And what did I see,
Comin' for to carry me home,
A band of angels comin' after me,
Comin' for to carry me home.
If you get there before I do,
Comin' for to carry me home,
Tell all my friends I'm comin' too,
Comin' for to carry me home.

Jinx wipes a few tears from her cheeks. Max reaches across and squeezes her hand. She smiles, and says, "I bet I can figure the code out, Henry. The chariot is a wagon or boat, ready to help the runaways, right? And the Jordan River could be the closest river for them to cross over. When they get separated, they would want their family and friends to know they are on their way. So they would send a message ahead of them."

"Why, Miss Jinx, that's real close. We got so many songs like that. Besides bein' secret code songs, they comfort us in the midst of our sufferin'," says Henry.

The carriage enters a woodland area with dense foliage and underbrush. A bubbling creek flows through on its way to a larger river. The day finally darkens.

Birds go to roost, and squirrels and rabbits rustle through the underbrush to their nests. Henry stops the carriage. "Whoa there, Thunder. Good old boy—we all need a water break." He unhitches Thunder, and he and Max lead the horses over to the streambed.

Petey bounces over to Jinx. *"I feel like something big is going to happen—not good, not good,"* he says. He continues to bounce like a rubber ball until he bounces right up into Jinx's arms. She buries her nose in his neck and hugs him.

"What's wrong, Petey?"

"I think people are coming, bad people," Petey says.

Jinx feels a chill run up her backbone and neck, as if someone touched her very lightly. She looks around in the gathering gloom and listens for the night sounds. Then Jinx realizes there are no night sounds.

> *It is perfectly still. A buzz starts in her ears until she no longer sees anything but blackness. Inside a dark globe she sees two dark forms riding horses, galloping down a dark path. There is a red haze around them. Red, the danger color. They feel dangerous. Running with the horses are smaller dark shapes.*

The buzzing stops and Jinx feels Max shaking her. She looks into his blue eyes, shaking off the rest of the vision.

"Come on, Jinx, where were you? I brought Dot back to the carriage and you were swaying back and forth with your eyes closed. What did you see?" Max's eyes are wide with concern.

Jinx tells him about the dark forms rushing towards them. "We have to be really vigilant, Max. They mean us harm."

"We'll continue on our way to Charleston tonight. Hopefully we can reach town before they meet up with us. It'll be safer in town," says Max.

They talk it over with Henry, saying that Jinx has a bad feeling about danger. Henry looks at her and says, "Miss Jinx, I learned a long time ago to go with your gut feelings on matters. We'll be watchin' the whole way into town. Should get there in another hour or so, accordin' to that last sign we saw."

This time Dot is harnessed up front, with Thunder in the rear. The brave group hurries on its way. The road narrows and enters a valley between some large hills. The terrain is rocky.

Max feels like the land is closing in on them, a good place for an ambush. *I don't like this at all. I hope that I don't have to fire my gun at anyone,* he thinks.

The noise and action hit them out of nowhere. Huge, baying dogs set upon them, and two riders swoop down out of the hills like birds of prey after rabbits. Thunder and Dot whinny in fear, rearing their front legs high in the air; Petey barks his head off, and Henry gives the reins a mighty slap on Dot's sides. She takes off at an all-out gallop, pulling the carriage through the rocky road. The carriage sways back and forth like a ship at sea.

The riders shoot into the air; rifle shots crack as warnings. The riders shout for them to pull up and surrender. Dot runs all the faster. Max pulls his pistol out of his belt and takes aim out the window with both hands on the gun. He pulls the trigger, and the explosion pushes him back against the seat.

"Max, no...don't shoot anyone!" Jinx is frantic.

"Whew, that gun has a kick to it," says Max, grinning. "I'm firing into the air to scare them off. They need to know we're armed, too."

"How can you grin at a time like this?" Jinx wants to know. She peeks out of the rocking carriage in time to see one of the riders pulling closer. In his hands is a lariat circling in the air.

"He's going after Henry!" she shrieks. The lariat flies up and over Henry; the children watch as Henry is jerked from the seat and down to the ground. Their carriage is a runaway itself, hurtling down a treacherous path.

Max and Jinx focus on Dot. *"Dot, stop. Calm down, girl. Pull up and stop..."*

It takes another mile to get through to the frightened horses. Thunder pulls back with all his weight as if they are having tug of war. Finally Dot calms into a canter, then a trot, then a tired walk. She stops and hangs her head, sucking great gulps of air into her lungs. Thunder whinnies and raises his front legs.

Max and Jinx jump from the carriage and each go to a horse to pat their long noses and calm them. Jinx hugs Thunder's neck—he is sweating from the run for freedom.

"We need to go, now. They'll come get us—listen to the dogs..." Thunder says.

The dogs catch up to them, swarming around like bees, barking into the air. Petey is disgusted with the dogs. He recognizes the hound pack. *"Brute, stop your pack from yelling, right now. Enough noise,"* Petey says.

That gets the big hound's attention. *"Petey? What are you doing out here? Master sent us after your driver's scent, and we caught him, all right. Okay boys, down—hunt's over,"* says Brute. The other hounds listen to the alpha dog and stop most of the baying. They mill around, waiting for their master. The wait is not long.

Max has the pistol pointed at the rider when he gallops up to the carriage. The man dismounts and walks up to Max with his chin up and a nasty grin pasted across his face.

"Put that gun down, boy, before you git hurt," says the man. The children recognize Jackson right away, the slave hunter they have met two times before, at John and Mary's farm and later at the Matthews' farm. Their spirits drag.

"You're the one who's going to get hurt. I'm the one pointing a gun. Now where's our servant, Hiram?" Max really does not feel as brave as his words. It takes a huge effort to keep his voice from quivering.

"If you want to keep your *'servant'* alive, you'll put the gun on the ground, and step way back. And we all know Hiram ain't your servant; his name is Henry. He's a runaway slave from North Carolina, and him and his brother got themselves into a spot of trouble up there in Christiana, Pennsylvania, too. He's goin' back to his owner, and you two can go on your merry way. Be glad we don't have ya arrested fer helpin' a runaway. Now put the gun down, boy."

Max and Jinx pass each other frantic silent messages.

"Listen to the man, Max. We don't have any choice."

"But Jinx...ahhh–I'm so furious. All this way and so close to Henry's boys, and now we lose Henry?"

"We'll go on and get Henry's boys, then pick him up on the way home. And pick up our other new friends, too. Buy them all and set them free. Jefferson and Janie, so her baby can be born in freedom; help JoJo if he needs it..."

"Listen to yourself, Jinx. We are WAY in over our heads. We might have to give our mission up."

"Now you listen to yourself, Max. Since when do you give up? Did you give in to those pirates and Blackbeard last summer? I've never seen you give in to any person or circumstance."

"Okay, for Henry's safety we'll have to let him go for now, or they may shoot him. I'll put down the gun."

"Well, little boy, what's it going to be? Time's up," says Jackson.

Max puts the gun on the ground in slow motion, raises his hands and moves back away from it.

Jackson gets the gun and tucks it in his belt. "Now git them horses and the carriage turned around, and follow me. I'll show you yer 'servant.' He never shoulda run in the first place."

Jinx and Max climb up in the driver's seat. Petey jumps up in Jinx's lap. She soothes the little dog, who is trembling with anger and growling.

"Wait, boy. I think you'd better hand me that shotgun up there," says Jackson. "Put your hands back up in the air, both of you."

"You want it, you got it," says Max, furious. He circles his arm holding the gun as if he is throwing a discus and hurls it way out in the darkness. They hear it hitting rocks and give off a small explosion as it goes off. Jackson glares at him and lifts his arm as if he is going to hit Max. Petey snarls and shows his teeth.

Jackson growls back. "Watch yer dog. He bit me once, but he won't bite me agin," he warns, with a dirty fist in the air. He rears his horse and rides away.

Max says, "Hurry, Dot," and turns the carriage to follow Jackson back a mile or so to where Henry was lassoed. They fear what they will see when they get there.

When the dejected children get to the site, they see Henry tied to a tree. There is rope around his neck and wrapped around the trunk, and his hands are tied to a limb up above his head. His head hangs down and his eyes are closed. They are afraid he is dead.

Max pulls on the reins to stop Dot and the carriage, but before they are completely stopped, Jinx flies out the door and runs to Henry.

"Oh Henry, what have they done to you?" she says. She checks him over. He looks bad. His face is bleeding all over with scratches from being dragged with the rope. His nice clothes are ripped and torn, and one of his boots is missing.

"It's not as bad as it looks, Miss Jinx. I'm banged up a bit," Henry says. His one eye is swollen nearly shut.

"Git back from him, girl," yells Billy. He's holding a gun on everyone.

"He needs first aid," says Jinx. She and Max are both tired of being bullied by these two men. Jinx runs to the carriage and comes back with some soothing ointment, soft towels and bandages. Max gets her some water in a pail from the creek. She dabs Henry's wounds and cleans his face with great care, then applies some ointment and bandages. The whole time she whispers to him, barely moving her lips.

"What are you going to do with us?" says Max.

Billy and Jackson laugh. "We don't want you. You're free to go. Yer servant here is going back to his real master, poor guy. Probably get forty lashes with the whip or worse. But we want to take a look inside yer carriage, first. Might be a few things we could use—like a treasure chest full of money. Billy, go see what's in there," says Jackson.

The teens look at each other. How did these men know about their money? Now Jinx is really mad. "You stay out of our private carriage. You're plain thieves, that's what you are, and the worst kind of men who sell other men back into slavery."

"Not for you to judge, girl. Ah, I see Billy has some big fat pouches. Bet there's wads of paper money in there—ain't so, Billy?"

Billy drags the pouches over to Jackson and opens them. "Yep, Boss, you heard right. Now we not only git money for the runaway, but we git all this bonus cash, too. Look at it all..." He reaches into one pouch and grabs a fistful of bills. The men laugh and slap each other on the back.

They load their saddlebags full of every last bill and coin from the pouches. Then they rifle through the rest of Jinx and Max's possessions, freely taking anything they feel a need for: provisions, Jinx's pearls from Mrs. Matthews, mess kits. The rest they dump on the ground as they paw through it, including their clothing.

Billy cuts Henry's arms down from the tree, and the men finally leave, dragging Henry behind them. Henry gives them a sorrowful glance over his shoulder, as he starts to run and trip along behind the horse.

"Jackson Merryweather, Junior, at your service," Jackson yells back, as he tips his hat.

All the children can do is watch Henry until he is dragged out of view. They know they can't report the theft of all their money, either, because of aiding a runaway. The teens sink to the ground amidst their ruined belongings, stunned beyond words.

Chapter Sixteen

The Mysterious Couple

After repacking what is left of their belongings, the children both sit up in the driver's seat, with Jinx trying her hand at the reins. Thunder trots along at a good pace. They hope to make it into Charleston, South Carolina, before midnight.

Petey rides on Dot's back behind the carriage, trying to console her. She feels it is her fault they were captured.

"No Dot, you were magnificent. We flew through the air like an eagle. It's the carriage that held you back. Both you and Thunder are faster than those thieves' horses," says Petey.

"Thank you, Petey, but we lost Henry. That's so bad," Dot says.

Petey licks her right behind her ears and makes her shake her head and neigh in laughter.

"Stop it, Petey; that tickles."

Max and Jinx have their own serious discussion.

"Jackson Merryweather, Junior. Now we know who this guy who continues to haunt us really is–the son of a no-good woman. His mother is the lady who owns the store in Lancaster. Remember Merryweather's Dry Goods? Eliza warned us about her spying on us. She must have told her son about seeing our money and buying supplies and having Henry as our servant," says Max.

Jinx nods in agreement. "That family's bad news."

Max has another thought. "Jinx, remember in the vision story about Henry and Edward, the part about the slave auction? There were posters tacked up everywhere in town that listed a Jackson Merryweather, Senior, as being the owner of the new group of slaves for sale. And Oscar told us, rumor has it he got killed in a fight with a government ship patrolling for illegal slave runners."

Jinx shakes her head slowly. "That's sad. A whole family involved in selling enslaved people and things like stealing and kidnapping. And we're victims of their hatefulness. I don't want to be a victim. They can't stop us. But what's the plan now, Max? We have no money left to buy Henry's boys back, or even buy Henry's freedom. We can't exactly wire home for money; can't rob a bank. I feel sick in the stomach. We can't give up, no matter what happens." She looks at Max for the answer.

Max scowls while he thinks. He feels so battered by the recent attack that he momentarily feels like giving up. Then he lifts his shoulders and takes a big breath of cleansing air.

"You're right. No way do we give up. We're not going to be victims. We *will* make this all work. I think we should get a room in Charleston tonight, maybe stay for two nights, to relax and plan. Lucky for us, those thugs didn't check our pockets. I have some money left. Not much, but enough to last for a couple of days. Do you have any money?"

"Yeah, same as you; some money was hidden in my pockets and under the cushions in the carriage. Good thing they didn't tear apart the carriage in their searching."

Max's eyes shift sideways and he grins about something. A plan flits into his mind.

"And what's with you grinning all the time, especially when serious stuff happens. Are you losing your mind, Max? Like when you shot off your first round with that awful gun. You grinned like a crazy loon... Oh no, tell me you really did not have a gun course at the academy, and that was the first time you ever shot a gun."

"I did so have a gun safety course. First time I ever shot off an antique pistol, though. But William Parker and Henry did take me out back of the barn to teach me how to fire a shotgun." Max grins again. "Now, I have a surprise for you about getting more money."

Jinx doesn't know whether to continue yelling at Max about the danger of guns or prod him to explain about the money.

"Ooooo, Maxwell M. Myers–you are so infuriating. So, what do you mean about getting more money?"

Max takes the reins back from Jinx. "You go relax, we'll be fine. After we rest up a couple of days, I say we go on to get the twins and then start home, gathering our new friends along the way."

"Okay, I'll play your waiting game." She leans back in the seat and gives a heavy sigh. "I need something good to happen, really soon. I feel like we both have a black cloud following us around." She closes her eyes.

The trees soon thin out, and they enter the outskirts of Charleston. The night is mild, and now they smell the faint scent of the ocean mixed with the perfume of blossoms. Palm trees, along with other broadleaf trees, line the streets. Spanish moss is draped over many trees, dangling low to the ground like spidery webs. The buildings are a mix of colonial wooden houses and tall Victorian brick buildings. Many of the buildings have balconies with pretty wrought-iron fencing. Large doors and windows are open to the mild night air on the second-story balconies, but most houses are dark. It is past midnight.

They find an inn on the main street and pull up to the front hitching posts. The hitching posts are iron, in the shape of horses' heads. A large brick building with tall white columns and a front veranda stands before them. A gilded sign hangs from one post saying "The Charleston Inn." Whicker chairs with cushions line the porch. Jinx dismounts and sinks right down into one.

"Ahhhh, I could fall asleep right here," she sighs.

"This looks like a really nice inn," Max says. "I don't think they want transients sleeping on their front porch. Would look bad to all the rich plantation owners who come here to stay," he teases.

"Are you calling me a tramp?" Jinx isn't too tired to rise to the bait.

Max laughs and turns to read an engraved sign on the elaborately carved double doors. He reads it aloud: "Welcome to Charleston Inn. After midnight, please ring the bell. The innkeeper will attend to your needs."

Max pulls on the doorbell chain. They hear a bell ringing inside, but nothing happens. Max pulls again...nothing. This time he pulls three times in a row. *Brrrring, brrriinnnng, brriinng...*

"Hold your horses, hold your horses. Isn't anybody patient anymore? Where's that lazy, good-fer-nothin' servant boy? Prob'ly fell asleep." An elderly man wearing a rumpled shirt and baggy pants opens the door and squints at the two children through bifocals. "Now what can I do for you? You're certainly too young to be out and about this late at night."

"Please sir, we need two rooms for a couple of nights," says Max. "We...we had a bit of trouble with highway robbers on the road earlier. They stole our servant to sell as a runaway slave and took most of our money, but I can pay you up front." Max pulls a few bills out of his pocket.

"All right, come along. I'll send for the groom. The servant boy can show you to your rooms. Your dog should stay in the stable with the horses. No animals allowed in the inn." He grumbles to himself as he turns to lead the way. "All this trouble so late at night; I'm too old for this job." He closes and locks the front doors, not noticing Petey scampering over to hide behind a plush chair.

The bell rings again, causing the elderly man to stop and turn, looking over his bifocals for his servant boy. He sighs and shuffles back over to open the doors again.

Two people stand before him. One appears to be a thin white man dressed in an immaculate black suit, with a vest and top hat. He has bandages on his hands and a swath of bandage on his face, making it difficult to see his features. He carries a white cane and wears glasses with a green tint. The other man is a bit taller and well dressed as a servant. His skin is very dark, and his broad face smiles at the innkeeper.

"Excuse me, sir. My master here, he needs a room for the night. We're headin' out on a big trip in the mornin'. You can see he's a invalid somewhat and has trouble speakin' and walkin'. Do you have room for him, please?"

Now the innkeeper really grumbles. "Why can't all you folks come sign in early evening like most people do? I gave the last two rooms to these children. I'm afraid there is no room in the inn."

The invalid turns towards Max, who slowly nods his head. The strange young man smiles at Max.

"You can share my room," says Max. He knows this is the way travelers of the era often do it, sharing a room with other travelers. Max is so tired he thinks he can fall asleep on the floor with an extra blanket and pillow, so the poor guy can relax in the bed alone.

"Oh thank you, son, thank you. My master's mighty tired tonight. We sure do 'preciate it. Mr. Innkeeper, sir, it's too painful for my master to sign in–his hands were burned in a fire. Can I scratch a mark for us?"

The innkeeper throws his hands in the air. "Forget signing in, all of you," he grumbles, turning his back and motioning for the white people to follow him. "I'll have you register in the morning. The kitchen's closed for the night, but I might be able to have the cook fix cold plates of food."

The servant takes the master's arm and gives him a gentle pat. "I'll help you to the room, Master," he says. Then he turns to the innkeeper. "Then I'll take care of the horses and carriage, sir. Y'all git your rest and don't worry."

Max, Jinx and the strange couple follow the grouchy innkeeper in through the lobby. He awakens a young black boy who sits slumped on a stool behind the front desk, half asleep.

"Sonny, wake up..." He smacks him over the head. "Show these people to their rooms on the second floor. Then go wake up Cook and have her fix some food for the guests. Get their bags, now." He hands them keys. "Good *night*," he says, as he turns to hobble back to his room behind the desk. He totally misses Petey again, sneaking out from behind the chair and running after Jinx and Max.

Sonny jumps up, holding one hand over his ear. He's trying hard not to cry with pain. Sonny gathers up their bags and almost runs to the stairway before he gets another hit. When they arrive at the first room, Max gives Jinx a big hug. He turns the key in the lock to open his door.

"See you in the morning, Jinx," he says, as the young man and his servant follow him into the room. "Will you feel safe enough with Petey tonight?"

"I'm so tired a hundred thieves could break in, and I'd never know it," she says. Jinx watches them go into their room. She especially watches the stranger, who hesitates and turns to look at Jinx. When the stranger sees Jinx watching him, he nods his head before he disappears into Max's room. Jinx hears the lock turn.

Jinx and Petey go down the hall to their doorway and slip quietly into the room. The room is pleasant, with a brass bed and quilt. Jinx thinks about the other quilt in the vision dream. Quilts seem to play a big role in this adventure. Another cushioned chair sits beside the bed, and Jinx sinks into it, tired to the bone and thankful to sit. After a short rest, she pulls off her boots and slips out of her dress. She washes up in the water from a pitcher. Pulling on her nightshirt, she muses out loud to Petey.

"You know, Petey, there is something very mysterious about that man in Max's room. He didn't even say one word."

"*She's very nice, and tired. They have a long way to go to Canada. Is Canada cold all year long?*" Petey says.

"No, Canada has some nice warm days in summertime. You meant to say *he's* very nice, not she, right?"

"*Does Canada have dogs? I think she should have a dog like me when she gets to Canada.*"

"Yes, Canada has dogs." Jinx slips under the quilt and pats the covers for Petey to jump up. He pops up in one leap, like a jack-in-the-box finally being freed. Jinx plays wrestle mania with Petey, one of their favorite games. They roll around under the quilt, Jinx laughing and trying to get Petey's paws, Petey yipping and trying to gum her wrists in his gentle jaws.

"You keep saying *she*. The stranger's dressed like a man, and his servant called him master. Why do you think he's a she?"

"*Because, I know.*" Petey rolls on his back to get a belly rub and kicks his legs.

"You're being silly. If he's a she, what is she doing in Max's room?" Jinx rubs Petey's furry belly.

About that time Jinx hears a gentle tapping at her door. She slips out of bed, grabs her shawl around her shoulders and goes to the door. "Max? Is it you?"

"Yes, Jinx, may we come in?"

Jinx unlocks the door, and Max and the stranger enter. "Better lock up again," Max says. "I'd like to introduce you to Ellen Craft."

Jinx watches in amazement as the young man removes his hat and his facial bandages. She sees a pretty female emerge, with short, curly black hair framing her oval face. Ellen Craft smiles at Jinx. "I thought I'd best stay with you tonight, if I may," she says.

Petey bounces in delight, saying, "*Told ya, told ya so...yip yip.*"

"Shhh, Petey. You'll wake the guests." Jinx hops back on her high bed. "Please, Ellen, sit down. I bet you have an exciting story to tell us, right?" When Ellen still seems a bit hesitant, Jinx grabs her tablet and pencil and makes a drawing of the hand with the stars surrounding it. She shows it to Ellen.

Ellen laughs in delight. She looks relieved. "Follow the stars. I see I can trust you both. Max told me some of your story. I want to thank you for going with Henry on the Underground Railroad, to get his little boys back safe in his arms.

"Me and my husband, William, is slaves from Macon, Georgia. We'd like to have our own children, start a family, but never in slavery." She shakes her head firmly. "So, we decided to run away to the North, to freedom."

Jinx can't help but look at Ellen's white face and hands. "But your skin is so light...excuse me, I shouldn't have said that. Please forgive me," says Jinx, blushing.

"Miss Jinx, don't be sorry. Don't you see; that's what makes our plan so perfect. My mama is a slave, too, but my daddy is the white master of the plantation.

"Them plantation masters, they often use a slave girl to father more slave children, to sell or work for 'em. Some of them children, they's white as their daddy, but with black blood in 'em, they still has to be slaves.

"So I can pass as a white woman. Only a white lady wouldn't be allowed to travel alone with a slave man, so I'm pretendin' to be a white, invalid gentleman travelin' with his servant. And since I don't know how to read and write to sign in at the register, we pretend I have burns and an illness. Did I fool you?"

"Sure fooled me," says Max. "I about fell off the chair when Ellen took off the bandages and showed me she's a woman."

"I thought I'd better tell you quick, Master Max, before you went to put on your nightshirt and got all embarrassed." Ellen laughs softly.

"You fooled us all, except for our dog friend, Petey," Jinx says.

Ellen smiles at Petey, who jumps into her lap. She pets him and scratches his ears. Petey looks at her with adoring eyes. "I'd love to have a little dog like Petey when we get to Canada. I think y'all must be pretty special. I can feel these things, you know? I can tell what people is like just by lookin' at them. They have a glow about 'em—different colors. You and Master Max, y'all have a golden glow. That's the best kinda glow, kind and gentle, helpful like. Some people has a darker glow, and the darker their glow, the darker their soul." She looks off, as if she is remembering a disturbing incident in her past.

"I've met so many brave, wonderful people on this trip, so many of you in slavery who are striving for freedom. Slavery is so wrong–it won't continue," says Jinx. She stops herself abruptly. She wants to tell Ellen about Abraham Lincoln and the Civil War between the North and the South, and how there will be freedom for all of the African Americans. *But who knows what kind of wrinkles I'd stir up in the Time Tunnel if I foretell the future,* she worries.

Ellen gives Jinx an odd look, and then she nods. "Word travels from plantation to plantation. We all try to learn as much as we can 'bout what's goin' on. I heard rumblin's of the South wantin' to pull out of the Union. Oh my, I see nothin' but troubles ahead."

Max catches Jinx's eyes and nods his approval. They had both decided they shouldn't be fortune-tellers to the people back in time. He yawns and stretches.

"Please excuse me, ladies, but we all should get some rest. I'll leave you to talk together. Miss Ellen, I am so glad to make your acquaintance. I'm privileged to know a young lady as brave and daring as you, along with your husband." He bows and leaves.

Ellen sits in amazement, with both hands covering her mouth. "To think of a white gentleman bowing to me–why I'm so honored..."

"You are the one who needs to be honored, Ellen. And I believe one day you and William will be remembered in history for your bravery and intelligence. Let's get comfortable. Would you mind sharing the bed with me?" says Jinx.

"I'd be honored, Miss Jinx."

"No, I'm honored, Miss Ellen."

"Then we'll both be honored," laughs Ellen.

Both young women laugh and whisper until sleep overtakes them.

Chapter Seventeen

Daring Escape

In the morning, Jinx can hardly contain herself until Ellen wakes. Jinx has washed up and is getting dressed when Ellen finally rolls over and stretches.

"Miss Jinx, that's the best night's sleep I've had since me and William took off on our journey. I thank you and Master Max for helpin' us last night."

"I'm so glad we met. Now it's time for you to be Master Craft, again, instead of Ellen Craft. Let me help you get your disguise on. I love secrets," says Jinx. "I rang the servant's bell to arrange for some fresh water to be sent to the room. The water closet for ladies is a few doors down the hall. The fresh water pitcher should be here when you return." Jinx has to smile to herself at the odd Victorian name for the bathroom.

Ellen's face clouds over. "I got to be so careful, Miss Jinx. I shouldn't be seen in the hallway by anyone. It could give away my secret."

"Let me peek out in the hallway. I'll give you an all's-clear signal when it's safe," says Jinx. She eases the door open and peers up and down the hallway. Finally she motions for Ellen to head out the door and watches her scurry down to the water closet.

Neither of the young ladies notices the Negro servant who steps out of a room a few doors behind them. She squints her eyes and quickly steps back into the room, where she watches in interest; only half of her face protrudes into the hallway. She smiles to herself, thinking about a few extra coins that might come her way if she talks to the right person.

When they join Max in the dining room, Ellen once more looks like a young gentleman of fine quality, who has had many medical problems. The dining room is elegant with deep red curtains at the windows and thick carpets from India under the tables.

The servant girl nods her head at them as she brings coffee, tea, toast, and jam. Next comes fried ham and eggs with fried yams. Breakfast ends with a tray full of cakes and pastries.

Their secret friend plays the invalid as best she can, pretending to have a difficult time cutting and eating her food. Jinx assists her throughout the meal.

They notice the innkeeper watches them through the dining room doors from the front room, behind his desk. He doesn't appear to be any happier in the daylight than he was last night. He walks over to their table, a stooped-over little man with white hair and gray whiskers.

"Everything satisfactory?" he asks.

"Yes, sir," says Max. "Nice soft beds—we all had a great night's sleep."

"Wish I could say the same," grumbles the old man. He looks at the invalid and asks, "Feeling any better? What did you say your name is?"

Ellen whispers in Jinx's ear. Jinx says, "He says he is somewhat better, but his throat is too sore to speak. Oh, Max, what time is it? We must get our new friends to the train station."

Max pushes his chair back. "Yes, our bags have been brought down by your servant, sir," he says to Ellen. "I believe I have cleared up our debt. So we must rush off. Fine breakfast," Max says to the innkeeper.

The three friends head to the front door; Ellen pretends to limp in pain, using her cane. William Craft is waiting with the carriage and horses. The innkeeper follows them out, scowling all the way. He watches Max help the invalid man and Jinx into the carriage, speak to William, the servant, and jump up into the carriage himself. Max slams the door, and William gives a gentle slap of the reins to Dot. Off they go on a short trip to the train station.

"Whew," says Max, wiping his brow. "Did you see the old man staring at us? I think we need to get you and William on that train heading North, before the innkeeper does too much thinking."

Before anyone can comment, Ellen's husband taps at the window behind Max. "I sees a horseman ridin' hard behind us, wavin' an arm. Should we pull up?" he asks.

Max sighs. Another problem, another decision to make. Jinx and Ellen nod yes, so Max tells William to pull over.

A young groom from the inn's stable gallops up and pulls on the reins of his golden horse. He rides bareback. They can see he is only a boy, his brown face shining with sweat in the warm morning sun. The day promises to be a hot one.

"Head groom from the stable sends a important message, Master," he says to Max.

"What is it?" says Max. It must be very important to have a young boy chase them down. The air turns tense as everyone strains to listen to the boy.

"Yes, sir...well, his sister works in the kitchen. She heard the upstairs maid talkin' to the innkeeper right after y'all left. The upstairs maid, she said early this mornin' she saw a tall woman scurryin' down the hall to the bathroom. Said she was in a nightgown and came outta the young miss's room, only she weren't the young miss.

"So the maid hid and watched; then she saw the young miss and the tall stranger come outta the room and go down to breakfast. Only now the tall stranger was dressed like a man.

"The innkeeper thinks somethin' big is up, and he called the sheriff. They's goin' to the train station. Innkeeper thinks y'all is cheatin' and tryin' to pass the tall stranger off for a white person. He's right angry at y'all..." says the young boy. He looks frightened for them, checking back over his shoulder to make sure he wasn't followed.

"All right, change of plans. Everyone stay calm," Max says. "You did a good thing, friend," he says to the young boy. He hands him a fistful of coins from his pocket. "Please share these among yourself, the groom and his sister. And tell them we send a thousand thanks."

"Thank you, sir," says the boy. He smiles from ear to ear at the treasure Max hands him. "I sure will share; I will, sir." He stuffs the coins in his pocket and turns the horse to head back to the stable.

William takes charge. "We'd best be goin' our separate way, Master Max," he says. "We'll slip into the woods and lose ourselves amongst the trees as best we can. We'll try to find a place to lay low 'til dark, then start off North."

Max has been deep in thought. "Ellen and William, maybe you should take Thunder to head off in the woods. Try to find a path heading North. When you get to another town you can hop the train. There isn't any way they'll know where you went. We'll take Dot and the carriage and head on down to Georgia, sticking to the back roads. What do you think?"

"You sure you wants to give up your horse, Master Max?" William asks. "We done all right on our own. We're pretty good at hidin'."

"We're able to help, please, William. It'll be safer, I think," Max says. He knows William is strong and proud.

"Then we thanks you, Master Max. We can leave Thunder at a safe place for y'all to pick up later," William says.

Thunder is proud to help the Crafts escape. He prances so much that Jinx has to settle him so he can be saddled. *I'll get them so far away the sheriff will never find them,* he brags. Then he realizes he is parting company with his friends. *But, will I see Dot and you all again?* he asks. He lowers his nose to nuzzle Petey, who has come to comfort him.

I'll miss you, Thunder, I'll miss you. But you have important work to do. I know we'll find you again... Petey says. He runs in circles around Thunder.

Jinx has an idea. Pulling the rest of the paper money out of her pocket, she hands it to William, along with her compass. "Please, can you have Thunder sent down to Savannah, Georgia, when you get to the next train depot, before you get on the train? That way he'll probably beat us there. The leftover money can help you on your way to the North," she says.

William helps Ellen to mount Thunder, then turns to smile at Jinx and shake Max's hand. "You bet, little miss," he promises. "No words can thank y'all enough for your help. God bless you both." Ellen waves and blows a kiss. William mounts and both lean low as Thunder takes off in a gallop.

"Goodbye, Thunder, goodbye...fly like the wind," Dot whinnies after him.

Dot is anxious to do her part in this latest adventure. *"Come, children; hurry. We must get out of sight on a back road. I know where to go. The horses in the stable last night were talking about all of the trails along the river—very beautiful and less traveled."*

They all hop up to the driver's seat. Max gives Jinx a smile and says, "I think you should ride in the carriage. There's an important surprise for you in there."

Jinx gives him a withering look. "I don't want to be alone."

"Don't worry, you won't be for long. Don't argue...git along, little doggie."

She hops back down and gets into the carriage, lifting her skirts to climb the steps. Jinx slams the door as hard as she possibly can. Dot takes off; she races the carriage off the main road, back along a river trail that heads South.

Jinx steams alone in the carriage, in a foul mood. *I'm sick and tired of wearing skirts that get in the way. I'm sick and tired of camping. I'm so scared of sneaking and hiding and waiting to get arrested. And we don't seem to be any closer to rescuing Henry's twins.*

"Oh, but my dear Jinx, you are so brave, and you have done so much already to help some enslaved people to freedom," a velvety voice purrs.

Jinx snaps upright, like her backbone has suddenly become an iron rod. She looks up. She looks all around and under the seat in front of her. Then she bends low to look under her seat. There lies her big orange-and-white cat friend, Poppy. She licks Jinx's nose with her scratchy tongue.

Jinx bites her lower lip and smiles through tears of relief at seeing her beloved friend. The furries are together again. She scoops Poppy up and hugs her, noticing Poppy wears small saddlebags over her back. The pouches are puffed out, full of something.

"Oh Poppy, you don't know how glad I am to see you. You wouldn't believe how much trouble we've had so far."

"I've been watching over you all. The path to reaching a significant goal is often filled with trouble and despair; staying the course is what builds character and makes reaching the goal so much more worthy," Poppy purrs.

Poppy closes her eyes as Jinx rubs the soft fur under her chin and around her neck. "Poppy, you truly are our little angel full of wisdom. Now let me help remove this heavy backpack you brought with you through the Time Tunnel. I'm curious—what's in it?"

Jinx opens the flaps, and bundles of 1800s money fall out–more than enough to pay for the freedom of the two little boys. Her mouth falls open. "But...where did you get this, Poppy?"

"Max only packed half of what was in the original treasure chest. You see, he did wire home for more money, so to say. That boy's mental telepathy is almost perfect. Or should we say purr-fect?" Poppy purrs happily at her joke.

"Well, now I know what he meant when he said not to worry about losing all of our money. The *JMP History Mystery Detective Agency* is back in business." She taps at the window, giving Max a big grin.

The black cloud that has been hovering over Jinx's head bursts into pieces and floats away. Her confidence returns full force; she is ready to deal with the rest of this remarkable journey, as long as her remarkable friends remain by her side.

PART THREE

Sweet Freedom

Chapter Eighteen

Georgia, At Last

Jinx tosses and turns in her sleep, kicking the light covers off of her body. She had been sleeping so well in the soft bed at the Savannah Inn, but now she is sweating and feels sick in her stomach. It's coming...the ending of the vision story about Henry and Edward. She feels it in her dreams. This one will be a bad one, the worst part of the story and a final piece of the puzzle in the lives of Henry and Edward.

Max? Where's Max? She reaches out her hands, but the room is empty and dim, and she feels so alone. Jinx moans in her sleep.

Max, the vision story...help me through it... Jinx sends her best friend a telepathic message, through her dreams. *Please Max, see it with me...*

Vision Story Part Six:
1843 River Bend Plantation of Willard Young, North Carolina

The field hands are in a constant state of turmoil today. They whisper in worried tones when Boss Man's back is turned. Their master hovers near death up in the big house, but no other news has come down to them in the fields yet.

Boss Man is extra harsh today, cracking his whip and beating anyone for talking. It is way past noon in the sweltering cotton fields, and Boss Man hasn't even given one break for food or water.

Master's family has been staying at the big house this past week–his mother and father, two younger sisters and one older brother. None of Master's siblings are married. Gossip from the house slaves has it that Master Willard Young's older brother, Arthur, has been taking control of the plantation, and he is holding Missus Young's hand and hugging her way too much, already. He is known to be stern with the house slaves even though it is not really his business.

Missus is so sad that she lets him take charge of all the business of running the plantation. She seems to sit in a daze by her husband's bed all day long. Her two young children are kept tucked away in the nursery with their nanny. She worries about what to do if her beloved husband dies. How will she manage?

She knows nothing about running a huge plantation, other than running her small household.

Finally the big bell up at the main house interrupts the quiet working day in the fields. Bong...bong...bong...it does not stop. Boss Man yells at them to stop working and take their lunch break.

"Go to your cabins until further notice. Anyone caught out and about will be shot—no questions asked," says Boss Man. He rides off towards the big house.

The field workers stand quietly, watching. Bong...bong...bong...the bell can mean only one thing. It is tolling the death of the master. They know their lives will change under the control of a new master, probably for the worse. All the field hands walk to their cabins, bowing their heads in honor of their kind master who has passed away.

Alem and Anwar walk to their small hut with Mama and Pap to await news.

"Do you think May Ella will be able to sneak down here from the big house, to tell us what happened?" Anwar asks his brother. Anwar thinks his brother is the luckiest man around to have found such a wonderful woman.

"I hope so. But she's Missus Young's personal hand servant. She may be needed every minute right now. May Ella likes the missus—says she's kind and fair to the house servants. Then when Master Arthur come things changed. He does lots of yellin' and throwin' things at the servants over triflin' matters," says Alem.

Their master has purchased Alem's sweetheart from the neighbor's plantation to replace another house servant who had run off. When she was recaptured, she was given her thirty whip-lashes and sent to the fields for hard labor.

A quick rapping at the door brings young May Ella into their home. Alem moves off the chair and embraces his sweetheart. She is a pretty girl, wearing a simple blue frock that almost reaches her shiny shoes. Her soft black hair frames a round face with a cute nose and a pert chin. May Ella's eyes shine for Alem. Then she turns serious.

"Poor Master took his last breath with Missus holdin' his hand. It's like he slipped away to Heaven in peace. No more rackin' coughs and fever. It's so sad. Missus wants to sleep in her own room for a while, before she talks with the undertaker and the minister," May Ella tells them.

"What about Master Arthur?" Pap wants to know.

At the mention of his name May Ella shivers. "I heard him talkin' to the Boss Man. He says he wants to address all the field hands after supper, before dark. I don't think the news will be good. Master was hard, but his brother is just plain cruel. He's been real nasty to the house servants. We're afraid of him; he's everywhere at once. You turn around and there he is, a-watchin' you with them evil eyes."

"I hope when things settle down our weddin' plans can go on," says Alem.

May Ella nods. "Nothin' will keep us apart, Alem. It will be fine. Right, Mama?"

Mama smiles and nods her head. "All in good time, May Ella, all in good time."

Anwar frowns and paces around the room. He does not like to be a prisoner in his own house. "Boss Man says stay home or get shot. What kind of life are we gonna have ahead of us? Ever since Master's been sick, things have gotten worse. Master kept Boss Man in line, made sure he wasn't too harsh with us field hands. Now we'll have another bad man in charge, like mean ol' Boss Man."

May Ella hugs Alem and gives Anwar a quick peck on the cheek. "I must get back. Mistress needs me to be with her, especially now. I love you all." She slips out and scurries back up the hill to the big house.

Soon after she leaves, a messenger runs door to door shouting, "Big meetin' by the red barn when you all hear the bell tonight. Master Arthur says spread the news to your neighbors. All field hands is to come out to the red barn." On he runs with the important message.

Right before dark the big bell rings again to gather the field hands for a meeting. A couple hundred men, women and children report to the big barn, murmuring and whispering, wondering what will happen to their plantation now that Master has died.

Arthur Young and his overseer, Foreman Alfred Dunn, ride their huge stallions from the livery stable to the front of the quiet crowd. Arthur looks splendid, dressed in his very best riding clothes and boots. He sits astride a pure white horse so he is way up above, looking down his nose at his slaves. Arthur resembles his brother with his light brown hair and sideburns and green eyes, but his good looks are spoiled by the sneer on his face.

He stares at the crowd in silence, riding back and forth in front of them, rearing his stallion and snapping his riding crop, until most of the enslaved workers look downward not daring to make eye contact, and the murmuring stops.

"*Much better*," *he roars.* "*I am your new master. I now own the plantation. I own you. You work for me now. Let there be no misunderstanding about who is in charge. I expect you to work two times harder than you did for my brother, God rest his soul. He wasn't cut out to rule over slaves. He was too soft on you and didn't let Boss Man do his job. If you continue to be lazy like before, you will be beaten within an inch of your lives.*"

Now Master Arthur rides up and down in front of the silent slaves again, looking them over. He stops before Alem and Anwar, amused. "*You two look exactly alike, are you brothers?*"

Alem and Anwar answer, "*Yes, sir.*"

Arthur slaps them with his riding crop. "*You say 'yes, Master.' Say it again.*"

Both young men gulp as welts appear on their faces. "*Yes, Master,*" *they say.*

"*Are you twins?*"

"*Yes, Master.*"

"*What are your names?*"

Each answers.

"*Alem, Master.*"

"*Anwar, Master.*"

Master Arthur is mighty displeased. "*What kind of names are those? African? You live in America. You will not be called by those names or use them on my plantation. What are your American names?*"

Alem makes the big mistake of looking up into the master's eyes. "*But Old Master, he let it slide. He didn't even know we still used our names: Alem and Anwar.*"

Arthur grabs Boss Man's bullwhip, cracks the whip around Alem's legs, and pulls him smack down on the dusty ground. The other slaves murmur in distress and edge back from this angry man. Anwar falls to his knees to help his brother.

"Well, I'm the New Master. Don't ever talk back to me. If you have no American names, tonight they will be given to you both. You will be Henry," he says to Alem. "And you will be Edward," he names Anwar. "Now, repeat your names."

Anwar answers first, "Edward, Master."

Alem is angrier than he has ever been in his lifetime. He blots out the distressed look of Anwar and his parents. The rest of the crowd is blotted from his view. He sees only a red rage and this hateful man's green eyes.

"My name is Alem, Master," he says firmly.

Arthur's whip flails again. "Say it. Say Henry!" he yells.

"My name is Alem..." The beating stings like nettles.

This time Arthur beats him over and over. "Your name is HENRY," he roars.

Alem tries to cover his head. The beating continues until he feels himself blacking out. His face is bleeding and his back is torn open.

Moments later, when he comes to, he is barely able to see the master sitting way up there on his horse out of his swollen eyes.

"Your name is Henry—say it."

Alem coughs blood out of his mouth and whispers, "Henry, Master."

"You finally got it right. Is there anyone who has a question?" Arthur asks the stunned crowd. They couldn't believe how savage the attack was on the two young men. "Then, back to your cabins.

Report to the fields before sunup. You can see well enough in the predawn to get an earlier start." He and Boss Man ride away, towards the big house.

Pap scoops his sixteen-year-old son into his arms as if he is a baby and carries him back home. "Don't you worry none, son. You two will always be Alem, my world, and Anwar, my brightest star. No one can take your names from you."

Mama weeps for her brave boys. It is time to teach them about the quilt. Now she knows her boys will not stay on the plantation forever. Soon they will reach for the stars.

"Ahhhhhh..." The lingering sight of Alem's beating is so awful and powerful that Jinx moans aloud, waking herself from the nightmare vision story. Her own ribs and back feel bruised. She leaps out of her brass bed in the Savannah Inn, grabs her shawl and stumbles into the hallway to pound on Max's door. Petey follows her into the room when Max answers the door.

"Max, did you see it? Did you share the vision story?" Tears roll down her face like a miniature rain shower.

Max nods, with tears glistening in his blue eyes. "I received your telepathic message. I saw everything. I can't believe the horrors they had to experience."

Jinx curls up in the chair beside Max's oak bed, with Petey in her lap. Poppy leaps down from the bed and rubs against Max's bare feet, purring. Max sinks back down on his bed.

"The beatings they received...stripping them of their very names; it is shameful and merciless," says Max.

The teens are silent, each reviewing in their mind the whole story that started when they sat on the porch swing with Aunt Merry. To read about these serious events in their history books is unsettling enough. But to take part in it and learn to know these people from the past as friends puts a heartbreaking, highly emotional spin on it. They each ferociously want to protect all of their new friends.

After a bit Max pours each of them a glass of water from the small pottery pitcher on his oak side table. Jinx gulps hers down. She is more determined than ever to find Henry's twins. She gives a large sigh and straightens her shoulders.

The morning sun lightens the sky in the east. "So, we're finally here in Savannah. I'm starving, believe it or not, after what we've witnessed. Let's meet in the dining hall in half an hour for breakfast. We can talk over our next plans. We've so much to accomplish..." says Jinx. She moves towards the doorway, noticing the bruised feeling passing away.

"Good plan. Let's try not to work ourselves into frenzy. We'll continue to take one step at a time. First step is to let the furries outside, right, Petey? I'll take care of that and see you soon."

"Open the window for me, please. I'm in a hurry," Poppy says. Max chuckles and pulls the tall window open. Poppy leaps out onto the roof, over to a big tree branch, and disappears below.

The teens laugh. "Petey, out the window for you, too?" Max teases.

Petey heads for the door and sits at attention, eyes big as saucers. He glances back over his shoulder at Max, half believing him.

Breakfast is eggs, potatoes, and ham scrambled together, with hot biscuits and molasses on the side. Max asks for black coffee, while Jinx drinks a frothy glass of milk that comes right from the cows at a nearby plantation. Petey and Poppy chow down in the kitchen.

The two friends eat in silence, both thinking about their incredible job ahead. A Negro servant comes to the table with a letter on a tray. He bows before Max. "Master Maxwell Myers?" he asks. Max looks at Jinx; both have a bad feeling.

"Yes, I'm Max Myers. What do you have for me?"

"A letter arrived for you this mornin', sir. Also, there is a message from the stable. Your horse has been delivered and is awaitin' you." Thunder is back, at least that is good news. Max takes the letter from the tray, and the servant takes his leave.

"Wait, don't open it. I know it's more bad news," Jinx says.

"Don't be silly; we've got to read it." Max breaks the seal and slides the letter out. He scans the contents, frowning and shaking his head. "You're right—more bad news." He hands it over to Jinx.

She reads it softly aloud.

My Dear Master Max and Miss Jinx,

I must tell you some bad news in hopes of attaining your help on your trip back North. I know you remember the family whom you helped escape from slavery at the River Bend Plantation in North Carolina: Harry, Ruthie, Sammy and JoJo. They have reached the safety of Canada with me, except for their older son, JoJo. The last night, when we were finally at the Saint Lawrence River border crossing, kidnappers snatched him before his horse crossed over. When they burst out from hiding behind a grove of trees, JoJo's horse reared in fright and threw him to the ground. The rest of the horses and riders swam across the river to the Canadian side in safety.

I had to physically hold his papa back from diving into the frigid water. He wanted to swim back for his son. But the kidnappers were armed and dangerous, so I convinced him to stay with me on the Canadian side. I promised him that I would contact you to rescue JoJo. If you are unable to return JoJo to them, then I will make other plans to rescue him on a return trip South. Remember, always "Follow the Stars."

Your humble friend,
Doc Alex Ross

The teens sit in silence, hands in their laps, eyes locked on each other. Max's mouth shows the smallest hint of a smile. "Well then, we'd best start a list of people to pick up along the way North. This could be very tricky," he says.

Jinx nods, her eyebrows stretched high. She leans her hand on her chin and taps a finger on her cheek, thinking. "Our number-one thing to do is rescue Henry's twins, now that we've finally reached Georgia. Next, we rescue Henry; we'll check his home plantation in North Carolina. If he's not there, I don't know what we'll do or how we'll find him. And I hope JoJo is back at the plantation in North Carolina where we first found his family. Oh, Max, what if they were sold to someone else? At least we know Jefferson and Janie are back at their Virginia plantation, because we saw them beaten there. And Edward is in Pennsylvania, waiting for the Christiana Resistance trial."

"Picking up Edward could be tricky; he's in jail," Max adds, massaging the beginnings of another headache on his forehead. "Other than that minor detail, I think your plan is right. We'll deal with any problems as they come up. If we worry too much ahead of time, we'll be bogged down in so much muddy thought that we'll never get anywhere. Take one step at a time; keep the faith. We have to believe that things will work out for the best."

"Oh my..." purrs Poppy. She has slipped in from the kitchen and winds her way around the ankles of both children. *"You two have managed to break your all-time record for piling up problems to solve,"* says their fluffy cat, who likes to tell it like it really is. *"But having faith is the way to move forward; you're correct about that. That is how those enslaved are able to seek freedom."*

Petey pushes his way out from underneath the long tablecloth that covers their breakfast table.

"Any leftovers? No? Then let's go, let's go, lots to do," Petey says. *"Thunder says he's ready for action. He says Ellen and William Craft made it to the next train depot, heading North. They send their love."* Petey crawls across the floor on his stomach, back legs stretched out, looking over his shoulder, and grinning a big doggy grin. Then he scampers for the door.

Petey makes them laugh; this breaks the tension they feel. Max heaves a sigh of relief. "Well, at least that's one less thing to worry about. I'm glad Ellen and William made it to the train." He pushes his chair back, places his napkin on the table and stands.

"I'll ask the desk clerk and the head groom in the stable for directions to the Smythe Plantation. Henry said he heard the men mention that plantation on the day his twins were stolen. The plantation can't be too far from Savannah. I'm sure everyone knows all the rich, important plantation owners around here. Ready, detective friends?" Max says.

Jinx stands. "I'll go upstairs and get our bags. You know, Max, this whole plan may be the *JMP History Mystery Detective Agency's* finest hour." Shoulders back and chin high, Jinx walks out of the dining room. Her faithful friend, Poppy, is by her side.

A proud Thunder pulls the carriage down the beautiful streets of Savannah, past the Colonial homes and Victorian homes and through the many elegant parks with spraying fountains and blossoming pink hibiscus. Spanish moss drapes over trees, hanging low to the ground. The city's overall look reminds Max and Jinx of the other southern city they had recently visited–Charleston, South Carolina.

Busy people walk the streets, going in and out of bakeries, clothing stores and the market, doing their daily shopping. Other carriages pulled by horses move along the streets near the dock, where ships from foreign ports load or unload their goods in large wooden crates.

Max guides Thunder onto a street heading west out of Savannah. Jinx sits with him high on the driver's seat, holding Poppy in her lap. Petey rides between them. Thunder has been doing a nonstop neighing of his news about his adventure.

"I trotted as fast as I could through the stream water. Ellen and William held on tight. No dogs could find us, no sir. We rode north the rest of the day and all through the night. Ellen saw the safe house first. It was a farm with a burning lantern on the fence post. I had a nice warm stall, and Ellen said they had a soft bed in a secret room in the attic. Then the farmer took us to town early the next morning, to the train depot. William gave him money to ship me back South. And guess what? Ellen and William headed North on the train, but I got to ride a train going back Down South. The train felt funny; it rocked and made a big noise. But could it ever go fast."

Max and Jinx laugh at his excited chatter. Dot puts in her bit.

"Now that he rode a train, there will be no living with him. And he'll be bragging to every horse he meets about saving those folks," Dot says. She is a bit jealous.

"Don't fret, Dot. Look at everything you've done so far to help some of the enslaved people. You carried Ruthie and little Sammy and me to help Doc Alex get them to his false-bottom carriage. You're as important as everyone else on this team. We couldn't do it without your help, too," says Jinx.

On they drive through the beautiful countryside, meadows filled with sweet-smelling flowers, trickling brooks, planted fields and narrow valleys. They look for the cotton fields of the first plantation west of town. They have been told that the Smythe family plantation house sits upon a hill and is called *Far View Plantation.*

Then they see it. A pure-white house sits up high, off in the distance. Cotton fields sprawl for acres and acres, filled with slaves toiling in the hot afternoon sun. Everywhere they see overseers on horseback watching over their group of workers. Some fields are being planted, others weeded, and still other fields are ready to have the snowy-white cotton fluffs pulled from the vines. This is the biggest plantation they have experienced yet.

"Here's the lane that leads uphill to the house," Max says. He pulls off to the side. "We finally made it to the plantation that has Henry's boys. This is what we've been planning for and struggling to reach—a big rescue of two little guys who don't even know we're coming for them."

"Is your stomach knotted like a piece of rope?" Jinx asks Max. "Mine is. I thought we'd never make it, and now that we're here, I don't know what to do or say. My heart is thudding its way right up into my throat so I can barely swallow."

"I feel the same way. But we better get ready to follow our usual plan of bluffing our way through, because here comes one of the overseers. Ready, set, here we go..."

The Boss Man takes his time riding up to the carriage, looking them over with one eyebrow raised and a lopsided grin. "Howdy strangers. Can I help y'all?" he asks in a southern drawl.

He sits astride a spotted brown-and-white horse. His straw hat covers his face with shadows. He wears typical work clothes: dusty brown trousers; a loose, white shirt rolled up at the sleeves and well-worn riding boots. His whip and shotgun lie secure against his saddle.

"Yes, sir. I'm Maxwell Myers and this is my friend, Margaret MacKenzie. We have business with the master of Far View Plantation. Are we at the right place?" Max ignores the sharp poke in the ribs Jinx gives him for calling her Margaret.

The man continues to look them up and down, with a slight frown and question marks in his eyes. "Yes, y'all found the right place. Keep followin' this lane. It'll take you directly up the hill to the big house. Good day to y'all." He tips his hat brim with two fingers and turns back to his job. "Water break," he bawls in a loud voice.

The weary field hands place their tools carefully on the ground and gather around the wagons filled with water buckets over by a cluster of trees. They share gourds and metal ladles full of water. Some drop in the shade for a brief rest. The ladles remind Max and Jinx not only of the drinking gourds the field hands use to sip water, but also of the dippers in the sky pointing the way North.

Max gives a slight tap with the reins. "Okay, Thunder, go on up the hill. Soon time for a big water break for you and Dot, too. Let's go, big guy."

As they draw closer, they can see the magnificence of the large white house. The main house is long and elegant with four roof-to-ground columns. At each end, huge extensions to the house run forward, perpendicular to the main house. They enclose a magnificent courtyard with a large fountain in front of the house. There are balconies on the second floor and a spacious veranda on the ground. Tall pecan trees line the driveway to the house, leading to a circular lane in front. The front lawn has fountains spraying water, flower gardens, and little paths with iron benches under the old trees.

Max and Jinx both find themselves shivering with anticipation and a tiny bit of fear. Will this go as planned? A black cloud chooses this moment to skim across the sun. As the day darkens, it doesn't encourage the *JMP History Mystery Detective Agency* one little bit.

Chapter Nineteen

Secret Plans?

A servant appears from nowhere and takes the reins from Max, who jumps down to help Jinx. Petey and Poppy leap off, staying close to the children. Jinx picks up Poppy, stroking her soft fur.

The silence of the afternoon is broken by the yipping of two fluffy, auburn-colored dogs that run around the side of the house. They look like little foxes. Petey begins yipping with them, exchanging information. The little fur balls jump up and down on Max and Jinx, calling out, *"Hello, hello. Welcome. Come play with us."* They are very friendly little puppies.

Two children run around the side of the house, laughing. The boy calls out to the dogs, "Duke, Duchess, stop that jumping. Come, right now. Come."

The dogs give lingering little yips of joy and licks before they run to the boy and sit by his side, wiggling all over.

"I'm sorry for our dogs' bad manners. My name is Colin Smythe, and this is my sister, Anne." He looks about the same age as Max, while his sister is a few years younger than Jinx.

Colin's hair is as black as a raven's feathers. He is shorter than Max, very fair skinned and slim. He is dressed in short pants with long stockings and high-top shoes. His white shirtsleeves are rolled up on this warm afternoon.

Anne is a tiny girl who looks much like her brother, only with softer features. Her long, black hair is tied back in a blue bow. She wears a pale-green long dress and tiny boots.

"Eddie, Henry, come get the dogs," Colin calls out.

Two small slave boys, dressed almost as fine as Colin, run from the rear yard to scoop up the puppies. They grin at the company in interest as they turn to go back around the house. Max and Jinx exchange glances. At last they have found Henry's little boys.

Everyone laughs at the comical, wiggling puppies' antics as they try to escape from the little boys' arms to run back. Petey and Poppy follow the small boys and puppies to the stable, where they will all be fed and given water.

"The pups are only twelve weeks old. Mama and Papa bought them as gifts for us. They are quite the rage in England. Pomeranian dogs come from a region near Germany. Queen Victoria herself loves them and brought some from Germany," says Colin.

Max puts out his hand to shake with Colin and little Anne. "My name is Maxwell Myers and this is my friend, Margaret MacKenzie."

"Please, call me Jinx," she says. "It's my nickname. I tend to often find myself in trouble." The children all laugh. "We've come to talk with your parents about some business," Jinx adds.

"Of course, come in to meet our mama. I'm afraid Papa is out checking his fields. He won't be in until later," says Colin. They follow him in to the main hall.

Like the other plantation house they experienced, this house is filled with rich treasures. Mahogany side tables filled with vases of hydrangeas and roses line the hall. There are benches and hall trees full of hooks for hanging cloaks near the front double doors.

Colin leads them to his mother's sitting room. Their mother rises and shakes the hands of Max and Jinx as her son introduces them. Anne runs to her side, to give her mama a hug. Mrs. Smythe's hair is also deep black. Her dark brown eyes are large in a very pretty face. She wears a lavender gown with hoops that comes almost to the floor.

"The puppies were so naughty, Mama. They jumped on our guests. But they did come when Colin called them. They tumble and yip and make us laugh," says Anne.

"Colin, you must follow through with daily training so Duke and Duchess learn their manners," Mama says. "But they are only small puppies; it will take time. Now, where are Eddie and Henry? Ah, here they come. Go get Cook to fix us some tea and cakes, boys. Be very careful when you bring the trays."

"Yes, Mistress," they both say. They bow and take their leave, glancing back over their shoulders at Jinx and Max.

The sitting room is filled with couches and chairs covered in soft blue and golden material. A family portrait hangs above a white-marble fireplace. Other pictures of still life, such as bowls of fruit and vases full of flowers, are hung on the walls. Thick rugs from India cover the floors. An open book of poetry sits on a small side table beside Mrs. Smythe's chair.

Colin and Anne sit alongside their mother, while she offers a soft couch to Max and Jinx. "Colin tells me you wish to speak about a business matter," she says. "Mr. Smythe handles all the business for the estate. But he should be home any moment, for teatime. Our great grandfathers may have immigrated to America from England, but you can't take away our British habits. We must have our tea," says Mrs. Smythe.

An average-size man enters the room. He has light-brown hair and green eyes. The children's looks favor their mother rather than their father, but when he grins, Max can see Colin's smile is exactly like his father's.

The two Smythe children run to their papa and hug him. He turns to study the company. "Hello, I am Frederick Smythe. I see you have met my wife, Mrs. Smythe, and my children."

Max jumps up and walks over to shake hands and introduce Jinx and himself. Jinx stands and gives a little curtsey. Max raises his eyebrows and smiles at her.

Eddie and Henry enter the room from a side door, carefully balancing trays laden with tea and small sandwiches and cakes. Eddie is a bit taller than his brother, but other than that, the eight-year-olds look like bookends. They are small for their age, round-faced with black-button eyes, and curly, dark hair. Their skin is the color of ebony. Dressed alike in tiny suits with jackets and white shirts, they look like miniature butlers.

Each boy places his tray on the serving table, and then they bow and go stand with their backs against the wall near the fireplace. They watch Max and Jinx with big, dark eyes.

A servant woman dressed in black comes to pour and serve tea. Next, she goes around with the tray of small plates and sandwiches.

Max and Jinx are starving by this time of the day. The ride from Savannah took a couple of hours, with no stop for lunch. They each enjoy the tiny chicken sandwiches and frosted cakes with the tea.

"Mr. Smythe, the young people are visiting because they have a business matter to discuss with you," says Elaine.

Frederick turns his green eyes on the children. He seems to be satisfied that Max is old enough to handle business affairs. "So Max, tell me about you and Miss Jinx. Where are you from, and why have you traveled to Far View Plantation?"

Max takes a deep breath. This is a big moment. He must make it sound convincing. "Well, Mr. Smythe, we have heard about your two slave boys who sit over there, Edward and Henry. You know how word gets around. We live up North, and word traveled up there about the cute pair of twins you acquired to be used as house slaves. We would like to buy them from you; it's as simple as that."

Eddie and Henry give a jolt on their stools. They look back and forth at Max and Jinx and Mr. Smythe.

The Smythes look at each other in surprise.

"I don't know... We've had them for almost a year. They are quite entertaining and very bright little boys," says Mr. Smythe. "They will soon begin formal training to be personal servants for Colin and me."

"Yes, we are quite used to having Eddie and Henry around. They are very useful doing house chores and waiting on us. And the children find them to be good servants for their needs," says Mrs. Smythe.

"But sir, we come prepared to pay a large sum for them. You can name your price, and I can meet it. They will be very well treated by us," Max says. He begins to have doubts about this working.

"Papa, please; Colin and I don't want to lose Eddie and Henry for our playmates," says Anne.

"Let's invite Master Maxwell and Miss Jinx for dinner. After dinner I'll give my decision," says Mr. Smythe. "Children, why don't you take our guests out to the gardens for some fresh air. Then show them each to a room to freshen up and rest. It is very nice to have you visit."

"Thank you both very much for inviting us to dinner," says Jinx. She has let Max do most of the talking, since this is how women are expected to conduct themselves during this time. *How far women have come with their rights,* Jinx thinks.

"Eddie and Henry, you may join the children outside," says Mrs. Smythe.

Max and Jinx nod their thanks again and join the children as they all go outside once more. When they reach the garden paths, the four animals begin to bounce around them in a great game of chase. Duke and Duchess, along with Petey and Poppy, run like a zoo full of escaped animals, barking and mewing, jumping and tumbling.

The children join in the chase and have a great time trying to capture the pets, running through a maze of stone paths and hedges. Finally, the children sink down on benches and the ground, laughing and breathing hard. The pets flop down also, after getting drinks from a fountain that lies low to the ground.

"Eddie, run and tell Cook we would like a pitcher of lemonade and some glasses," Colin orders. Eddie scampers off and soon returns with a tray. He and Henry pour and serve. They stand back and wait.

"Oh, please—you both have some, too," Anne says.

Grateful, the two slave boys pour some lemonade for themselves. They watch Jinx and Max with questions in their eyes. Jinx notices them watching. After a while, she goes off to the side and sits by the boys, while Colin, Anne and Max walk the paths in a maze made of clipped hedges.

They are very cute twins, as alike as two buttons on a sweater. Jinx smiles and puts her hand in the dust, picks up a stick and traces around it. The boys look at each other and then watch her in fascination. She adds the five stars around the hand. Eddie and Henry each take a quick, short breath and look at Jinx.

They speak for the first time. "Where did you see that, Miss Jinx?" Eddie asks.

"I saw that on a quilt." Again the boys look at each other.

"Do you know the meaning of that picture, Miss?" asks Henry. He and Eddie are taking a big chance with their questions.

"Yes, it means 'follow the stars.' I learned about it from a special man, your papa. Max and I have come a long way to help you find your papa and uncle. But it will be very dangerous. Your master may not sell you to Max and me. Then we'll have to help you run for freedom. Do you understand? You have to trust us. Where do you stay?"

"We live with the cook, Miss. Her cabin is close by the kitchen at the back of the big house," says Eddie.

He and his brother grab each other in excitement. *Could this be true,* they think, *or are we dreaming?* They cry at night because they miss Papa so much.

Eddie pinches Henry's arm. "*Ouch,* that hurt. What you thinkin', Brother?" says Henry.

"I'm checkin' if this is true or if we're dreamin'," says Eddie.

He grins at his brother, who gives him a little shove.

"Well pinch yourself next time," says Henry.

"Why do you want to help us, Miss? We don't even know you. You and Master Max popped into our lives out of nowhere," says Henry. He doesn't quite trust this white girl.

Jinx laughs at their antics. "We want to help you because we helped your papa and uncle to get to a safe house up North. We don't believe in slavery. We believe everyone should be free. We promised your papa we would find you and take you to safety.

"Here's what you should do—when you go home tonight, you make a small bundle of things that you want to take along on the trip. The lighter your bag, the easier it is to travel. Then you listen for an owl calling. That's the signal that it's time to go. Maybe your master will sell you to us, but I'm not sure. So be ready to go late at night, just in case."

Jinx wipes out the symbol she has drawn in the dust. The boys grin at her, their dark eyes shining with joy.

Jinx turns and sees Anne standing nearby watching them. Her stomach clenches, and her heart flutters. *How long has she been there?* Jinx thinks. *Did she hear any of the plans?* Jinx had kept checking, and thought the other children were not close, but then she got so involved in making plans with the boys. This could mean trouble; but Anne only smiles at Jinx.

"I came to visit with you. Tell me about up North. I've not been on a trip that far away," Anne says. She sits with Jinx until the bell rings to call them all in to prepare for dinner. The children walk back to the big house together.

Anne lags behind to walk with her brother. Jinx looks over her shoulder, biting her bottom lip. *Please, please, I hope Anne didn't hear the plan,* Jinx thinks. *If she has, there's no telling what kind of trouble Max and I might experience. If we're arrested as slave stealers, we could be thrown into jail. Then our mission to save our friends would be put on hold indefinitely...and we would be trapped in the past.*

Chapter Twenty

Colin's Decision

Jinx and Max only have a brief time to wash, change clothes, and talk over the plans before dinner. They have been invited to stay overnight. When Max hears about Jinx's discussion with the boys, he is pleased.

"I don't quite know what to think, do you, Jinx? I have a feeling Mr. Smythe won't sell the boys, and then we'll have to do it the hard way. I'm glad you laid some plans with Eddie and Henry," says Max.

"Uh, Max, there's one more thing to tell you. I tried very hard to make sure Anne and Colin were with you while I talked with the twins, but at the end when I turned around, there was Anne. I sure hope she didn't hear anything."

"That could make it rough, especially if she tells her parents. Don't worry though; you did a great job of preparing Eddie and Henry. I couldn't get away from Colin. He's a nice kid, but boy, can he talk. He was full of questions about life up North. He heard about the train routes that run north and south and is anxious to take a train ride," says Max. He squeezes her hand. "We'll soon find out if Anne heard and told her parents, or if we can buy the boys. We'll deal with it, even if we get thrown out of here."

A servant dressed in a black uniform taps at Max's bedroom door, inviting them to dinner. "Your pets are being fed on the kitchen porch," she says softly. She bows and backs out.

Both Jinx and Max are dressed in their finest clothes. Each had the service of a house servant who insisted on helping them; the servants poured fresh warm water in a basin for washing, brushed their clothing, polished their boots, helped comb their hair and assisted in dressing. Max and Jinx thanked them and pressed some coins in their hands to help them and their families.

Now they walk together down the long, spiral stairway to the large hall. Another servant bows and shows them into the dining room. It is as elegant as the other plantations they have visited. Everything is shined and polished, from the serving tables to the beautiful trays, bowls, and dishes. Candles are lit, and servants stand waiting quietly by the side. Eddie and Henry are nowhere to be seen.

Mr. Smythe stands up and gives his guests a genuine smile. "Ah, Miss Jinx and Master Maxwell, you both look fine this nice evening. Come join us." He pulls out a chair for Jinx and nods at Max as they both sit.

Anne gives Jinx a shy smile, while Colin speaks out to his guests. "I'm so glad you came to visit. It was such fun to have new friends to play with this afternoon."

A smiling Negro woman in a black dress and a frilly white apron delivers a huge ham to the center of the table. It smells of delightful spices and is glazed with honey and raisins.

"Anne, would you say the prayer, please?" asks her mother.

While the shy little girl says a quiet blessing, Jinx finds it hard to concentrate. *These are decent people, but they hold people in slavery to do all of the hot, dirty work of running a plantation,* she thinks. *How can one person hold another person against his will when the United States Constitution says all men are equal?* Jinx and Max have talked about this dilemma over and over.

After the blessing, Mr. Smythe stands and carves the huge ham into thick slices, while the servers bring trays of sweet potatoes, corn, tomatoes, breads, and rolls. Max again sees the stark difference in the lives of the rich owners of the plantations and their slaves living in squalor. *How can the slave owners not see the injustice?* Max thinks.

Dinner conversation is pleasant. Max and Jinx find it is easier to talk about the people they have met on their journey south, especially about their adventure with the tornado.

Desserts are fresh peaches in cream and vanilla frosted cake. Afterwards, Mr. Smythe clears his throat. "Maxwell, if you would kindly join Colin and me in the library while the ladies go to the music room, we can discuss business. Then we'll join them so you can hear how well my Annie plays the pianoforte."

Jinx gives Max's hand a squeeze for good luck under the table, and they smile at each other. Whatever the decision, they feel confident with other plans.

In the library Max gazes in awe at the high shelves filled with classic books of varied themes. There are novels, poetry, and Shakespeare, atlases, natural history, world history; the library included everything a well-bred Southerner would need for a good education.

Mr. Smythe motions for the boys to be seated; then he sits in his favorite leather chair near the fireplace. He lights a cigar and puffs a bit, looking into the air, deep in thought. Colin and Max talk softly about their horses and dogs.

Mr. Smythe finally looks at Max and begins to speak. "I asked Colin to be here because I think he is old enough to begin taking part in plantation business. Maxwell, I'd like to know the real reason you wish to purchase the boys." He watches Max with his intense eyes.

Max sits up straighter. His mind is a whirlwind of thoughts. *How honest should he be? What kind of danger will his words stir up for the twins, for Henry and Edward, for Jinx and himself?*

He fixes his blue eyes back on Mr. Smythe, takes a breath and says, "We would like to reunite the little boys with their father, sir. We believe they were too young to be taken from their parent. Families should be together."

"I see. Are you an abolitionist? Do you think that slaves should be set free?" says Mr. Smythe. He has cut right to the point.

"Yes, sir, I guess you might say my friend and I are abolitionists. I was never put into a situation before now, where I had to define myself as an abolitionist. If believing that all people should be free to pursue their dreams of a good life, then I am definitely an abolitionist." Max glances at Colin, who has been listening with interest.

Mr. Smythe smiles and stubs out his cigar. "Colin, what do you think of this situation?" asks his father.

Colin sits straighter, also. He is proud to be asked for his opinion on business matters and to be here with his father for the first time. He looks at Max.

"But Max, we treat our slaves very well. They only get whipped if they disobey our commands. Our plantation is one of the largest around, with hundreds of acres. We need many working slaves for the welfare of the plantation."

Max winces at Colin's words about whipping the slaves. "I understand that you need workers, Colin. But why not pay them for their hard work? Even a small amount would give validity to them as people," says Max.

"That would cut into our profits. It wouldn't be a sound business decision. And they're only slaves, Max, not like you and me. They are like our livestock–our cattle and farm animals. They are a good asset for our plantation," says Colin.

"There's where we differ in opinion, Colin. The slaves *are* exactly like you and me. They're people, with thoughts and feelings and dreams the same as any one of us." Max sees a broad, deep chasm between the Smythes and himself. He shakes his head sadly.

Mr. Smythe watches the two young men as they talk about this serious matter of slavery. The hot topic has always bothered him deep within his heart. But his father and grandfather before him have held slaves. It is the way things have always been done in his family. Even the founding fathers, George Washington and Thomas Jefferson, held slaves on their plantations. How, then, can it be so wrong?

"Thank you for being honest with us, Maxwell. I respect you for your opinion, but I strongly disagree. And I'm afraid I have decided to keep the boys here. My little Annie would be heartbroken to lose her playmates, and the boys show great aptitude for being trained to be superb house servants. Well then, shall we join the ladies?" Mr. Smythe stands and leads the way out of the library.

Colin motions for Max to stay behind until his father is gone. "You know, Max, you made some good points. I must think more about slavery. I hope we can remain friends."

Max turns and places his hand on Colin's shoulder. "Even though we differ in opinion about slavery, I want you to understand that my offer to pay for the boys, rather than steal them, is made in respect for your right to your own opinion. I hope you do think it over. And, yes, we can still be friends." The two boys smile.

When the boys reach the music room, Annie is already playing a pretty waltz by Strauss. Eddie and Henry are now standing in the rear, intently watching her fingers fly on the keyboard while swaying to the beat. All of the pets have been brought back to the big house; they lie upon cushions on the floor. The Pomeranian pups are sound asleep, exhausted from their rough-and-tumble play all day long.

Jinx, Petey and Poppy look at Max as he enters. He gives them a tiny, sad shake of the head. Jinx looks down, disappointed by the outcome. It seems that nothing will be easy on this trip.

Eddie and Henry were anxiously waiting on Max to return with the answer, also. When they see his face and the sad negative shake of his head, their eyes slide to Jinx. She notices their look and ever so slightly nods at them. They know what to do; they will be ready to go when they hear the hoot of the owl.

After another song, Mr. and Mrs. Smythe excuse themselves for the night. "Now, don't stay up too late, children. Miss Jinx and Master Maxwell must get started on the next part of their journey tomorrow morning. Breakfast will be early." The children give their good nights to the adults.

When they are alone, Eddie jumps up. "Miss Annie, could me and Henry try to play on the piano? One song, please?"

Henry joins his brother. "Please, Miss Annie?" he begs.

Duke and Duchess wake up, run to the little boys, and jump up and down at their legs, giving little yips. Petey joins in the excitement of the puppies.

"Let's play, let's play, let's dance, yip, yip, yip."

Poppy stretches her back and yawns.

"I've had quite enough puppy wildness for the day. Where do they get all that energy? They are worse than Peter with all that jumping and yipping," she purrs.

Jinx smothers a laugh, leans down and strokes Poppy. "Soon time for bed, Poppy, old girl," she murmurs.

"Yes, you may try to play a song," Anne says to the twins.

Eddie and Henry take their places on the bench. They make a big show out of jostling each other and pushing back their jacket sleeves. Then they carefully place their hands on the keys and look serious. Eddie starts and Henry joins in with the harmony. They begin to play an easy little melody, unfamiliar to everyone.

The other children look at each other, smiling. How can this be?

When they finish that, they place their small hands in their laps. Then they break into a soft singing. The tune and the words capture everyone's attention. Even the dogs stop playing and come to sit and listen to the Negro Spiritual, *"Wade in the Water."*

Wade in the water.
Wade in the water, children.
Wade in the water.
God's a-gonna trouble the water.
Well who're these children all dressed in red?

God's a-gonna trouble the water.
Must be the children that Moses led.
God's a-gonna trouble the water.
Who's that young girl dressed in white?
God's a-gonna trouble the water.
Must be the Children of the Israelite.
God's a-gonna trouble the water.
Who's that young girl dressed in blue?
God's a-gonna trouble the water.
Must be the Children that's comin' through.
God's a-gonna trouble the water.
Jordan's water is chilly and cold.
God's a-gonna trouble the water.
It chills the body, but not the soul.
God's a-gonna trouble the water.
If you get there before I do
God's a-gonna trouble the water.
Tell all of my friends I'm comin' too.
God's a-gonna trouble the water.

Eddie and Henry finish their song. Both sit in silence, looking at their hands beneath the piano keyboard. The other children stare at the boys, caught in the moment. Then they clap and cheer.

"Where...how did you learn to play that little song on the piano?" Anne asks.

Both boys grin at her. "We watched you, Miss Annie. We saw your fingers on the keys every time you practiced. That's all it took," says Henry.

"I was thinkin' the black and white keys on the piano are like you and Master Colin, and me and Henry, you know? But they're standin' side by side, not apart like we has to do," says Edward. Anne tilts her head, thinking about the statement.

Max and Jinx nod in agreement. "You are all wonderful musicians," Jinx says to the twins and Anne. "You've got real talent for music."

Anne makes eye contact with Jinx and stares deeply into her eyes. Jinx can tell Anne's thoughts are elsewhere. Then Anne smiles.

"Don't know what a mu-si-shin is, but if it mean we like to sing, then me and Eddie sure is mu-si-shins," Henry says. "We'll take the animals out for you." They bow and leave with the furries to go outside.

The big hall clock bongs ten times. The children head to their rooms, saying good night. Max whispers to Jinx as she goes in her bedroom door, "Wait until two o'clock. Everyone will be sound asleep, I hope. I'll tap at your door, and we'll go down the back servant stairs and out to pick up Eddie and Henry. Say your prayers for safety." He hugs Jinx and leaves.

Jinx can't sleep one wink. Petey is restless, too. *"Is it time yet, is it time to get the twins?"* he asks about every ten minutes.

"No, it's not time. Try to rest, Petey; you're making me jumpy."

"I told Thunder and Dot to be ready to go," Petey says.

"What a good little guy you are, Pete-o. Where would I be without you by my side?" Jinx strokes his silky fur and tries to rest.

Jinx is dressed in her everyday traveling dress and boots and has her bag ready to go when the hall clock bongs two chimes. She and Petey wait by the door for Max.

When he taps, they sneak down the hall to the servant stairs and are soon outside by the cook's hut, behind the big house. Everything is silent; even the birds and insects and frogs by the fountains are asleep. The night is starlit, and the air has cooled. Jinx shivers and pulls her shawl closer. The air smells crisp with pine scent and the aroma of the garden roses. It seems like the entire world is hushed and waiting.

Max and Jinx kneel in the cool grass with Petey and Poppy by their sides. "Who whooo, who whoo..." Max gives an owl call.

Through the back window of the hut drop two small, tied bundles of clothing. Then they hear a scrambling, and two little forms climb out of the window and drop on top of each other.

"Oomph..." says Eddie when Henry lands on him.

"Shhhhh...I ain't that heavy," says Henry.

The twins' eyes seem to glow in the dark, like Petey and Poppy's eyes do. They quiver with barely contained excitement.

Petey leaps up to the window and disappears inside. Jinx and Max look at each other in surprise. Now what is Petey up to?

"Petey, get back here. Now is no time to go exploring," Jinx thinks it to her terrier, rather than saying it out loud.

"Be right there. Something important left behind," says Petey. There is more scrambling, and Petey appears in the window, tugging at something, trying to pull it out. *"The Pomeranians told me about the twins' favorite blanket. I want them to have it for the journey."*

All of a sudden two little fur balls drop out of the window and help Petey finish tugging. A quilt falls to the ground. Duke and Duchess jump up and down, kissing the twins. For once, they are totally silent.

"Our Freedom Quilt," say the boys. They sink to the ground and cuddle the dogs. They hug and kiss them goodbye once more, before they carefully drop them back inside the hut.

In the center of the quilt is a big patch. On it is a brown hand with five yellow stars around it. It's the quilt and symbol that Jinx saw in the first vision she had of the twins being taken away from their father.

"Our Grandmamma wrapped us in it when the bad man came and took us. It has the path to freedom on it. She taught our papa the path, and then she taught us. It'll help us git up North, to freedom," Henry whispers.

Jinx helps the boys roll up the quilt, and then the group makes its way to the horse stable. Jinx thinks about this big night ahead. She feels her heart thudding. She says another silent prayer for safety and success.

Max tries to pull the barn doors open without making too much noise. His only thought is to get Thunder and Dot hitched to the carriage and to be on their way back to Savannah.

Everyone hustles into the barn and stops short. In the moonlight they see Colin step from behind the carriage and stand blocking their way. He folds his arms over his chest and stares at everyone, one person at a time.

Chapter Twenty-one

On the Run

Max walks around Colin and throws their bags into the carriage. Thunder and Dot neigh to their friends and prance in their stalls. The twins hide behind Jinx, afraid this dream of seeing their papa again will be ripped from them.

"Hello, Colin. What are you doing up so late?" Max says. He puts his hands on his hips, facing Colin.

"Anne talked with me before dinner tonight. She told me about Jinx's plans with Eddie and Henry," says Colin.

"Why didn't you tell your father?" Max asks. He cocks his head. He is not sure how this conversation will end.

"Because I've been thinking about the points you made on slavery. For the first time, I actually heard someone talk to me who has a different opinion. I've never really thought about it before. Our family has always had slaves. It's my way of life."

Max smiles at this southern boy who has become a friend. "So, what do you think now? Have you changed your mind about owning slaves?" he asks Colin.

Colin uncrosses his arms and smiles back at Max. "I'm not sure, but that's a good thing, isn't it? You've planted a seed of doubt in my mind. However, there is one thing that we both can agree on."

"What's that?" Max says.

"Children should never be taken from their family. Anne and I talked it over. We both want the boys to go with you, back to their father."

Colin offers his hand to Max, who grasps it. The boys hug, slapping each other on the back, like friends do.

Max reaches into his bag and pulls out a wad of money. "We can pay your father—what do you think? Would one thousand or two thousand dollars be enough?"

Colin shakes his head. "Put your money away, Max. My father is very rich; he doesn't need your money. I'll stall him from finding out as long as I can. When the boys turn up missing tomorrow, I'll tell my father the truth: I have a different opinion than he does, and I decided to send the boys back to their father. I'll take the blame and his punishment. We'll see if he'll treat me like a young businessman or tan the hide off my backside." He rubs his back end. Everyone laughs.

"But Colin," Jinx says, "if you take the money, you can tell your father you made a sound business deal now that you're included in the family business. Maybe it'll go easier on your backside."

Colin grins and shakes his head no, again. "I have a suggestion for you, Max; I think you should leave your carriage behind in Savannah, and take the first train out of town in the morning. The train will get you much further away, faster. Even if my father decides to look for the twins, he'll never know where you've gone. But I think he will honor my wishes; he's a good man, overall," Colin adds.

"He must be a good man. He's got a good son," says Max.

The boys get the horses and carriage ready. Before they load, Jinx runs to hug Colin. She kisses the side of his face. "Thank you, Colin, for your friendship and your help. Tell Annie I say thank you, too. Tell her that letting the twins go is a good thing to do. I'll never forget you and Annie."

Colin puts his hand on the side of his face and turns red, much like Max when Jinx teases him. He grins at Jinx.

"Goodbye, Miss Jinx. Goodbye, Eddie and Henry. Best of luck to you." He shakes the twins' small hands. Then he turns to Max one last time. "Max, I feel that big changes will come to the South by the time I'm a grown man. It's in the wind already. Who knows?" He salutes them as Max drives the carriage out of the barn and down the hill away from Far View Plantation.

We know, Max thinks. *We already know that big changes are coming for the better, but at the cost of many lives given up in service to the country.* He smiles in the moonlight and urges Thunder into a trot, heading back towards Savannah.

It is six a.m. and barely light. Max, Jinx and the boys stand on the platform beside a hissing, black engine. Jinx holds Petey in her arms. Poppy lounges in one of their bags of clothing.

The day is cloudy and cool, and the air smells of oil, cinders and burning coal. The steam from the huge smokestack rises straight up in the air before it drifts away.

Max looks up at the steam engine, amazed at its giant size and shape. His mind compares this train to the streamlined modern-day trains. *This dinosaur comes out in first place, in my opinion. It's a beauty,* Max thinks.

They have a few hundred extra dollars in their pockets, because they have sold the carriage at the livery stable. They couldn't bear to part with their faithful horses, so Thunder and Dot are being loaded into a cattle car partly full of animals farther down the line.

Max carries a hurriedly made-out document saying his family owns the little boys. He hopes they won't be challenged. They need to get out of here as fast as possible. He thinks of his friend Colin and smiles.

A black porter in a blue uniform and cap carries their luggage onto the passenger car. People hustle to step up into the train cars as a conductor in uniform calls, "All a-bo-aaard."

The conductor who calls for boarding is an older white man with wispy white hair and a beard. He takes his cap off and scratches his head, looking at Jinx, Max and the little boys with kind brown eyes. "I'm afraid these Negro boys can't ride with you, Miss. Negroes ain't allowed in the white folks' cars. The car for colored folks is down the line."

"Oh, of course," says Jinx. "But they are so small, I don't trust letting them alone with strangers."

"Miss Jinx, we be all right alone. We're big boys now," Eddie says.

Henry agrees. This whole train ride is an adventure for them, although they have a great fear of being caught and sent back to the plantation for punishment. Little Henry shivers. *I seen the beatin's and whippin's that happen when the slaves try to run for freedom,* he thinks.

Petey speaks to Max and Jinx. *"I'll go with the boys. I'll watch over them."*

Jinx looks at Max. He nods. "I'll tell you what; Petey will ride with you. He's a great watchdog." Both boys like this idea. Jinx hands Petey over to Henry. "Take good care of each other," she says.

The conductor takes the boys by their hands and leads them away. "They'll be fine back there, Miss," he says, smiling. "I'll check up on 'em when I go through the coaches."

Jinx and Max go up the steep iron steps and into an elegant train car. It is lined with dark-stained oak. The seats are covered in brown velvet and the backs can be swiveled front to back. They find their luggage loaded in the overhead rack and reverse one of the seats so they can sit facing each other.

The brakes hiss as they are released, and the train jostles its passengers as it starts down the tracks. It gives off a departing steam whistle: *whooo, wooooo.* It makes Jinx and Max think of the similarities between the real train and the Underground Railroad.

"We've learned so much, haven't we?" Max says.

"Yes, and much of it's pretty harsh," says Jinx.

"The negatives are important, because they teach us lessons about what's right and wrong in life, but we should also try to think of some positive things that have happened to us and the people we've met," Max says.

"Okay, we've learned how to handle horses and a carriage," says Jinx.

"We've formed lasting friendships with some brave Africans striving for freedom," says Max.

Jinx feels her spirits lift once more. Max always knows how to help her when she's feeling down. He either makes her laugh with his silliness or puts a positive spin to their discussions. "We've learned that we can push our gifts farther than ever before, and that our problems eventually work out for the best," she says.

"How about all of the black and white people we've met who are part of the Underground Railroad? These people risk being arrested and put into jail for breaking the Fugitive Slave Laws, to help the runaway slaves to freedom. Can you believe how well organized it is? It's truly amazing," says Max.

"Might I add something to the 'positive thoughts' game? You two have grown in wisdom and strength through all of the struggles you have mastered so far. I'm very proud of you," purrs a velvety voice. An orange-and-white, furry head peers out of the corner of their bag in the overhead rack. Poppy looks at her boy and girl with green, slanted eyes. She gives them each the cat caress of a slow blink of her eyes and loud purring.

"Thank you, Poppy," says Max. "Your opinions about us matter a great deal."

Jinx gives Poppy a cat caress back by slowly closing and opening her eyes at Poppy. Poppy purrs louder and jumps down to Jinx's lap, where she curls up in contentment.

The train moves on through the Georgia countryside and into South Carolina. Acres and acres of plantation land pass by; sometimes the field hands pause when they hear the train and wave.

The steady rocking of the train car soothes the children's tattered nerves and gives them some much-needed rest as it heads towards their destination of Wilmington, North Carolina.

"Next stop *Wil-ming-toooon...*" Jinx is awakened by the old conductor's voice. Max comes through the doorway from the other end of the car and sits back down across from Jinx.

"The little guys are fine," Max says. "I was back visiting with them to make sure they were all right. They made friends with the other people in the car by doing their funny little antics, and Petey helped entertain the rest of the time. Henry and Eddie are quite a handful." Max laughs and shakes his head.

"I know; but I think both boys are so intelligent. Can you believe how well they sing and play the piano by ear? I can't wait to find Henry. He'll be excited to see how they've grown. My stomach is doing twists just thinking about it. What's the plan?" She looks out of the window at the countryside bathed in late-day sunshine. "Do we move out tonight?"

"We'll do some checking at the train depot about where Arthur Young's plantation is located. And we'll have to get a few supplies to put in the horses' saddlebags. I hope Thunder and Dot had a good ride on the train," says Max.

The train slows down with lots of hissing and brake squealing. It gives a few toots of the steam whistle–*whoo wooooo wooooo*. The children look out of the window and watch the Wilmington train depot slowly appear. They see people watching and waving for their relatives on the train. The train chugs to a halt at the wooden platform. The riders gather their bags and begin to make their way to the doors.

"Let's get our bags and get off the train. You can watch the bags while I go get the boys," says Max. Jinx nods.

As soon as they step off the train onto the platform, Max leaves Jinx and runs back to the boys' coach. He waits impatiently for the people to depart, then, not seeing the boys, his heart gives a lurch. He finally runs back up the steps into the car. Henry and Eddie are lying on their seat fast asleep, covered by their quilt. The kind old conductor waits by their side. When he sees Max, he gives a broad smile.

"There you are, Master Max. I didn't want to leave these two little rascals alone 'til you picked them up. They only fell asleep the last hour," says the man.

"Wake up, boys–time to go." He jostles the little boys awake.

Petey pokes his sleepy head out from under the quilt.

"Are we here?" he yawns.

Max scoops Petey into his arms. "Yes, we're here. It's time to move out, guys. Get your bags."

Once awake the boys jump up, ready to go. Grabbing their bags and quilt they run for the door. "Goodbye, Mr. Conductor," says Henry.

"Thanks for watchin' out for us," adds Eddie.

"Good luck to y'all," says the conductor. He nods goodbye to Max and walks on to check the other cars.

"Come on, guys, let's find Jinx. Then we go get Thunder and Dot," Max says.

They find Jinx, tapping her toe and looking all around. The little boys run up and hug her, almost knocking her over.

Jinx laughs to see their excitement. "Miss Jinx, Miss Jinx, that train ride was so fine. Some nice folks gave us some cornbread and drinks of water. We told them all about our plantation home. But we didn't tell them our secret." Henry whispers the last part.

Eddie chatters on with his comments, too, as the group heads for the livestock cars. They can hear mooing, clucking, and oinking as they reach their destination. The animals are not happy to have been crowded together on the long ride. Thunder and Dot neigh from one of the less-crowded cars, anxious to see their people.

"Ooooo, the smell of you pigs is disgustin'..."

"Well, you chickens don't smell any better than us!"

"Mooooo-ve over, Sadie. Tell the other cows to give us some rooo-m."

"Maaaaa-x! Get us off this traaaaa-in," Dot begs.

Max grins while he shows the paperwork that says he owns the two horses. The men unloading livestock lead them down a ramp. They throw their saddles and other equipment in a pile as they check off Max's list.

"Now I've ridden the train, too, like Thunder," says Dot, *"but I can't say I enjoyed it. Too much motion. I'm glad to get my hooves back on firm ground. I like to be the one in motion."* She makes a flapping sound with her lips and shakes her head.

"I love the speed," says Thunder. He paws the ground with one front leg and snorts. *"I wish I could run as fast as a train."*

Jinx helps Max put the saddles and bridles on the horses. They tie the bags onto their sides. Then Max leads the little group down off the platform and out to the street, away from the action and noise of the depot, and ties the horses to a hitching post on the main street.

"Wait here, everyone. Let me do some asking around about the plantation we need to find," says Max. He jogs back up to the depot and disappears inside.

Max looks around the depot platform. He sees some barred windows with ticket sellers behind them. A few vendors hawk their wares: roasted nuts, fruit, fresh rolls, and flowers.

The long wooden benches are almost empty, as most people have either found their friends and family or boarded the train to move on to another town. He walks over to a ticket window and waits for a turn to talk to the ticket seller.

"Hello, sir. I'm looking for directions to the plantation of Arthur Young. Do you know him?" asks Max.

"Not familiar with that name, son. I'm new to the area. Joe, do you know of a Young Plantation?" he calls out to another ticket seller.

"Yeah, he has a pretty big spread northwest of here, 'bout ten or twelve miles away. He raises some livestock along with cotton. Runs them in to the auction at the stockyards once a year–pigs, chickens, and cattle. He took over the plantation when his brother, Willard, died. Remember?" says Joe. He leans front to see who wants to know. When he sees Max, his eyebrows rise. *Why would a boy want to know about that plantation,* he thinks. Curious, he decides to close his window and take a break.

Max gives his thanks and leaves in a hurry. *It's almost sundown,* he thinks. *We better buy some supplies before the stores close and head out of town. We can camp out tonight. Best to get away from the busy town and nosey ticket sellers.*

When Max returns, Jinx decides to take the boys with her to the store, leaving Max on guard duty. Henry and Eddie can barely contain their excitement of actually seeing a store in a big city. The plantations have been their whole life before this adventure.

As they enter the store, the boys run to the candy counter and stare at the jars and jars of penny candy. "Miss Jinx, look, look...so much candy, all different colors," Eddie says.

"You and Henry choose what kinds of candy you would like," says Jinx. She gives each boy a few coins to spend. *That should keep them busy while I gather some supplies,* she thinks. *Most of our things were stolen by Jackson and Billy or left behind. We need some basic things like food and utensils.*

They hope to get help from people along the Underground Railroad, but for now they need to plan on being alone and camping with the boys. *I remember Henry telling us 'we don't find them, they'll find us,' so we'll have to trust that piece of wisdom.*

Jinx picks out cans of fruit and beans, along with tins of meat. The pile grows with eating utensils and cups. She finds small rain slickers for the twins.

The storekeeper is a tall man in dark pants, a striped shirt and an apron. He is as thin as a skeleton, with deep-set eyes. Of course he is very interested in this girl with the two little Negro boys. *Most unusual,* he thinks. *This girl isn't treating them like they're her servants... something is definitely weird about the situation.* Smiling, he totals the purchases and puts everything in a few sturdy paper bags.

"Where you headed, Miss?" he asks.

Jinx gives a tiny smile. *Why is everyone always asking hard questions,* she thinks. "Boys, are you still trying to choose your penny candy?" She hurries over to the candy counter, pretending she didn't hear the man. Jinx hustles their decision-making and waits by the door as the boys pay. Then they all run back to where Max waits. Each boy has a sweet piece of hard candy in his cheek.

Max has been tightening the gear and checking for rope and other small tools in his own bag. When Jinx comes up to him, he notices her frown and wrinkled forehead. "What's wrong?" he asks.

"It seems like people are always watching us and questioning us. The storekeeper was asking nosey questions," she says. "I dropped my guard and wasn't treating the boys like servants. I...I let them pick out some penny candy."

"Ah, Jinx, I hope no one noticed. It's hard to keep your guard up every second of the day. I noticed the ticket seller at the depot was very curious about me, too. So we'd best get going. Let's get you mounted. Then I'll help one of the twins up. Who wants to ride with Jinx?" he asks.

Petey jumps up and down off of all four paws. *"Me, I want to ride with Jinx, me...me..."*

Poppy is already nestled in one of the packs on horseback. She gives a heavy sigh and tucks her head back in the bag. They can hear her mewing about excitable dogs and children.

Both boys ask to ride with Jinx, so Max reaches down and picks up two twigs lying in the dirt by the wooden sidewalk. "Okay, whoever pulls the short stick gets to ride with me," he challenges.

Both boys love the little game. They eagerly choose their stick and line them up to see who wins a ride with Jinx. Eddie has the short stick.

"Ahhhh ha, you lose, Brother," Henry says to Eddie. Eddie gives him a friendly shove.

Max grabs Henry and swings him up in the saddle in front of Jinx before they get into a wrestling match. He puts Petey across the horse in front of Henry. Then Max gives Eddie a boost up and mounts himself.

Both boys look around until they spot their quilt rolled up and tied down behind Max. "Our quilt will help tell the way," Eddie says. Satisfied, he pops another candy into his mouth.

Thunder paws the ground, eager to get some exercise.

"Easy, big boy. Let's not take off in a dead heat. A nice trot will do to start," says Dot, shaking her pretty, polka-dotted head.

"Why walk when you can run?" neighs Thunder.

It is dusk, and the stars are beginning to shine. Max and Jinx both look for the dippers that point the way to the North Star. They follow the road out of town, anxious to find Henry.

No one notices the ticket seller standing in the alley beside the store. He watches as they trot away. Then he raps on the door of the store that has now closed. He would like to talk to his friend, the storekeeper, to see what he knows about the strange little group that has just departed from town.

Chapter Twenty-two

Moses

The boys are both sound asleep, leaning back into their new friends' chests. Max keeps an eye on the stars and also checks his compass to stay on a northeast route. Sometimes they have to leave a main road and go through wooded land and across streams and through the swamps with those pesky, biting insects. It is hard to gauge the miles by horseback.

Jinx watches the land, anxious to see the cultivated fields of cotton, wheat or corn that indicate a plantation. She wonders how they will find Henry, or even know that it's the correct plantation. "Max, what's the plan to find Henry?"

"We sneak into the slave quarters and try to waken one of the slaves. Ask them–they know each other well. They'll help us."

Jinx thinks about this for a while. "We need a miracle, don't we?" she says, not really wanting an answer.

"Miracles happen all the time," Poppy says. *"Angels walk amongst us—just ask them for help."*

The trail follows a river. It twists around a hill of rocks, out of the earthy-smelling woods, and downward to a bigger road. Fields of cotton meet their eyes, all lying silent and empty on this moonlit night. Their hearts begin to pound and anxiety builds. This could be the Young Plantation.

Max leads Thunder along the river and through a small valley; then he follows the fields to where the buildings can be seen in the distance. They halt behind a grove of apple trees, out in the fields. A ground fog from the river swirls around them, lightly touching them with misty fingers.

"Beyond the big barn, way out there, are the slave quarters," Jinx whispers. "Should I stay here with the twins while you go check things out?"

"Good idea," Max says. He gives Eddie a little shake. "Eddie, we're getting down off the horse." He helps the sleepy boy to the ground and leads him over to an apple tree to join Jinx and Henry. The boys now become excited and wide awake.

"Are we here? Is this where Papa is livin'? How will we find him?" Their questions come fast and furious.

"Shhh...be calm, boys. Max will check it out. Our job right now is to stay silent and hide here," says Jinx. The boys grab each other and shake with excitement.

Petey jumps down and sniffs the ground and the air. He starts to follow his nose towards the slave quarters. *"This is it, I can smell Henry's scent, he's here, he's close by..."* says Petey as he takes off.

Max runs after him, silently communicating to him to wait up. *Petey, wait up...wait for me...* When they get close to the shacks of the slaves, Max grabs Petey in his arms and stops to get his breath.

He and Petey peer around the corner of the little building. It doesn't have a rear window, and Max doesn't want to go around to the front where he will be more visible. They move to the next building. *Great, a rear window,* Max thinks. He picks up some small pebbles and tosses one through the opening. No one comes. Another toss. This time a head pokes out, looking around. It's a young man, with his wife behind him asking who is out there.

"Some white boy and a dog," he answers. "What you want, white boy? I don't need no trouble."

"I'm looking for a man named Henry. Is this the Young Plantation?" Max asks.

"You got the right place, but Henry, he ain't walkin' too good right now. He really got the whip for runnin' this last time. The thought of tryin' to run again got beat right outta him."

"Where is he?" Max is anxious to find Henry and be gone into the night.

"He chained up in that big barn over there, so he can't run at night. Now you'd best move on 'fore someone hears you and gets Boss Man awake. Big trouble then." The head pulls back into the hut, and a wooden window flap is closed in Max's face.

Max puts Petey back down. "Go find him, Petey."

Nose to the ground, Petey takes off in search of his friend, Henry. He sniffles and mutters as he runs. *"Sniff sniff...not good. I smell blood mixed with Henry's smell. Sweat and tears...sniff sniff."*

Petey stops at the small side door of the barn and scratches in the dirt, frantic to get the door open. Max tugs the door. It opens easily. He sneaks slowly through and walks toe to heel, listening for a sound that Henry is somewhere in the barn. They hear a soft moan of pain. Petey disappears again in the dark. *"Here, over here, quick, quick,"* says Petey.

"Petey, what...? Is it really you, my little friend?"

Max walks toward the stall where he hears the weak voice. Henry sits huddled in the corner, hugging Petey to his chest. Petey kisses Henry's face all over. Max leans down and puts a hand on Henry's shoulder. He sees that Henry's once-fine clothes are tattered and torn. Henry has a blanket wrapped around his back; it is covered in dried blood.

"Henry, we've come for you."

"Master Max, I've been prayin' that you would find me. But I'm chained up—how do we get me outta these chains?"

Max realizes that Henry wears cuffs around his ankles and is also chained to a big post. "Where are the keys kept? Who has chained you here?"

"Boss Man, he has the key ring. He chains me up every night, now. And I have to wear the ankle chains when I works in the field. It's hard to walk around; sure can't go far. That's my punishment for runnin' two times. But I'll never stop tryin', not until I'm dead."

"Henry, don't talk like that. We have your boys. They're safe with us, and they need their papa. So let's figure out how to break these chains."

Henry grabs Max's hands in shocked disbelief. "You mean it, Master Max, you really found my boys?"

Max grins and nods his head.

"No need to break the chains," purrs a soft voice. *"Look what I've found hanging on the door of Mr. Boss Man. I slipped in through his window, and there they were. Time to go, everyone."* Poppy drops the key ring in Max's lap.

"Oh, Miss Poppy, you is one fine cat," says Henry.

"Thanks, Poppy. You really are a fine cat." Max picks her up for a quick face cuddle into her soft fur. He remembers another time when Poppy stole some keys to set Max free from pirates.

When Henry stands, free of his chains, the blanket slips to the ground. The full moon shines in the window and falls on Henry's back when he turns. Max stares, horrified at the crisscross stripes of oozing red that haven't healed.

"Henry, I am so sorry...I swear we will get you and Edward and the boys to Canada, so you will never have to be beaten again." Max feels a fresh push of energy. Max picks up the blanket and wraps it around Henry. "Let me help you, Henry. Now we're set to go."

Henry clutches the blanket to his chest. "Thank you, Master Max." Tears fall down his cheeks. "Stick to the shadows, now. I can't wait to see my boys. Are they fine? Are they healthy?"

"Wait until you see how fine your boys are, Henry. You'll be so proud of them."

Max leads Henry back out to the grove of trees. They crouch low and run. The two furries lag behind, watching for any sign of danger.

Far out in the fields, the little boys strain to see when their papa is coming. When they spot Max, Jinx has to hold them back so they don't forget and burst out into the open.

The reunion is emotional for everyone. Henry runs to his boys and scoops them up into his arms. The boys sob into their father's strong chest, calling, "Papa, Papa..." over and over. Max and Jinx both cry along with them.

Papa finally puts his boys down and stands back to take a good look at them.

"Why, Master Max, I don't believe these are my boys after all. My boys is little tiny beans, not big strong boys like these two."

The boys start to giggle through their tears. "Papa, we is too your boys–really. We growed fast," Eddie says.

Jinx gives Henry a tender hug, careful not to squeeze his raw back. "Welcome, Henry," she says. "It's so good to find you. I've got some cooling balm for your back."

"My back can wait; first, let's git goin' far away from here. We need to be hidden by daybreak," says Henry. "Boys, tell Miss Jinx and Master Max the secret plan."

They grab their quilt and point to the bottom patch. "See this blue river, here? It's to remind us to wade in the water when we can, to keep the slave hunters and hounds from trackin' our scent," says little Henry. "So, first we has to cross the big stream, and keep followin' the North Star."

"And the next patch, it shows a big, scooped-out rock. It tells about a place we can hide, behind the scooped-out rock in a real cave," Eddie adds. "Our Grandmama made this Freedom Quilt to help Papa and Uncle, and they told the secret code to me and Henry. Some of our people who made it to freedom, they sent word back to tell others 'bout the path to freedom. Grandmama used to wait up late at night for the secret messenger. He'd come a-tappin' at the back window of our cabin."

Max and Jinx are impressed. "Then let's head for the river and find that cave to hide in tonight. We have to make plans to find JoJo at his plantation. We'll tell you about him as we ride," says Jinx.

"Well, Thunder, think you can hold big Henry and me?" asks Max. Thunder snorts and paws the ground.

"I think that horse knows 'xactly what you say," says big Henry.

"Henry isn't your real name, is it?" Max says.

"No, Master Max," Henry says softly. "It's Alem, means 'the world' in the language of my people."

"I think it's time to reclaim your name, don't you?" says Jinx. "Then we won't get mixed up with two Henrys."

"You're right, Miss Jinx. My name is Alem, and I'd be right pleased and proud to have you call me Alem."

"And Uncle's real name is Anwar," adds Eddie. "It mean 'the brightest.' Papa told us the story of comin' to America. He said we was old enough to hear the tale, even the bad parts. It was a hard journey for Papa and Uncle."

Jinx and Max glance at each other. They know the story well from their painful visions.

"Now it's time for my sons to take their own hard journey to freedom," says Alem.

The group mounts the two large horses and heads out to the river so they can cross, in search of the safe cave for the night. All is quiet and peaceful in the dark shadows of the woods.

❀ ☙ ❀

"*Grrrrrrrr...*" Petey stands with Poppy at the mouth of the cave. Both animals have bristled fur; Petey's is a ridge from head to tail, like a razor-backed wild hog, and Poppy's tail looks like a bottlebrush.

Jinx sits bolt upright, searching the darkness of the cave and the opening out into the inky blackness. The others are sound asleep after locating this small cave behind a rock pile with the scooped-out rock.

"What is it, Petey?"

"*Horse and rider.*"

Jinx pushes her blanket back and crawls over to Max, who is hidden beneath his own blanket. "Max, wake up. May be trouble." She tugs on his arm.

Both Max and Henry snap to wakefulness and join Jinx at the cave's entrance. The night is mild and silent; even the wildlife sleeps. Then comes a stealthy sound of a lone horse picking its way through the last of the woods and entering the area filled with pebbles and gravel leading to the cave.

They see a dark-colored horse with two riders—men dressed in dark clothing.

"Everyone to the rear of the cave," hisses Max. "I'll keep watch." The others grab the boys and bedrolls and hustle to the back wall of the small cave. Fear fills the cave like an unwelcome ghost.

The first rider dismounts and makes his way around the rocks, keeping behind them as if afraid of being shot. "Hello?" he calls out in a low voice. "Anyone here? We're friends."

Max lies on his stomach in the shadow of the cave opening, watching. He thinks he recognizes the voice. It's the ticket seller. If he has tracked them, it could mean nothing but bad news.

Petey stops his low growling and starts wagging his stubby tail. Before Max can grab him, he runs out to the man. *"Petey, no."* But it's too late. He runs right up to the man and jumps up and down for attention.

"Ah, the riders are friends. This is good news, indeed," Poppy says.

"Hello, pup. Tell yer people we mean no harm," the man says. He scratches Petey behind the ears.

Max feels cautious. It's been very hard to tell the difference between friend and foe on this trip back in time. Everything is so secretive and in code.

"What do you want? How do you know us?" Max calls out. "We're armed, so don't try anything." *I might as well bluff my way through this,* Max thinks.

"I saw you at the train depot. I'm the ticket seller who knew the Young Plantation. You seemed...well, scared, as if you were into something over your head when you asked about the plantation. When I saw you with the little Negro boys loading up camping gear, I did some checking around. I figured whatever you're up to, you could use some help. You're delivering some parcels, I'd guess. Am I correct?"

Max feels a hand on his shoulder that makes him jump. It's Alem. "He's a conductor, Master Max. 'Delivering parcels' is code on the Underground Railroad for helping runaways. We can trust him."

Alem and Max get up and dust off their pants. Jinx and the boys join them. Henry and Eddie run to their papa and grab his waist, standing not behind him, but at his side. They've not only grown in stature; but they've also grown in courage. They're ready to help Papa fight for their freedom.

By this time, the second rider has dismounted. A smaller man dressed in a baggy brown coat, loose-fitting pants and a battered, straw hat walks over. He has a bandanna wrapped around his neck and lower face. Max and Jinx are surprised to see he is a black man. But even though he is short, there is an air of strength and confidence about him.

Both riders walk closer. "My name is Frank Dixon," says the big man. He offers his hand to Alem and Max and dips his hat at Jinx. "I've brought someone for you to meet. This is Moses, one of the best conductors on the Underground Railroad."

Alem draws in a big gulp of air and moves to greet the smaller man, falling on his knees. He grabs one of Moses' hands and big tears start washing down his face. "I...I've heard many a story of you, Moses, how you've led many people to freedom and come back for more. I'm honored to meet you. Boys, come shake the hand of a great person, named after Moses in the Bible, who led his people to the Promised Land."

Moses shakes the hands of the little boys. They look at him with big round eyes. They know the Bible story.

"Now then, you get up off your knees. Moses is what some folks call me, but I'm just plain Harriet...Harriet Tubman. I'm here to help y'all get further up North to safety."

She takes off her broad-brimmed hat, unwinds the bandanna and smiles at the astonished group. Standing before them, holding a rifle, is a commanding woman. Jinx and Max feel an immediate sense of relief; someone else is here to take charge.

They see an oval face with a huge scar on her forehead, soft brown eyes and brown curls. For the second time on their journey, Max and Jinx have been totally tricked by a woman dressed as a man to fool the authorities.

They remember Poppy's words of encouragement: *"Miracles happen all the time. Angels walk amongst us, just ask them for help."*

Chapter Twenty-three

Wanted–Dead or Alive

The group stays in the safety of the cave through the next day, resting and talking. They send the horses out to a meadow in the woods to graze. Petey and Poppy make their rounds, sleeping in different laps and being petted and spoiled lovingly.

Harriet tells them about Frank getting word to her of the two white children with the two little Negro boys, and how she decided to check on them and help them go North if they needed her help. They assure her that her help is desperately needed. This is the first time Max and Jinx actually feel their trip will be successful, and that they can do a bit of leaning on someone else for support. They marvel again at the organization of an Underground Railroad that runs from deep in the South all the way to Canada.

They can't risk building a campfire to heat food for fear the smoke will attract someone to the cave, so the group eats the crackers and jerky Jinx has bought.

"Miss Harriet, how did you get that big mark on your head?" asks a curious Eddie. The very evident sign of an old injury has bothered him.

"Hush now, Eddie. That ain't polite to mention Miss Harriet's scar," says Papa.

Harriet gives a soft laugh. "That's all right, Alem. It makes for a good story. Would you boys like to hear it?"

Eddie and Henry nod their heads, grinning, and they scoot closer to sit in front of Harriet.

"When I was 'bout fourteen or fifteen years old, I was in town with the mistress one day. Well, it happened that I heard a commotion in the store, so Miss Nosey Me goes in to see what was happenin'. It seems a runaway from my farm had gone into the store to beg for some food, and the overseer was already in there and recognized that runaway. He grab that poor slave man by both arms and shook him 'til his teeth rattled. Guess what happened?" says Harriet.

"You got in a fight with the bad man?" Henry guesses.

"That's close. That overseer, he shouted at me to help tie up that runaway slave. But I run right up to that overseer and shoved *him*. 'You let him go. Don't you hurt him,' I said. I pushed him a hard one, let me tell you. He lost his grip, and the runaway took off for the door," says Harriet.

"Then what happened? Did the bad man hit you?" Eddie asks.

"Quick as a flicker that overseer picked up a heavy weight from beside the scales on the store counter, and he heaved it with all his might at the runaway. 'You stop him, stop him **now**!' he ordered me. But I was already backin' up, ready to run away, too. Instead of hittin' the runaway man, it hit me smack on the forehead. Put this big dent in my ol' hard head and knocked me clean out. When I come to, I was home in my own bed with my mama prayin' for me. I almost didn't make it. That's a true story."

Eddie takes Harriet's hand. "I'm sorry, Miss Harriet. That must have hurt awful bad. You were so brave to help the runaway."

"I still get some bad headaches and have some blackout periods, too. But I guess I knowed then it was my duty to help my people escape from slavery. I pray for that runaway and hope he made it to freedom," Harriet finishes softly.

Jinx moves over and sits beside Harriet and takes her other hand. "I know about those terrible headaches. I...get them, too, when I have really vivid dreams about bad things that have happened."

Harriet looks into Jinx's eyes and nods wisely. "I sensed we has some things in common, Miss Jinx. We both has duties to help people, don't we?" She squeezes Jinx's hand gently.

Max and Alem move over to the cave opening to watch the sunset. It is a glorious one, with reds, oranges and yellows. The low clouds are backlit with golden light. They urge the others to come see it.

Miss Harriet begins to plan for the night. "We've got to try to pick up your JoJo before I lead you to the state border," she says. Max has already told the others and Harriet the story of Doc Alex and JoJo's family.

Harriet knows many of the plantations in the area. "Where is he, Master Max?"

"At a plantation named River Bend," Max says.

Alem gets a startled look in his eyes. "Oh, Master Max, if only we'd known last night...that's my home plantation. You was so close to him..."

Max lets his head fall back and closes his eyes. He gives a heavy sigh. "It's my fault. I always look at one detail at a time, and I forget to look at the big picture. I never thought to ask the name of your plantation. I remembered it by the owner's name of Young."

"It's no one's fault, Max," Jinx says.

Harriet snaps into action. "I know the way back real good. I'd like Miss Jinx to come with me. We's both small and can slip in and out fast with the boy."

Jinx nods her head, glad Harriet has entrusted her with the plan.

"We'll have to take Dot and Thunder. It's not all that far. We should be able to git back and continue on our way later tonight. Maybe we'll even git to the next safe house tonight," says Harriet.

The dark is coming fast. Max goes out of the cave and takes a good look around. Then he whistles through his fingers for the horses. It's not long before they hear them trot out of the woods. Max pats them both on their smooth necks.

"Is it time to go?"

"We're tired of waiting."

"The meadow grass was delicious."

"No one saw us, we kept hiding."

Both Dot and Thunder are full of pep and very chatty after their restful day. Max and Jinx get Dot's saddle and bridle and start to prepare her for the secret trip back to Alem's plantation. Max saddles up Thunder.

He helps Jinx and Harriet mount, after giving Jinx a big hug. "Go get 'em, partner," he says.

Jinx has become a good horseback rider. She gives Dot a gentle kick with her booted heels and off they go, back into the woods. Harriet leads the way astride Thunder. Tonight they have no moonlight to show the way; the sky is cloudy. The birds are at roost, but they startle a few rabbits and a fox and send them scrambling as they wend their way through the underbrush amongst the dense trees.

Harriet gives some soft directions when needed. She and Jinx ride close together where the path allows. She asks Jinx a question.

"Miss Jinx, you mentioned 'bout your headaches when you have certain dreams. Are they like visions of things to happen in the future?"

Jinx hesitates, not sure about how much she should tell Harriet. "Yes, they are visions, but usually about things that have happened in the past."

"Ah, yes, I see. Mine are of things to come. They help me know how to help my people. So, we's sisters of a sort. That's a good thing," Harriet murmurs.

"I like it that we can understand and share something together," says Jinx. "My Aunt Merry understands what I go through, also. She helps me a great deal when I'm...home."

"I sense you's very far from home," Harriet says. But she ends the conversation at that point.

It seems to take longer than it did before until they finally approach the River Bend Plantation. Tonight it looks familiar to Jinx. She points out the big barn.

"Max went in behind the big barn to the slave cabins. He said he threw some pebbles in a back window of one of the cabins and talked with them about Henry...I mean Alem."

Harriet directs Jinx to go for JoJo. "Miss Jinx, I believe you need to go get JoJo. I'll stay here with Dot."

Jinx nods, taking a deep breath. She suddenly realizes how easy it has been to let Max be in charge. *Time to do my part,* she thinks.

Jinx slips down off of Dot and gives the mare a rub on her long nose. Dot bobs her head in thanks, knowing it is important for her to be a very quiet horse right now.

"Miss Harriet?" Jinx says.

"Yes'm?"

"I know my job is to get JoJo, but...what about all the others I'm leaving behind? I feel so guilty," Jinx whispers. "They all need to come with me to freedom, right now." She lowers her head because she knows this is impossible.

Harriet places her finger under Jinx's chin and gently lifts her head. "Now, now, Miss Jinx, the time has to be right. There's thinkin' and plannin' needed before anyone goes for freedom. You knows that. It's JoJo's time to run for it, and you're part of the plan, so you git goin', gal."

Jinx nods, feeling instantly better. She crouches low and runs through the long grass to the back of the barn. She listens, but hears nothing except the thudding of her heart and a rushing sound in her ears. *It's only my bad nerves,* she thinks. Jinx gives herself a pep talk. *You can do this!* Jinx darts looks all around; then she runs for the slave cabins.

She approaches a group of cabins from the rear and hides behind the first one. She's breathing heavily, trying to calm her nerves. Jinx decides to try Max's plan and looks around for a few pebbles. No window. She moves to the next one. Ah, good, there is a little window. Jinx tosses a pebble. Right away a head appears.

"Now who's there? Can't a family rest their tired bones without bein' disturbed every night?" A weary head peers out at her.

Jinx guesses this is the cabin that Max bothered last night. She bites her lip to keep a nervous laugh from boiling out. "Please, one last time. Do you know a boy named JoJo, about ten years old?"

The person sees it is a white girl this time. He scratches his chin and shakes his head. "You one brave girl," he says. "The Boss Man is real mad that Henry disappeared again. And they finally got that boy, JoJo, back after his whole family run away. Now you want to make more trouble takin' him back? My, my, it gonna be a bad day tomorrow."

"Where is he? Please?" Jinx asks.

"You knows I'm gonna get the stick fer helpin' you, don't you, gal?" he says.

Jinx hadn't thought of this; now she feels horrible. *There's no easy way to do this,* she thinks. *Now what should I do?*

The man disappears for a moment, and Jinx thinks he has abandoned her. She turns to go back to Miss Harriet, when she hears a scrambling at the back window. A thin form drops to the ground and hugs her with all his might. It's JoJo.

"There he is, Miss. And God help you if Boss Man finds y'all. He's plannin' on goin' out with a band of men and hounds to search tomorrow, real early. They's puttin' a poster out, too, with a reward on Henry's head. Wanted, dead or alive. I jus' hope I can bear the whippin' for lettin' this boy go. But rather me gettin' the whip than a little ten-year-old boy. Good luck." The back window flap slaps closed once more.

Chapter Twenty-four

Safe House

The group has grown to seven people now with the addition of JoJo–too many for the two horses to carry. Their speed has been drastically reduced. It is decided to pack the horses with provisions and have the three boys ride.

The others want Alem to ride, also, because his injuries are far from healed. Besides the horrible stripes on Alem's back that are still bleeding, his ankles are raw and infected from the rusty cuffs that he had to wear day and night.

"No, please, I can walk fine. Let the women ride," Alem says.

Jinx goes to him and takes his hand. "Alem, you need to let us take care of you right now. You need to rest and heal. The lotion that I have to put on your sores can't work if you won't take care of yourself."

"Papa, the quilt say to keep goin' North 'til we find a house with four acorn trees in front of it. That's a safe house. If we can make it there tonight, we can all rest again. They might have more medicine that can help you," little Henry says.

"Yes, please, Papa, ride with us," says Eddie. They are so afraid of losing their father again. Gentle Dot bobs her head and nickers. So Papa hops up on Dot's broad back with his boys.

"The boys is right about the house with the acorn trees," Harriet says. "That sound like Miss Beth's safe house to me. I knows exactly where she lives. She welcome us, for sure."

It is settled. They head North, back into the woods to the middle of a stream. Harriet knows the way to the next safe house and heads the group with confidence. They walk at a brisk pace, leading the horses.

JoJo holds Poppy in his lap, sitting astride Thunder. He strokes her soft fur as she purrs deep in her chest. She softly repeats to JoJo her good news about angels walking amongst them. JoJo smiles and nods his head.

"I knows, Poppy. An' Miss Harriet is our angel," JoJo whispers in Poppy's ear. Poppy twitches her ear and gives JoJo's arm a lick with her scratchy tongue.

Petey runs on ahead, scouting the path. He returns often to report that all is clear.

Max talks with Harriet as they slosh through the cold water. "This is really how most of the runaways make their way to freedom, isn't that right? They walk the path through woods and swamps by night and hide by day. Most don't even have a horse or a guide, do they?"

"That's right, Master Max. Their thirst for freedom is so strong they run without shoes on their feet and with only the clothes they wear on their backs. They is so beaten down, they finally run without one clue where to go or how to get North to freedom. Often they fail. But word 'bout how to go North is spreadin'."

"I've been up North and back South a number of times leadin' my people, and I'm gettin' to know the paths and the safe houses open to runaways. You has to know the signals and signs to look for."

"I know some signs to look for," says JoJo. "Maybe a lantern lit and hung on a fence post, or maybe a quilt folded over the fence. Mama was so afraid to run, but Papa kept pushin' and plannin'. I...I was scared, too. I see things, like I told Master Max. It come true, didn't it? I saw my family 'round the supper table, but I wasn't there."

Max reaches up and pats JoJo on the leg. "And what did I tell you?"

JoJo grins at Max in the dark. "You said Doc Alex and you and Jinx wouldn't let that happen. You'd watch out for me. That's what kept me goin'. Too bad I was fast asleep the first time you come to that window. I woulda knowed your voice in a flash, Master Max."

"Well, we've got you now," Jinx says. "And we'll go with you the whole way to Canada. This will be the biggest walk Max and I have ever taken, right, Max?"

Miss Harriet encourages the boys, impressed with their knowledge. "You boys is ready to reach freedom, umm hmm. You learned your lessons right good about how to be safe. Never forget to watch out, though, every minute you're on the trail North, 'cause them slave catchers is good trackers. Your job is to stay one step ahead."

The low chatter helps to pass the time. Sometimes the walkers take a break for a while and hop up on one of the horses with the boys. They walk, and walk, and walk some more, on through the night. When they come to some swampy marshes, Harriet leads them right into the mud.

"Harder for the hounds to track you if you stay in the streams and swamps," she warns.

The swamps are terribly humid and filled with biting insects. Thick, ropey vines twist around trees and low vegetation, making the way through difficult. Tall, old cypress trees pop right up out of the water. Scum wraps around their feet and legs, and more than once they hear the splash of some critter sliding into the water. Max and Jinx both worry about alligators and water moccasins biting them.

Poor Jinx must have the same bruises and open blisters on her feet as I do, Max thinks. *But she doesn't complain one little bit about her own problems. She's always looking out for everyone else.*

Alem finally falls asleep from exhaustion, with his arms wrapped tightly around Eddie and Henry. His big head nods to the beat of the horse's legs plodding steadily onward.

Near dawn, Harriet halts them at a woods' edge. In a small clearing sits a pretty farmhouse and a small barn. They can see four trees planted in a group.

"This is it, the safe house," Harriet says. "See—a dim lantern swingin' on the fence post, almost out of oil after the long night."

Max says, "I'll go to the door; wait back here, everyone."

But Jinx says firmly, "I'll go. It's my turn." She looks towards Harriet, who smiles and nods at her young friend.

Jinx and Petey take off across the clearing to the four trees. She almost skids and falls when her feet hit what feels like marbles. Jinx's tired mind can't imagine what this many marbles are doing under the trees. Then she realizes what they really are and laughs. "Marbles... Petey, I can't believe I thought someone booby-trapped the safe house with marbles under the trees."

"*Acorns, silly,*" Petey says.

A faint pink shows in the eastern sky. Jinx can hear a rooster: *cock-a-doodle-doooooo.* She also realizes the cows in the barn have been mooing. The side door to the little farmhouse opens, and a woman carrying a lantern hurries towards the barn. Jinx figures she is going out to milk the cows. *I don't want to scare her,* she thinks.

"Petey, go to her, little guy. Let her know we're here," Jinx says softly.

Petey scampers over near the barn to the woman and gives a little bark. She stops in amazement.

"Why, what are you doing out this early, little dog?" The woman looks around. "Do you have a master?"

Petey keeps yipping and making little runs towards the woods, then back to the woman again. Jinx can hear him saying, "*Yes, yes... we're here. We need help at your safe house. Back here in the woods...*" But of course all the lady hears is, "*Yip, yip...yip, yip, yip.*"

With her lantern held high, the woman turns and looks towards her four acorn trees.

"Is someone there?" she says.

"Yes, please, I have a delivery...a load of...of potatoes?" Jinx tries out some of the secret code. *If the lady thinks I'm crazy, I won't know what to do.*

The woman peers into the lantern light, searching for the person who goes with the voice. She walks over, finding Jinx. "You poor, dear child. You looks exhausted. Lead me to 'em," says the lady.

Jinx sees a friendly, black face smiling at her in the lantern light. "My name is Jinx...well, Margaret is my given name, but I prefer Jinx," she says, relieved.

The gentlewoman's smile broadens, and she follows Jinx to the woods' edge to meet her load of potatoes. If she is surprised at the size of the group, she doesn't show it. "Come, dear people. Follow me in the side door. I'll take care of y'all. You've reached the right place."

The woman sees Harriet then, and becomes even more excited. "Miss Harriet, it's so good to see you again. I can't wait to hear 'bout your adventures. We'll leave the horses in the barn on the way. I'll rub 'em down and feed 'em when I get to the cows. Ol' Bossy won't be happy to wait any longer, but we'll have some good, creamy milk for breakfast. Oh, I'm Beth, for those who don't know me." She fills the silence with her soothing chatter.

Henry steps up. "I'm Henry, and this is Max, and JoJo, and my twins, Little Henry and Eddie. We're lookin' for some help along the path to freedom, Miss."

"I think y'all came to the right place," Miss Beth says.

"Thanks so much for your offer about the horses, but I think I have enough strength left to take care of them. Jinx, care to help me?" Max says.

"You bet, partner." She wants to tell him about the wanted posters. They watch the others go into the house. Both teens sigh with relief. Safe for the time being, they hope.

They turn and look at each other. "We haven't had much time alone since we started the trip," Max says. "I'm used to talking with you, bouncing ideas off each other."

"I feel the same way, Max." Jinx finds a big horse brush and starts to work on Dot. Max gives Thunder a good brushing while he listens.

"You need to know what I found out when Harriet and I picked up JoJo. Harriet already knows about this. The family who had him was in the same cabin where you asked about Alem; talk about co-incidence. JoJo says he never heard your voice. The man wasn't too happy about being disturbed by pebbles at his window two nights in a row." Jinx says.

Max laughs. "You're kidding me; what are the chances JoJo would be at the same place? So what did you find out?"

"The Boss Man must have gotten into big trouble for losing Alem again. He's being sent out at daybreak to begin a search. They're getting a posse together with men and hounds and sending out wanted posters, and they put a huge reward on Alem's head."

Max pauses from his brushing and stares at Jinx. "It's a good thing you found out about that. We'll tell Harriet. I guess we need to tell Alem, also. It'll upset him, but knowing about the wanted posters will help us all to be extra vigilant."

He finds some folded horse blankets in a pile, so they cover Dot and Thunder and lead them to some empty stalls. Jinx finds a barrel of oats with a small feeding bucket sitting nearby. She places some feed in their troughs.

"Ahh, great rubdown. Felt good after our long trip," says Dot.

"I'm starving, snort, snuffle..." says Thunder, with his mouth full. *"Thanks for the chow."*

"Now Thunder, use your manners, no talking with your mouth full," says the ever-gentle Dot.

Another horse whinnies his welcome.

"Hello, friends. Glad to meet you. Where'd you come from?" says the handsome brown stallion from a stall further back in the barn.

Jinx and Max give their horses a goodbye rub on their velvety noses and walk from the barn to the house. They notice the shades are all pulled down tight so not a crack of light shows from within.

The sun is on the horizon, and birds are chattering and swooping around on their morning search for bugs and worms. The day will be clear and sunny.

The kitchen is warm and comfortable. The group sits on benches around the big wooden kitchen table and talks to Beth about their journey. The three boys are so tired, they keep nodding off into their arms laid on the table.

Beth has the woodstove going full blast with iron griddles on each burner. Bacon sizzles and spits, grits bubble in a pan, and eggs stand in a bowl waiting to be cracked over another griddle and cooked. She pours hot coffee for the adults, who cradle the big, warm mugs in their hands.

Beth is a large woman with skin as dark as a black coffee bean. Her graying hair is pulled neatly to the back of her head, but wisps of fluffy hair have already pulled loose and frame her face. She wears a long, plain dress covered with her kitchen apron. Even though Beth is aging, she has strong hands and a straight back.

"My husband Mitchell, God rest his soul, passed on last winter. We been freed from slavery many years back. It's a lot a hard work to keep our little farm goin', but my grown children lives nearby, and they plants the fields and harvests the crops. I take care of the milkin' and gatherin' eggs in the chicken coop, and I sells the extras at the village market. It works out real good. I been in this farmhouse mosta my life, and I plans to die here, too. But I'm sure not ready to go yet," she laughs.

"It's good of you to help the runaways, Beth," Jinx says. "It must be a constant danger for you and them."

"It's the right thing to do. Mitchell and I got active as a safe house way back when we first got our freedom papers. Miss Harriet, here, she visited a few times now with her special deliveries. Never could understand the thinkin' of some people to hold human bein's in captivity. They seem to think their slaves is happy little families with a roof over their head and food on their tables. That's sugar-coatin' it, if you ask me." She shakes her head slowly, all the while cooking and serving up platters of good food to her guests.

"A course I has to have my freedman papers 'vailable all the time, in case I'm questioned. I could be snatched up and sold Down South quick as a flicker flies. I been lucky, I guess," Beth adds.

The little boys wake up fast when they smell the fragrant aromas of food in front of their noses. They all tuck into their mounds of food after Beth offers a simple blessing to God for delivering these people safely to her doorstep.

"Next step is warm baths and fresh clothes and good sleep for everyone," Beth says. "Nice clothes is important, 'cause if black folks is spied in good clothes they's not quite as likely to be thought of as a runaway. Just makes 'em a little bit safer."

Alem finishes his food and wipes his mouth on a linen napkin. "Thank you for this good food, Miss Beth," he says. "Boys, please give Miss Beth your thanks, jus' like your grandmamma taught you."

All three boys chime in with their thanks and run to give Miss Beth a hug.

"Now, I'm goin' out to milk those cows while y'all get these boys to bed. It'll take some time to heat up water for this group," says Alem.

"Papa, we don't need no baths, really. We don't mind. We's not dirty," says Eddie. JoJo and Henry nod their heads in agreement.

The others laugh at the three boys; all are covered in swamp mess with dried mud on their faces. "Oh yes, everyone gets a bath," says Papa. "Even us big folks'll wash up and be glad for it." He still clutches the torn, dirty blanket around him.

Miss Beth sees the raw welts that wrap around Alem's ribs and the bleeding circles of skin around his dirty feet. She shakes her head at him.

"Mr. Papa, you ain't goin' nowhere 'til you have the first hot bath, and I can treat your wounds. If we don't get them wounds cleaned out, you could get a bad infection, and you know it," Beth says.

"Ha, Papa, you has to get the first bath." The boys tease their papa. He gives in to Beth's wisdom and starts to haul buckets of water to be heated.

After bathing in Epsom salts and scrubbing the grime off of himself from head to toe, Papa dresses in fresh cotton pants. Miss Beth uses vinegar to disinfect the raw wounds on his back and ankles. Papa doesn't even flinch at the stinging of the vinegar. She wraps clean strips of cloth around his back and chest with great care. Then Papa finishes dressing in a new shirt and knitted socks.

Miss Harriet and Beth continue to supervise the heating of those big buckets of water on the stove and getting the boys cleaned up for bed.

Jinx and Max go out to milk the cows. Poppy and Petey follow along, hoping for a little of the fresh milk.

"We're learning all kinds of new things on this trip, right, partner?" Jinx asks, as she tries her hand at pulling on the teats of a cow. Nothing happens, so she pulls harder.

"Ouch, who are you? Obviously don't know how to be gentle, that's for sure," says the cow.

"Sorry," Jinx whispers. She tries a gentler squeeze and is rewarded with a squirt of milk into the bucket.

"Better," says the cow, munching the straw in her feeding trough.

Max chuckles at their private joke of talking animals. He calls Jinx. "Hey, would you look at this?" He milks with two steady hands and fills his first bucket in no time. Jinx looks at him, impressed, until he aims at her and squirts her face.

"Not fair," she says, mopping her face with an arm. "Watch this; ready, Poppy?" She aims a squirt at Poppy, who opens her mouth and laps at the stream of milk. Then she runs back and sits to rub a paw over her face and lick the remains of the milk.

"Where's mine, where's mine?" says Petey. He jumps up and down and does a flip. Jinx shakes her head and grins at his antics and fills a small bowl with the milk.

Miss Beth comes out to help. After they dump the fresh milk into big tins with lids, she shows them the little cooling house built over a brook. They store the milk cans in the cool stone building, standing them in the bubbling, cold spring water until Beth can get the milk to market.

Beth shows them how to pick the green leaves of the watercress plants growing in the cool water, to use in her salads. They each taste a leaf of the crisp plant.

"Tastes a bit like radishes," Jinx says. "A nice little burn on your tongue. I like it." Max agrees.

The sun is up and shines on a beautiful North Carolina fall day. Soon everyone is washed and resting in various beds in the farmhouse. The rest period is brief.

Beth goes about her chores until she spots a horseback rider coming fast. She runs back to the house, ready to act if it is danger approaching. To her relief, the man is a friend and fellow stationmaster on the Underground.

He is out of breath and grim. "Beth, if you have passengers, you need to git them hidden fast. Word from town has it that a slave catcher is headed your way with the sheriff. Someone saw some action over here before sunup."

"Thanks for the warnin', Paul. I'll take care of it." The messenger takes his leave. There is hardly time to spare. Beth runs to the house to awaken the adults.

"Miss Harriet, you and Alem get the boys. You gotta hide in my secret room. Max and Jinx, you play the part of lost folks who stopped for advice. I'll tell 'em you headin' out after a warm meal. I hope to heaven you can act. Now go on, and make up the beds. Mustn't appear that they all been slept in," says Beth. She is calm and in charge and knows what to do.

She gathers the runaways in the kitchen and goes over and opens the pantry doors. Canned goods and other household supplies stand on side shelves. Hooks with coats, sweaters, and aprons are on the back wall. Beth pushes on the back wooden wall. It slides to the side. Everyone is amazed to see another small room, hidden between the walls of the kitchen and sitting room. Alem and Harriet take the boys' hands and lead them into the room.

"Be brave, boys. It'll be very dark in here," says Harriet.

"We can do it, right?" Eddie asks his brother and JoJo. They nod their heads, even though they are scared to death.

Beth slides the wall closed and shuts the pantry doors. "Now, let's put away the breakfast dishes and have some tea, friends," she says to Max and Jinx.

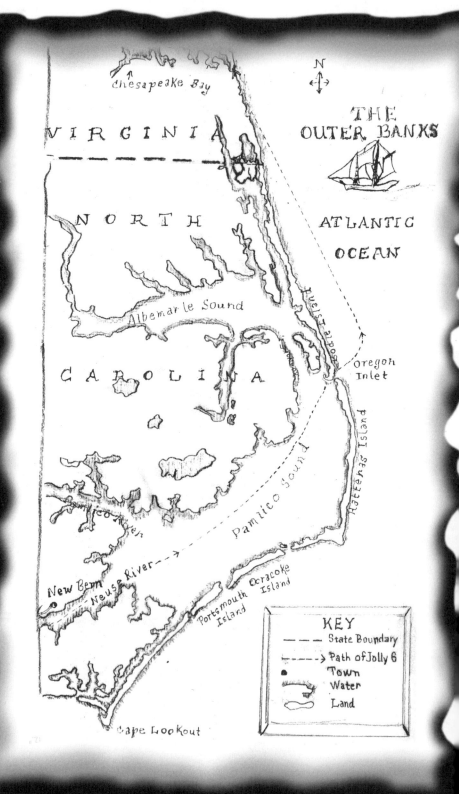

Chapter Twenty-five

The Jolly G

Horses trot in the lane and up to the farmhouse. There is hard pounding at the door. Petey barks, and Poppy jumps out of Beth's lap. They all catch their breath and get ready for a confrontation.

"Open up, Miss Beth, it's the sheriff here," says a gruff male voice.

Beth walks to the door and opens it. "Why, Sheriff Smithson, what brings you out to the farm? Come right in." She stands back as the sheriff and another man enter. The stranger shifts his eyes all around the kitchen, taking in the details.

The sheriff takes off his hat and holds it in his hands. He has red hair and a red beard. His hazel-green eyes look apologetic. He has known Beth and her husband for a long time. But duty calls.

"This here's Alfred Dunn. He's an overseer from a plantation farther south. He's lookin' for some runaways; they're a slave man, name of Henry, and a little slave boy 'bout ten years old called JoJo. They went missin' a day apart, and he thinks they headed up through here together. The man has a price on his head." He drops a wanted poster on Beth's table.

Beth tilts her head and reads the poster with interest. She looks back up at the men, puzzled. "One thousand dollars is a hefty reward. But why would you think they're here?"

The stranger walks closer to Beth. He has a jagged scar across his left cheek and a stubbly growth of a beard. His bad odor almost makes Beth take a step back, but she refuses to back down in front of him.

"Someone spotted some action over here about sunup. Says they saw you with some people and horses. Now what would you be doin' with a group of people that time of day?" says Dunn. "And do you got papers on you, woman?"

"That's 'bout the time you folks stopped in, ain't so, Master Max?" Beth says. "Sheriff, these fine folks got a bit lost and stopped in for directions. And you knows I never sends no one away hungry."

The sheriff nods his head in agreement. "Yes, she got her freedman papers, Dunn. I've knowed her and her husband, God rest his soul, for many a year."

Max and Jinx try to look as innocent and pleasant as possible. Jinx nods her head and smiles, and Max gets up to shake the sheriff's hand. "Hello, sir. Nice to meet you." They all ignore the rude stranger.

"Well then, ya won't mind if I look around, will ya?" asks the stranger. Beth looks at the sheriff, who shrugs his shoulders as if to say it's out of his hands.

"I can't say I likes the thought of a complete stranger pawin' his way through my house, but go ahead. I've nothin' to hide." Beth stares at the stranger until he looks down.

"I'll check the barn," the sheriff says.

Boss Man Alfred Dunn starts in the kitchen, opening the pantry doors, and then he goes through the rest of the rooms, downstairs and upstairs. Beth follows, glaring at him. *Uppity black woman,* Dunn thinks to himself. He finishes by tromping down the basement stairs, then back up. Not happy, but having nowhere left to look, he goes out to the sheriff.

"Nothin' here. I'll be on my way. Gotta get back to the posse," Alfred says. He mounts his horse and waits for the sheriff.

The sheriff walks back in to the porch to say goodbye. "Beth, be careful what you're doin'. I'd hate to ever have to arrest you for breakin' the Fugitive Slave Law. Good day to you," the sheriff says, in a low voice. The sheriff tips his hat, mounts, and rides back towards town with the other man.

Beth hugs both Max and Jinx. "You was perfect. I believe havin' you here saved the day." They wait another hour to make sure the men don't return. Then Beth goes to the pantry and releases the runaways.

Beth and her fugitives have peach pie to celebrate. Even Petey and Poppy lap up a bit of pie and cream.

"Now, everyone, soon time to gather your belongin's. I need to get you movin' on your way. There's a number of plans how to send you on," says Beth.

"Miss Beth, Max and Jinx needs to get on up to Richmond, Virginia," says Harriet. "They want to try to pick up a married couple.

They's slaves who tried to run, but got recaptured. The plantation's called Acorn Acres, outside of Richmond."

Beth looks at Harriet. "Should we move you by boat? It'd be faster than walkin

Harriet thinks about it and checks for everyone's opinions. "Miss Beth has a friend who sails along the coast, fishin' in a large sailboat. Only most of the time his catch is another kind of fish, if you know what I mean. He could get us all the way up to the Baltimore harbor. We could stop off near Richmond along the way. I do think this would be a good way to go."

"That would be wonderful, Miss Beth," Alem says. There is a catch in his voice. He becomes overwhelmed by all of the good people putting their own lives in danger to help him and his family.

Jinx and Max agree. "That's a great way to move more quickly than over land," Max says.

Eddie runs for the quilt. He spreads it out on the kitchen floor and calls everyone over. "Look, this here block tells us to go by boat," he says. His small brown hand points to a beautiful patch with blue waves and a white sailboat. "Granny knew, somehow..."

"Then it's decided. My son told me he's in port now. I'll get word sent ahead to him through my son to wait for y'all. I'll take you there myself, on my milk wagon. I have my normal afternoon deliveries to make, so no one'll question me on the road. But y'all will have to lie flat in the false bottom of the milk wagon for a few hours. It'll be a bumpy ride. Boys, you ready to be sailors?" asks Beth.

The boys are round-eyed and speechless at the thought of traveling in a boat. If it wouldn't be for the constant threat of getting caught, this would be another highlight in their young lives.

Harriet and the other fugitives lie in the false bottom of the milk wagon, sometimes being jostled so hard their teeth rattle. Alem lies on his stomach, his head resting on his arms, to protect his sore back. Jinx and Max ride up top with Beth, holding Petey and Poppy. Thunder and Dot are tied to the rear, and Beth's big brown stallion, Caesar, pulls the wagon with little effort.

Beth stops at a few houses along the way to deliver milk, vegetables and eggs. They arrive at the market in the village of New Bern in the late afternoon.

The Neuse River runs into a finger of the Pamlico Sound here, so the rich odor of fish and salty backwater fills the breeze. Beth guides Caesar down a back alley, off onto a rutted path that leads away from town to a rundown dock.

Max and Jinx see an old two-masted sailboat bobbing in the late-day sun. The name *Jolly G* shows on the side of the wooden boat in faded black paint. No one is about except the seagulls gliding through the air and a large blue heron standing off to one side in the marshy reeds, fishing for its supper.

Beth, Max and Jinx jump down from the wagon. Petey and Poppy travel off through the grasses to explore.

"We're here at the boat. It's almost sundown, and then y'all can come out of hidin'. But we shouldn't risk it yet. Here are some sandwiches and tea for you," says Beth, as she lifts a panel in the false bottom of the wagon to give the group in hiding some fresh air.

The sounds of scrambling, stretching, and a few moans of stiffness fill the air.

"We can manage a bit longer, Miss Beth. Is you all right, boys?" says Alem.

"Yes, Papa, but it's mighty hard. I wanna run as fast as I can," says little Henry. The other boys murmur their assent.

Petey returns and jumps onto the wagon. He wiggles in under the false bottom and crawls over the boys, licking them and tickling them with his soft, furry body. They giggle and hug him, forgetting their woes.

Sundown is another beautiful, rich display of crimsons and purples. Poppy returns with a small fish for her supper. They all freeze when they hear a song being whistled merrily. Two men stride down the path, carrying armloads of bags.

"Why, Miss Beth, I see you've arrived in time for our nightly sail," says a black-bearded giant of a man. He wears trousers tucked into high rubber boots, suspenders and a loose, checkered shirt. A tall Negro man, who is dressed in coarse clothes, a sailor's cap and rubber boots, follows the white man. They also wear broad smiles. When the supplies are loaded into the boat, they quickly return.

The men help the hidden passengers out of the wagon. Beth introduces everyone to the sailors. "Meet Captain Gus and his first mate, Samson," she says. "They'll get you safely up the coast, all the way to Baltimore."

"And this is the *Jolly G*," says Gus. "The G stands for Gus, of course," he roars. Everything is huge about the man, even his voice.

He looks over the strange group of travelers: seven people, a dog, a cat and two horses. He pulls on his black beard and says, "We have Moses with us, I see. And lots of animals...so now I guess I'm about to become Noah. Welcome aboard the ark."

"I want to thank you, Capt'n Gus, for changin' your plans and sailin' North for us," Miss Harriet says. "You've saved the day more than once now, by stealin' away in the night with my runaways."

"Miss Harriet, you know I'll sail you to the moon and back if that's what it takes. You're the bravest woman I know." Captain Gus takes Harriet's small hand into his hands that are as big as hams. Then they all turn to Miss Beth.

It's time to say goodbye to Beth. Some tears are shed as the runaways think about this brave black woman who has saved them once more with her daring acts.

"Now, now, no time for tears. You got miles to go. Best wishes to y'all," Beth says. She hugs them and leaves quickly. She knows they must hurry on their way to safety, and who knows–she may have a load of potatoes at her back door when she gets home.

Harriet helps the boys from the rickety dock, down the plank onto the *Jolly G.* Alem stays behind to help with the horses.

Thunder and Dot have been munching on some of the swamp grasses.

"Not bad, chomp, chomp," says Thunder.

"A bit too salty," Dot adds.

"All right, Thunder, let's get you aboard the boat," Max says.

Thunder stops munching grass and looks from Max to the boat. *"Ohhh, I don't know about this...too much water out there...too deep,"* he worries. He rears up, and then tries to back away.

Jinx tries to calm him. "Thunder, it'll be like the train ride with that nice rocking movement. You won't even get your feet wet," she says.

Thunder shakes his head and snorts, not believing her.

JoJo jumps back up on the dock and takes his shirt off. He gently covers Thunder's eyes and strokes his nose. "Let me help you, Thunder," he whispers into Thunder's ear. "You won't have to look; follow me. I'll take care of you, boy. Come now," he says. He leads Thunder down the ramp into the boat and to the part of the deck covered over with a roof.

Everyone praises JoJo, who grins shyly and puts his head down.

"Such a fuss, Thunder. There's nothing to it," says Dot. She moves down the ramp and into the boat with no trouble. But she goes over to Thunder and rubs his neck with her head, to soothe him.

Petey jumps right into the boat. Poppy takes her time.

"Neither in nor on the water is my favorite place to be," she grumbles. She lifts her paws daintily and walks down the ramp. Once on the deck, she finds a dry space to sit and begins to groom her fur.

A few steps lead down into the cabin at the bow. The cabin is spacious, allowing for sleeping room. There is a small door under a chest that leads to the very belly of the boat. A secret room down there makes a good hiding place for runaways.

Out on the deck are the fishing nets, rolled and stored at the side. Other gear, including some large rods, bait buckets and tackle boxes are stored in racks along the stern. Another trapdoor on the main deck leads to the bottom, where the fish are stored after a big catch.

The sails are tied down to the mast with ropes, but the two sailors now unfurl them and make ready to cast off. The night winds are kicking, perfect for setting sail.

"We'll move night and day if the weather holds," Gus tells them. "Samson and I take turns grabbin' a few hours of sleep. We'll be out in the Pamlico Sound tonight, headin' for the northern Outer Banks. Then tomorrow we'll clear the Outer Banks and head out into the Atlantic coastal waters."

"How 'bout I take my turn in the sound tonight, Capt'n Gus, and you take the *Jolly G* around the islands tomorrow durin' the day? Be more people out on the water tomorrow that might want to know what a black man's doin' with a sailboat. You won't draw no attention," Samson says. He looks at the group.

"Captain Gus, he bought my freedom some years back. He's as good a man and a sailor as you'll ever see," he grins. "We've been runnin' slaves up the coast to freedom for the past few years. Never been stopped yet," he reassures them.

Gus goes into the cabin to get some sleep. The adults want to keep the boys awake until daybreak if they can, so they will sleep during the day. They soon find that is no problem.

"Miss Harriet, will you tell us some more stories about when you was a little girl?" Eddie asks. They all gather around Harriet and get seated on side seats or cushions. The boys take turns holding Petey and Poppy, cuddling them in their laps.

"My life as a little girl was like yours, I expect. I lived in Bucktown, Maryland, with my mother and father. We was slaves on a small farm. I was workin' hard by the time I was six years old. I had to go out on cold days and check those ol' muskrat traps in the icy cold streams, in my bare feet. And those big traps were so hard to pull open. I shivered and shivered all over from the cold.

"One day I remember gettin' myself into double trouble. I was in the farmhouse kitchen. There on the table sat a pretty, blue bowl with sweet, sweet sugar cubes in it. Well, I never tasted sugar, but I wanted one so bad. So I sneaked my hand in that bowl and got one to pop into my mouth. *Ummm,* it was so good; it melted in my mouth. I turned around and guess what?"

"You got caught by the master?" JoJo says.

"Yes sir, there stood Master glarin' at me. But I didn't want to get whipped, so I took off runnin' so fast Master couldn't catch me. Guess where I hid?"

"I know, I know, you hid in the barn, under the hay," says Eddie.

"No, not in the barn," says Harriet.

"How 'bout in the woods?" asks Henry.

"No, not in the woods. I hid in the pigsty, with the dirty pigs and hogs."

"*Oooooooooooh,*" the boys all say, giggling. They try to imagine living with the pigs.

"How long did you hide?" Eddie asks.

"Four days and nights," Harriet says.

"But what did you eat?" asks Henry.

"I ate the slops they threw in for the hogs."

"*Ooooooooooh*," the boys say again.

"Well, finally I decided I better give myself up and take the punishment, because I couldn't stand one more day with the pigs. I was a stubborn little girl, but I knew when to quit. So I went back in to the big house. And I got whipped twice, once for stealin' sugar, and once for runnin' away."

"*Oww,*" JoJo says, rubbing his backside.

Everyone laughs, including Samson, who steers the course through the night water for the sailboat.

"Did you decide then to run for freedom someday, Miss Harriet?" Jinx asks.

"Yes, I made up my mind someday I would be free and never git beaten for anythin' again. But it did teach me honesty; I'll say that. It's never a good idea to steal, boys. That's the lesson for tonight."

The sails snap in the wind, and the sailboat makes its way North. The group lies back to watch the stars. Max takes Jinx's hand and gives it a gentle squeeze. "Next stop–Richmond," he says softly. "We're getting to the end, day by day. Look up there; it's the Drinking Gourd."

The Big Dipper's pointer stars show the way to the North Star, which shines so brightly that night.

Samson starts singing in a beautiful, bass voice:

Follow the drinkin' gourd,
Follow the drinkin' gourd,
For the old man is a-waitin' for to carry you to freedom
If you follow the drinkin' gourd.

Harriet joins in, and soon the rest of the travelers sing along in soft voices, wondering how this journey will turn out.

Chapter Twenty-six

Bad News

Back on land, the night air is crisp and filled with wood smoke drifting from the big house and the small slave cabins on the plantation. It is a chilly, late October night; there will be frost on the pumpkins by morning. Summer crops have been harvested and winter wheat planted. The moon is full and round, and the stars crackle like fireworks.

Three riders, sitting astride Dot and Thunder, stop by the stone bridge that had given the teens shelter from a tornado weeks ago. Miss Harriet, Max and Jinx sit in silence, studying the plantation.

Petey is along as a trusty watchdog. His keen ears can pick up sounds unheard by human ears.

The *Jolly G* waits for their return at a rundown dock outside of Richmond, Virginia. Miss Harriet has guided them inland, where Max and Jinx hope to find their two recaptured friends and get them back to the boat before daylight.

All is quiet and dark. Everyone should be asleep now, so the two time-traveling teens are ready to sneak into the slave-cabin area to search for Jefferson and Janie.

They wonder about their two friends, who were runaways seeking freedom way back when their trip South first started. Have they recovered from the beatings they received when they were caught and brought back to Chester Matthews' Acorn Acres Plantation? Will they want to run to the North again? Did Janie have her baby in captivity, instead of in the freedom that they wanted so badly? They are excited to see them again.

The rest of their freedom-seeking group is back on board the *Jolly G*, waiting for their return. This will be the last stop in the South to rescue people, and Max and Jinx want the attempt to go well. Then they will sail on up to Baltimore, so close to Pennsylvania and freedom.

"Okay, Max, ready or not, here we go," Jinx whispers. Petey jumps down from Dot's saddle and runs ahead. They tie the horses to a nearby tree branch, give them pats, and the three slip into the shadows of trees and outbuildings close to the slave quarters.

Miss Harriet holds them back with her arm extended. "Never rush into it," she cautions. "You don't know when the slave driver might be makin' some night rounds, 'specially if there's been a Negro that run recently. He'd be real cautious that no other slaves try to run, 'cause the master'd be mighty unhappy with him."

Max nods his understanding. They lie in wait behind a cove of trees for more than an hour, but it appears that no one is making rounds this night. They decide to go on to the cabins.

Harriet motions for them to stop at the rear of a cabin in the middle of the group. She goes around and raps on the side of the cabin; then she peeks her head around so she can see the front door. A person comes to the door and pushes it open. A man sticks his head out to see who is there. He gives a puzzled look when he sees Harriet.

Before he can speak, Harriet says, "Please, we're looking for a couple named Jefferson and Janie. She was expecting a baby. Do you know them?"

The man lowers his head. He gives a large sigh and says, "Wait, I'll come around back." The window closes, and he soon joins them.

He is a middle-aged man, thin as a stick, with stooped shoulders from years of bending over in the fields. His curly dark hair is mixed with gray. He looks even more confused and concerned when he sees Max and Jinx.

Petey licks the slave's hand in greeting. His face is filled with the sorrow that comes from seeing bad things and feeling years of suffering.

Max and Jinx exchange a look of foreboding. Something feels very wrong.

"I'm sorry to tell ya'll the bad news. Jefferson and Janie...well, they met with real rough times. Janie never did recover from that whippin' she got for runnin'. It brought on her baby too soon, and the poor little thing didn't have a chance. Janie and her baby died from complications soon after.

"Jefferson, he went wild with sorrow after he lost Janie. One day he put down his tools in the fields and run. The Boss Man ordered him to stop, but Jefferson kept on runnin.' He wouldn't stop for nothin'.

So Boss Man shot him dead. He didn't need to shoot him that many times, but he's a mean one. Now they's both gone. But they have their freedom now, up above with the good Lord." He points skyward and shakes his head.

Jinx and Max don't know what to say. Finally, Max says, "Thank you for speaking with us. We're friends, and we hoped to help them..."

The man nods and says, "No one's runnin' right now. They put on extra guards, 'specially at night. So be careful when you leave. They's makin' rounds, out around the back fields. You's good people; thanks for carin'. " He slips away, back into his cabin.

"I was afraid they'd be watchin' real close," Harriet says. She sees how devastated the teens are and pats their shoulders. "Come now, ain't no more you can do here. I'm real sorry 'bout your friends, but we need to get goin'. Not safe around here tonight." She looks with great concern around the perimeter of the dark cabins.

Max rubs his forehead, and Jinx feels tears sliding down her cheeks. But there is no time to grieve. They must get out of here without being caught. Petey leads the way through the shadows again, back toward the horses. *"Grrrrrrr..."* Sudden growling from Petey warns them of danger.

The dark shape of a man on foot runs from the front of a building at the edge of the property. "Who's there? Stop...Stop, I say..." There is a blast from a shotgun.

Petey leaps and knocks Jinx down to the ground, then yelps in pain. *"Yip, yip, hurts...,"* he says, as he crumples to the ground.

Max scoops Petey up, grabs Jinx's hand and drags her to her feet. They tear off, running for the horses; the man runs after them, yelling at them to stop.

Another man farther away on horseback rides towards the action, shouting and firing his shotgun into the air. A few heads poke out of slave cabins, then quickly disappear back inside.

The teens and Miss Harriet reach the horses and mount. Max feels an iron grip close on his ankle. He kicks the man, trying to break loose. The man cries out in pain when Max boots him in the face, and he falls to the ground. Thunder and Dot streak away, galloping with all their might. The man on horseback gallops after them, shouting for them to stop.

They run the horses for miles, trying to lose the other rider. Miss Harriet, holding on to Dot's reins, has them zigzag in and out of woods and streams, behind rocks and finally back to the swamp. Jinx can barely hold on to Harriet's waist. By the time they reach the swamp, they have lost the guard from the plantation. Harriet has them pull up, way back in dense trees and underbrush.

Jinx almost falls off Dot and sinks into the mud in her haste to reach Max and Petey. She gently takes Petey from Max, her heart thudding and dread filling her chest like concrete.

She sees blood on the front of Max's shirt from holding Petey against him.

"Petey, Petey..." is all she can say. She cuddles the little dog's still form, terrified that he is dead. Blood covers her fingers. "Max..."

Max dismounts from Thunder, and they put Petey on a blanket on solid ground. Max places his ear against Petey's chest and detects a fast pitter-patter. "He's alive, Jinx. His heartbeat is strong. I think he was hit with some buckshot. Here, in his side and back leg."

Petey opens his eyes and sees his best friends' worried expressions. *"Okay, but it hurts,"* he says, and then closes his big brown eyes again.

Harriet tears a scrap from her dress and dips it in the nearby water to clean Petey's wounds.

"We have to get him to a vet or doctor or someone. He took that buckshot for me; he knocked me down to keep me safe," Jinx says.

"Petey's a good dog, a hero," says Harriet. "I know a doctor in town who helped me before when one of my runaways got shot. We'll go there. I know he's a good man. He'll take care a your little Petey, for sure. Let's saddle up."

They wrap Petey in a blanket and mount up again to head back to Richmond. Jinx holds her best friend close with one arm, the other around Harriet's waist.

The horses are upset about their little friend.

"He's such a brave dog," Dot says.

"We'll get him help fast. Count on us," says Thunder.

The teens feel dazed by all of the night's bad news about their slave friends and Petey being shot. They don't speak again except to urge the horses on towards town and help for their little buddy.

Near morning, they ride into town and stop in a dark alley. "Now look for a sign that says *Joseph Small, MD.* Tell him Miss Harriet sent you," Harriet tells them. "I'll ride Dot back to the *Jolly G.* It'll be safer for us all if I'm not seen with you come daybreak. You think y'all can find the way back out to the old dock?"

Max and Jinx nod. "We'll see you there, Miss Harriet. Thank you for helping us tonight. What would we have done if you hadn't been with us?" Jinx says.

Harriet smiles. "Everything will be fine, y'all will see," she says. She turns Dot around and heads out of the alleyway and back to the safety of the swamp.

Max and Jinx knock until the sleepy doctor comes to the door. "Miss Harriet sent us to you. Our dog has been shot and needs help. Please sir, will you look at him?" Jinx says.

The doctor takes immediate action. "Come in, come in. When Miss Harriet calls for help, I don't waste any time–I know it's important." He ushers them into a side patient room where they can place Petey on comfortable towels. Then the doctor hustles back out to prepare for surgery.

Max and Jinx lean over the table that holds Petey, stroking his face and ears. Around him lie various little knives and tweezers and a basin of warm water. Petey rests on a clean towel, only opening his eyes once in a while to whimper softly.

The doctor comes in with a little cup of liquid and a clean cloth. He doesn't match his name. Dr. Small is a very large man with a round belly and red cheeks. He is a pleasant man, and he assures the teens that Petey will be fine.

"So, was this cute little bugger out raiding someone's chicken coop?" says Dr. Small.

Here we go again, thinks Max, *more lies and secrets and hiding*. "Well, sir, he sure was out somewhere, exploring I guess. Someone fired buckshot at him." He glances at Jinx, and she nods, giving her friend a tiny smile.

"It's all right; I know Miss Harriet gets into some tight spots. No one has to know about this. You're safe with me. Now, young lady, I need you to dip this cloth into the liquid and hold it to your pup's nose. It's chloroform; it'll put him under so he won't feel the pain of me digging those pieces of lead out of his side. Basically a new thing, chloroform is. It was invented a few years back, and it comes in real handy for surgery. That's right–good job." He watches Jinx hold the chloroform close to Petey's nose.

Jinx can smell the sweetness of the chloroform and wishes she could take a big whiff herself and go to sleep for a long while, away from all of the sadness. But instead, she sighs and continues to pet her dog's soft ears. Petey sighs, too, and slips into deep sleep.

The doctor shaves Petey's right side and rear leg with lather and a straight blade so he can see the entrance wounds better. "Ah, there we go, looks like four or five pieces got him. Not so bad after all," says Dr. Small. He cuts a bit and prods with tweezers. The lead shot makes little clinks when the doctor puts them into a small metal bowl.

"There, I think I got them all. He's a lucky dog that he didn't take a full blast. Then he'd be in trouble." Dr. Small cleans the wounds again with antiseptic and wraps a soft, cloth bandage around Petey's sides and back leg. He looks like a little mummy.

He hands Max the remaining bandage and a small bottle of pills for pain. "If he seems to be in pain, give him the tiniest bit of one pill twice a day. This is strong stuff; be careful with it. But he's a terrier; they're tough little dogs. Terriers don't let anything slow them down for long, right?" He chuckles.

"Thank you, Dr. Small. We really appreciate you taking the time to see Petey," Jinx says.

"What do we owe you, Doctor?" Max says.

"Oh, twenty-five cents for materials should do it," says Dr. Small.

Dr. Small goes over to a sink and washes his hands. Turning back to the two, he shakes their hands. "Well, glad I could help you. I keep a few Jack Russell terriers myself–great hunting dogs. Try to keep him down and resting a few days. He'll be back to normal soon. Good luck to you."

Jinx wraps the patient up in a blanket, and they take a sedated Petey back out to the horses. "I'm starving," she says, surprised that she can even think of food after last night's adventures.

"Me, too. Let me go order some food at the inn. We'll eat on their porch. You can sit on one of the rockers in the sun. I'll see if they have some apples for Thunder, too."

Jinx sits in the autumn sunshine and rocks Petey as if he is a baby. His sweet eyes are closed, and he sighs in his sleep. Her tired mind tries to process the events that have happened. Max soon joins her, with ham and eggs on brown bread and some tin cups of tea for breakfast. They lay Petey gently in the sun on the wooden porch between them.

"I'm anxious to get away from here and back to the *Jolly G,*" Max says. He avoids speaking about last night. They eat for a bit, silent.

Petey awakens, sniffs the food, but falls asleep again. "Poor little guy," Max says. "He's not even hungry–unusual for him."

"Max, I need to talk about what happened last night," Jinx says, getting teary-eyed. She takes a big gulp of tepid tea. "Why did that have to happen to Jefferson and Janie? They were innocent, decent people. They deserved so much better."

Max swallows his bite of sandwich. "I know," he says softly. He looks at Jinx, his best friend, sitting on the porch of some inn in 1851 Virginia, in a bedraggled dress and scuffed boots. He ducks his head and smiles.

"What?" Jinx says.

"Poor Jinx...there you sit in your dirty dress, like some time-traveling vagabond. I can tell you're upset. You haven't even mentioned your precious Phillies trying to reach the playoffs."

"That's right, I wonder how they're doing. Hope they're beatin' your Mets." She starts laughing with Max, harder and harder, until she dissolves into sobs. Max pats her hand.

"I needed that," Jinx says finally, feeling much better. She dives into the rest of her food.

Max gets up and feeds apples to Thunder. Thunder takes a large drink from a public watering trough. *"How's Petey? He looks bad, all wrapped up like that,"* Thunder says.

Max rubs Thunder's nose. "He's all fixed up, Thunder. Your friend will be stiff and sore for a while, but he'll soon be back to normal."

Max turns to Jinx. "You know your question about Jefferson and Janie? I wonder, too. I don't think there is an answer to why two good people had to die in that tragedy. Why did any of this slavery happen? Why do wars happen? Why does bad stuff happen to good people? It's the way of the world. As Time Travelers, called back to help people in history, we've been pretty lucky. This is the first time we've lost someone. That's really tough to accept, Jinx. But it's not possible to save everyone. I know we want to, but real life doesn't work that way." Max rubs his throbbing forehead.

"You're right, of course. But we have to try, right?" says Jinx.

"Right, partner. Now, we have some other really good people waiting for us, so let's get going." Max picks up the bundle of Petey and holds him until Jinx gets mounted, then he hands him off.

He mounts and turns their horse to the road out of town. They travel the remaining miles out to the countryside and into the marshes to find the old dock where the *Jolly G* awaits their return.

Wanted Dead or Alive

Large Bounty-$1000-on the Head of
Runaway Slave
Goes by Name of Henry
Very Dark Negro Man
Medium Tall
Ears Stick Out
Back of Hands Scarred
Owned by Arthur Young
River Bend Plantation, North Carolina

Two men stand across the street, hiding behind a horse and buggy that are tied up at a hitching post. "I can't believe it's them two kids again," says Jackson Merryweather to his sidekick, Billy. "They're everywhere, up and down the coast. They're definitely stinkin' abolitionists, helpin' runaways." He pulls a folded wanted poster out of his coat pocket.

"I wonder..." says Billy, as he looks at the poster they ripped from the wall of a storefront. "Sounds like that slave we captured from them kids more than a month ago. Tall, dark guy, ears stuck out; he musta escaped again. Think they've got him hidden somewhere?"

Jackson's snake-like eyes watch the teens. "It'll be worth followin' them. Let's get back to the livery stable for the horses now, before they leave. Hurry..." The men turn down the side alley and begin to run.

By the time they return to the main street, there is no trace of the teens and their horse.

"Drat it all," Jackson says. "They gave us the slip. But we found them once, and we can find them again. That slave'll be worth big money now, dead or alive. Sounds like the owner has had it with that slave runnin' all the time. This should be fun." He rubs his hands together.

"I like your thinkin'," Billy says, chortling in glee. "Let's get trackin'."

They smack their horses and gallop out of town. Both nasty men are sure they can find their prey, earn some money, and have lots of fun doing it.

Chapter Twenty-seven

The Trial

It's a cold November evening aboard the *Jolly G*. The boat is in the upper Chesapeake Bay, close to Baltimore. Spirits are high. The voyage has been a good one, with only one day of stormy weather that had the travelers seasick.

Petey is now up and limping around, proudly showing his healing wounds to everyone. He is the star and hero of the day. Even Poppy follows him around and fusses over him. His fur is growing out in little clumps, and he keeps scratching at the wounds.

"Petey, no, you'll scratch the wounds open," whispers Jinx.

"*They're itchy,*" Petey says.

That is a good sign he is healing, Jinx thinks.

"*Peter, I think you're up too soon. You must rest more. Those were very nasty wounds—I am extremely concerned for your recovery,*" Poppy says.

"*Thanks, Poppy. I'm glad you're my friend,*" Petey says.

"*Well, I do care about you, very much,*" Poppy says, a bit embarrassed to be admitting how afraid she really has been of losing her friend. Petey doesn't know that Poppy stayed by his side, day and night, until he started to improve.

Thunder complains to Jinx and Max about wanting to be on dry ground for good, while gentle Dot sleeps most of the time. Poppy keeps the boat free of mice and rats that seem to hop onboard whenever they make a short stop at another hidden dock to pick up hay and oats and supplies.

Captain Gus calls the travelers to come see the city in the dim light. "We're close to Baltimore. I'll soon be droppin' y'all off. Then it's only a short journey by land to the Pennsylvania border."

The group cheers. Captain Gus and his mate Samson have gotten them to Baltimore in days instead of the weeks it would have taken them by foot.

"We can use the Freedom Quilt to help us again," says young Henry. Alem hugs his son.

"You and Eddie tell the folks about some of the other patches on the quilt," Alem says to Henry. The twins run to get their quilt and spread it out on the deck. The moonlight falls on the beautiful quilt, lighting up the unusual patches.

"This here patch looks like a bear's paw. It reminds us to look for little paths through the tangled woods, the ones that bears and deer make. They usually lead to water. Walkin' in water is safer. It throws our scent off the track and makes us harder to find," says Henry.

"Look here at this one," says Eddie, not to be outdone by his brother. "It looks like flyin' geese. We can follow them North if we see them in the sky."

Henry puts his hand on his hips, after wagging a finger at his brother. "Now what else did Granny tell us? You could end up headin' back the way you's runnin' from if you forget this rule."

"I know, I know. Everyone knows that geese fly North in the spring only. If it's fall and you see them, you gotta keep them behind you and head the way they come from," says Eddie. He gets up and shows them how to look backwards for the geese if it's fall and ends up tripping over Poppy.

Poppy runs to a far corner, muttering, *"Keeping little boys in confined spaces is not a good idea."* She smoothes her ruffled fur and checks for other damage.

Henry grabs him and rolls on top of Eddie, and they begin to wrestle and giggle.

"I guess we'll learn more safety rules from the quilt later," Alem says, shaking his head and smiling at his boys. It is hard to believe that he has his precious children back again after losing them for a year.

"All right, time to quiet down and get our things together," Harriet says.

"Yes, we're dockin' way out in the marshes, but noise travels in the quiet of the night," Captain Gus says. He and Samson guide the sailboat into a rickety dock that sticks way out into the water. They seem to know where all of the old, hidden docks are on this journey.

Harriet gathers her group together and has them sit around her. "I want you to listen real good now. We always have to watch out for kidnappers. This here state of Maryland is patrolled by all kinds of lawmen and slave catchers who want to make our lives a livin' nightmare. 'Cause it's next to Pennsylvania, a free state, there's lots of runaways tryin' their hardest to get there. So, boys, you have to be extra serious and quiet. If we drop our guard, we're easy pickin's for those bad men. They'll snap us up quicker than a bullfrog grabbin' a fly. Do y'all understand?"

The boys, wide-eyed and quiet, nod their heads.

"We can do it, Miss Harriet. We's old enough to help get us to freedom," says JoJo.

"All right then," says Harriet. "My papa trained me to be a tracker in the woods. He taught me how to walk so quiet no person or animal would know I was behind 'em. He taught me how to live in the woods, how to find food, what plants and berries are good to eat. I thank my papa every day for bein' the father he was, who loved me so.

"So, boys, I'm goin' to train you, too. I was a little bitty girl when I first learned, so you're plenty old enough to become good woodsmen. Are you ready?" asks Harriet.

The three boys are excited. They grin at Miss Harriet, anxious to learn how to slip through the woods and fields as quietly as a fox.

"Then it's time to pack our belongin's and take our leave. And don't you forget to thank these good men for sailin' us to Baltimore," says Harriet. The little boys adore her as their teacher.

It's a major ordeal to get the horses unloaded, along with the seven travelers and their belongings. JoJo again leads a nervous Thunder up a makeshift ramp to the old dock. He and Thunder have formed a close bond during the boat trip.

Once on firmer ground, the horses are loaded and packed with saddlebags. Captain Gus and Samson go around the group and solemnly shake hands.

"I wish you smooth sailin'," the captain says. "With Miss Harriet helpin', I know you'll make it to freedom." Samson gives his best wishes, and he and the captain head back to the *Jolly G*, swaying in the water. They plan to leave right away, heading back South, out to the open water and safety.

"Goodbye, goodbye, thank you," the three boys say, and they wave to the brave sailors who helped them along the Underground Railroad. Everyone waves until the sailboat vanishes from view.

Alem's back is much better, so he and Max insist the women and children should ride tonight. Miss Harriet knows of a safe house not too many miles from their landing place. They head off through the marshes with its foot-sucking, wet grounds, bulrushes, and tough grass, with Petey and Poppy tucked up on the horses' broad backs.

Miss Harriet rides up front on Dot, guiding the troops again. Max walks to the rear, holding Thunder's reins, with the little boys astride. Jinx walks with Henry in between, both casting their eyes left and right.

Everyone must help be the eyes and ears for the group. They must maintain a constant vigil for slave catchers. All remains calm, but it takes the rest of the night to make it to the safe-house farm. It is early daylight when they reach the wooded property near the fields.

The next danger lurks along the main road that runs by the farmland. Wagons loaded with produce are already on the road heading to the markets in Baltimore. Harriet halts the group in the woods, so they can discuss their options. They get down on their stomachs in the brush.

Harriet points out the huge, bundled haystacks and corn stalks in the fields across the road. The fields are chock full of these bundles, waiting to be brought into the barn and silos to feed the livestock for the winter.

"If we can make it to the field, we can dive in under them haystacks or hide in amongst the cornstalks," she says. "That way Master Max and Miss Jinx can ride to the farmhouse to alert the owners that we's arrived. We should be able to hide in the fields and sleep through the day until the safety of the night arrives," says Harriet. She is the expert on ways to avoid being seen and captured. She sees many dangers with her quick mind and sharp eyes that her runaways may not see.

"We don't wanna hide in no pigsty like you had to, Miss Harriet," says Eddie. The other boys start to giggle.

Harriet smiles at their innocence. "Now, boys, remember, this is serious business. You can see how many strangers are travelin' on the road. If they see a group of Negroes like us, they'll be mighty suspicious. Not everyone is friendly like the wonderful folks you've met so far."

They stop smiling and nod their serious little heads at Miss Harriet. They want to show the grown-ups that they understand.

The adults all love the boys, silliness and all.

Miss Harriet continues her instructions. "When we tells you to go, you scurry over the road and run into the field. Go over to a big haystack and kneel down. Use your hands to part the hay and burrow into the middle, quick as little rabbits going into their homes. Do you understand how to do it?" she says.

The three boys nod their heads again, brown eyes glistening with the excitement of it all.

Alem puts his big arms around the boys and hugs all three. He points to the field. "In the middle is the biggest haystack of all, see it? That's the one for you three boys. Now you have to try to sleep, not giggle and wrestle and attract attention. Can I trust y'all?"

JoJo says, "I can make sure we're good and quiet." He feels that since he is two years older than the twins, he'll be the leader. He frowns and squints his eyes at the twins to show them he is in charge.

They wait in the brush until later in the morning when the traffic slows down. While they wait, the adults talk in hushed tones.

"Alem," Jinx says, "did you get to practice your letters and words at all?"

"Yes, Miss Jinx, you'll be surprised how many words I can sound out now," Alem says proudly. "Mama had a little Bible that she got a long time ago, but none of us could read. She give it to me one day, and I keep it in my pocket. Well, I pulled my Bible out ev'ry night and practiced, and soon I could read some verses."

He reaches inside his pocket and pulls out a small book. Alem opens his Bible. "Listen boys: 'And ye shall know the truth, and the truth shall make you free.' Those are great words." He closes his Bible and puts it back into his pocket.

"That's so good, Papa. I'm real proud of you," says Eddie. He and Henry snuggle closer to their father.

Jinx has tears in her eyes. "We're all proud of you, Alem."

"I can't wait to teach my boys to read. Boys, you know one of the worst things that the white owners do to us–they try to keep us in ignorance. They made a law sayin' we's not allowed to read and write. Some of them even think we's too dumb to learn. But Miss Jinx, she taught me anyways, and I thank her for it.

"I want to learn to read good 'nough to read Mr. Frederick Douglass' book about slavery. I heard about him. He's a good man, a runaway slave who learned from the white street boys in Baltimore how to read and write. And now he's workin' hard to tell everyone how bad slavery is. He's my hero, boys."

"Papa, you's my hero," says little Henry. Eddie and JoJo nod their heads in agreement.

At midday the traffic on the road almost comes to a halt. Everyone is either home for lunchtime or at his destination. One by one, the boys are sent to the field. JoJo streaks across the road first to dig out a burrow for the boys, who quickly follow. Then Harriet scurries to the field to hide, followed by Alem.

Jinx and Max miss spotting the lone horse rider on the road, because they are mounting Dot and Thunder, preparing to head to the farmhouse. When they cross the road they see the thin man on horseback, off to the side, peering around the long field that shimmers in the early November sunlight.

"Uh, oh," Max says, "now what?"

The stranger hales them, so they have to stop to see what he wants. The man points to the field.

"Did you two happen to see a Negro man cross this road and go over there, somewhere?" he asks Max and Jinx. He appears to be a well-dressed, wealthy man.

"We were busy with our horses," Max says, always careful to avoid lengthy answers that could get him in trouble.

"Well, I saw him. I don't know what he'd be doin' comin' out of the woods and hustlin' over to this property. I hope it's no runaway tryin' to steal chickens or food. Maybe I should look around." He dismounts and walks into the field.

Max and Jinx stare at each other with wild eyes, afraid he'll go near one of the bundles of hay and hear someone make a noise. They both dismount and follow him into the field.

As the man nears the biggest haystack where the boys are hiding, Jinx begins to sneeze and cough. "Oh dear," she says loudly. "I believe the dusty field is making me sneeze. Well, I don't see any sign of a Negro man."

"We're going to visit the owners of this farm. We'll be sure to tell them about the man," Max adds.

"Well, if you're sure..." the stranger says. "I guess I did my duty. We have to be on the lookout here in Maryland, 'specially since we're so close to Pennsylvania. Those good-for-nothin' runaways are always tryin' to cross the border to a free state. Well, good day to you then." He tips his broad-brimmed hat to Jinx and walks back to his horse to ride on his way.

"Phew, another close one," Jinx says. "Good job, boys," she says to the haystack. They don't hear one peep out of the boys. Jinx smiles.

Max and Jinx get their horses and ride in the long lane, past their hiding friends, to meet the owners of the safe-house farm.

The travelers sit once again around some kind strangers' big oak farm table in their comfortable kitchen. Supper is served by the glow of oil lamps. The food is abundant: delicious homemade crab chowder full of white crab meat, potatoes, onions, and carrots. Loaves of bread and strawberry jam are passed around the table. The adults enjoy hearty, black coffee; the children, rich milk. A dark chocolate cake has been baked that day, so dessert is a special treat.

They have been given a chance to wash and dress in clean clothes again, and it is truly appreciated. The men and boys now wear fresh flannel shirts. Harriet and Jinx were given pretty cotton dresses that come to their ankles.

Thunder and Dot are bedded down in a safe barn. Poppy and Petey have met the family cat, Dusty, and share some food over by the kitchen stove.

"Finally, someone I can speak with who understands cat language," sighs Poppy.

"Yes, I see you have a dog. That must be very challenging at times," Dusty says.

"Challenging doesn't begin to describe the trials and tribulations of having a dog for a friend. But he is a good dog, overall. He's quite the hero right now..." And the cats go off to chat.

Dale and Ruth Blevins live on the farm with their two daughters, Debra and Julia. The girls are near the ages of JoJo and the twins; Debra is ten and Julia is eight. When the meal is finished, Ruth says to the girls, "Why don't you take the boys to the parlor and play with your toys? The adults have important things to talk about."

Jinx and Max feel older than the adults in many ways, especially after experiencing the tragedies and triumphs of this trip back in time.

"Wouldn't it be great to go with the kids and play games and not have to worry about the next move on the trail?" murmurs Jinx to Max.

Max gives her a sad smile. "I agree," he says. "We'll definitely need some downtime after this trip."

Debra and Julia are delighted to lead the three boys off to play games. They are soon spinning wooden tops, shooting marbles, and marching Julia's collection of carved animals into a little Noah's ark.

Poppy has fun batting the marbles around the parlor with Dusty, while Petey steals little animals out of the ark to make the children laugh and chase him.

Alem notices a pile of newspapers on a bench against the kitchen wall. "May I look at the papers?" he asks Dale.

"Of course, feel free to look through all the papers. There's some interesting news filtering down from the North. Friends sent a copy of Frederick Douglass's *North Star* paper."

"I've heard about Frederick Douglass," Jinx says. "Alem told us he's a Negro freedman, working against slavery." She also remembers learning about him in history class but chooses not to mention that fact.

"That's right, Miss Jinx; he's becoming quite famous as an abolitionist, working not only for the slaves, but also for women's rights," Dale says.

Max and Jinx sit on either side of Alem and spread out some of the newspapers, including the *Baltimore Sun*. Alem is the first to spot the story in the *North Star*. He gasps and grabs hold of Jinx's and Max's arms.

"Miss Jinx, Master Max...here's news about what happened over at Christiana. Help me read about it," Alem says. They all listen with interest as Max begins to read the article out loud.

When Alem finishes reading he turns to Max and Jinx, his trusted friends. "We need to go there, to watch the trial, to be there for my brother."

November 20, 1851 Philadelphia, PA

CHRISTIANA RESISTANCE TRIAL ABOUT TO BEGIN

The trial against 3 white men and 27 Negroes who took part in a riot and fired upon Federal Marshal Henry Kline and Edward Gorsuch, a slave owner from Maryland, is about to begin. The resistance against authority took place on the farm property of William Parker, the known leader of a Negro underground resistance group, on September 11.

Gorsuch was in Christiana, Pennsylvania, to collect his runaway slaves. When the marshal and Gorsuch arrived to reclaim his property, Parker and his group holed up inside and refused to turn over the runaways. Words exchanged between the men quickly escalated into shots being fired, wounding Gorsuch's son, Dickinson, and killing Gorsuch.

A large crowd of neighbors, both Negro and white farmers, had gathered during the fight, making identification of suspects difficult. Parker is missing and assumed to be on the run for Canada.

The accused are being held at the Moyamensing Prison in Philadelphia. Castner Hanway, one of the accused white Quaker neighbors, will be the first to be tried. Trial will be held on the second floor of Independence Hall in Philadelphia as soon as the last jury member is chosen.

The charge brought down by the Honorable John K. Kane, United States District Judge, is: Treason against the United States of America. The jury will be asked to decide two things:

1. Did the defendant, Castner Hanway, participate in the altercation, aiding, abetting, or assisting the Negroes in any way?

2. If he did, is the offense treason against the United States?

Thaddeus Stevens, a well-known Lancaster, Pa., lawyer, will lead the defense team. The Attorney General of Maryland, Robert J. Brent, leads the prosecuting attorneys. The Honorable Judges Robert C. Grier and John K. Kane will preside over the trial.

"I don't think that's a good idea, Alem," Max says. "You know there's a serious bounty for your capture. You won't be safe, even in Pennsylvania. Think of your boys–do you want to risk losing them again and maybe being captured or shot?"

Alem slowly lowers his head. He places his elbows on the table and covers his face with his hands, rubbing his eyes. They hear his shallow breaths and feel his frustration and anxiety.

Jinx places a hand on his arm. "Alem, I know where we can go to be safe. Let's head back where we started from–to Mary and John's farmhouse, near Lancaster. We can wait there to hear the news from Philadelphia. I know Anwar will be freed, Alem. I can feel it in here." Jinx places her hand over her heart.

Alem nods through his tears. "Both of you's right, my friends. What goes 'round comes 'round. It's right that we should end up back at the beginnin' of this trip we took together. We'll take the boys to Master John and Miss Mary."

Dale breaks in, "I know this must be hard for all of you. When should we move you out, Miss Harriet? We have a freedman who helps us out on the farm, an old man from Down South who came to us one night. We purchased his freedom. Now he drives a covered wagon for runaways at night to the next two safe houses, which should get you to your destination."

Harriet looks around at her group of refugees, wishing that she could let them rest. But she has had a blackout spell that always means trouble. "We needs to get movin' again," she tells them. "It's important to go now."

Max and Jinx nod. If Miss Harriet has a strong feeling about keeping on the run, they trust her judgment.

They all exchange hugs and thanks with Dale and Ruth for the wonderful supper and fresh clothes. Then the hustling begins; there are belongings and boys to round up and horses to get saddled. Within a half hour they slip through the dark night to the side of the barn, where a cloth-covered Conestoga wagon with a team of mules awaits them. Thunder and Dot are fully packed with their belongings and saddled, also ready to go.

Harriet and the boys clamber into the wagon. Petey and Poppy nestle together on blankets piled under one of the side benches. The wooden wagon is painted a shade of blue as light as a robin's egg. The tan canvas canopy is held up by curved pieces of wood, so it seems like they sit inside a tent. The wagon carries boxes of pumpkins and gourds, packed for market.

Dale shows them the false-bottom entrance inside the wagon in case they need to hide. Ruth hands them a clean pillowcase loaded with good food for their trip—rolls and chicken and ham, ripe red apples and sweet green pears.

Alem is about to climb aboard the front of the wagon to sit with the driver when he hears a chuckle. An old Negro man with bushy white hair comes from the shadows of the barn to the wagon. He is dressed simply in his brown trousers, scuffed boots and red shirt. His straw hat is in his hands, and his red bandana is tied around his neck.

"Ah, Little Man," he says, in the language of Alem's people in Africa. "I see you made it this far in life, heading for sweet freedom. You may be taller and older, but you still have that fire in your eyes," he says to Alem.

Alem turns to look at the old man. A broad grin flashes across his face as he recognizes him. "Grandfather. You look the same to me as that day long ago when I was a young boy right outta Africa, and you drove the wagon I was in to the slave camp. Now you goin' to drive me to freedom. Come, we must shake hands."

Alem grips the old man's hands and pulls him into an embrace. They look at each other and laugh again, happy to be crossing paths one last time.

Max and Jinx also remember the man from their first vision of Alem coming from the slave ship. "Hello, sir. We're Max and Jinx. What may we call you?" asks Max.

"I think 'Grandfather' will be good enough," he says. Grandfather climbs aboard the seat in front and offers a strong handgrip to Alem to pull him up. "I can't call you Little Man anymore, can I? So I'll call you Big Man. We have much to talk about these next few days, don't we, Big Man?"

The three boys stick their heads out of the canvas-covered wagon; they're interested in this story.

"Hello, Grandfather," they all call out.

"Hello, Little Men," Grandfather returns with a smile. He shakes the reins and the mules begin to pull the Conestoga wagon out the rutted farm lane, followed by Max and Jinx mounted on Thunder and Dot.

The Blevins family waves goodbye to the departing group once more, before they return to the warmth of their farmhouse to await a new group of freedom seekers.

Jackson Merryweather and his friend Billy step out of the livery stable in Baltimore with frowns on their faces. It has been the same story all along the way from Virginia to Maryland. They have stopped at their usual places for news on runaways, but no one has spotted two teen-age children with a tall Negro whose ears stick out.

"I don't git it," Jackson says. "There's no trace of 'em anywhere. It's like they've disappeared from the face of the earth."

"*Maybe they took the train, or even a boat,*" *says Billy.*

"*Yeah, but we checked the pier and the train depot. No one remembers them at all. And two kids with a black man would stick out.*"

Billy gets a look on his face. "*Didn't your ma say they had somethin' to do with that Christiana fight?*"

"*Yeah, why?*" *says Jackson.*

"*Because they were talkin' about that Christiana fight in the bar today and how a big trial is startin' soon. They arrested some of the white guys and a bunch of Negroes involved in shootin' at the deputy marshal and killin' that Gorsuch guy, and the judge says it's treason against the United States. Gonna be a real big trial in Philadelphia.*"

Now Jackson nods his head and smiles. "*I think it's time to visit Ma again and see if she knows anythin' more about those two kids. If we can find 'em, we can find that runaway slave. I'd bet my horse on it. Time to head home.*"

The two men clap each other on the shoulders and head back to the stable to get their horses. There's money to be made, and they mean to have it.

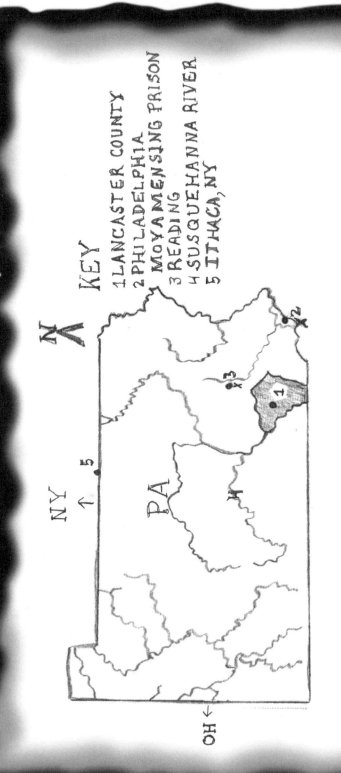

PENNSYLVANIA

KEY

1 LANCASTER COUNTY
2 PHILADELPHIA
 MOYAMENSING PRISON
3 READING
4 SUSQUEHANNA RIVER
5 ITHACA, NY

N

NY
↑ 5

PA

OH →

Chapter Twenty-eight

Homecoming

It's the third night on the run from Maryland. Harriet and Grandfather have been very cautious, only going twenty or thirty miles each night. Tonight they should reach the farm of John and Mary Martin. Jinx and Max feel as if they are going home, back to Conestoga Courage Farm, even if it is 1851.

It's a cloudy, cold night. Light snow has been falling. The mules plod along at an even gait on a backwoods path barely wide enough for the wagon. The trees have shed their leaves and seem to be asleep with the wildlife. All is whispery quiet in the snow-white wonderland, except for the creaking of the wagon wheels.

Max and Jinx ride inside the wagon tonight with their runaway friends. They have been talking about the trial, worrying about its outcome and Anwar's health. A cold, damp jail cell is a terrible place to be held in November. If they are declared guilty as charged, it will be the death penalty.

Harriet has a big announcement for the group. "We'll reach Pennsylvania tonight. I think Max and Jinx can help you all get the rest of the way up through New York State into Canada, so I'll be leaving you soon after we get to the Martin safe house.

"I already talked with Grandfather; he's taking me back down South where I'll pick up my family. I got word that my niece, Keziah, and her children are to be sold at the slave auction. If that happens, I'll never see them again. I must rush back and try to find them..."

Jinx grabs her hand. "Miss Harriet, you came into our lives at just the right time, when we needed you the most. Words can't describe how much we love you for the work you do, helping your enslaved people reach freedom. Thank you." She hugs Harriet.

"Yes, thank you, Miss Harriet, thank you..." Everyone takes a turn to give her a big hug.

"Now, now, it'll be fine. You have two good friends there who'll show you the rest of the way north to Canada. I already met up with 'em a time or two back when I was bringin' a group through. They's mighty fine people, mighty fine."

Before tears start, Harriet says, "How 'bout another story to make you laugh, boys?"

"Oh, yes, Miss Harriet...a story; tell a story," say the boys. They take their quilt to sit on and slide in close to Harriet's feet.

Harriet leans down and smiles at her three brave boys. "Once, I was down in Bucktown, Maryland, on a rescue mission. Well, that was real close to where my master lived, and I sure didn't want to run into him. So, I got an old gray suit and a beat-up gray hat and dressed up like an old man. Now I wanted a couple'a animals as part of my disguise. Guess what I bought?"

"Dogs," Petey barks.

"I'm sure it was cats," says Poppy.

"No, horses," say Thunder and Dot.

"Hee-haaaw, mules," say the two old mules pulling the wagon.

JoJo giggles with Max and Jinx, because he can hear the animals talk, so he says, "Did you get some puppies, Miss Harriet?" The others look around at the animals, which are barking, mewing and neighing, and wonder for a moment what all of the clamor is about.

"No, I got me a couple'a chickens. I pulled my hat way down over my forehead, tucked them chickens up under my arms, and strutted my way down the road. Sure 'nough, with my bad luck, guess who I ran into?"

"Oh, no, not your old master?" young Henry says.

"Yes, sir, that's exactly who was coming my way, walkin' to town in a nice, white suit. So I had to think fast. When he got close enough, I acted like them chickens got away from me. I kind of threw them at him–you know how chickens act when they're upset. Those chickens started flappin' and cluckin' and scratchin' and flutterin' and squawkin' all around him. I tried to catch 'em by the feet, and he yelled, 'Get away from me. Get them birds away from me.' I took my good ol' time."

By now the boys and adults are laughing out loud, picturing the squawking birds.

"Did that man's fine, white suit git dirty, Miss Harriet?" asks Eddie.

"Oh my, yes. By the time I caught them chickens in that dusty, dirty road, his fine white suit was dirty gray. He tried to brush himself off, and I said in a deep voice, 'Sorry, sir, mighty sorry,' and I walked as fast as I could in the opposite direction. He never did know who really passed 'im on the road. Those old chickens did a good job helpin' me," she ends her story.

The boys clap their hands. "Miss Harriet, we'll always remember you by the good stories you told," says Eddie. The other boys nod their heads and give her more hugs.

Harriet moves out to the driver's seat with Grandfather. The snow has picked up. Two or three inches coat the ground, and Grandfather's hat is covered in snow. "We're close now. The horses and mules will soon have a warm barn," Harriet tells him.

Jinx pokes her head out of the wagon, and Max and she guide Uncle the rest of the way home. When they enter the lane and see a warm glow of lamplight from the kitchen windows, Jinx feels an immense weight lifted from her chest.

"There's no place like home...there's no place like home," Max whispers in her ear.

She laughs and puts her hand on Max's shoulder. "You've got that right, partner. Petey, Poppy, come look—we're home."

Alem, Max and JoJo have rubbed down the horses and mules, fed them, and now come stomping their boots and shaking snow off of their coats onto the farmhouse porch. They enter the kitchen, ready for warmth and good food. Joining the others, they pull chairs up to the table.

Fragrances of roasting pork and sauerkraut make everyone's stomachs growl with hunger. Mugs of hot cocoa and coffee warm hands around the table.

Mary had been the only one home to greet the runaways at the door. She was very surprised and happy to see Max and Jinx again. Now, gazing at the teens, she marvels at the feat they have accomplished.

"Now that everyone is here, we can catch up on news," Mary says. "John is in Philadelphia, attending the trial of Castner Hanway. He wanted to be there for Edward," she says to Alem. "Whatever the jury decides about Mr. Hanway is vitally important, because that decision will tell whether the others will go to trial or be let free."

"That's so good of Master John," Alem says. He feels better, knowing someone who cares is watching out for his brother.

Mary is very excited to have a visit from Harriet Tubman. She has heard about this little lady who has already made a name for herself along the Underground Railroad. Mary is also delighted with the three little boys who have been entertaining everyone with their tumbling tricks.

"Now we have a big problem," Mary jokes. "When I call for Henry, both of you will come running. We'll soon have the same problem with the Edwards, because I have faith that big Edward will be released and come home from Philadelphia with John."

Eddie and little Henry giggle. "No, we won't," says little Henry.

"That's right, Miss Mary. Papa is usin' his real name now, the one his papa and mama gave him in Africa. His real name is Alem," says Eddie.

"And Uncle Edward's African name is Anwar. Their names mean 'the world' and 'the brightest.' So we won't get mixed up at all," says little Henry.

"Alem—that's a wonderful name. You shall be Alem to John and me, also," says Mary.

Alem beams with pride over his boys.

"Now let's have our supper. The Pennsylvania Dutch believe it is good luck to eat pork and sauerkraut on New Year's Day. I know we're a few weeks early, but I figure it can't hurt to have some extra luck. So eat hearty, everyone." Harriet and Jinx help Mary serve up large plates of mashed potatoes, pork, and sauerkraut. After Henry recites a meal blessing, they dig in.

Poppy and Petey eat the mashed potatoes and pork, but neither likes the sauerkraut much. Petey tries it first. His lips roll back and his tongue tries to force it down. Poppy sniffs at a strand and watches Petey.

"Um...it's a bit sour," Petey says.

"That would be why it is called sauerkraut," says Poppy.

"I guess we should both try to eat some for good luck, for Anwar," Petey says.

"You're correct—for Anwar," Poppy says.

They both grab a bite of sauerkraut and force it down. The looks on their faces have everyone else laughing, as the hungry group eats its way through two helpings of the meal.

The snow continues to fall, softly covering the ground like a blanket of cotton. It reminds the freedom seekers about how far they have come in their quest, and how much farther they must go.

After a day of rest, Harriet calls her little boys together for one last story, another true story told from her heart. "Now, my brave boys, I want to talk with you about the rest of your trip North. I'm sendin' Master Max and Miss Jinx directly north through New York, then west to cross over the big Niagara River into Canada.

"There's a village named Owen Sound in Ontario. You'll be truly free there. Lots of our people are makin' a good life for themselves in Owen Sound. You're to meet up with Doc Alex at the crossin'. He'll take you on into Canada and help you get settled. You remember how I told you never to let your guard down?"

The boys shake their heads solemnly. "Yes, Miss Harriet. Yes, Miss..." they say.

"Do you think y'all are safe now, here in Pennsylvania?" asks Harriet.

"Well, it's a free state—no slavery allowed," Eddie says.

"But we ain't really free, is we, Miss Harriet?" Henry says.

"That's right, little Henry, we're not really free. Just 'cause Pennsylvania don't allow no slavery don't mean you's free. Y'all don't got no freedom papers, and even if you did, them slave kidnappers will steal you away in a flash and sell you to a chain gang. You must stay on watch every minute of the day and night so's you don't get snatched. Y'all got to help the others keep watch, because you are runaways, and you will be sent back to worse punishment than you ever had in your life."

"We promise to help. Right, Henry? Promise, Eddie?" says JoJo.

The three little boys spit on their right hands and promise to stay serious and alert when they travel.

"Miss Harriet, what's a chain gang?" Henry asks.

Harriet gets a faraway look in her eyes; then suddenly her head rolls back and her eyelids flutter. She sways for a few moments while Max and Jinx jump to their feet to help her.

With a jerk, her eyes snap open and she sits straight again. "I 'bout blacked out, didn't I?" Harriet asks, when she sees how startled everyone is.

"Yes, Miss Harriet," Jinx says. She stoops beside her and takes her hand, patting it. "Are you all right? Could someone please get Miss Harriet a glass of cold water?"

Max brings water and a cool cloth, which Harriet places on her forehead.

"I'll be fine in a minute; don't y'all worry none. That's what happens sometimes 'cause of that balance scale weight that hit me in the head. I black out and fall over.

"That's why I knowed I had to run for freedom, boys. I couldn't be sold to no chain gang and have to walk all the way Down South. What if I had one of my spells?

"I hope you never has to witness a chain gang, or be part of it. It's an ugly, hopeless thing to see. The Boss Man, he puts manacles on your hands and feet and chains your feet to a partner. Then they put thirty or forty of you in a long line, with a big ol' chain runnin' from front to back. They poke you and prod you and use the whip. You better keep up walkin' all the way, for days and days, in rainstorms or blazing sun. If anyone gets sick or falls, you get dragged along until you either get back up or die. If you die, they leave you by the side of the road.

"When I was half-grown, our master came to the cabin one day and grabbed two of my sisters to sell to the chain gang goin' South. My one big sister, she had a little baby, and they ripped that baby right out of her hands and gave him to another woman. I saw my sisters chained up in the gang and marched down the road, gone forever." Harriet's head drops low and one single tear rolls down her cheek.

Everyone is stunned beyond words. What horrible treatment. Jinx continues to hold Harriet's hand and pat it gently. But Harriet doesn't stay down for long.

"So that's why I run away. I'll sneak Down South to help others and find my family members to steal away North, as long as it takes for us all to be free."

The boys have listened in silence, awed at the thought of a chain gang. What a magnificent woman and heroine for them all. Now they clap for Miss Harriet. She smiles, but she pats the air for them to stop.

"I ain't no one special. I'm one little woman tryin' to do my job in life. Boys, I truly hope you get the freedom you deserve, so you can figure out what your job in life is all about," says Harriet.

The boys jump up and go to her with hugs. She kisses each boy on the forehead. Then Harriet sends the boys out to the barn to say thank you and good night to Grandfather, who feels more comfortable bedding down in the barn with the horses.

In the morning, Harriet is gone, along with Grandfather and the Conestoga wagon, having slipped away in the shadows of the night as she so often does. A powerful presence has left their company and will be sorely missed.

Thanksgiving passes with a big feast. The Christmas holiday season comes. The boys have a good time decorating the house with evergreen-scented boughs and a Christmas tree.

They all use their creative minds to make little presents for each other out of wood scraps and Mary's pile of cloth and needles. This keeps the boys occupied and happy. But always, always they are aware of the chance of slave catchers and kidnappers. They stay in during the day, only venturing outside after dark.

One day a letter arrives from John, giving them hope.

My Dearest Mary,

The trial days are tedious and lengthy. They are full of testimony that is questionable. Thaddeus Stevens and his lawyers are sharp as tacks. They bombard the witnesses for the prosecution with such a barrage of questions that their heads are spinning. This is a good thing—it makes the jury think they are making up lies to cover themselves.

One day they brought all of the Negroes into the courtroom so the jury could see them. They were dressed alike in neat clothes, with their hair carefully brushed. I was able to make eye contact with Edward. He was so happy to see me that he smiled. I noticed he has a wracking cough and looks very thin. No doubt the horrid, damp conditions at the Moyamensing Prison have many of the men ill.

A group of good-hearted, white churchwomen actually cooked Thanksgiving dinner for the three white men and the Negroes on trial. I heard there was so much of the feast left over, they had enough for other prisoners in the wards. What good people.

The defense team will be finishing soon. I may not make it home for Christmas Day, but I expect to be there shortly after. The whole trial hangs on the balance of whether or not Castner Hanway is declared guilty of treason. We shall continue to pray for the jury to make a correct decision.

I remain your loving husband,
John

Mary finishes reading the letter out loud. Everyone sits quietly, thinking and hoping for the best. It sounds like it won't be much longer. Max and Jinx again feel so frustrated that there is nothing anyone can do but wait. Finally, Eddie speaks up.

"I think we should wait and not have Christmas Day until Master John and Uncle Anwar are home from Philadelphia. It won't really be a happy day without them, will it?" Eddie says.

"That's the spirit, Eddie. I think you're right. Let's take a vote," says Max.

"What does *vote* mean?" asks JoJo.

"It means you get to help make a decision about something important," Jinx says.

The boys, and even Alem, are excited. They have never been asked to take a vote on something important.

"Okay, all of you in favor of waiting to have Christmas Day until John and Anwar return, raise your hand and say *aye*," Max says.

Arms shoot to the ceiling and a resounding aye is shouted.

"Anyone opposed, say *nay*," Max adds.

Everyone looks around to see who might say no. They all laugh.

"The ayes have it. We shall wait until our friends John and Anwar return," says Max.

The boys cheer and tussle each other, tumbling to the floor in happiness. Petey and Poppy jump on them while the adults laugh.

Later that evening, when everyone has gone to bed, Jinx taps at Max's door. She is wrapped in a big quilt. Max comes to the door and slips out to the hallway to sit with his friend. They both huddle in the quilt for warmth, as the house becomes very cold overnight to save on wood and coal.

"Max, do you know how this trial turns out?" Jinx asks.

"No, I don't. Isn't it strange how we are learning so much of our history by going back and reliving it? I wish I did know."

"We couldn't tell everyone, though. But it would make our wait better, that's for sure," Jinx says. "What's the plan to get this group to Canada? We've come so far, but often the last leg of a journey is the hardest."

"I've been thinking about that. Miss Harriet is right. If we go almost straight up north through Pennsylvania, then northwest through New York, we could have them cross at Niagara Falls into Canada. We'll have to take it one safe house at a time, until we get there."

"Right...one safe house at a time. We need to post a letter to Doc Alex Ross to be on the lookout for us. Mail it when we're ready to move on, so he can gauge the time. He could have a boat ready for us to cross the Niagara River," Jinx suggests.

"That's a really good plan, partner," Max says. "Of course, we'll hope it's not too close to the falls, or we'll all go over. Not a good scene," he jokes. Little does he know how those words will come back to haunt him.

"I've never been to the falls, have you?" Jinx says.

"No, but I remember Doc Alex saying he has helped runaways before cross at Niagara Falls, New York. So we'll finally get to visit the falls." Conversation drifts to an end.

Petey and Poppy come looking for their friends. They snuggle in under the quilt and get cozy on laps. Their two humans lean against each for support and are soon sound asleep. The old farmhouse sighs and settles around its inhabitants, protecting them as it has others for a hundred years before.

It is now a few days into the New Year and there is still no news from John. Max and Jinx help Mary with the farm chores: chopping firewood, gathering eggs, and milking the cows.

Jinx and the boys bake cookies and pies and cakes with Mary, and she teaches the boys their alphabet letters. They are anxious to read like their papa and are learning fast.

It is a quiet period with no danger approaching the house. Yet Alem, Max and Jinx never forget to be on guard duty, always watching and listening when they are outside at night or inside by day. Petey and Poppy help with the guarding; their ears prick up at the least bit of unexplained noise.

They have the boys practice drills where they must run to the hidden room in the basement, or go to the trapdoor in the barn if they are outside at nighttime. The boys take it very seriously and become adept at disappearing quickly.

Alem discusses his fears daily about he and the boys being spotted at a white farmer's property. "With every day that goes by, it's more likely we'll be kidnapped by slave hunters," Alem says. "I heard 'bout the Negro church in Lancaster that helps us runaways. Wouldn't it be better to hide with them folks? We fit in there. Here, we stick out like a bunch a sittin' geese that shoulda flown South for the winter."

Max and Jinx nod. "You're right, Alem. Mary, what do you think?" Jinx asks.

Mary smiles at her special group of friends. "That's a wonderful idea, since you're waiting for Anwar to come home here, and not passing through quickly like our usual guests. Alem, I can get word to Reverend Bailey of the Bethel African Methodist Episcopal Church," she says. "He'll know exactly what to do.

"The good folks at Bethel AME are experts at hiding runaways right in amongst the church members. They'll dress you in the right clothes, so you don't look like runaway slaves. You'll feel safer, I'm sure," she adds.

A couple of days after the decision, a Bethel AME member arrives in the darkness of night to pick up Alem and the boys, and they slip away so secretly that Jinx and Max never hear them go. The house seems empty and still the next morning without the little boys and Alem.

One market day, Jinx and Max decide to ride in to Lancaster with Mary to mail a letter to Doc Alex. Alem and the boys remain safely hidden with the church members.

They all bundle up in heavy coats, as the day is a cold one. A few inches of snow lie on the ground, and the sky is a brilliant sea of blue. The sun makes blue-gray shadows in the snow. Thunder and Dot are both hitched to the wagon to give them a run.

The road is frozen solid with chunks of snow and hard ruts, making for a bumpy ride. Breaths of condensation rise from their mouths and noses and float away in the crackling cold air.

"Isn't it a glorious day?" Mary says.

The teens agree. Jinx has the letter in her pocket, addressed to Doctor Alexander Ross, Windsor, in Ontario, Canada. They hope this important letter reaches him.

"Would you please ask for my mail?" asks Mary. "I haven't been to town because of the weather. Maybe there is news from John."

"Wouldn't that be great?" Max says. "Yes, of course, I'll ask for your mail."

He gets a jittery feeling in his stomach, hoping for good news. They've been waiting at Mary and John's home too long now. Each additional day is more dangerous for their runaways being discovered, even though hidden with the church members.

When they pull into town, Max and Jinx part company with Mary, who heads to market to drop off her eggs and a can of fresh milk. They walk down the street toward the post office, which sits beside Merryweather's Dry Goods Store.

"Um, Max...is this a good idea, us being spotted here in town by that Merryweather lady? What if she sees us and tells her son, Jackson?" says Jinx.

"We were so anxious to post this letter we didn't think about that. You're right," Max says. He pulls his hat down low. "I'll take the letter inside. Maybe you should head back to market and find Mary. We shouldn't be spotted together." Max says.

Jinx hands over the letter and scurries back the opposite direction towards market. Max hurries inside and posts the letter. He goes up to the window and waits for a clerk to appear. A middle-aged, short man with black hair and a crooked nose finally comes over. He has a potbelly but is thin as a stick otherwise.

"Good day, young man. Sorry I took so long. It seems everyone is out posting mail on this nice day after all of the stormy weather. What can I do for you?" he says.

"Hello, we're visiting with John and Mary Martin. Mary is over at the market and sent me to fetch her mail, if there is any," Max says.

"Why, yes, I remember a letter. I was sorting through the mail that arrived earlier. Her husband's been in Philadelphia for a while, I see," says the nosey clerk. "He must have important business to be away from the farm so long." He looks closer at Max, hoping for some gossip to share around town. After all, his job is pretty boring, he thinks.

"I suppose so," Max says, taking the letter and turning away.

"Wouldn't have to do with that trial of those Negroes that murdered that southern fellow, would it?" says the clerk.

Max pretends he didn't hear him. "Have a good day, sir," he says and walks out the door. He ducks his head and hurries, trying not to break out in a panicked run. *I don't want to attract any more attention,* he thinks.

Max doesn't see the man come out of the post office door and go next door to Merryweather's store. He finds Jinx and tells her about the nosey man. "I'm sure he was digging for news," he says. "We've got to move Alem and the boys out soon. It's too dangerous to stay put any longer."

"Calm down, Max. Maybe this letter will tell us what's going on with the trial, and we'll be able to plan better," says Jinx.

They enter the market to find Mary and see her across the aisle delivering her baked goods and eggs to a stand holder, who pays her for them. "Hello, you two. Any letter for me, Max?"

Max pulls the letter, a bit crumpled, from his pocket and hands it to Mary. "Let's hope it has good news," Max says. He shares his story about the nosey mail clerk with Mary.

She gives him a worried look. "Let's get back to the wagon and open the letter."

They all sit on the wagon bench holding their breath as Mary opens the letter. Mary skims the letter and then glances at them with a puzzled look on her face. "It's very brief. John says he'll be in on the noon train with a surprise for us...let's see the date...why it's today. It should be about noon. Let's go meet his train. Dare we hope?" They all think about Anwar.

The train station isn't busy at noon on a Monday. Most workers have taken an earlier train. A few people wait on the platform and watch for the train to pick up friends and relatives. Max paces up and down, unable to shake his scare over the post office clerk's nosey questions.

They hear a whistle–*whooo, wooooo.* Then with a huffing and chuffing, the black giant rounds the bend and pulls in to the station, hauling a full load of cars behind it. They anxiously watch people making their way down the iron steps to the wooden platform.

When it seems like everyone has departed, they hear a shout from farther down the platform where the Negro passengers have come off the train. It's John, waving his arm and hurrying towards his wife, holding a very thin black man by the elbow.

Everyone runs to meet them. It's Edward, or Anwar, as they have come to call him. He looks haggard and pauses to cough, but no one can mistake him for anyone other than Alem's twin brother, with a smile on his face larger than life.

John is breathless with the news. "Thaddeus Stevens and his team have gotten an acquittal for Castner Hanway. Everything has fallen apart for the prosecutor. They have released most of the people that were arrested, and the rest will probably be let go by the end of the month." He grabs his wife and hugs her.

The postal clerk and Widow Merryweather shiver in the cold air, watching from the alley near the train platform. They hide alongside the last building on the corner. The storekeeper pulls her shawl closer against the bite of the January wind, and slowly she nods her head. She has a cruel smile on her lips.

"Yes indeedy, those are the same two children I saw months ago with Eliza Parker, right after that mess over there in Christiana. Now they're with Mary Martin while her husband has been gone to Philadelphia. And that Christiana trial is going on at the same time. I don't believe in coincidence. Those two are involved in helping runaways, sure as my name is Agnes Merryweather."

"I figured you'd be interested, my dear," says the postal clerk. He has been courting the widow this past fall and winter, hoping to marry

her in the spring, and have his name on the store sign instead of hers: Stumpy's Dry Goods. "I'm sure Jackson will be interested in following them again. He made some good money before, and now I understand that same slave ran again and has a heavy bounty on his head."

They continue to watch as the train pulls in. When they see John Martin get off the train and escort a tall black man over to his wife and the children, the good widow's false teeth about pop out of her big mouth. She pecks her beau's cheek with a wet kiss and turns for the store.

"Oh my, yes, Jackson will certainly be interested in this juicy bit of information. Come along, Stumpy," she says. Her broad backside swishes side-to-side as the big woman strides down the alley, back to her store.

The little postal clerk has to run to keep up with the widow. "Yes, my dear. We must get back to work."

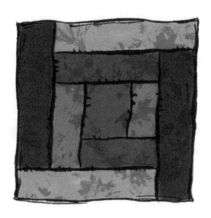

Chapter Twenty-nine

Christmas Day at Last

There is turkey and ham for the celebration dinner, with sweet potatoes and stuffing, baked corn and green beans, biscuits with molasses, and so many choices of cookies, cakes, and pies that they could feed an army. Food is the universal comfort that brings people together to share experiences, either in sadness or in joy. Today, the meal is all about joy.

In the bitter cold darkness last night, behind the white barn near the woods, Jinx, Max, and John had waited for another "load of potatoes" to be delivered to the Martin farm. Stamping their feet and jumping to keep warm, Jinx and Max whispered to each other about how different they felt this time around. They had entered a world so foreign to them, and traveled its treacherous paths. Apprehensively, they thought about the last part of the journey.

Out of the shadows and running low, a group finally approached. It was Sister Carolyn and Sister Deborah from the Bethel AME Church in Lancaster who safely delivered Alem and his three boys. The two women slipped back into the darkness, not even staying for a cup of hot tea to warm their frozen hands and feet.

Edward takes his African name back with pride; he instantly turns back into Anwar. Little Henry and Eddie sit on either side of their uncle and eat with one hand on a fork and the other arm wrapped around their Uncle Anwar's waist. Petey and Poppy sit below the boys and enjoy the tidbits of the feast that the boys sneak to them under their bench.

Anwar is quiet, choosing not to speak much about his harrowing experiences in the prison. His smile says it all–to be back among his real family and his adopted family of white friends is the most precious gift he could have received this Christmas season.

After the feasting is over and the meal is cleaned up, they gather around the Christmas tree and exchange little presents. Alem has whittled tops and painted them in bright red and blue for the boys. He gives Jinx a small wooden dog, painted brown and white like Petey, and a wooden puzzle to Max. It is a cup on a handle. Attached to the cup with a piece of string is a small wooden ball. The trick is to flip the ball in the air and catch it in the cup. Max tries over and over to catch the cup, missing every time. The boys giggle and show Max how easy it is.

John has brought sticky ribbon candy home from Philadelphia for everyone to sample. It is rippled in red, green and white and tastes pepperminty good. He has a beautiful shawl for his wife. Mary has in turn knitted warm scarves for everyone. She has helped the boys make pretty cards on scraps of paper and sign their names with pains-taking care. They pass them out with pride.

Even Petey and Poppy get a present from the boys: Poppy, a felt mouse cut out and sewn together, and Petey, a stuffed toy with a bell sewn inside. They have great fun flipping and batting their new toys around. Alem has shown Max how to whittle whistles with little carved roosters on top for the boys and Jinx. Of course Jinx has to lead the boys in a tooting concert.

Jinx passes out warm mittens for everyone that she has helped Mary to knit, after Mary taught her the craft of knitting. They are in different colors, and Jinx is very proud of the pairs that she finished on her own. Now the boys march around wearing their new scarves and mittens and blowing their whistles.

Max admires his pair of mittens. They hadn't planned on cold weather when they first started the trip in September, because they really hadn't thought about the trip taking months to accomplish. He puts on his mittens. "These fit perfectly, Jinx. I'm really impressed with your new talent. That can't be easy, clicking those big needles together and getting them to actually make something."

Jinx gives him a smile and a toot on her rooster whistle before she slips it into a pocket. "Thanks, Max, and thanks everyone for your gifts. This has been a Christmas to remember." They all agree.

At sundown, they light candles and sing Christmas carols for John and Mary, not caring in the least that they are celebrating the holiday almost two weeks late. Mary prays for their safe journey to Canada. The group feels at peace.

Then the serious packing begins. It is time to head out to the next safe house. The weather has turned a bit milder, so it is a good night to go. Max hopes they can travel about twenty miles tonight. John insists they use the wagon with the false bottom.

"You'll get farther along each day if you can all ride instead of walking. My neighbors and I will build another wagon. It's not the first time I've sent a group out in our wagon, and it won't be the last," John says. He refuses Max's offer of paying for the wagon.

Max glances at Jinx. She nods, giving him a secret smile. She and Max read each other's thoughts very well. She will write a note of thanks and leave some money on her bed for the Martins to help fund their mission of service for other runaways.

When it's time to load the wagon, they notice the boys are nowhere to be found. In fact, no one has seen them for the past hour or so. They are not in the house, so they send Petey outside to track them down. Jinx and Max follow him, feeling a bit tense; the boys are missing—where did they go?

"Sniff, snort...out here, out here in the barn," Petey says. He follows tracks and scents in the snow right out to the softly glowing barn. It glows with the blue-colored halo that the teens saw before the big trip ever started. They look at each other with big eyes before Jinx pushes the door open.

The inside also gives off a dim, blue glow. They hear the boys talking in low voices as they squat around the open trapdoor in the floor.

"Okay, boys, what are you doing out here? You gave us a bit of a fright when you went missing," says Jinx.

JoJo closes the trapdoor with a bang, and the boys fold up their papa's pocketknife with grins of satisfaction. "We're sorry, Miss Jinx. But we spent so much time practicin' hidin' in the secret space under the trapdoor that we wanted to carve our names on it so people in the future will see we had to hide there and think about us," says JoJo.

"That's a great idea, isn't it, Max?" Jinx says. He nods his head and gathers the little boys together to go back inside.

"I know people will find those names someday for sure," Max says.

Finally, the group is packed up and ready to move out. The twins and Jinx nestle underneath the Freedom Quilt, all dressed in warm coats, hats, and new mittens and scarves. JoJo chooses to ride with Max on Thunder. Alem and Anwar will take turns driving Dot and the wagon.

Mary hands up a big bag of leftovers from the Christmas feast, enough to keep them going a long time. John gives them directions to the next safe house going North. He shakes hands once more all around.

Inside the wagon, Eddie points to a patch on their beloved quilt. It's the one with the hand and stars all around it. "Follow the stars to freedom," he says. They all place their hands on the dark-colored hand in the patch for good luck.

John and Mary wave goodbye as the wagon heads out the lane in the dark of the night. They try not to get too attached to the groups of runaways. It can be a heartbreaking thing. They usually do what they can for them and send them on their way, not knowing if the runaways will make it North to freedom or be recaptured and sent back South.

But this bunch is different. They feel a real connection to Jinx and Max and have been caught up in the drama of Alem and Anwar, the lost twins and the whole Christiana Resistance incident. Adding JoJo and his sad story to the mix finally did it–they have fallen in love with this brave little bunch of people.

There is no guarantee that things will always turn out as they wish just because they are devout, church-going folks. But it gives John and Mary the faith to go back inside their home and pray for a safe trip to freedom for this ragamuffin band of friends.

Chapter Thirty

Niagara Falls

*J*oJo *thrashes in his sleep. His dream is so real he can feel the numbing coldness. There is water and ice everywhere—water that roars and splashes high off of rocks, sending spray flying through the air. It is dark and bitterly cold. The water numbs JoJo's hands and feet, freezing his whole body and making him shake so hard his legs and arms knock together.*

He is sucked under and pushed back up by the thundering water. Swimming as hard as he can gets him nowhere. He is dragged towards the edge of the world. His arms reach out for dark figures on the side of this nightmare river, but they are so far away he will never touch their reaching fingers. He swirls around and around like water ready to go down a drainpipe and then he goes down...down...down...head over heels, lost in the pounding water.

"*Helpppppp mmeeee...*" JoJo screams aloud and sits upright, trembling in fear and shivering uncontrollably. Jinx reaches for the boy and hugs him tight, wrapping him in an extra blanket. His eyes are wide in shock, and he continues to fight the water of his dream, but Jinx keeps calling his name and telling him he is safe. Finally he collapses against her, sobbing. Alem pulls the wagon over to the side and waits for the boy to calm down.

"It's the same dream, Miss Jinx; it's a vision like the others I've had that came true. Will they always come true, will they?" asks JoJo.

"No, not always, JoJo. When I have my visions, sometimes they are only a warning or message that I have to figure out, like a piece of a puzzle," Jinx says. "And even if they do happen, the ending might be something totally different."

"You mean like my vision where I saw my family at the supper table, but I wasn't there, and then you and Master Max rescued me?"

"Yes. I know you will get to see your family again and be safe in your mama's and papa's arms. I feel it right in here." She taps her heart. "Now try to relax," Jinx says.

The young boy shakes off the bad dream and gives Jinx a little smile. "Thank-you, Miss Jinx, for loving us and helping us." He pushes back away from Jinx and fixes his big, dark eyes on her.

"Miss, I had another bad dream the other night. I was all growed up and so far from home. It was a real hot summer day. I was with a bunch of men who had guns. There were big boulders everywhere on this hill, and we hid in them, because this other bunch of men was after us. They wanted to kill us for some reason.

"Some was on horseback and others was afoot. Little boys was playin' on drums, then a man in my group yelled, '*Charge men, chaaa-arrrrage...,*' and he led us up over those boulders and right into a big fight. There was explosions and guns crackin' and smoke and blood... it was real bad, Miss Jinx. You could smell death.

"One of our men had a cloth with red and white stripes on it, and I saw the other group had a cloth that was all red with a big blue cross on it. All of a sudden I got hit with a bullet in my belly. The pain was so awful I woke up holdin' my belly, and I had a bellyache all day. It still hurts sometimes. What does it mean? I know you has visions, Miss Jinx. Tell me the truth, do you think I'm gonna die that way?"

Max has been riding beside the wagon, listening to Jinx give support to the little boy. He hears JoJo's story. Jinx looks at Max for help, but he freezes. They both know what battle is taking place in JoJo's vision.

Jinx thinks for a moment before she talks. She pulls JoJo tight again and whispers in his ear. "You have to let that dream go, JoJo. No one can predict the future for sure. Let the dream help you be aware, so you can help yourself to be safe in the future. But don't fear the future. That's no way to live."

She can feel JoJo nod his head and hug her tighter. Finally he pulls back once more. "I want to ride on Thunder with Master Max, please."

Max gives a deep sigh of relief. *Jinx handled that really well,* he thinks. Smiling at JoJo, he motions him to come ahead. He knows Thunder means a lot to JoJo, so he reaches over the side of the wagon to pull him up. JoJo and Thunder talk with each other often, and sure enough, JoJo whispers his fears into Thunder's ear as soon they begin to move again. Thunder's ear twitches. Max can't hear JoJo, but he hears Thunder's answers.

"Don't you worry, JoJo, I'll never leave you behind. You're safe with me. Always grab my mane and hold on," says Thunder.

It has been another week of running by night, and hiding by day. The weather has become even colder and snowier the farther north they've gone. Most days it snows a few inches, making for treacherous roads.

They have met more wonderful people along the way who have offered warm shelter and hot food, but they worry that the slave catchers always seem to be only a few steps behind. Not knowing when the enemy will strike has become wearisome to the travelers.

Because of the high reward offered for the capture of Alem, they have had some nerve-racking experiences. In Lampeter, Pennsylvania, they barely escaped captivity by dashing through an underground tunnel that ran catty-corner from one brick house to another big stone house on the square.

They found much support from the African churches in the North. Someone set some hounds on them when they were near Reading, Pennsylvania. By luck, a member of the Bethel African Methodist Episcopal Church found them and hustled them in town to the church basement, where they were hidden. Those churchwomen cooked up a big feast for them, pretending it was a church social that night. All of the members rallied behind them to attend the sermon and the supper. "Amens" resounded that night, along with singing and dancing.

From there they were sent to Saint James African Methodist Episcopal Zion Church in Ithaca, New York. There, the whole community seemed to be involved with offering help to fugitive slaves. Slave catchers seldom found runaways in that town, because the townspeople were so well organized.

Tonight they are finally cutting over to the northwest corner of New York, heading towards Niagara Falls. They hope and pray that Doc Alex Ross has received their letter and will have someone with a boat watching for them. They are in a forest of evergreens and thick brush, following wildlife paths through the trees. Fir boughs and heavy brush scratch at the wagon like reaching fingers as they push their way through, broadening the path.

The animals all react to the sound before their humans can hear it. Petey and Poppy crawl out from under the blankets and quilts and jump up on the seat beside Alem and Anwar, their ears pricked up. Dot and Thunder twist their heads and snort and whinny.

"Master Max, what do you think is goin' on? These animals hear somethin' we don't, for sure," says Alem.

The boys poke their heads out of the covers and watch the star-studded sky and moonlit terrain. It is a calm, clear night; nothing unusual is happening.

After riding a bit further, Max and JoJo circle back to the wagon, and Max holds out his arm to stop them. "Do you feel it?" he asks.

They sit tall, using all of their five senses. A very slight trembling can be felt vibrating through the wagon and the horses' bodies. A cold, crisp smell is in the air. Max waves them ahead. The trembling increases, and now their ears pick it up. It sounds like faraway thunder, but the night is clear, and it's winter, not thunderstorm weather.

Max smiles. He knows what's going on. They ride closer, and the noise increases, until rumbling and crashing sounds fill the air. They ride right out of the forest and into a magnificent frozen wonderland. They feel as if they are at the top of the world. A wide river falls over cliffs and hits far below. Mist from the waterfalls coats everything around with a crystal layer of ice. The trees sparkle in the moonlight. Their faces can feel the cold, wet mist from the falls.

Jinx points across the way, where other waterfalls rumble over more cliffs. "See over there–those other waterfalls?" she yells, above the crashing sound of the water. "That's Canada! We made it to the border." She and the twins are so excited that they jump to the ground and hug each other, doing wild dances.

Little Henry runs to get the quilt. He has remembered a special patch. "Everyone, come see! It's the great falls. Look, look... Granny even found out about them great waterfalls and made this block to show us the place to cross over to freedom." He shows everyone the patch with blue water falling over a brown cliff.

Alem and Anwar throw their arms around each other, and then they shake Max's hand. "Now we have to find Doc Ross and his boat. Wouldn't want to swim across the Niagara River tonight, would you?" Alem says to his brother.

"That's for sure," Anwar says. "I'm finally feelin' better–hardly any coughin' left, so I don't feel like a swim in that river."

Jinx realizes that JoJo isn't standing with them. Her heart gives a little double beat when she looks around to find him. JoJo stands back away from the happy group; he stares at the falls with big round eyes not blinking, as if he is in a trance. Then he starts to back up even farther.

Jinx knows what is wrong–it's his vision of the water. He saw himself caught in this swirling river, being dragged towards the edge of the cliff. He was dreaming of Niagara Falls. She runs to him and grabs his hands. "JoJo, listen to me. We won't let anything happen to you. Doc Alex will get you safely across."

"No, Miss Jinx, I can't go, don't you see? The last time I tried to cross the border at another spot my horse reared up, and I fell off while everyone else made it across the river. And I got kidnapped away from my family. Now it's gonna happen again...I'll never get across..." He stands trembling in the darkness.

"Stop it. Don't think that way." Jinx takes his hand and leads him back to the wagon, along with the twins.

Max remounts Thunder. "We need to go farther upriver, away from the falls," he says. "The boat will be at a safer location, I'm sure." They barely get going before Petey and Poppy put up a barking and yowling fuss. Petey hits the ground running, back towards the woods.

"Danger...yip yip yip, danger...kidnappers coming," Petey calls out.

With the sound of the falls roaring in their ears, they missed the hounds baying from a distance. Now the hounds burst out of the woods and set upon them, jumping, snapping, and barking.

There's a giant flash and *ka-boom* as something explodes beside the wagon, then comes a second flash followed by another explosion. A wagon wheel blows to pieces, and the riders are thrown sideways. JoJo is thrown clear off the wagon to the icy riverbank.

Someone has thrown some small sticks of dynamite at the group to frighten and disorient them. The explosions terrify gentle Dot. She drags the three-wheeled wagon closer to the raging river before Alem and Anwar can finally pull her to a halt.

Two men on horseback gallop out of the forest, shooting in the air. Smaller flashes and gunshots sound off. "Hands in the air, all of you, hands in the air," screams Jackson Merryweather. The group listens to him. They are terrified they will be shot.

It is a chaotic scene: the thunder of the falls, the hounds baying, Jackson and Billy shooting off their guns and their mouths, Petey barking, Poppy yowling. Max and Jinx are furious. They've come so far, only to be stopped by this man and his partner who have been thorns in their sides the whole trip. They can't fail now, but what can they do?

Petey finds Jackson's lead dog, Brute, and jumps on him, nipping his ear to get his attention.

"Brute, stop your yelling. Get your pack under control," Petey says.

"Owwwww, my ear. Oh–it's you, Petey. Why'd you bite me?" Brute whimpers.

"Sorry, old boy. It was the only way to get your attention," Petey says. He leads Brute over to the side, and Brute's pack follows him, finally beginning to calm down.

Max dismounts from Thunder, and Jackson and Billy make their first and last mistake by dismounting as well. Max watches Jackson go over to the riverbank, slipping and sliding on the icy ground, to grab JoJo around the waist. He has a gun, which he points at the boy in his possession.

"Now, I need that slave named Henry to get on his knees so Billy can tie his hands behind his back," Jackson says. "I don't want to hurt this boy, but I will shoot him if anyone tries anythin'."

"Jackson, we're in Canada," Max says, trying to bluff his way out of the bad situation. He is frantic to try anything. "Give it up, and let these people get on with their lives."

"They don't have no lives of their own. They're slaves and the property of that plantation owner. That one slave alone has a $1,000 reward on his head, dead or alive, and I mean to get that reward. And the Canadian border is halfway across that river. We's in the good old U-S of A. Do ya think I'm dumb?" Jackson says.

But Jackson and Billy will not get the reward; Petey and Poppy see to that. It all happens in a flash. Poppy leaps from the damaged wagon seat right into Billy's face as he walks by to tie up Alem. She digs in her claws and bites his nose, not letting go. Billy drops his gun and the rope and tries to pull her off, only making her scream louder than a Tasmanian devil and dig in harder. Max dives for Billy's gun, and Alem grabs the shotgun.

At the same time, Petey leaps in the air and knocks over Jackson, who drops his gun and JoJo. Both man and boy slide on the icy bank, trying frantically to grab on to something to keep from slipping into the raging currents of the Niagara River. Jackson grabs and claws at JoJo to stop his slide and actually drags JoJo along with him into the freezing river. The current immediately picks them up and starts moving them closer to the falls.

Quick as a bolt of lightning, Thunder leaps into the river and swims with powerful kicks toward his friend, JoJo. Jackson tries to grab hold of Thunder, but Thunder merely tosses him off and continues on to JoJo. JoJo does exactly as Thunder told him after his nightmare: *"grab my mane and hang on."*

Alem holds the shotgun on Billy while everyone screams for Thunder to swim harder. The Niagara River pulls Jackson and Thunder with it, but Thunder bursts into a more powerful swim and cuts back over to the bank, where Max and Jinx brace themselves against a giant tree that has fallen halfway out into the river. The icy river water sprays them as they grab at Thunder's reins and help him struggle back onto the bank. JoJo has his arms and hands entangled in Thunder's mane and his legs squeezing Thunder in a death grip.

Jackson screams for help, but there is none to be had for him as the river drags him ruthlessly on to the cliff's edge, and he is sucked over the lip. Jackson is there one moment, gone the next, dropping seventy feet down into the churning water and rocks below.

Chapter Thirty-one

The End of the Rainbow

A roaring bonfire warms the travelers' frozen bodies and heats water for hot coffee and tea. JoJo's frozen, wet clothes have been removed, and he is wrapped in dry clothes and covered from head to toe in numerous blankets, including the Freedom Quilt.

Now Thunder is the hero. He is wiped dry and covered with blankets. He stands by his boy, JoJo, and nuzzles him over and over to assure himself that the boy is safe and alive.

The sun is about to rise in the east on the frozen landscape. As it does, the ice-coated trees and brush begin to sparkle like millions of diamonds, taking away the breath of the huddled friends. Another awesome sight begins to glow. Jinx spots them first and calls out in amazement.

The rising sun's rays shine through the ever-present mist and cause a multitude of rainbows to break out, arching from one side of the falls to the other. Exclamations fill the air as they all jump to their feet to witness the spectacular sight of so many brightly colored rainbow bridges.

Eddie shouts, "We don't need any boat to cross the river; we can climb those rainbows and slide down the other side into freedom."

"That's right, boys, and an Irish legend says that a pot of gold is at the other end of the rainbow. Think how many pots of gold you would have if that were true," says Max.

"We don't even need them pots of gold, do we, boys? There's somethin' more precious than gold at the end of them rainbows," says Uncle Anwar.

The twins go stand by Uncle Anwar and Papa. "I know what it is," says little Henry. "It's sweet freedom. Right, Uncle Anwar?"

Billy is tied up and sitting near the fire; he hangs his head in fear. He is still in shock, having seen his friend go over the roaring falls to certain death. The hounds are close by having some chow with Petey and Poppy. The group must decide what to do with their prisoner. Right now, they all choose to ignore him.

A wagon from the distance pulls closer, startling everyone for a few chilling moments until cheerful shouts come from the two men aboard. "Hello, hello, friends! We've found you, finally," Doc Alex shouts. The Negro man with him can barely wait until the wagon gets close enough before he jumps from the seat and runs towards them, yelling, "JoJo, I came for you...JoJo!"

Climbing out of the igloo of blankets, JoJo tears off running for his father. "Papa, I was so afraid I'd never see you again." He tackles him around the waist.

His father grabs his boy in an embrace and spins him around. "I am so sorry...I'll never leave you behind again, never—I'll die first."

"It's all right, Papa. Miss Jinx and Master Max and big Thunder, they all took care of me," says JoJo. He's proud to introduce his father to everyone.

Doc Alex pulls up in the wagon and gets down to give handshakes and hugs all around. "Not very far downriver there's a wonderful spot to cross over to Canada on the Niagara Suspension Bridge. It's built over the narrowest point from shoreline to shoreline. Wait until you see it. It's a modern marvel."

The group packs to move one more time together. Max and Jinx decide to ride to the bridge before they leave their friends. They're curious to see this bridge to freedom. They watch Billy as they pack.

Billy looks bedraggled and beaten. His face will bear scratch marks from Poppy for a long time, and his nose is swollen from her bite. Poppy isn't at all sorry. She walks around him, spitting and hissing, like a big, orange prison guard.

Max and Henry walk over to Billy and stand above him, staring. Billy can't even make eye contact.

"What are you going to do with me? Please don't leave me tied up here, helpless. I'm afraid of bears and wolves," Billy whines.

"As far as I'm concerned, you deserve to be eaten by bears and wolves," Max says. "But I won't lower myself to your level and have you killed by wild animals. It's bad enough that Jackson was lost going over the falls. Who knows, maybe he made it to shore alive after the fall–we can hope so. No, I'll untie your hands and leave you to unknot the rope around your feet.

"You can take your horse and Jackson's horse and go back to the town to get medical help. After that, I don't care what you do. I hope to never see you again. And I suggest that you change your occupation to something that helps people instead of hurts them." Billy's head goes even lower in disgrace.

"Alem, do you have any words you want to say to Billy?" Max says.

Billy raises his head and stares at them. "I won't talk to no uppity, runaway *SLAVE*," he shouts. He spits on the ground near Henry's feet.

Alem shakes his head. "I don't believe I have anything to say to this man. He'll have to stand before someone a lot bigger than me on Judgment Day. Have a good day, sir."

Billy defiantly glares at the whole group. *If I ever get a chance to fight to keep slavery, you better believe I'll take it. I'll have my revenge for Jackson's death,* he thinks.

Max takes a knife, cuts the rope off Billy's wrists, and he and Alem turn their backs on him and walk away. The excited group moves into Doc's wagon, leaving their ruined wagon behind. Jinx and Max mount Thunder and Dot. JoJo runs over for one last hand up to sit with Max atop the horse that saved his life. Off they go to find the magic bridge, leaving Billy to struggle with a tightly knotted rope around his feet and around his conscience.

They follow the Niagara River down the gorge to a spot right before the whirlpool rapids, enjoying the roar of the falls and the mist. It is a day filled with bright, aqua skies and hope.

The bridge really is a sight to see. There are four wooden towers, two on each side of the river. Thick cables hang suspended between them, anchored to the rocks 220 feet below. A heavy oak plank roadway, eight feet in width, is laid amongst the cables, going about even hundred and sixty feet across the river. It sways in the wind.

"Here we are at the bridge to freedom," says Doc Alex. The group stands in silence, staring at the swaying bridge.

Doc Alex laughs. "I know what you're thinking, but trust me–it's perfectly safe. There hasn't been one accident in the three years since it was built."

Right after he says it, they watch two mules pull a wagon loaded with logs across the bridge and move on toward town. "See? Nothing to it," Doc adds. "All aboard."

Suddenly the group realizes that goodbyes must be said for the last time. After all the tragedy and triumph, and the hundreds of miles spent on the roughest trail imaginable, it all comes down to one simple bridge that will lead Alem, Anwar, Eddie, Henry, JoJo and his father to freedom.

Max and Jinx dismount and hug Dot and Thunder's solid necks. They each whisper goodbyes and thanks to the gallant horses.

"JoJo, Thunder must be your horse to love and protect, since he loves and protects you. Dot will go with you, Alem. I know you will treat her well. In their saddlebags you'll find enough money to give you all a great start on a homestead and some land in Owen Sound," says Jinx.

"*I'll miss you,*" Dot neighs. "*You're good friends. Thanks for taking such good care of me.*"

"*I...I don't know what to say.*" Thunder paws the ground with his right hoof. "*It was an honor to help everyone. Thanks for letting me go with JoJo. I'll take good care of him.*"

Max solemnly shakes hands with everyone. Jinx goes around and hugs each of her friends. It is an emotional scene for the group. Before any more thanks are given, Max has one more important thing to say.

"Alem, I never could get you to stop calling us master and mistress. Now you are truly going to be freedmen. Please, when you say good-bye, can you call us just by our names?"

Alem and Anwar grin from ear to ear. "Goodbye, Max. Goodbye, Jinx. Thank you, friends, for giving us our lives back," they call out.

The boys finish their hugs and goodbyes to Petey and Poppy.

"You know, don't you, Petey and Poppy are the finest dog and cat in the whole world?" says Eddie.

"That's right, they're heroes for saving our lives," little Henry adds. He pulls their Freedom Quilt tighter around him.

Petey jumps high in the air and does a flip for joy, while Poppy sits up on her haunches and waves both front paws.

"Safe travels back to your home," JoJo whispers, as he winks at Max and Jinx. "Maybe I'll see you sometime in the future. Who knows?"

Doc gives a solid slap of the reins to his horse, and the travelers take their final ride on the Underground Railroad. Max and Jinx wave until they are across the bridge, out of sight.

The JMP History Mystery Detective Agency walks slowly back along the fir-tree forest road, leaving the thundering roar of the falls behind. They walk in silence, lost in thought. Max puts his arm around his friend's neck, pulling her closer. She pokes him in the ribs with her elbow, making Max laugh.

"Time to go home, Jinx?"

"I'd say it's way past time to get home," says Jinx. "I have that stunned feeling that happens at the end of all our adventures. It's always like...I can't believe we actually did that whole thing. Wow, what were we thinking? That was a wild ride."

"I know what you mean. I feel dazed and exhausted. We've been gone for months on the trail. How about you two, Petey and Poppy?" says Max.

Petey is his usual terrier self, running ahead, circling back, sniffing, jumping, digging at hidden things under snow clumps. *"What? What? Tired, you say? Not me—let's find some more new friends. Maybe Brute can come home to play..."*

Poppy gives a delicate cat sneeze. *"I could go for a warmer clime,"* she says. *"I'm feeling a bit chilled. Peter, stop kicking up snow clumps— ugh, you hit me again."*

Max picks up his brave cat and tucks her into his coat. "I think we're far enough away from everybody and everything. It's safe. Time to catch the Time Tunnel. I'm sure Aunt Merry anxiously awaits our return."

Jinx grabs her terrier in mid-leap and hugs him to her chest. "Petey will crash big-time when we get home. He's just in his typical nervous frenzy of exhaustion." She kisses his head.

They stop near a small pine tree with a pile of rocks around it. Max and she know what to do. They join hands and try to clear their minds. That's not an easy thing to accomplish after all they have experienced on the Underground Railroad.

Jinx and Max close their eyes, breathe deeply, and let the soothing darkness sweep over them, helping to clear away their jumbled thoughts. They think of the spot near the barn where they left Aunt Merry on that warm summer night. There is a Time Tunnel peculiarity that no matter how long they've been gone, they return to the exact moment they left. Each thinks of that moment in time.

The great whooshing noise fills their ears as the four are pulled into the tunnel of darkness, spinning and swirling through time, to be dumped out on the ground near Aunt Merry's barn. Aunt Merry stands where they left her.

It is nighttime in the late summer again, with the song of the crickets playing their fiddles and the pond frogs flicking their tongues and singing songs. The whole sky is filled with stars, so big and close that Jinx feels as if she can touch the drinking gourds.

Aunt Merry lifts her eyebrows and smiles at her Time Travelers. "I suppose you have quite a story to tell me, right?" she says. "Welcome home."

Epilogue

Conestoga Courage Farm

The campfire crackles and shoots sparks into the night air. The *JMP History Mystery Detective Agency* sits in front of the fire on the evening after their return, enjoying the feeling of home and safety. Petey snoozes in Jinx's lap, as she runs her fingers through his silky fur.

Aunt Merry watches Max and Jinx through the flames, sitting across from them, and she wonders what looks different about the two teens. Are they taller and older? Or is it the confidence they emit? Maybe the way they sit, with their shoulders back and their chins up–tired, but proud?

Poppy rests in Aunt Merry's lap. Aunt Merry strokes Poppy's soft head and chin, causing the big orange-and-white cat's purr engine to go into overdrive. Then she notices the shadows of sadness around both teens' eyes. That's different, too. *They have seen some hard things and learned some tough life lessons,* Aunt Merry thinks. She waits.

"Aunt Merry, we saw some really bad things. Watching the harsh treatment of those enslaved people was one of the worst things I've ever had to do. Some of our friends were beaten and whipped until their backs were raw and bleeding. And...and two of our friends died in slavery, and their little baby, too, before we could get back to help them," Jinx says. Her eyes fill with pain and sorrow.

"Ah, yes. That must have been horrible. Did you feel helpless at times?" says Aunt Merry.

"Yes, during most of the trip," Jinx says. She gives a short laugh. "You know that story you told us about Patty Cannon and her gang of slave stealers? You were right. There were plenty of other people just as nasty."

"But life has balance," Aunt Merry says. "Never forget that. Goodness, evil, hope, despair... Sometimes the balance shifts to the dark side, but that's why there are people like you and Max, to bring life back into balance. But you are only one person, Jinx; you can't burden yourself with thinking you must save everyone. If you are able to save one single person, it's worth the trip."

"That's what Max told me," says Jinx, smiling at her friend.

"You're right, Aunt Merry," says Max. "Balance. Good and evil. Along with evil people, we met so many more good people, both black and white, who worked on the Underground Railroad to help the enslaved Africans to freedom. It was so extraordinary, the organization of it all.

"We met this plantation family—the Smythes, who had bought Alem's twins. They were nice people, good in many ways. They thought they weren't abusing their slaves. But those long, harsh hours of work picking cotton were horrible.

"I had a good talk with the son, Colin, and his father. We disagreed on the slavery issue, but Colin and I both learned a lesson. I heard their viewpoint. They saw slavery as a way of life that had been in the family for many years. To make a profit, they said they needed their slaves to work the fields.

"I suggested to Colin that if they could pay the workers even a small bit, it would give them dignity. But he said that wouldn't be a sound business decision. He said they were just slaves, not people like he and I. That was an eye-opener for me. How do you change that mindset?" Max says.

"But Max, tell Aunt Merry what happened," Jinx says. "It was one of the really great things about the trip."

Max grins and nods. "When we tried to sneak out with the twins that night, there was Colin, waiting for us in the barn. At first I thought he would call his father. But he said I had planted a seed of doubt about slavery in his mind, and that he and I agree about one thing I told him: no children should ever be taken from their parents to be sold into slavery. He gave us the go-ahead to take Eddie and Henry back to their papa."

Jinx is on a positive roll now. "Aunt Merry, most people we met were so wonderful. We got to meet Harriet Tubman. What a brave woman. She ran back and forth from the South to the North to help her people escape slavery, and she just spit at danger. Oh, the stories she told had us laughing, and crying. And brave Eliza and William Parker, right over there in Christiana, and how Thaddeus Stevens, the lawyer, defended the black people and the white farmers arrested for their part in the uprising. Then there's John and Mary Martin, who ran the safe house right here on our farm." Her eyes now sparkle in the firelight with the memories.

"Don't forget Ellen and William Craft. Their plan was ingenious, with Ellen dressing up like a white man and pretending to be an invalid all wrapped in bandages," says Max. He shakes his head in amazement.

"She was so brave, Aunt Merry. Can you imagine doing that, and having a brave husband who talks your way right into an elegant inn? I wonder if they made it to freedom? I wish I could visit with her again, for one last time," Jinx says.

Aunt Merry claps her hands together in happiness. Her two gifted children will be fine. *They are born to be Time Travelers,* she thinks. "Kids, what a great thing for you both. If you two would draw a balance scale and fill each side, one with negatives and one with positives about your experiences on the Underground Railroad, I bet the scales would tip way over to the positive side. And you are the good people who made it happen.

"I'm so proud of you both. You have accomplished unbelievable things," Aunt Merry says. "But I do see shades of sadness in your eyes. These travels back in time tend to age you beyond your years. Don't forget to take time to just be kids. Protect yourselves in between by playing and having lots of fun."

Aunt Merry gets up and hands Poppy over to Max. "I'm heading in to the house. I'll fix some sandwiches and tea for you. You've both got to be exhausted. Now don't stay out too late." She leaves the two friends and the furries to sit in the comfort of the dying campfire embers.

"Kind of funny how one minute we're running a team of horses in a carriage, living on the trail, responsible for our runaway friends' lives, never getting enough sleep, fighting with slave catchers, and in the blip of a Time Tunnel nanosecond we're back home, with Aunt Merry reminding us not to stay up too late," Jinx says.

"And I love that," Max says. "I'm so glad to be home again with Aunt Merry watching out for us. Remember in the middle of the trip when we both wanted to play games with the little kids and not have all that heavy responsibility? Now it's all over...time for us to relax and play. We did it, partner." They shake and bump fists on it.

They watch the sky in silence for a few moments. Jinx points to the constellations. "There it is, that old Big Dipper. Think back to when we were playing that game, trying to guess what's in the Big Dipper, Max."

"Um hum," Max murmurs.

"Well, I know now for sure what's in it–freedom. It's full of sweet freedom," Jinx says.

Max smiles at her, gets up and throws a shovel full of dirt on the last of the embers. Suddenly he stops short and stares at the barn. Jinx follows his gaze. The barn is glowing blue.

"Aha, Detective Max, the barn seems to be calling out to us once more," Jinx says. She's excited. "It wants to tell us something or show us something."

Max groans. "Where do you get all that energy? I am so ready to crash that I don't think I can even walk over there, let alone handle one more mystery."

Petey and Poppy take off like rockets hurtling toward the building. *"Come on, yip, yip, the barn is blue; it has something for us, come on..."* says Petey.

"And where do they get all of their energy?" Max says. He groans some more.

Jinx pulls him by the hand until she has him running with her. "That's it, old boy. Let's check out this one last thing."

Max lets Jinx open the door. She notices a warm tingle, like a little shot of static electricity, when she touches the door. It goes through her and into Max's hand.

"Ouch, that smarts," Max says. He shakes his arm.

The blue glow warms them when they enter. The first thing they notice is the floorboards seem to be lit up in the middle of the barn floor. The friends walk over and look at them.

They kneel down and shove the hay and debris to one side. The trapdoor is now in plain view.

"Ahh, the hiding space. Something must be in there again. Go ahead, Max. You open it," Jinx says.

Max grabs a small shovel to pry open the trapdoor. It falls back with a dusty thud. Again, they get a brief shot of electricity, through their feet this time.

Petey puts his front legs over the edge to peer into the hidden space. *A present, a present from the twins, yip, yip,* Petey says. He's very happy to see the surprise that is lit up in the corner–the Freedom Quilt, folded up in a neat pile.

"But how could it have gotten here?" says Jinx.

"Maybe Alem and Anwar and the twins sent it to Mary and John, hoping that somehow they would get it to us. Who knows?" Max says. They grin at each other.

Max jumps down to get the quilt and hands it off to Jinx. Pulling himself back up, he watches as Jinx opens it to shake off the dust. They both miss seeing a piece of paper fluttering to the floor. Other than a few small worn spots, the quilt looks good as new. They lay it over a nearby stall rail to trace the path of secret message blocks. A storm of memories comes tumbling back.

The blue, running river to walk in, to throw off the hounds; the gray-stone pile, with a scooped-out rock to show them a safe cave to hide in; the four oak trees with their little brown acorns at a safe house; the bear's paw; the flying geese; the white sailboat on the blue ocean; the beautiful waterfalls...each patch lovingly made and telling a tale of bravery and hope.

Jinx looks downward and finally sees the paper that was wrapped in the quilt. It's an old envelope, yellowed with age. She picks it up and shows Max.

"Look here; it's a letter, and it's addressed to me. The envelope is so old that I bet it came from the past. Another miracle. Max—I love this! It says:"

Miss Jinx MacKenzie
Care of John and Mary Martin
Lancaster County, Pennsylvania

Jinx opens the envelope very carefully. It is indeed a letter, full of good cheer and news from Ellen Craft, the young woman who disguised herself as a rich, invalid man. Jinx and Max plop down on some hay bales while she reads the letter aloud.

Dear Miss Jinx,

> *It was a wonderful treat to meet you and Master Max at the beginning of our adventure to freedom. Thanks to you and Master Max for risking your lives to help us escape. We did indeed make it to the next town to catch a train North. Our trip to Philadelphia took eight days using the train, a steamer and some ferry connections.*

> *On the train I had the incredible bad luck to sit beside an old white man who had been to dinner at my plantation and knew me well. I pretended to be deaf and spent my time looking away from him and out the window. I fooled him!*

We spent three weeks resting in Philadelphia with a white family named Ivens, who cared for us with love. That's where I finally learned to trust the white people who sincerely wanted to help our runaway folks.

Traveling on to Boston, we lived there for two years. We made many appearances to speak out against the evils of slavery.

Our former owner heard of our abolitionist work, and he sent two slave catchers with warrants for our arrest for breaking the Fugitive Slave Laws. Our lives became dark and frightening once more, as we had to go back into hiding. We fled onward to Portland, Maine, then to Nova Scotia, before we could arrange for passage on a steamer sailing to Liverpool, England.

Miss Jinx, I never thought I would become so educated and so accepted by people! The British people were wonderful. The abolitionists there helped us once more to spread word of the harsh treatment and horrible existence that American slaves had to endure. William and I also studied with Lady Noel Byron, the widow of the famous poet, at her Ockham School for the rural youth. We taught others the skills we learned on the plantation in return. It was a good exchange for everyone.

I told you I never wanted to have my babies while living in slavery. My dream came true. I have five beautiful children, named Charles, Brougham, William, Ellen and Alfred. Of course Ellen's brothers spoil her and are very protective of their sister.

We are soon heading home to America, since the Civil War has ended with freedom for my people. Freedom, Miss Jinx! You can't imagine what this means to us. We shall return to Georgia and hope to open a school for the Negro youth. The freed slave people need to be educated if they wish to improve their lives, so the best place to start is with the children. And believe me when I say none of my students will ever feel the cruel whip for misbehavior.

I wanted to share our success story, so I hope this letter somehow reaches you. I often think of you and Master Max and wonder how you are and what life has brought for you both. I wish you all good things and will continue to pray for you, my brave friends. Thank you, and God bless you.

> *Your friend truly,*
> *Ellen Craft*

Jinx quietly folds the letter up and returns it to the envelope. She gives a ghost of a smile as she looks into Max's eyes. The letter of thanks from Ellen finally brings closure for their experiences on the Underground Railroad. Jinx brushes a soft kiss against Max's cheek; then she jumps up, pulling Max to his feet.

"Look, here," Max says. The blue light still highlights the trapdoor.

Poppy's tail twitches with interest. *"I believe this will be a very nice surprise, also,"* she says.

Petey runs over and jumps on the open trapdoor.

"Come on, over here, look at this, yip yip!" he calls out. *"Sniff, sniff... good smells, the little boys were here!"*

"I'll never look at this trapdoor the same way again, now that we know its history," Jinx says. "Do you suppose the boys' initials...?" She remembers the three little boys huddled over the secret room's trapdoor with their pocketknife, laughing and so proud of themselves for learning their alphabet letters.

She and Max kneel down to inspect the underside of the trapdoor. There it is, a little message from time past, lit up in blue:

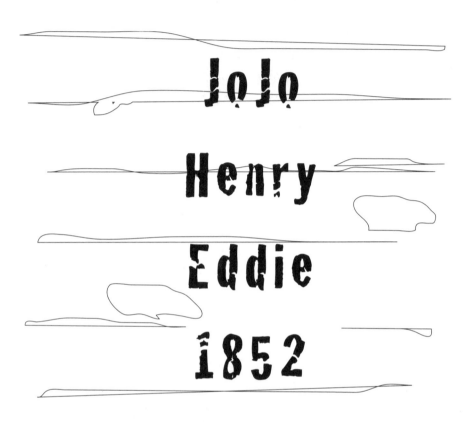

Jinx traces the carved letters with her finger, remembering the bright little boys who made it to freedom. They did their best to carve their names into the trapdoor, so people in the future would know they had traveled on through to freedom.

"Angels walk among us," Poppy reminds them, batting at Max's arm with her paw. *"Those three little boys were our angels."*

Jinx finally turns to her best friend, Max. He has the Freedom Quilt over his shoulders. He motions to Jinx to come share the quilt, and they leave the barn and walk slowly back towards the lit windows of the cozy farmhouse. They wear the quilt like a cape of courage.

Petey runs ahead, but Poppy waits by the barn, watching until the blue glow fades and snuffs out. Then she turns and follows her friends, her tail forever up and waving like a little flag.

"Job well done, friends. Job well done," she purrs. Poppy wrinkles her furry face in a little cat smile, full of love for her dog friend and her children.

THE END

Appendix I

A Letter to My Readers

Dear Readers,

Writing this story started out with an interest in the Underground Railroad, which ran right through my home area of Lancaster County, Pennsylvania.

It has been a long journey with Jinx, Max, Petey, and Poppy, and little did I know how many fascinating, real characters I would meet during the dangerous trip to the South to rescue Henry's boys, and then North to Canada and freedom. For example, put Henry Box Brown on your research list. I love his story of mailing himself in a big crate, out of slavery, to freedom in Philadelphia, Pennsylvania. These people are truly amazing!

All of the characters I chose to put in the novel became real to me, and I hope you feel their awe-inspiring bravery by the time you finish reading the story. Following this Letter to My Readers are lists of persons and places that may interest you and encourage you to do research on the Underground Railroad.

My wish is that my story, *Ghost Train to Freedom*, inspires you to learn as much as you can about America's period of slavery. Think about the thousands of enslaved Africans who sought freedom, against all odds, on the Underground Railroad. Remember both the black and white Americans who helped them, against the law, and with little regard for their own safety. Out of the pain and suffering of slavery comes an amazing American story of love, strength, and perseverance to help us better understand and respect everyone.

Sincerely,

Faith Reese Martin

Appendix II

Historical Background

People

Real people in history, who played an important role in the novel:

Cannon, Patty: notorious leader of a gang that stole African Americans to resell as slaves

Craft, Ellen and William: Ellen disguised herself as an invalid white man traveling with his Negro servant to make their way to freedom

Cross, Doctor Alexander: Canadian doctor and ornithologist (person who studies birds) who passed out survival kits and led slaves in the South to freedom

Douglas, Frederick: African American abolitionist, who educated himself and spoke out strongly against slavery

Gorsuch, Edward, and his son, Dickinson: Southern plantation owners who went to Christiana, PA to reclaim two enslaved men who had run away from his plantation; Edward was shot and killed

Hanway, Castner: the Quaker farmer who was arrested and placed on trial after he came to the aid of William and Eliza Parker during the Christiana Resistance

Parker, William and Eliza: former escaped African Americans who settled in Christiana, PA, and helped other runaway slaves to freedom; his home was the site of the Christiana Resistance

Stevens, Thaddeus: lawyer from Lancaster, PA, who defended Castner Hanway on trial for treason against the United States, and won his acquittal (freedom)

Tubman, Harriet: known as Moses, for leading many enslaved people to freedom in the North

Other Important Persons of Interest

Some other real people in history, who played an important role in the era of the Underground Railroad:

Beecher Stowe, Harriet: wrote the controversial novel, *Uncle Tom's Cabin*, in 1852, about the evils of slavery

Brown, Henry "Box": a runaway slave who mailed himself to freedom in Philadelphia, PA

Brown, John: a Negro revolutionary abolitionist who led an unsuccessful armed raid against the white authorities at Harper's Ferry, West Virginia in 1859; he was executed later that year

Coffin, Levi: Quaker abolitionist in Indiana and Ohio

Garrett, Thomas: Quaker abolitionist from Wilmington, Delaware

Hamilton Smith, Lydia: African American abolitionist and close friend of Thaddeus Stevens, the lawyer for the defense of Castner Hanway

Ripley, John: abolitionist in Ripley, Ohio

Still, William: African American abolitionist

Smith Haviland, Laura: Quaker Underground Railroad conductor and abolitionist, and suffragette and social reformer for women's rights

Places

Some important places along the Underground Railroad route:

Bethel African Methodist Episcopal Church, Churchtowne, Lancaster, PA: safe house for runaway slaves

Bethel African Methodist Episcopal Church, Reading, Pennsylvania: safe house for runaway slaves

Christiana, Pennsylvania: setting of the Christiana Resistance, at the home of William and Eliza Parker

Moyamensing Prison, Philadelphia, Pennsylvania: held those arrested after the Christiana Resistance

Niagara Falls, Canada: passageway to freedom in Canada for the escaped African Americans

Niagara Suspension Bridge: the first bridge to cross the Niagara River from New York, USA, to Canada

Owen Sound, Ontario, Canada: free settlement for many of the runaway slaves

Philadelphia, Pennsylvania: a gateway to freedom city; site of the famous trial for the Christiana Resistance participants

Saint James African Methodist Episcopal Zion Church, Ithaca, New York: safe house for runaway slaves

Songs

African American Spiritual Songs from the story, used as secret codes to help escaped African American slaves find their way North to freedom:

Follow the Drinking Gourd

Swing Low, Sweet Chariot

Wade in the Water

Appendix III

Glossary of Terms

Definitions of some of the terms used during the era of the Underground Railroad

Abolitionist: a person who believed slavery was wrong and worked to help abolish, or end, slavery

Agent: a person who would help to guide runaways along the Underground Railroad

Conductor: a person who led escaped, enslaved African Americans to safety along the Underground Railroad

Follow the Drinking Gourd: secret code in song, that instructed the runaways to look for the Dipper constellations in the sky to find the North Star, which would help guide them northward

Freight: secret code for a group of runaway, enslaved African Americans

Load of Potatoes: secret code for a group of escaped African Americans

Parcel: secret code for runaway, enslaved African Americans

Passengers: secret code for escaped African Americans

Safe House: secret code for a safe place to stay along the Underground Railroad

Station: a safe hiding place along the Underground Railroad

Station Master: the owner of a safe place to stay for runaways

Underground Railroad: a secret network of people who helped to hide the escaped enslaved Negroes and guide them to the next safe place to stay, as they made their way from slavery in the South to freedom in the North

Appendix IV

Mama's Freedom Quilt

The common view of slavery in the Civil War era is of slaves working in the fields and as house servants. In Chapter 12 of *Ghost Train to Freedom*, Max tells Jinx how surprised he is to find workshops with skilled artisans on the Matthews plantation in Virginia.

The coastal and inland communities of Africa that were raided by slave traders were often highly developed. It was not uncommon for the plantation owners to place orders with the slave traders to capture people with particular skills that they needed, such as crop management, blacksmithing and ironwork, animal husbandry and needlework.

Even though they had been enslaved, the Africans preserved their skills and cultural traditions and passed them on to new generations. Keeping these traditions alive was a great challenge. Not only did they have to cope with the difficulties of their slavery, but they were also forbidden from learning to read and write, and they were not allowed to own property.

So, the resources available to make items such as clothing and quilts were scarce for black women like Mama! There were no fabric shops available to slaves. They had to scrounge for whatever scraps of fabric they could find, often amongst that which had been discarded by the main house.

The colors in the quilts of the 1850s would have been very different from those today. Back in that era, the pigments available for dying fabrics were much more muted, and fabric makers lacked the technology to produce the vibrant hues to which we are accustomed. The quilt blocks on the following pages show some of the traditional patterns that may have been used in freedom quilts, along with Mama's own blocks.

Ghost Train to Freedom

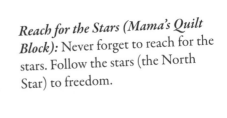

Reach for the Stars (Mama's Quilt Block): Never forget to reach for the stars. Follow the stars (the North Star) to freedom.

Log Cabin (Traditional): Look for a cabin with this quilt over the fence. It is a safe house.

Shoofly (Traditional): Look for free Africans who will help you on the Underground Railroad. But beware; you can't really trust anyone, for sure.

Drunkard's Path (Traditional): Walk in a crooked path, never in a straight line. If you weave back and forth, you will be harder to track.

Mama's Freedom Quilt

Flying Geese (Traditional):
Follow the geese when they fly North in the spring. They'll lead you to food, water, and places to rest.

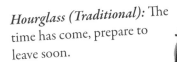

Hourglass (Traditional): The time has come, prepare to leave soon.

Cross Roads (Traditional): Look for the cross roads of a town in the North, on the trail to freedom.

Sailboat (Traditional): Look for a sailboat to take you to freedom.

North Star (Traditional): Follow the North Star in the sky to head North, to freedom. Look for the Big Dipper. Two of its stars in the bowl point to the North Star, the last star in the handle of the Little Dipper.

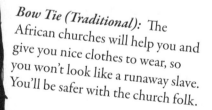

Bow Tie (Traditional): The African churches will help you and give you nice clothes to wear, so you won't look like a runaway slave. You'll be safer with the church folk.

Mama's Freedom Quilt

The Stream and the Rock Pile (Mama's Quilt Block): Cross the stream to look for the rock pile with the scooped out stone. There is a cave to stay in.

Bear Paws (Traditional): Follow the bears' tracks over the mountains. They'll lead you to food (berries and fish) and water.

Wagon Wheel (Traditional): If you see the wagon wheel quilt on a fence, get ready to move out that night.

The Stream (Mama's Quilt Block): Walk in the water to throw the hounds off of your trail. They can't smell your scent in water.

Oak Trees (Mama's Quilt Block): Look for the four large oak trees with the acorns on the ground, in the yard of a white farmhouse. This is a safe place to hide.

Rock Pile (Mama's Quilt Block): Look for the big pile of rocks with a scooped out stone. There is a cave to stay in, hidden behind the rock pile.

Appendix V

About the Author

Faith Reese Martin grew up in Lancaster County, Pennsylvania, an area rich in American history dating back to colonial times. Having taught fourth and fifth graders for thirty years in the public school system, she finds some of the best mysteries and adventures to share with children are those told in the history of America.

The author enjoys the meticulous research involved in creating historical fiction. Faith is especially excited when lesser-known historical facts come together to form a framework for a new story.

She also has a heart over-flowing with love for nature and all of its creatures. The ocean and the woodlands, dogs, cats, and other critters–all play a large role within the settings of her stories. These interests inspired Faith to create a series of historical adventure books designed for young readers, entitled the *JMP History Mystery Detective Agency*.

Faith taught in the Lampeter-Strasburg School District, Lampeter, Pennsylvania. She has a Bachelor of Science Degree in Elementary Education from Mansfield University, Mansfield, Pennsylvania, and a Masters Degree in Elementary Education from Millersville University, Millersville, Pennsylvania.

When not buried in a suspenseful mystery book, Faith enjoys playing alto sax in a forties Big Band and hand bells in her church choir. She resides in Lancaster County, Pennsylvania, with her husband, Robert, and her two dogs, Archie, and Lady.

Please visit her website to say hello to Jinx, Max, Petey and Poppy, at: www.faithreesemartin.com, or write to her at: ghostwriterfm@verizon.net

What early readers say...

"Through the eyes of teenage time-travelers, experience the dangers of a journey to sweet freedom on the Underground Railroad…Through this adventure, Author Faith Reese Martin gives readers a realistic glimpse of the cruelty of slavery and of the courage and triumph of those who provided safe houses, those who guided runaways, and those who traveled the Underground Railroad to "sweet freedom." This story is a touching reminder of the value of freedom and of the bravery of those who were willing to risk their lives for it."

Sherry Eshleman
Fourth Grade Teacher
Lampeter-Strasburg School District, Lampeter, PA

"Faith Reese Martin knows how to grab hold of her readers on page one and keep them hooked all the way through to the end. Weaving together history, mystery, time travel, action, and suspense—along with a good helping of humor—she spins tales that are intriguing, imaginative, and altogether enchanting.
The main characters in her JMP History Mystery Detective Agency series, Jinx and Max, are believable and lovable. Their pets, Petey and Poppy, are quirky and engaging. In each book the readers are given an opportunity to learn about a specific time and place in our country's history while going on a wild adventure right along with the characters."

Susan Hendricks Barry
Sixth Grade Reading Teacher
Martin Meylin Middle School, PA

"Author Faith Martin provides an engaging presentation for her student audiences. Her presentation combines entertaining personal anecdotes within a discussion of an author's life and work. Faith's teaching background is evident in her feel for what details interest kids. Without hesitation would I recommend Faith for your school's author visit!"

Katherine Stehman
Elementary Librarian
Lampeter-Strasburg School District, Lampeter, PA

Note to Teachers and Book Clubs

Each book in the JMP History Mystery Detective Agency series can be used across the curriculum as a novel study in reading or an accompaniment book for history courses.

Each novel has an in-depth guide for literary studies. Skills include: vocabulary study, discussion questions, art and history connections, literary elements, and writing activities.

Also, a *History Research Guide* accompanies *Ghost Train to Freedom*. This guide is designed for young readers and provides a basic history of the Underground Railroad. It also includes links to a website with additional information and links to encourage young readers to explore this important era for themselves.

These study guides provide teachers with valuable tools for lesson planning and student activities in the areas of literary and historical studies.

For more information about these guides visit: www.ghosttraintofreedom.com

Author Visits

Faith Reese Martin, along with her puppet friends, Petey and Poppy, is available for presentations and readings in schools and libraries.

For more information, visit her website at: www.faithreesemartin.com, or email her at: ghostwriterfm@verizon.net